Contents

Completely
blank
page
↓

The Intro

Right now at this exact millisecond...
Hello, I'm Barry Loser.

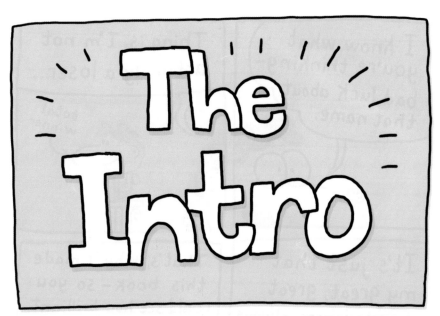

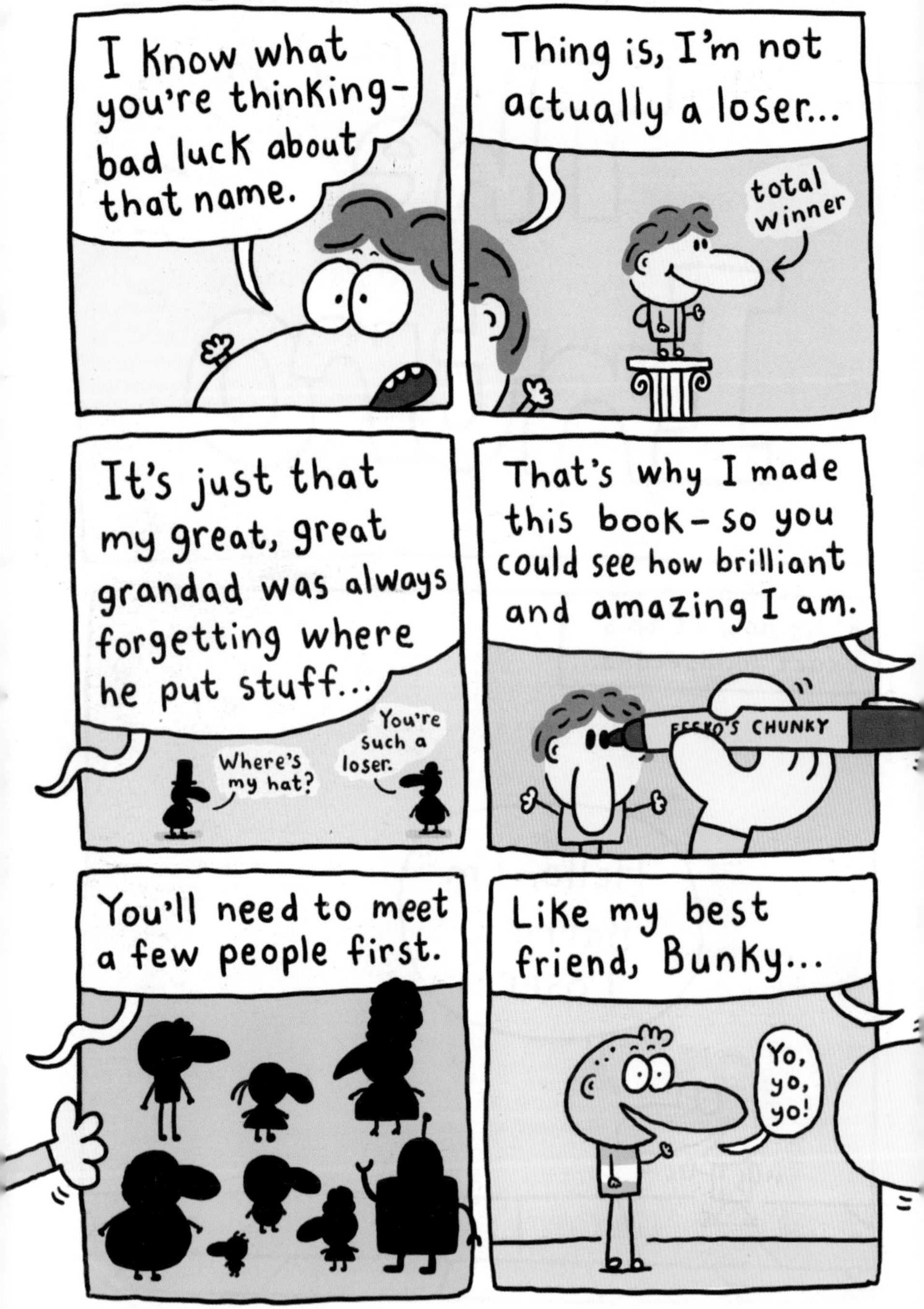
I know what you're thinking- bad luck about that name.
Thing is, I'm not actually a loser...
total winner
It's just that my great, great grandad was always forgetting where he put stuff...
Where's my hat?
You're such a loser.
That's why I made this book - so you could see how brilliant and amazing I am.
FESKO'S CHUNKY
You'll need to meet a few people first.
Like my best friend, Bunky...
Yo, yo, yo!

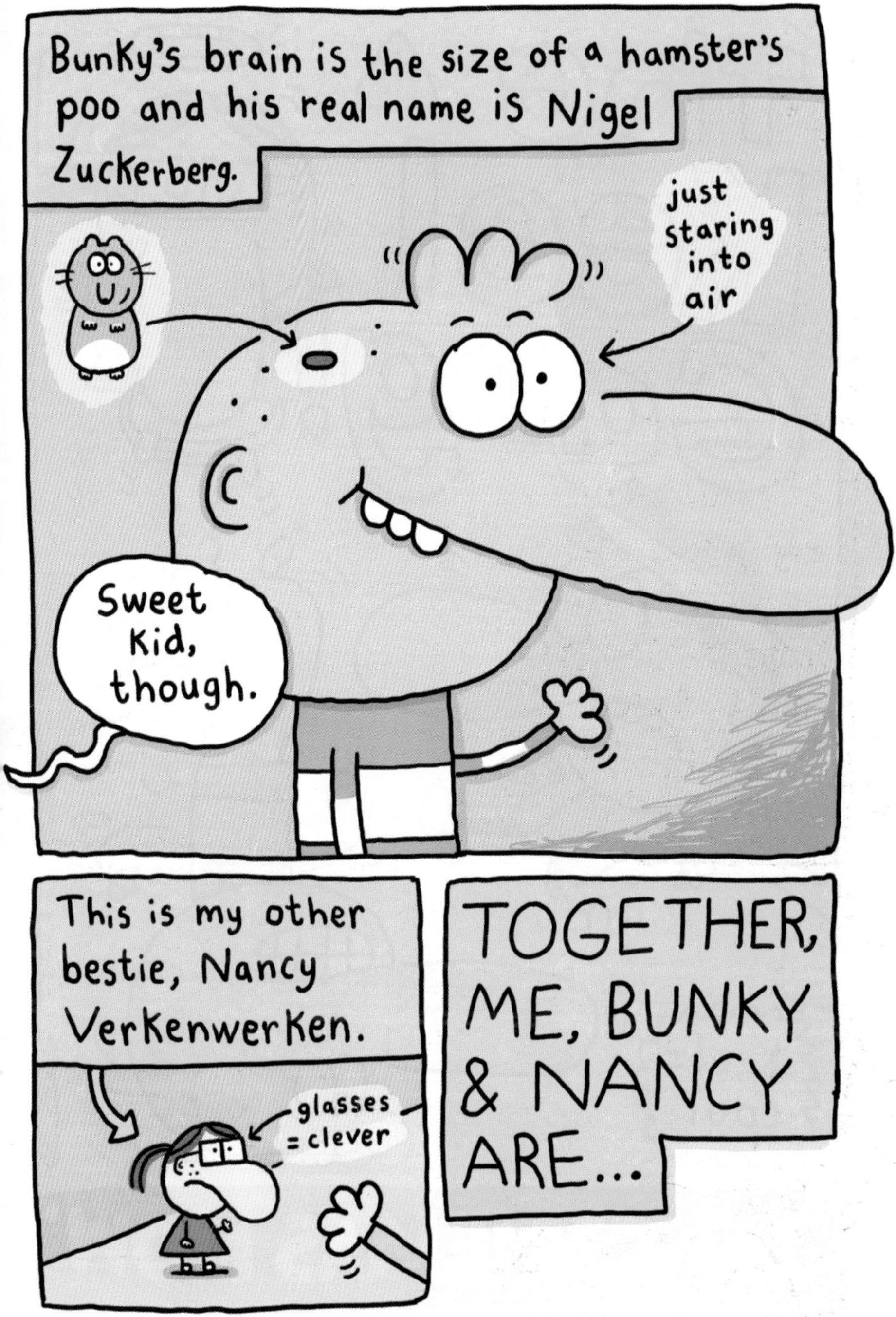

Bunky's brain is the size of a hamster's poo and his real name is Nigel Zuckerberg.
just staring into air
Sweet Kid, though.
This is my other bestie, Nancy VerKenwerKen.
glasses = clever
TOGETHER, ME, BUNKY & NANCY ARE...

(Turn page)

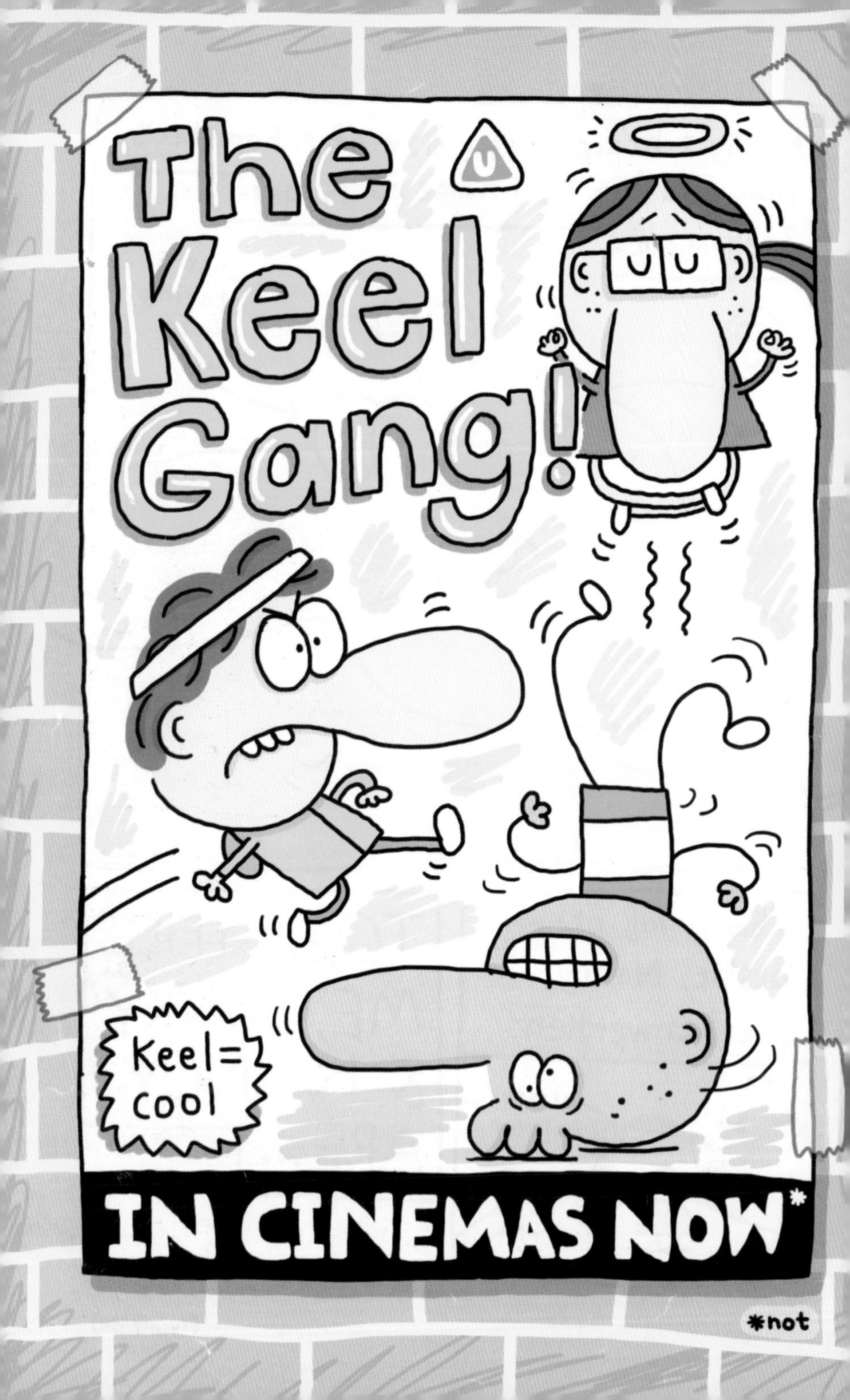
The Keel Gang!
Keel= cool
IN CINEMAS NOW*
*not

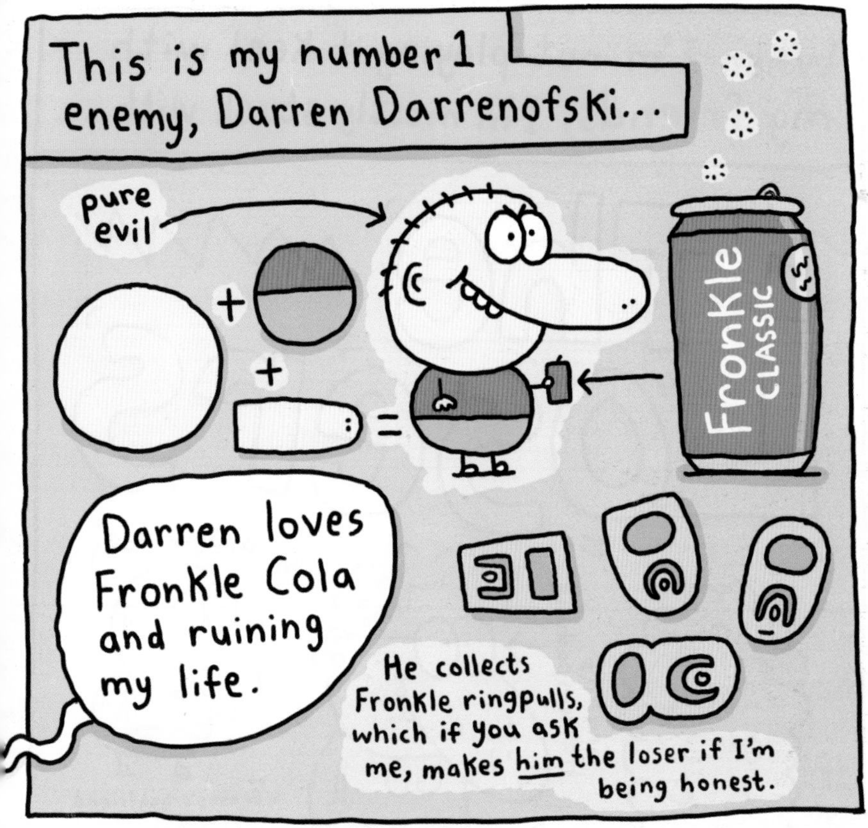
This is my number 1 enemy, Darren Darrenofski...
pure evil
Fronkle CLASSIC
Darren loves Fronkle Cola and ruining my life.
He collects Fronkle ringpulls, which if you ask me, makes him the loser if I'm being honest.

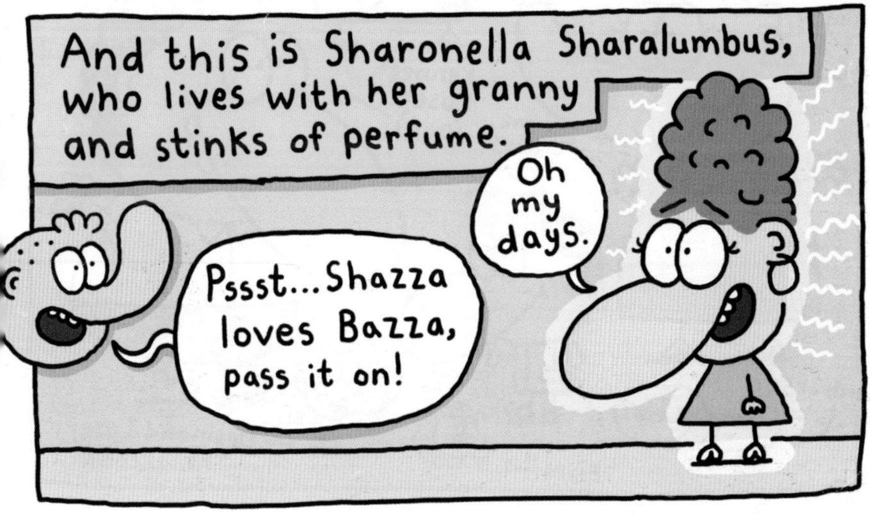
And this is Sharonella Sharalumbus, who lives with her granny and stinks of perfume.
Oh my days.
Pssst... Shazza loves Bazza, pass it on!

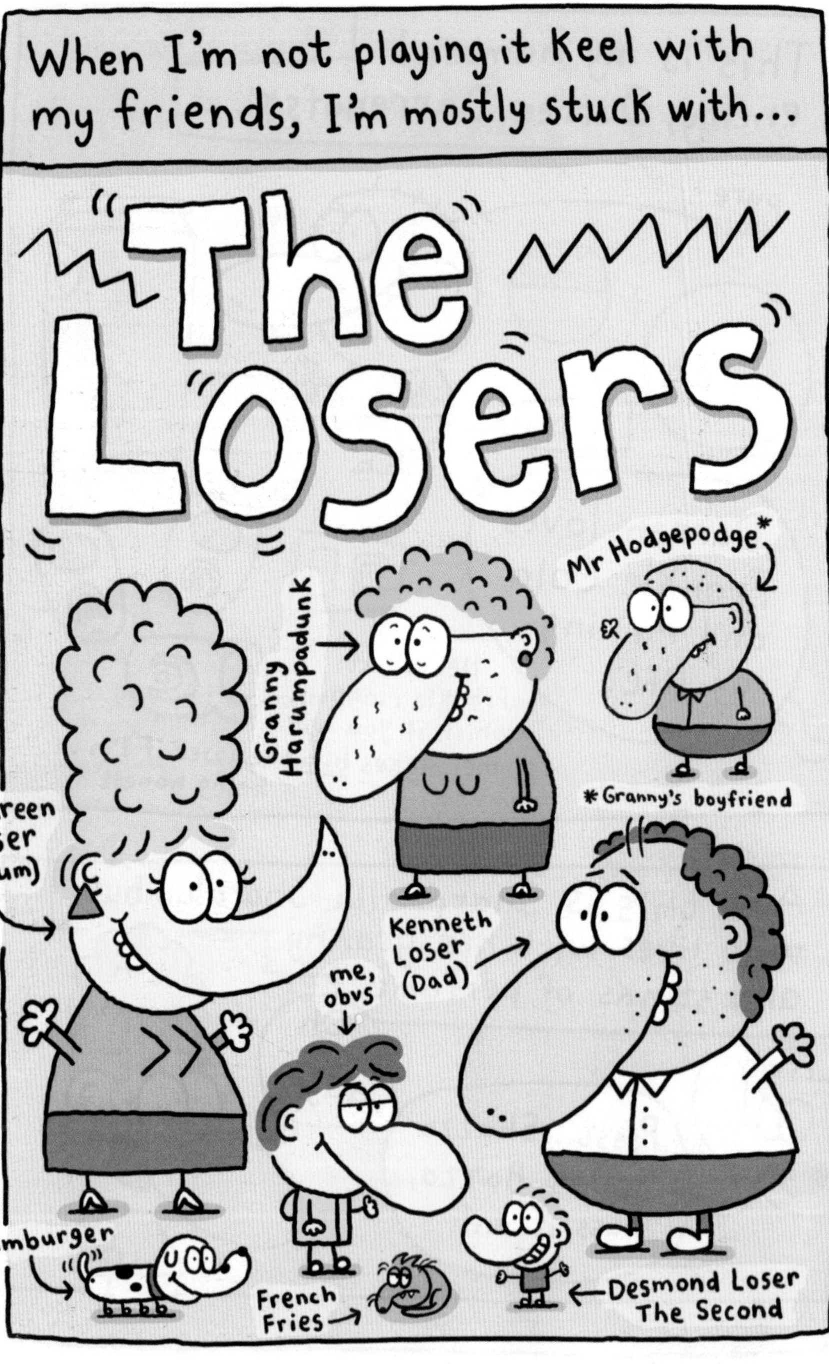
When I'm not playing it Keel with my friends, I'm mostly stuck with...
The Losers
Mr Hodgepodge*
Granny Harumpadunk
*Granny's boyfriend
Maureen Loser (Mum)
Kenneth Loser (Dad)
me, obvs
Hamburger
French Fries
Desmond Loser The Second

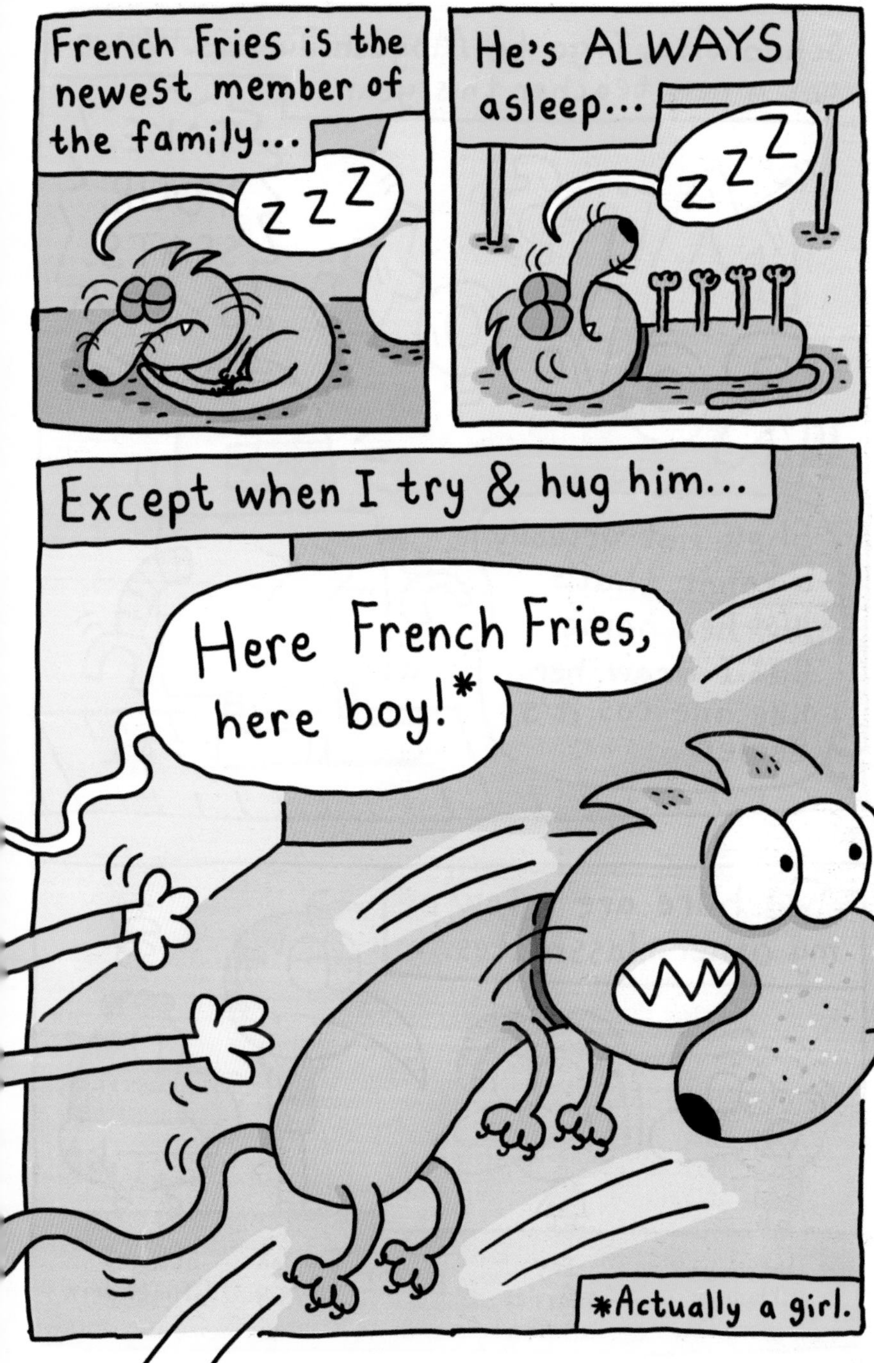
French Fries is the newest member of the family...
ZZZ
He's ALWAYS asleep...
ZZZ
Except when I try & hug him...
Here French Fries, here boy!*
*Actually a girl.

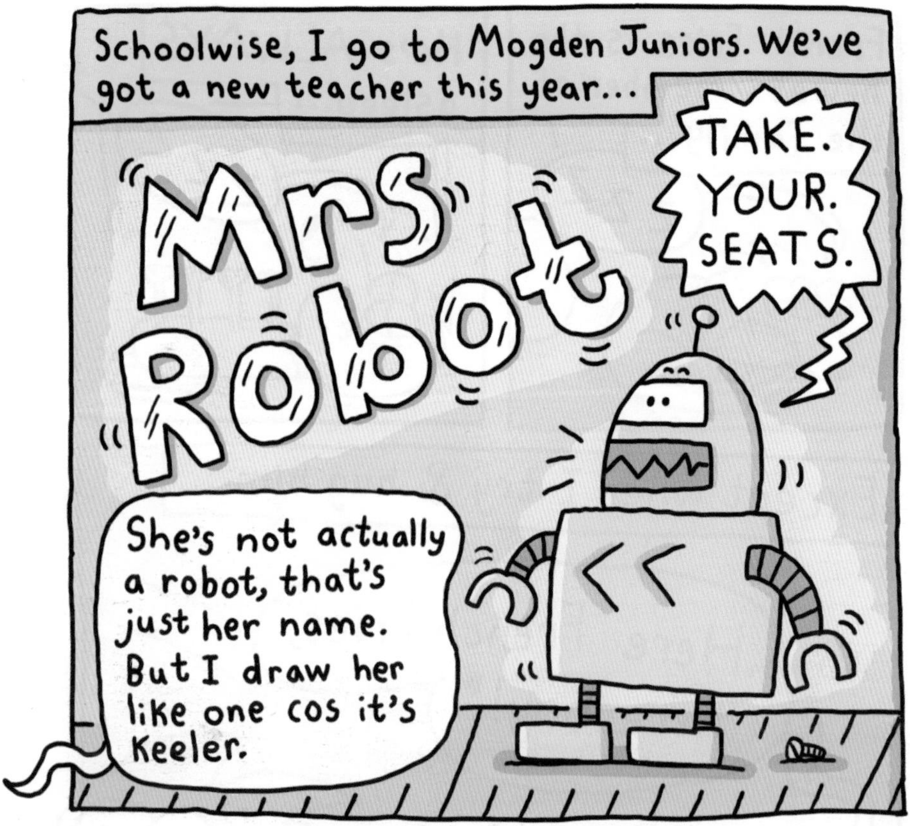
Schoolwise, I go to Mogden Juniors. We've got a new teacher this year...
Mrs Robot
TAKE. YOUR. SEATS.
She's not actually a robot, that's just her name. But I draw her like one cos it's Keeler.

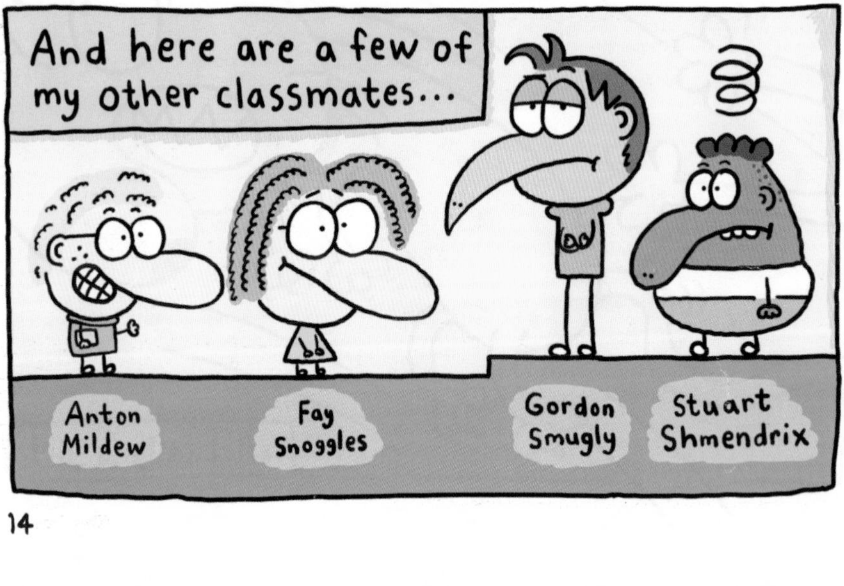
And here are a few of my other classmates...
Anton Mildew
Fay Snoggles
Gordon Smugly
Stuart Shmendrix

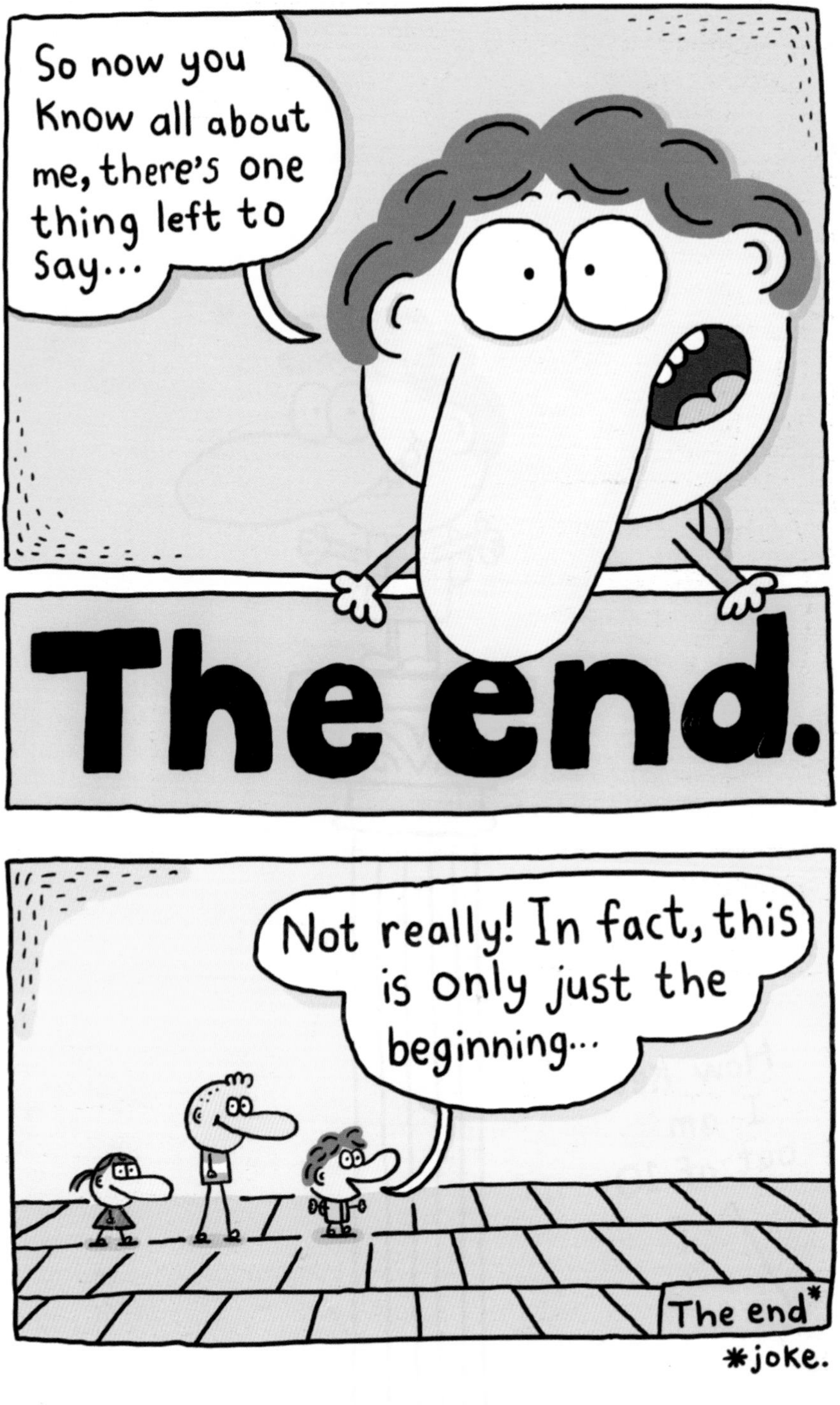
So now you Know all about me, there's one thing left to say...
The end.
Not really! In fact, this is only just the beginning...
The end*
*joke.

How keel
I am
out of 10

Episode 1

(Un) Happy Bday

Starring Barry Loser

That's me!

On the way to school one Spring morning...
Ah, isn't nature a wonderful thing!

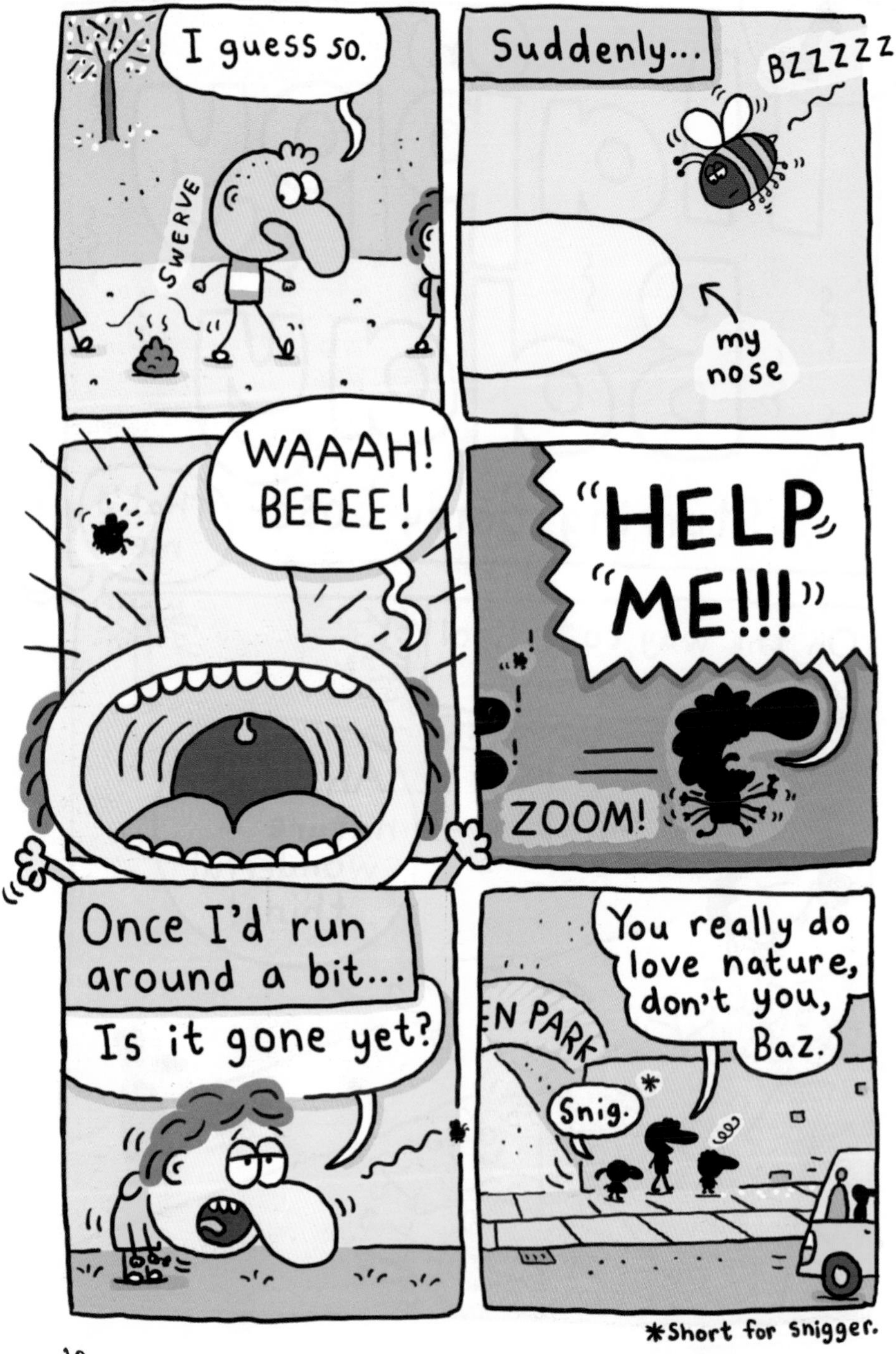
I guess so.
SWERVE
Suddenly...
BZZZZZ
my nose
WAAAH! BEEEE!
"HELP ME!!!"
ZOOM!
Once I'd run around a bit...
Is it gone yet?
EN PARK
You really do love nature, don't you, Baz.
Snig.*

*Short for snigger.

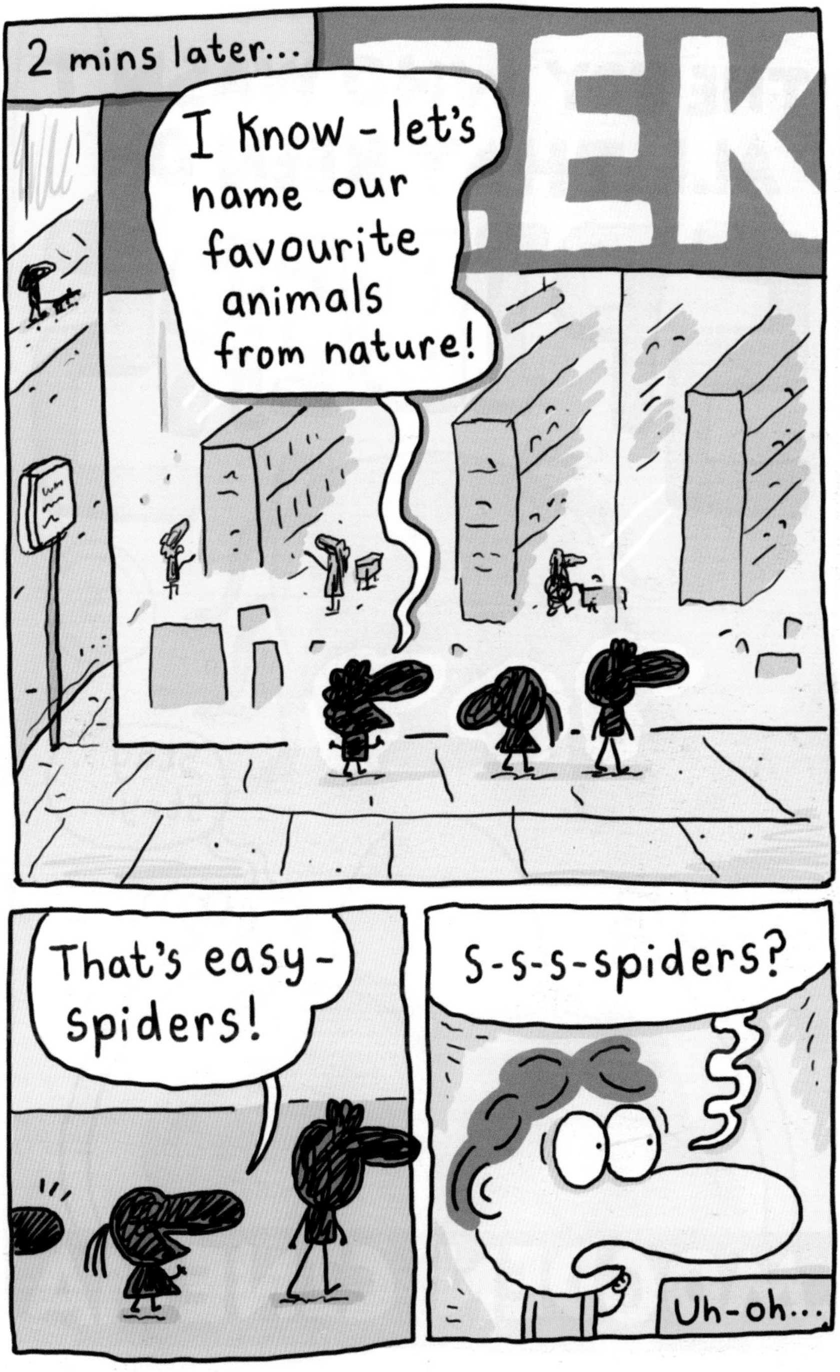
2 mins later...
EEK
I Know - let's name our favourite animals from nature!
That's easy - spiders!
S-s-s-spiders?
Uh-oh...

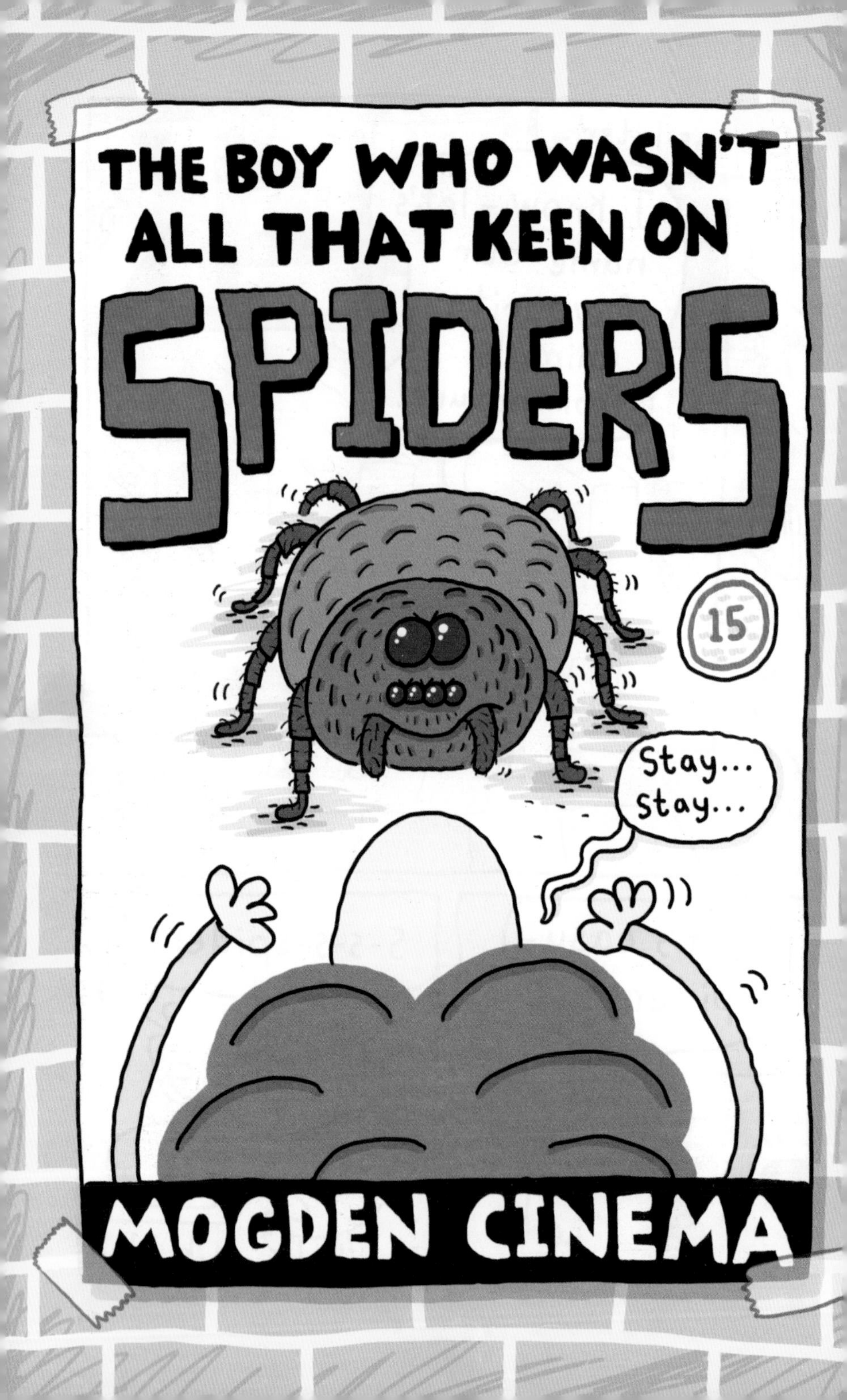
THE BOY WHO WASN'T ALL THAT KEEN ON SPIDERS
15
Stay... stay...
MOGDEN CINEMA

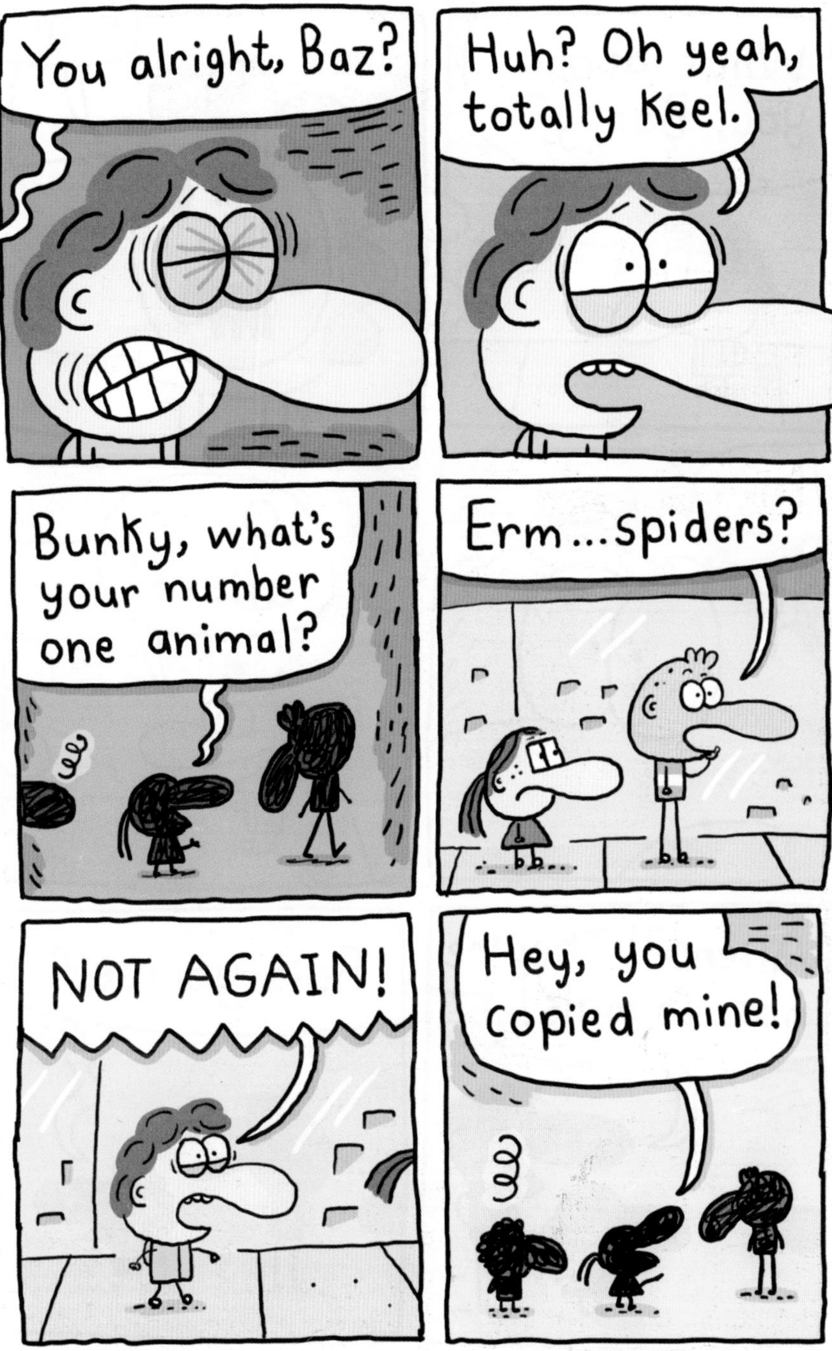
You alright, Baz?
Huh? Oh yeah, totally keel.
Bunky, what's your number one animal?
Erm...spiders?
NOT AGAIN!
Hey, you copied mine!

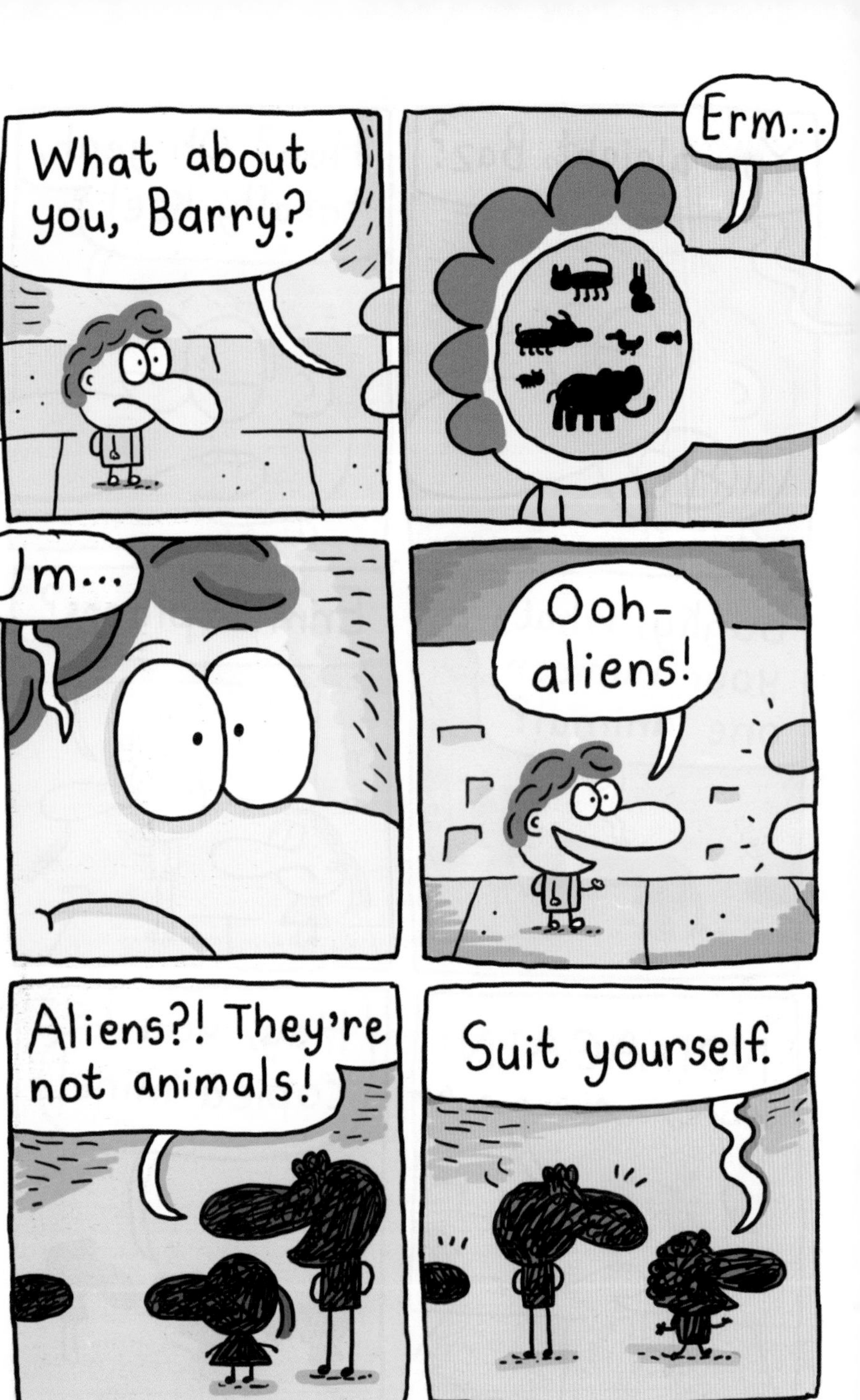
What about you, Barry?
Erm...
Um...
Ooh- aliens!
Aliens?! They're not animals!
Suit yourself.

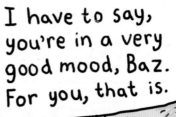
Anyway...

I have to say, you're in a very good mood, Baz. For you, that is.

Must be the joys of Spring.

Plus of course, my bday's just around the corner!

Just around the corner...

Just around the corner? It's ages away!

Yeah, mine's much closer.

Mine as well.

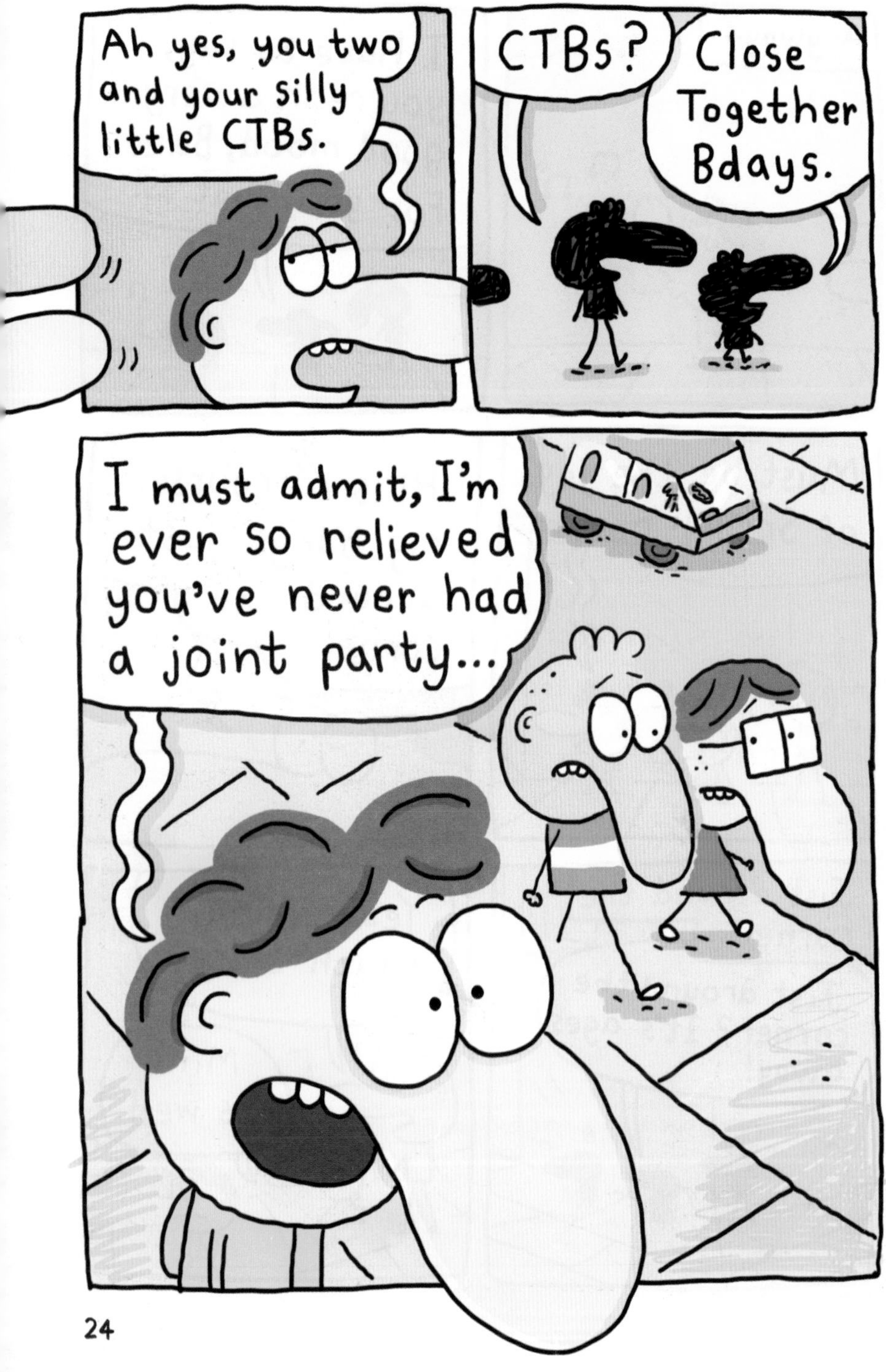
Ah yes, you two and your silly little CTBs.
CTBs?
Close Together Bdays.
I must admit, I'm ever so relieved you've never had a joint party...

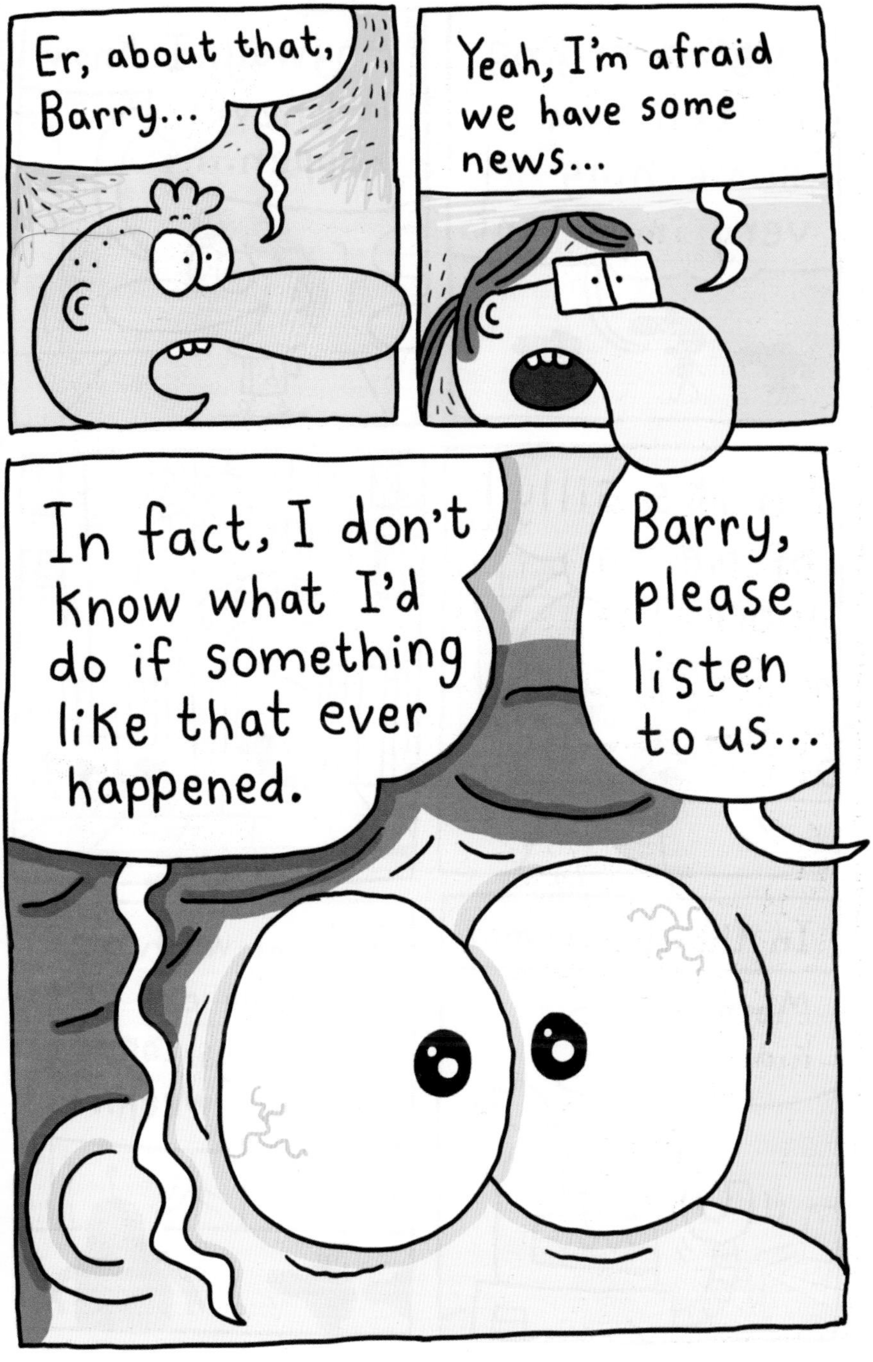
Er, about that, Barry...
Yeah, I'm afraid we have some news...
In fact, I don't know what I'd do if something like that ever happened.
Barry, please listen to us...

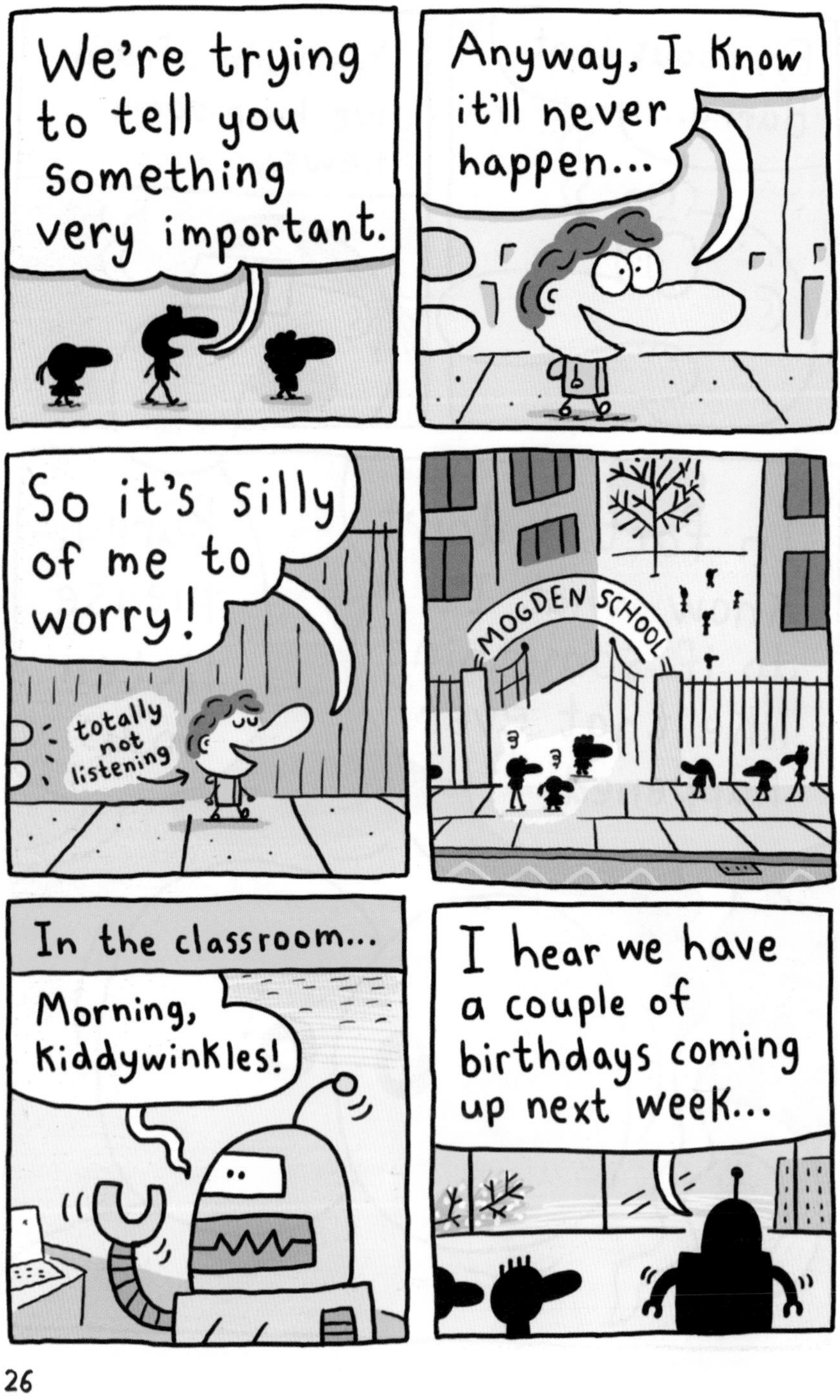
We're trying to tell you something very important.
Anyway, I Know it'll never happen...
So it's silly of me to worry!
totally not listening
MOGDEN SCHOOL
In the classroom...
Morning, Kiddywinkles!
I hear we have a couple of birthdays coming up next week...

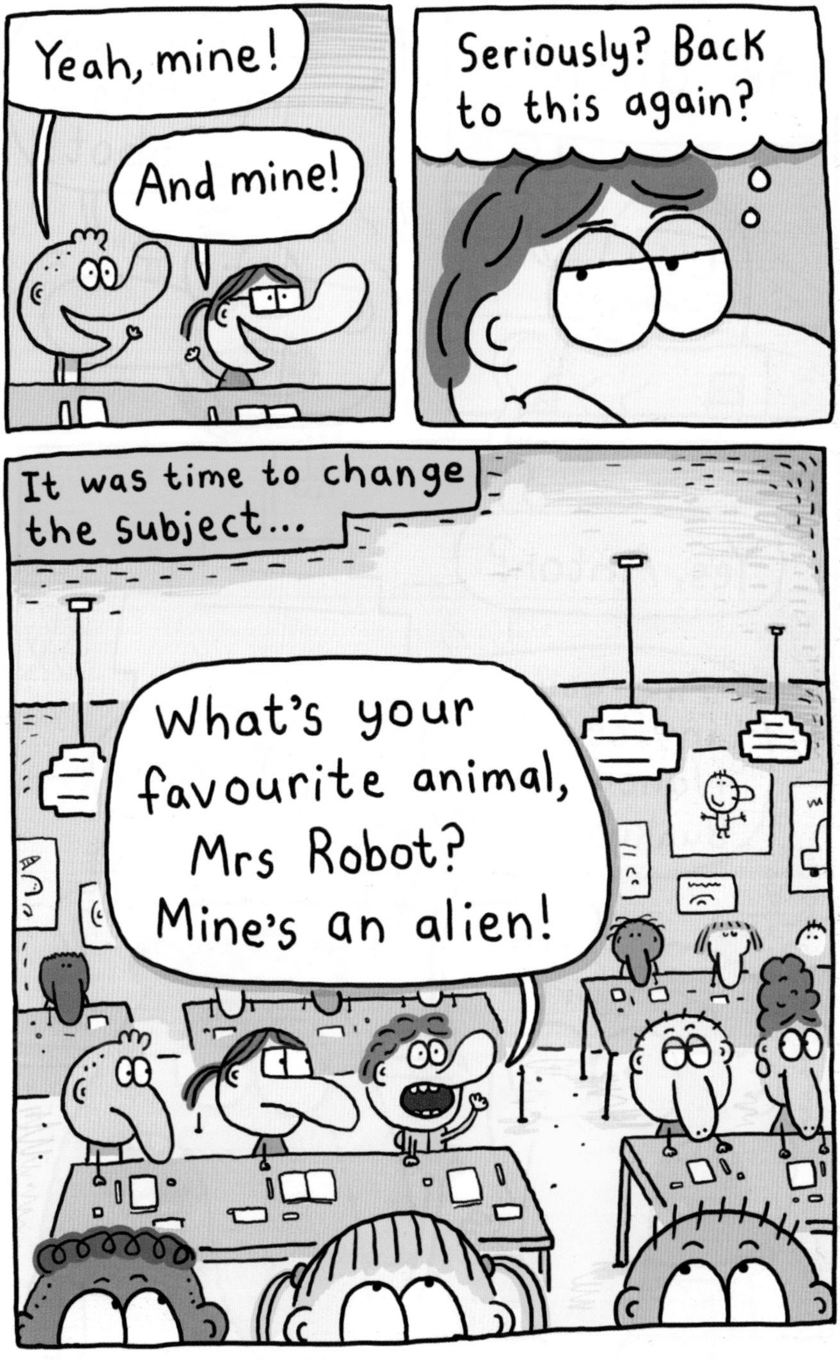

Yeah, mine!
And mine!
Seriously? Back to this again?
It was time to change the subject...
What's your favourite animal, Mrs Robot? Mine's an alien!

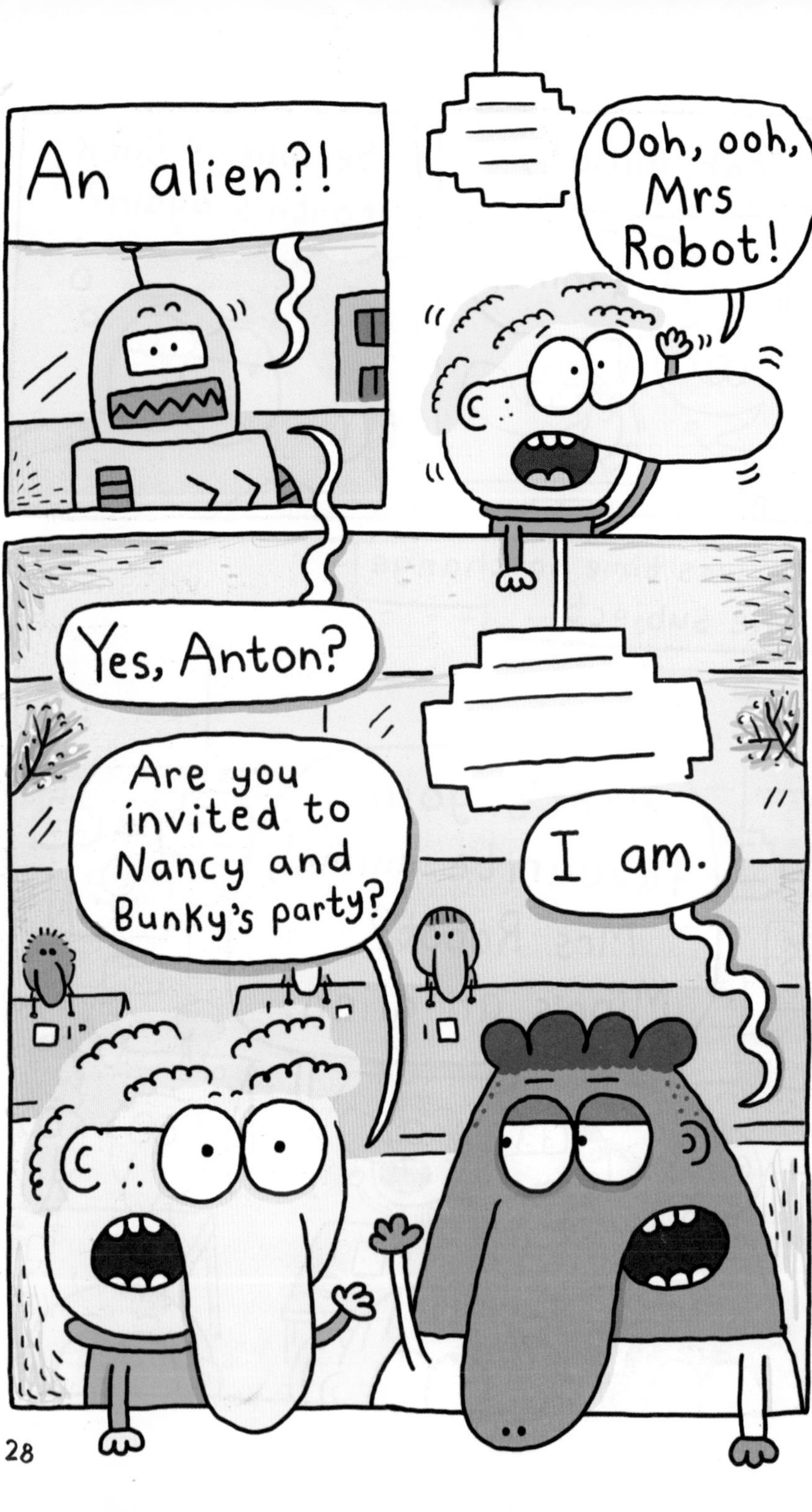
An alien?!
Ooh, ooh, Mrs Robot!
Yes, Anton?
Are you invited to Nancy and Bunky's party?
I am.

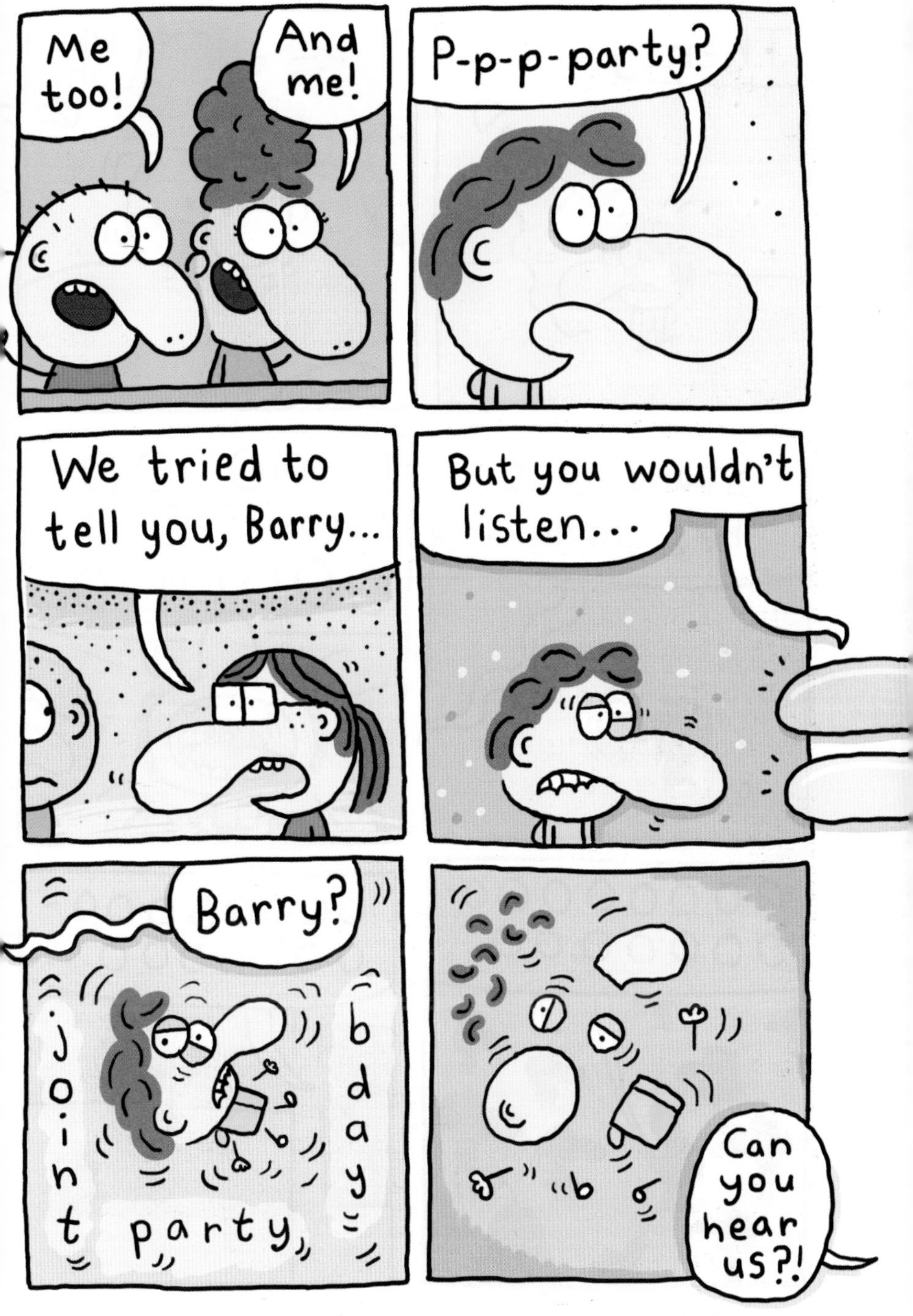
Me too!
And me!
P-p-p-party?
We tried to tell you, Barry...
But you wouldn't listen...
Barry?
joint party, bday
Can you hear us?!

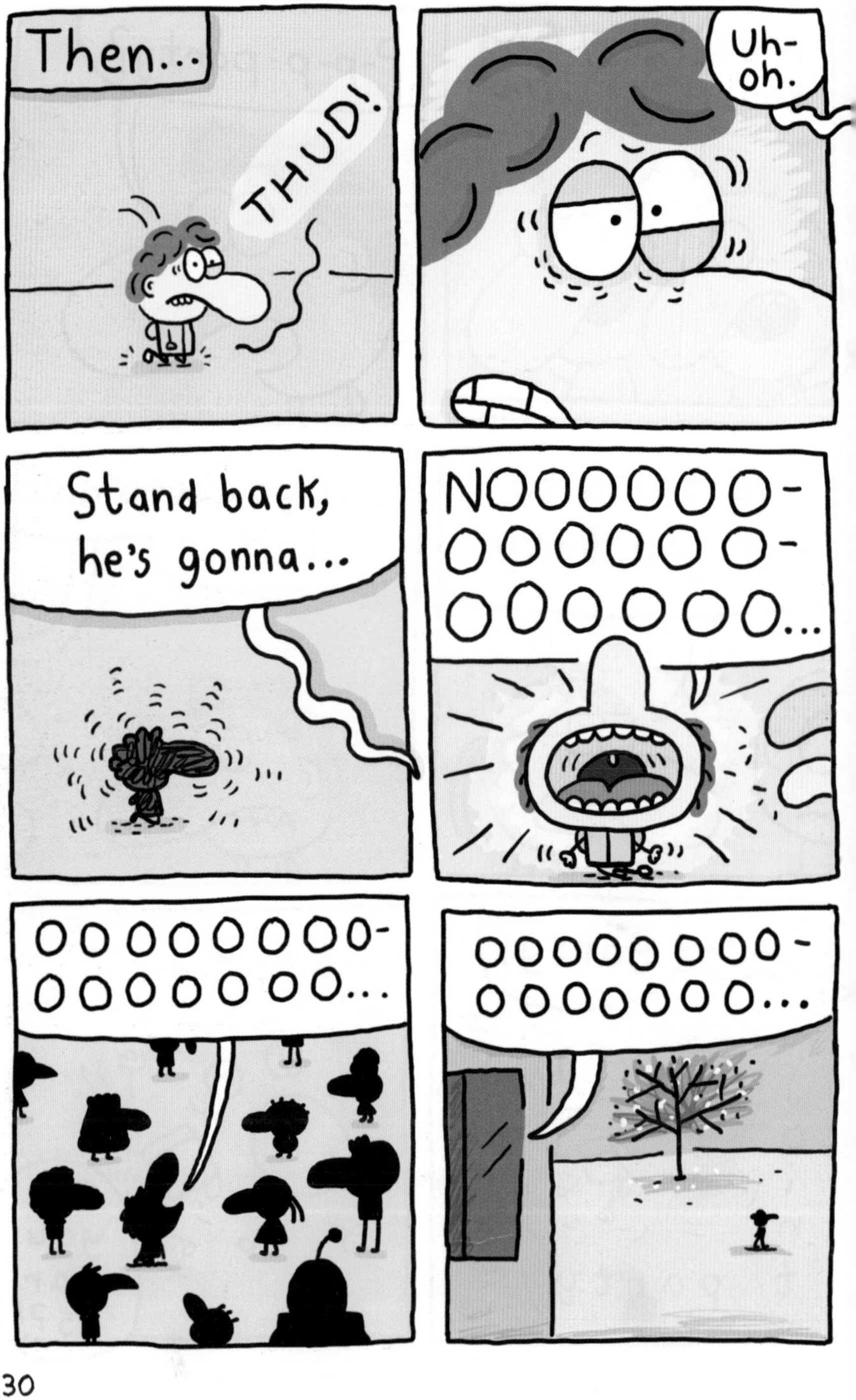
Then...
THUD!
Uh-oh.
Stand back, he's gonna...
NOOOOOO-OOOOOOO-OOOOOOO...
OOOOOOOOO-OOOOOOOOO...
OOOOOOOOO-OOOOOOOO...

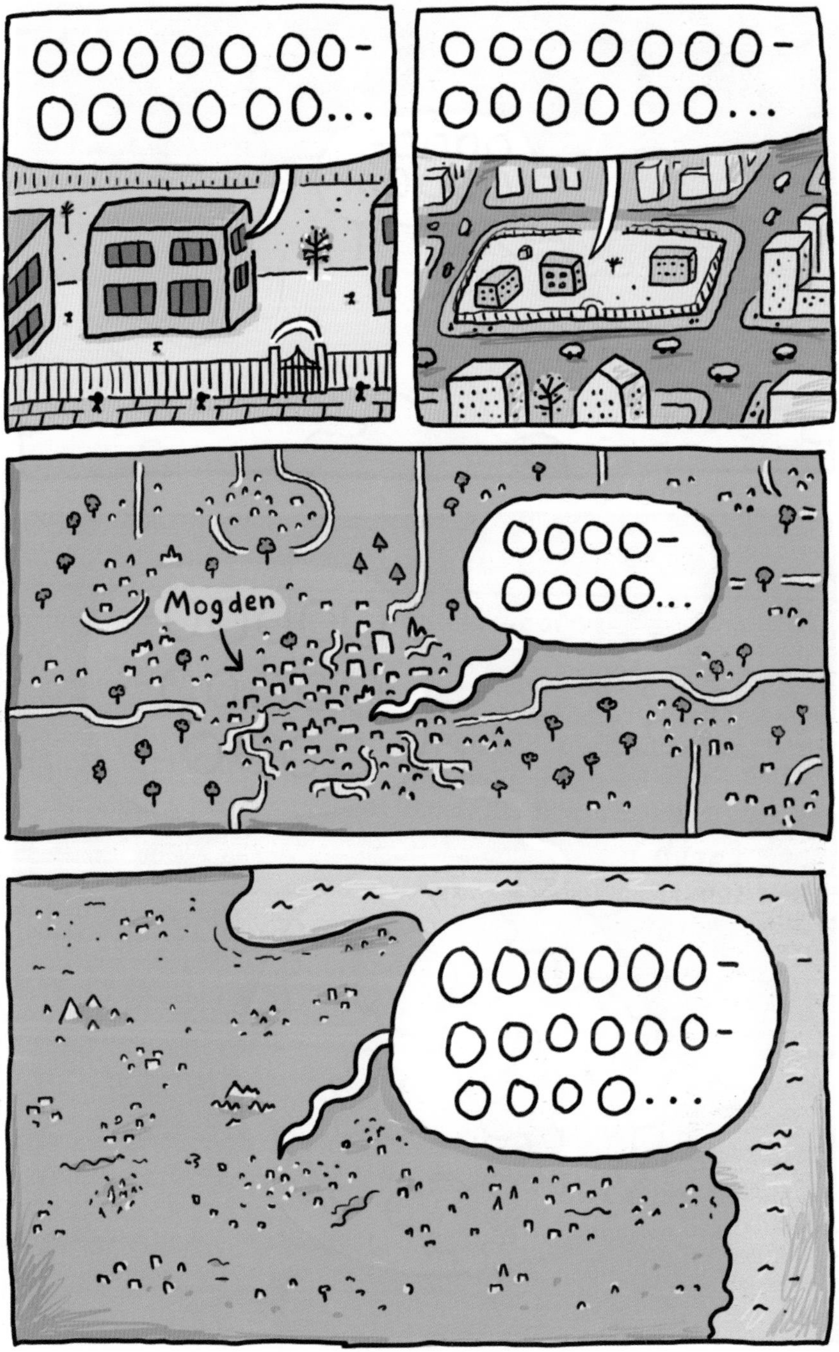
OOOOOOO-
OOOOOO...
OOOOOOO-
OOOOOO...
Mogden
OOOO-
OOOO...
OOOOOO-
OOOOOO-
OOOO...

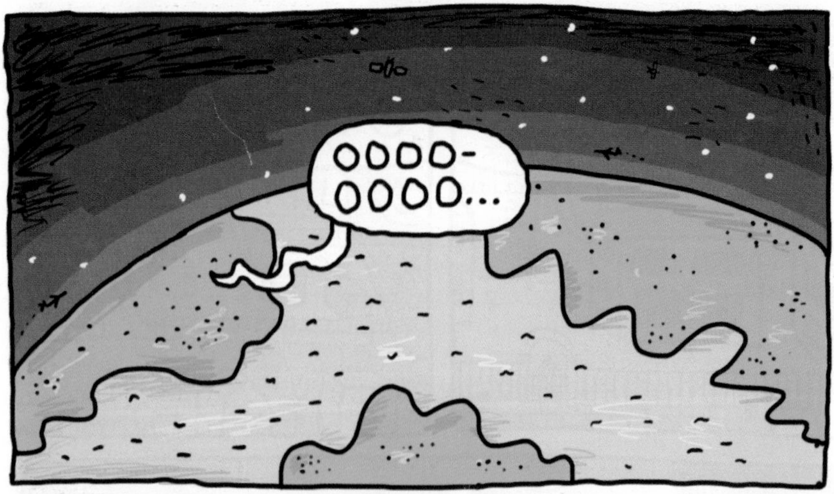
OOOO-
OOOO...

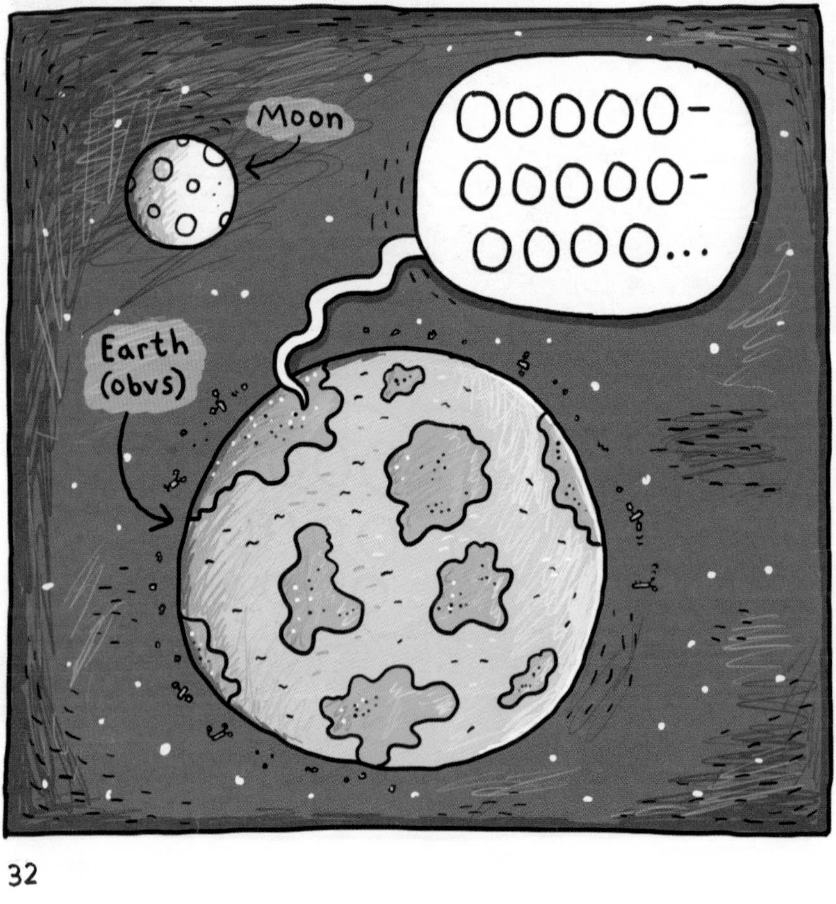
Moon
OOOOO-
OOOOO-
OOOO...
Earth
(obvs)

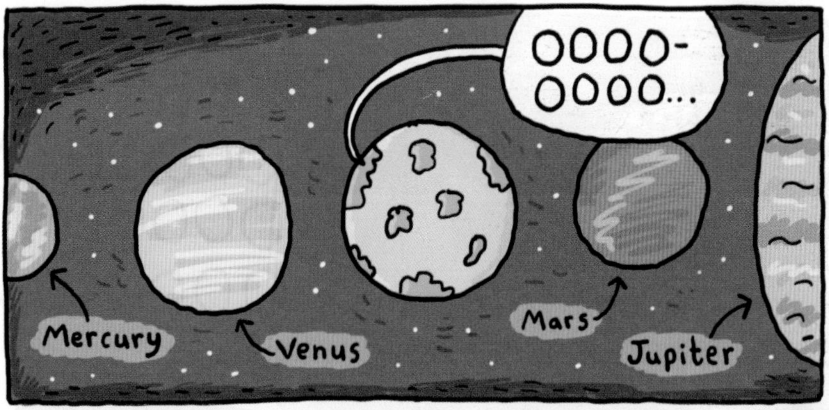
OOOO-
OOOO...
Mercury
Venus
Mars
Jupiter

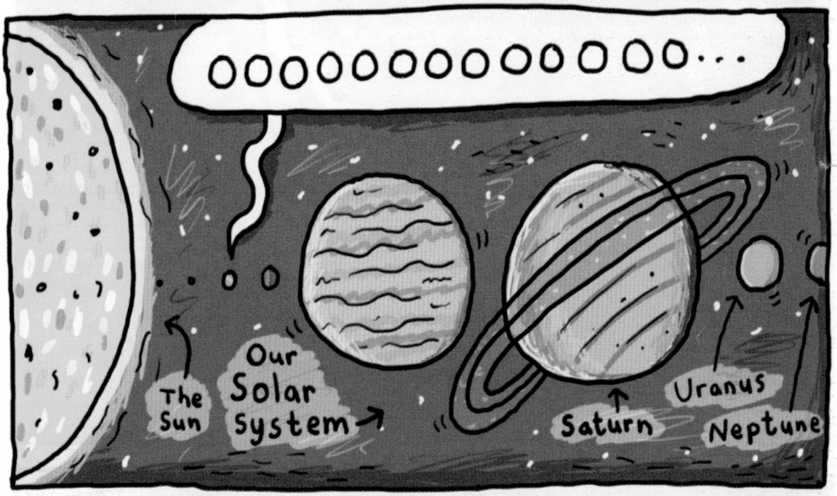
OOOOOOOOOOOOO...
The Sun
Our Solar System
Saturn
Uranus
Neptune

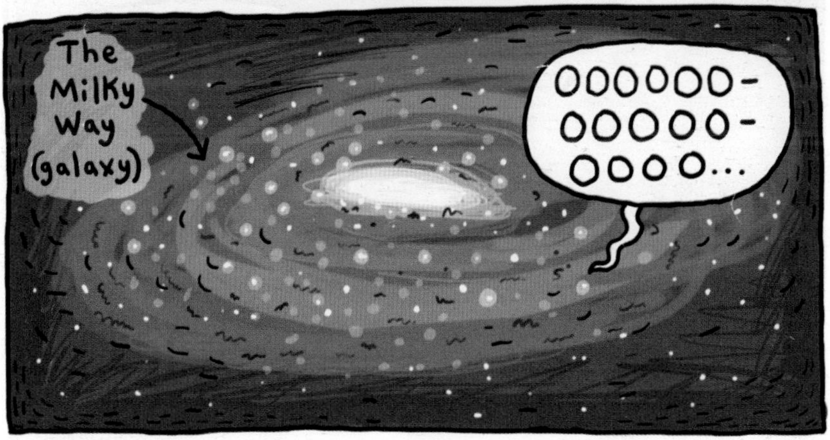
The Milky Way (galaxy)
OOOOOO-
OOOOO-
OOOO...

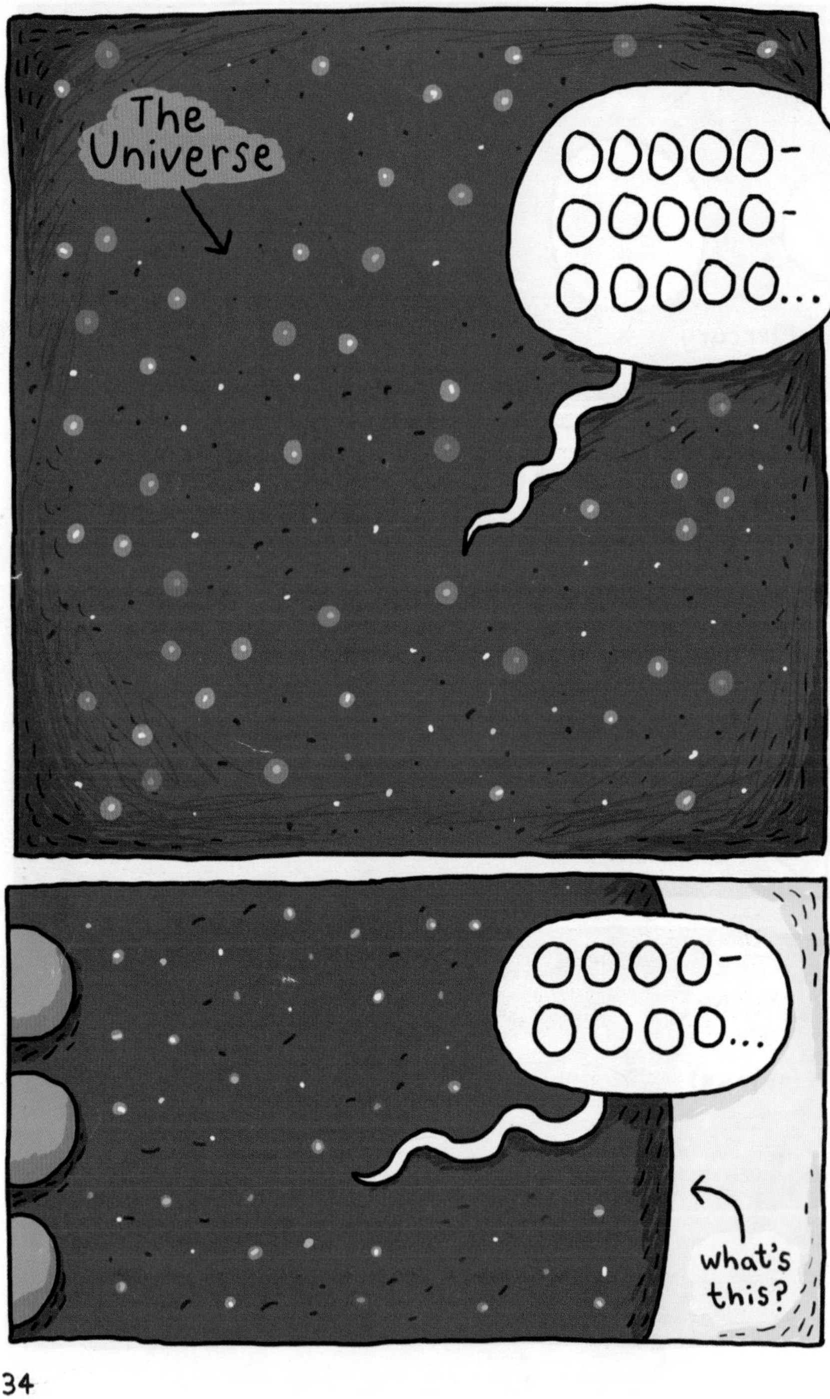
The Universe
OOOOO-
OOOOO-
OOOOO...
OOOO-
OOOO...
what's this?

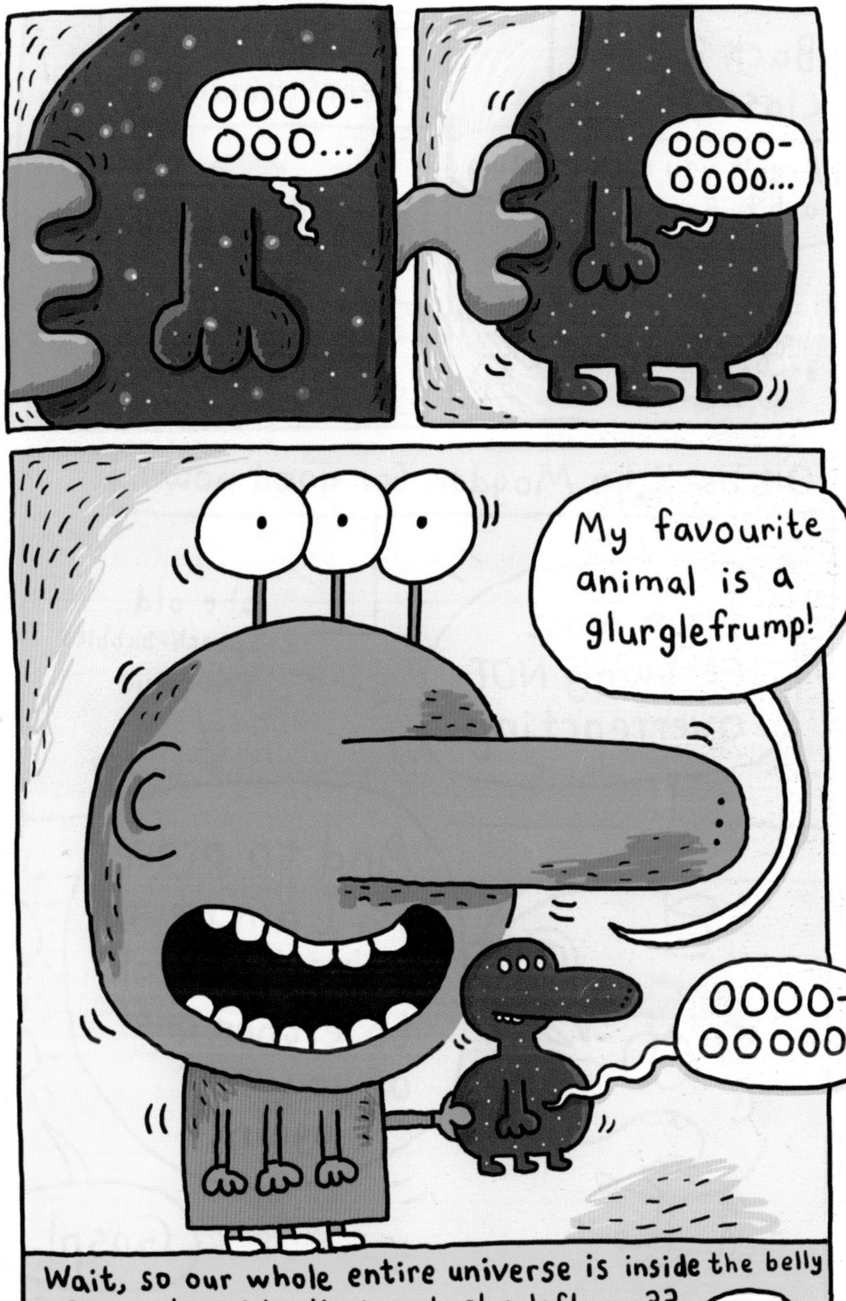
OOOO-
OOO...
OOOO-
OOOO...
My favourite animal is a glurglefrump!
OOOO-
OOOOO.
Wait, so our whole entire universe is inside the belly of some loserish alien's pet glurgleflump??
Yep!

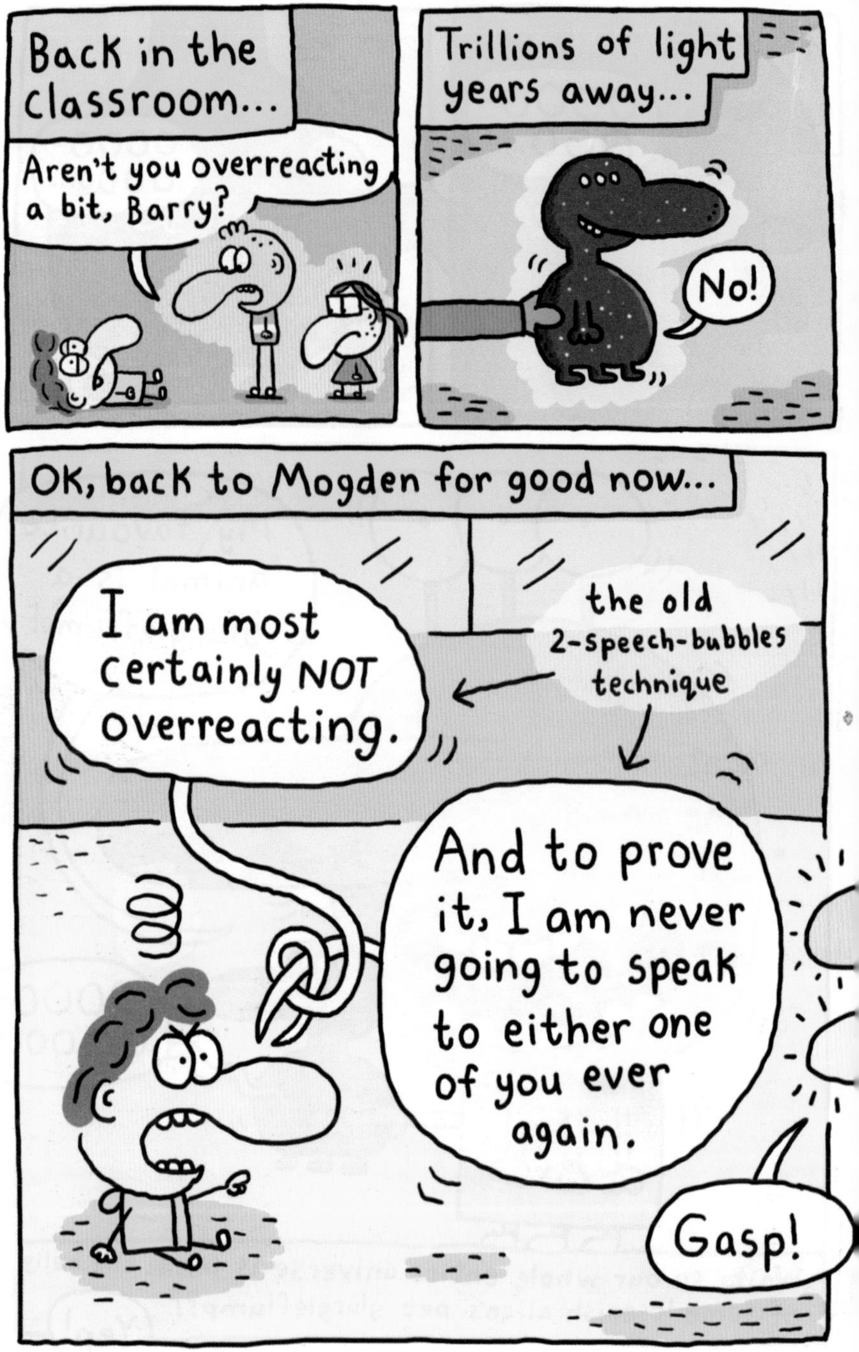

Back in the classroom...
Aren't you overreacting a bit, Barry?
Trillions of light years away...
No!
OK, back to Mogden for good now...
I am most certainly NOT overreacting.
the old 2-speech-bubbles technique
And to prove it, I am never going to speak to either one of you ever again.
Gasp!

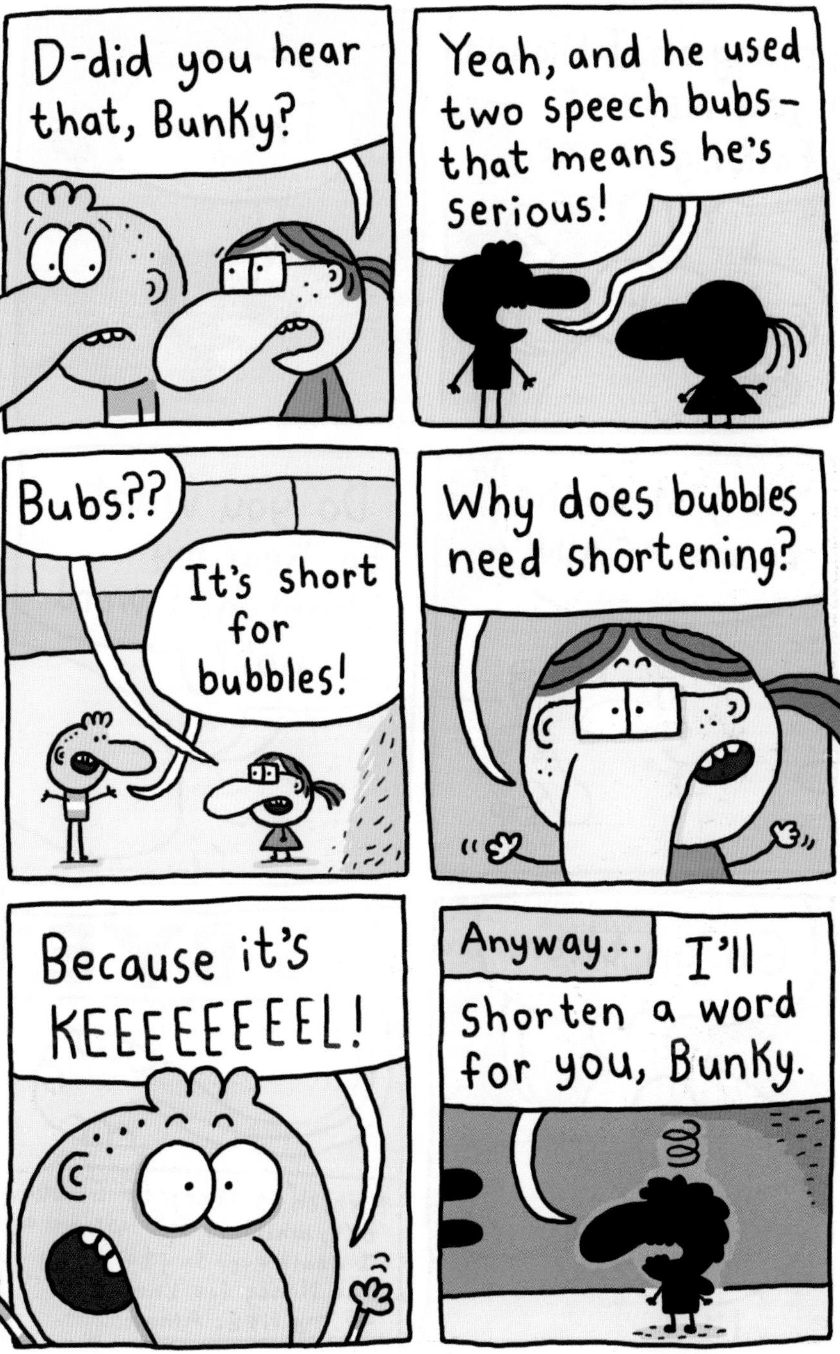
D-did you hear that, Bunky?
Yeah, and he used two speech bubs - that means he's serious!
Bubs??
It's short for bubbles!
Why does bubbles need shortening?
Because it's KEEEEEEEEL!
Anyway...
I'll shorten a word for you, Bunky.

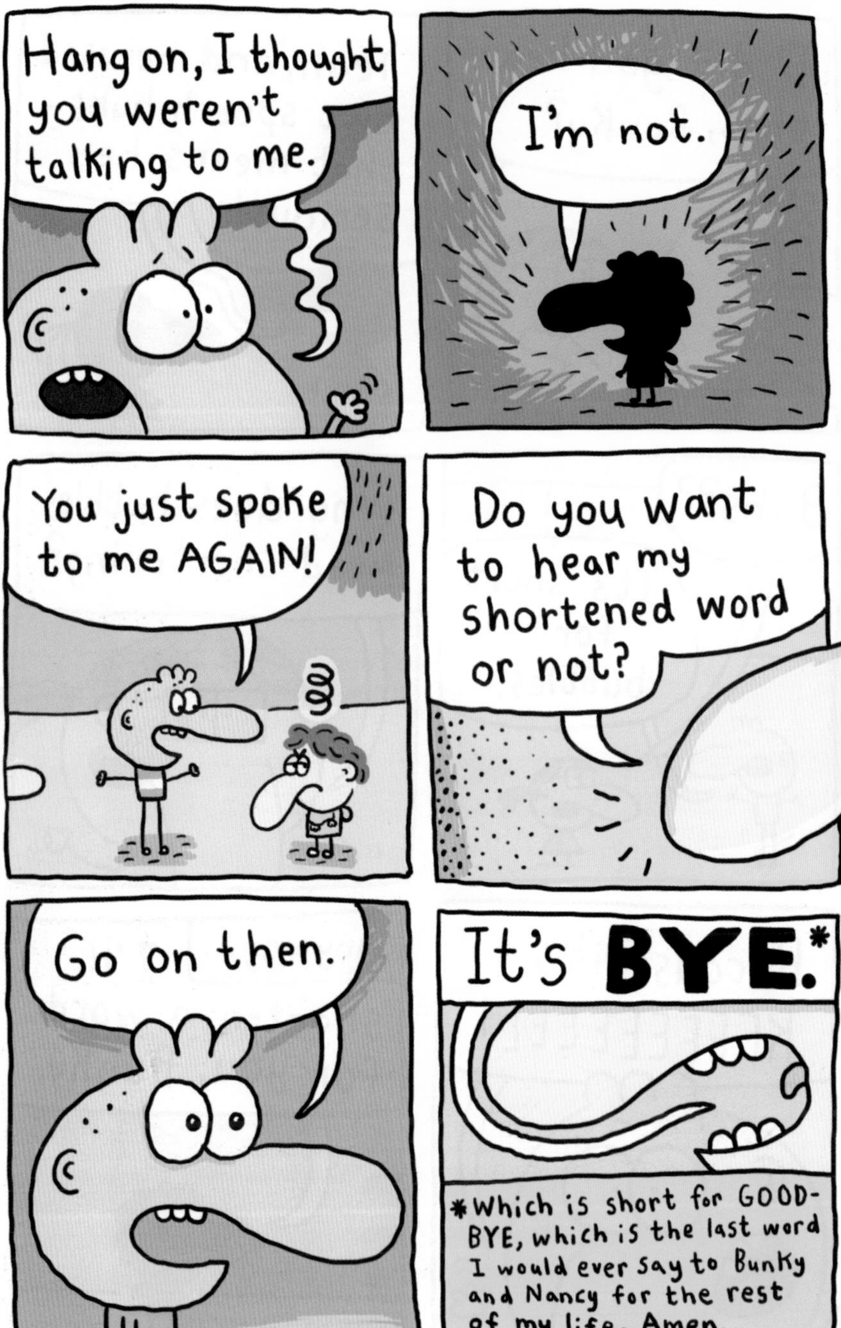
Hang on, I thought you weren't talking to me.
I'm not.
You just spoke to me AGAIN!
Do you want to hear my shortened word or not?
Go on then.
It's **BYE.***
*Which is short for GOOD-BYE, which is the last word I would ever say to Bunky and Nancy for the rest of my life. Amen.

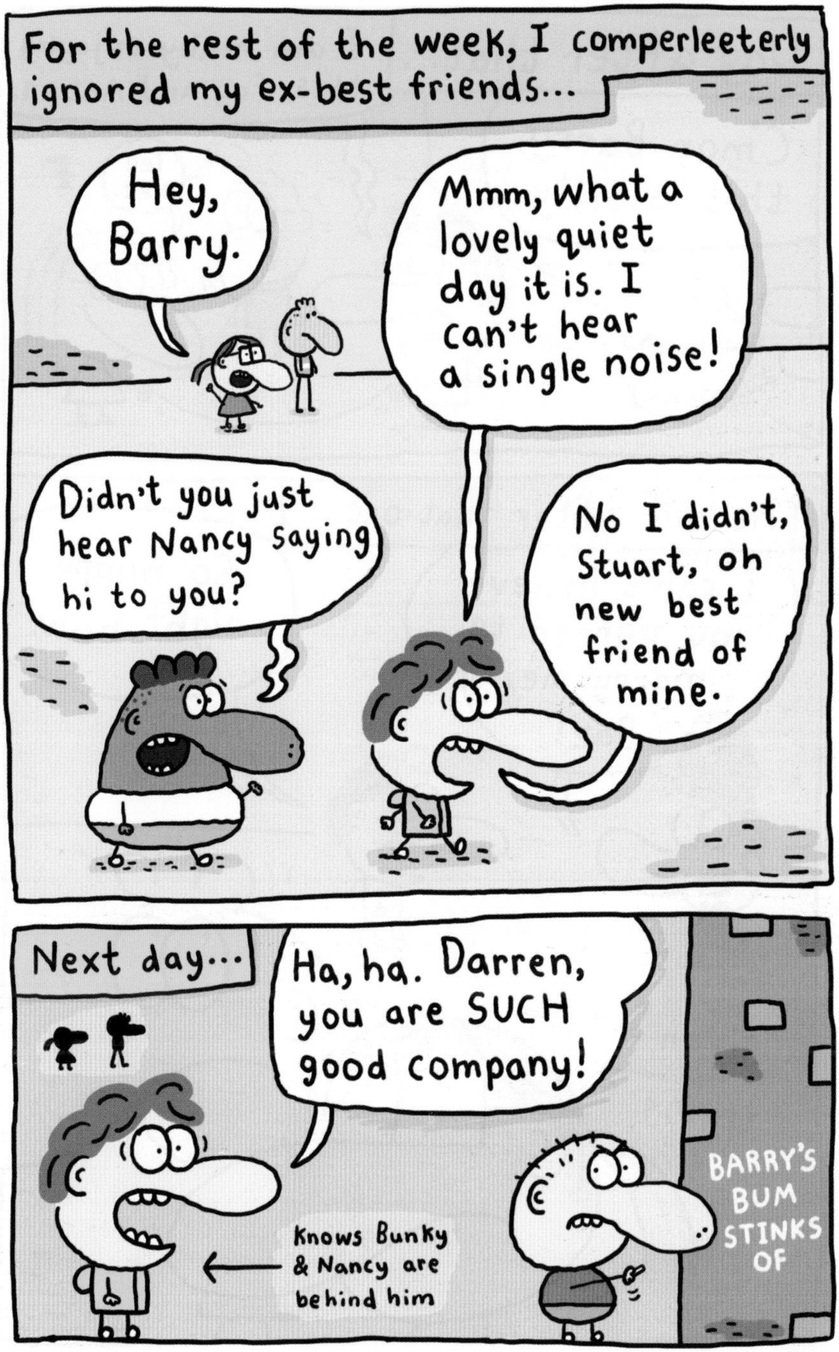
For the rest of the week, I comperleeterly ignored my ex-best friends...
Hey, Barry.
Mmm, what a lovely quiet day it is. I can't hear a single noise!
Didn't you just hear Nancy saying hi to you?
No I didn't, Stuart, oh new best friend of mine.
Next day...
Ha, ha. Darren, you are SUCH good company!
Knows Bunky & Nancy are behind him
BARRY'S BUM STINKS OF

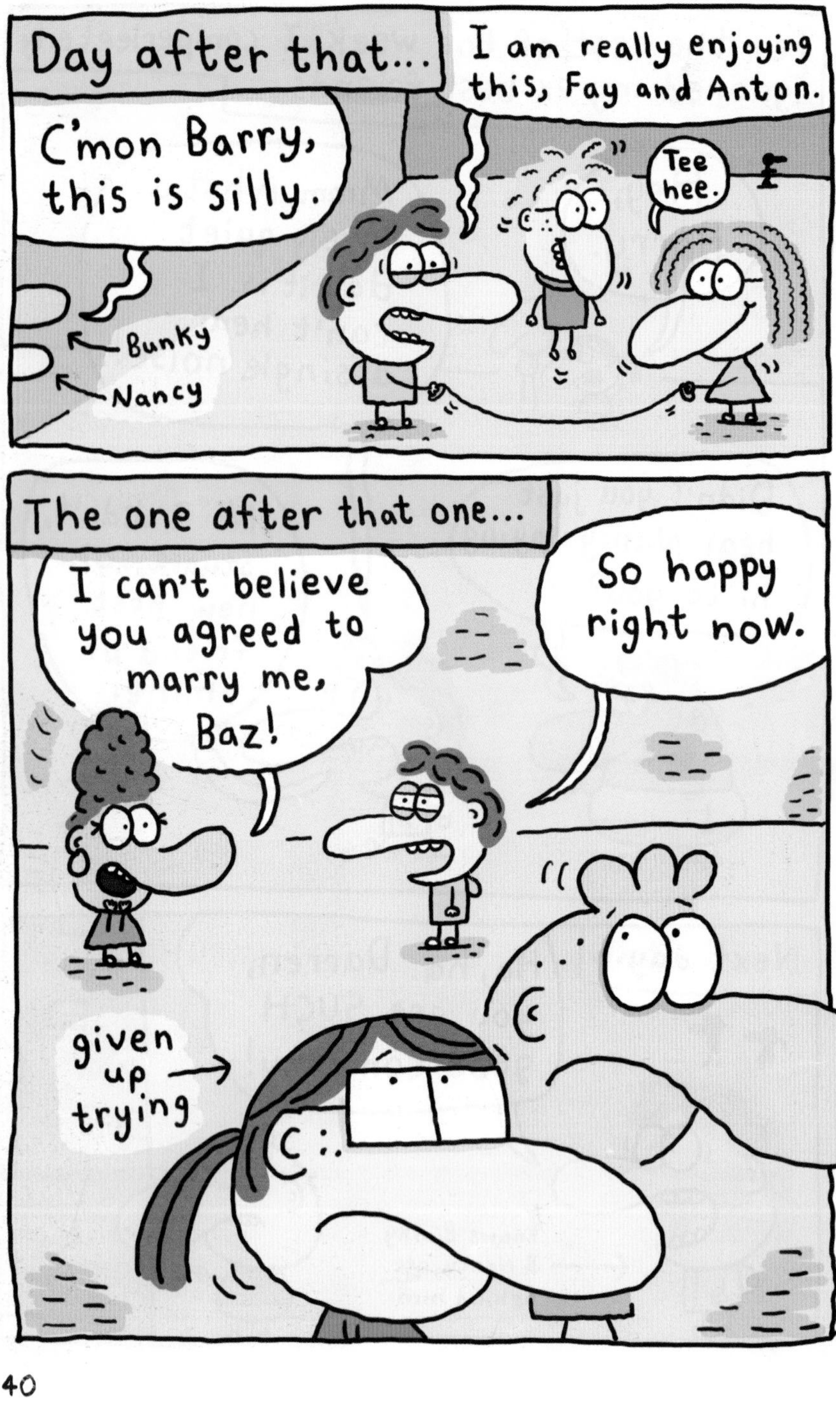

Day after that...
I am really enjoying this, Fay and Anton.
C'mon Barry, this is silly.
Tee hee.
Bunky
Nancy
The one after that one...
I can't believe you agreed to marry me, Baz!
So happy right now.
given up trying

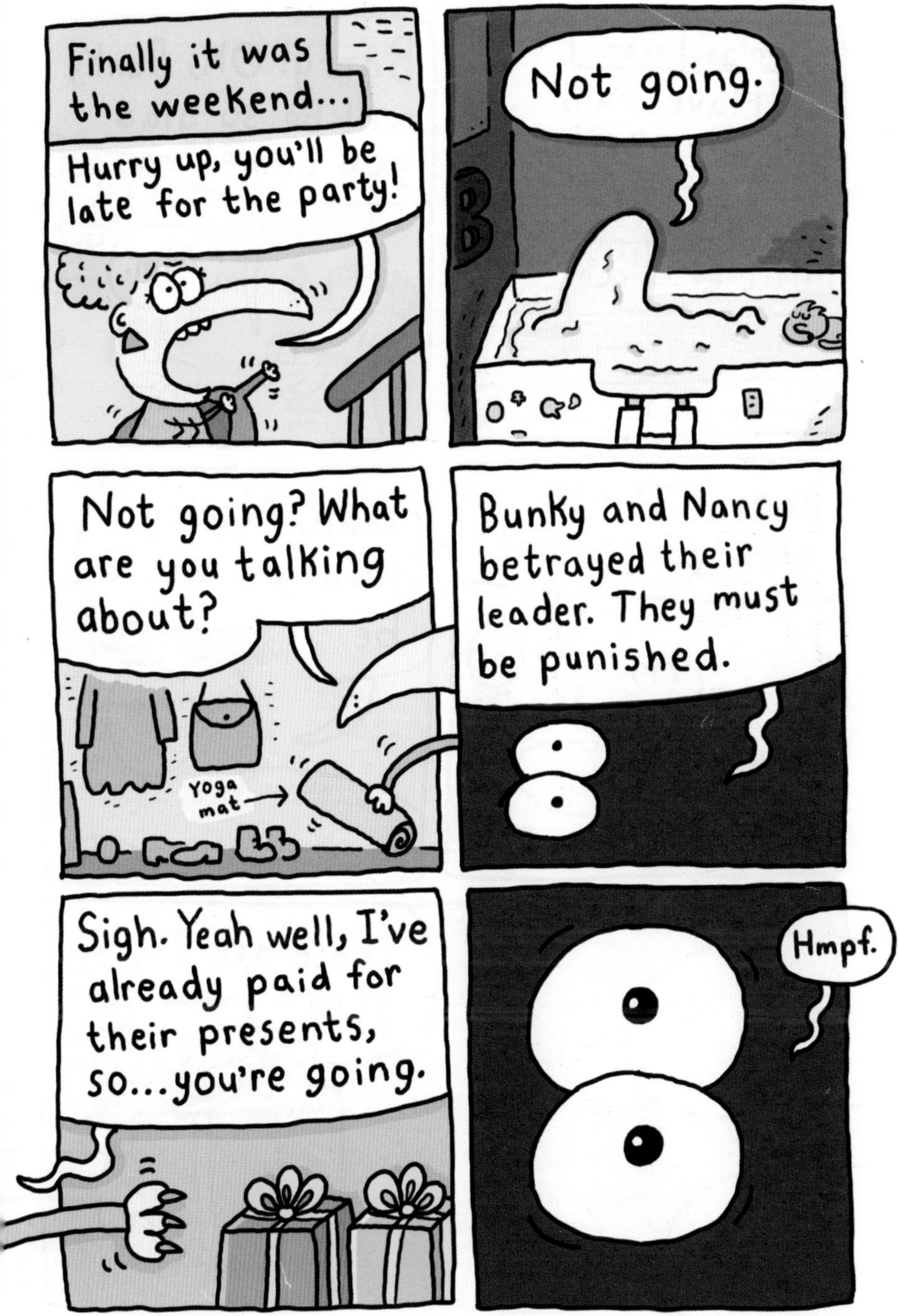
Finally it was the weekend...
Hurry up, you'll be late for the party!
Not going.
Not going? What are you talking about?
Yoga mat
Bunky and Nancy betrayed their leader. They must be punished.
Sigh. Yeah well, I've already paid for their presents, so...you're going.
Hmpf.

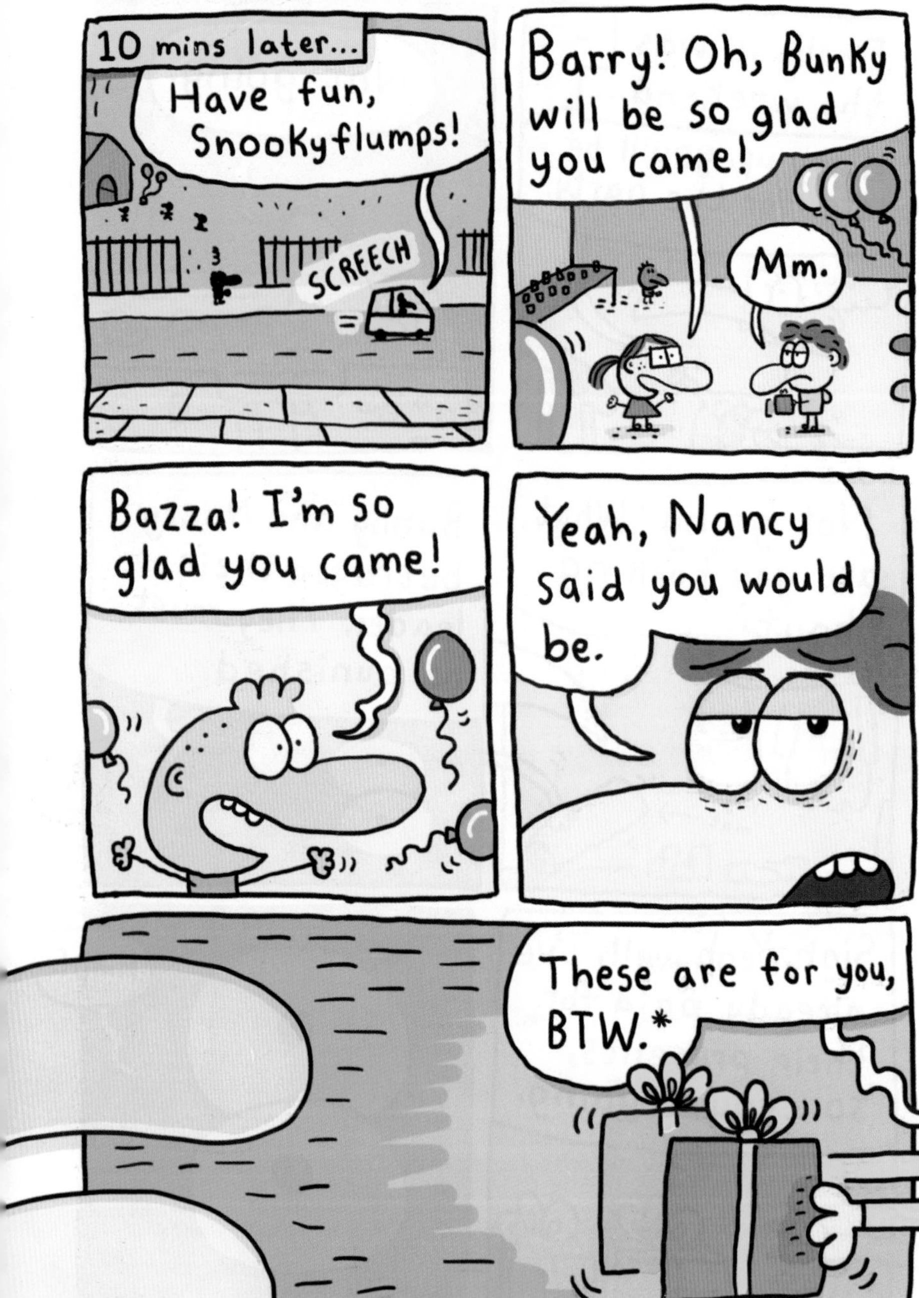
10 mins later...
Have fun, Snookyflumps!
SCREECH
Barry! Oh, Bunky will be so glad you came!
Mm.
Bazza! I'm so glad you came!
Yeah, Nancy said you would be.
These are for you, BTW.*

* Short for 'by the way'.

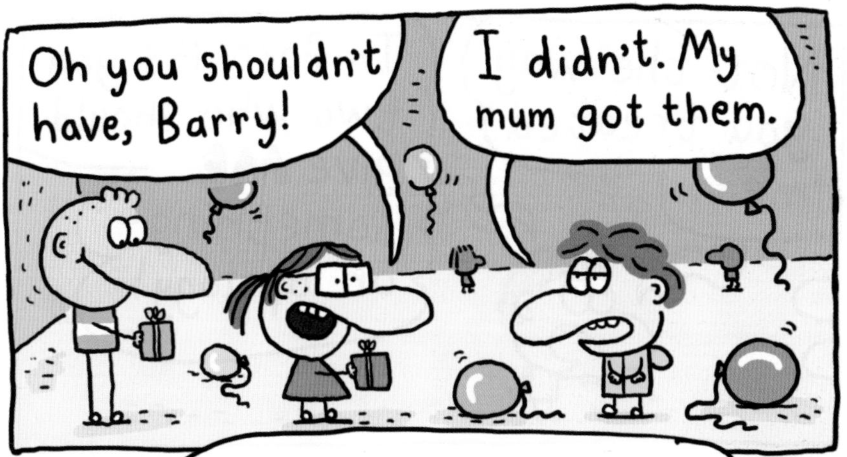
Oh you shouldn't have, Barry!
I didn't. My mum got them.

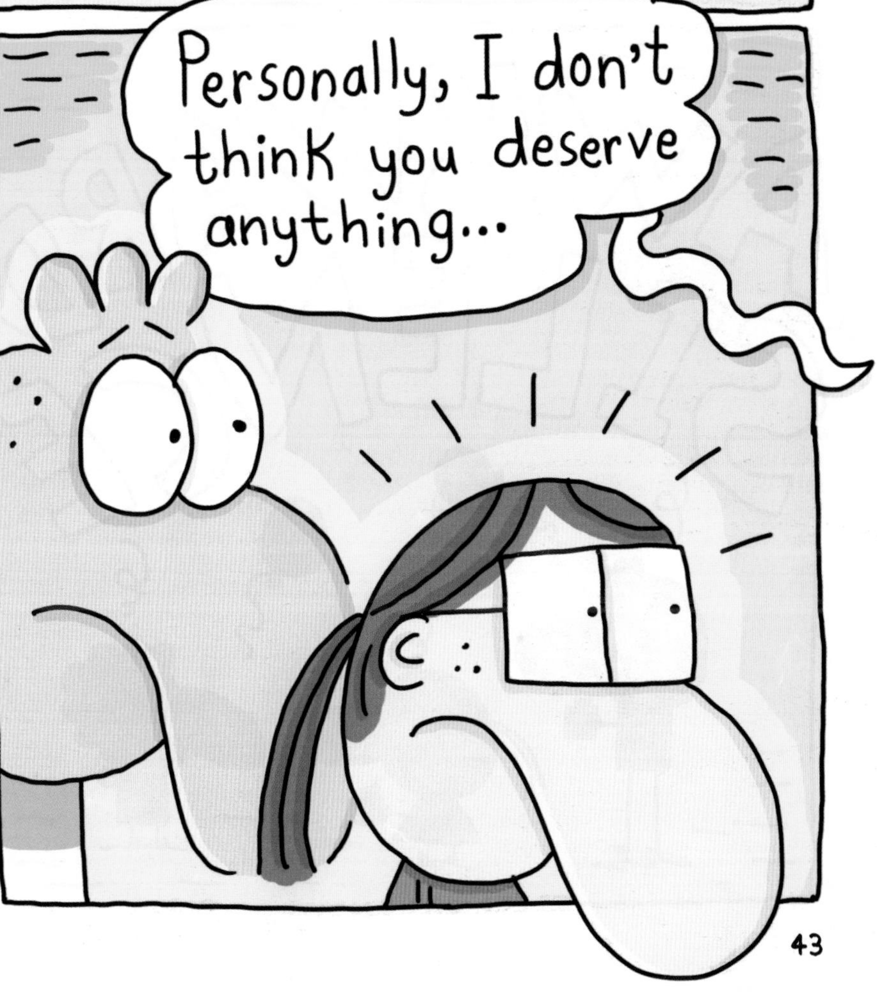
Personally, I don't think you deserve anything...

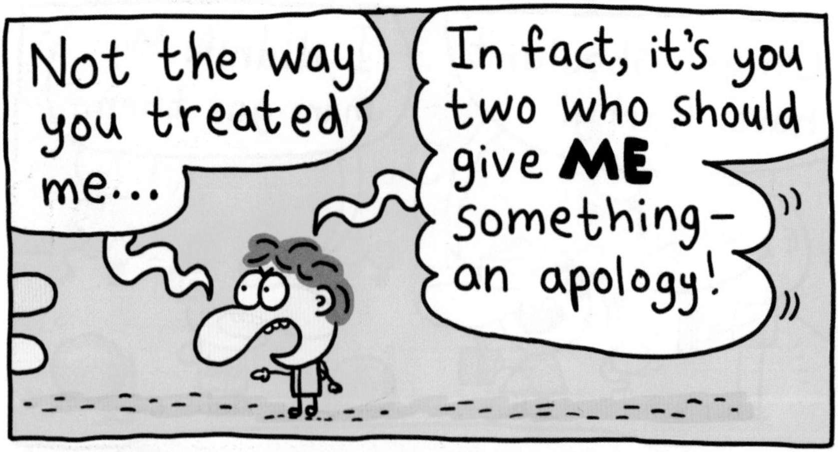
Not the way you treated me...
In fact, it's you two who should give **ME** something– an apology!

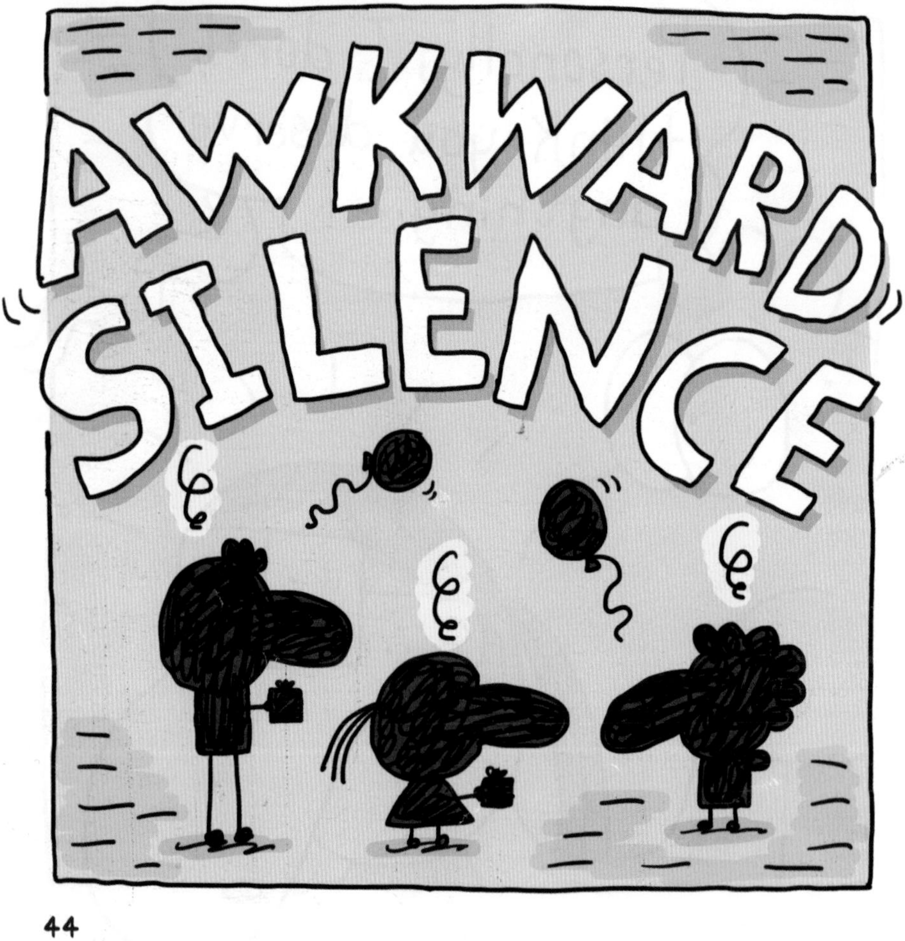
AWKWARD SILENCE

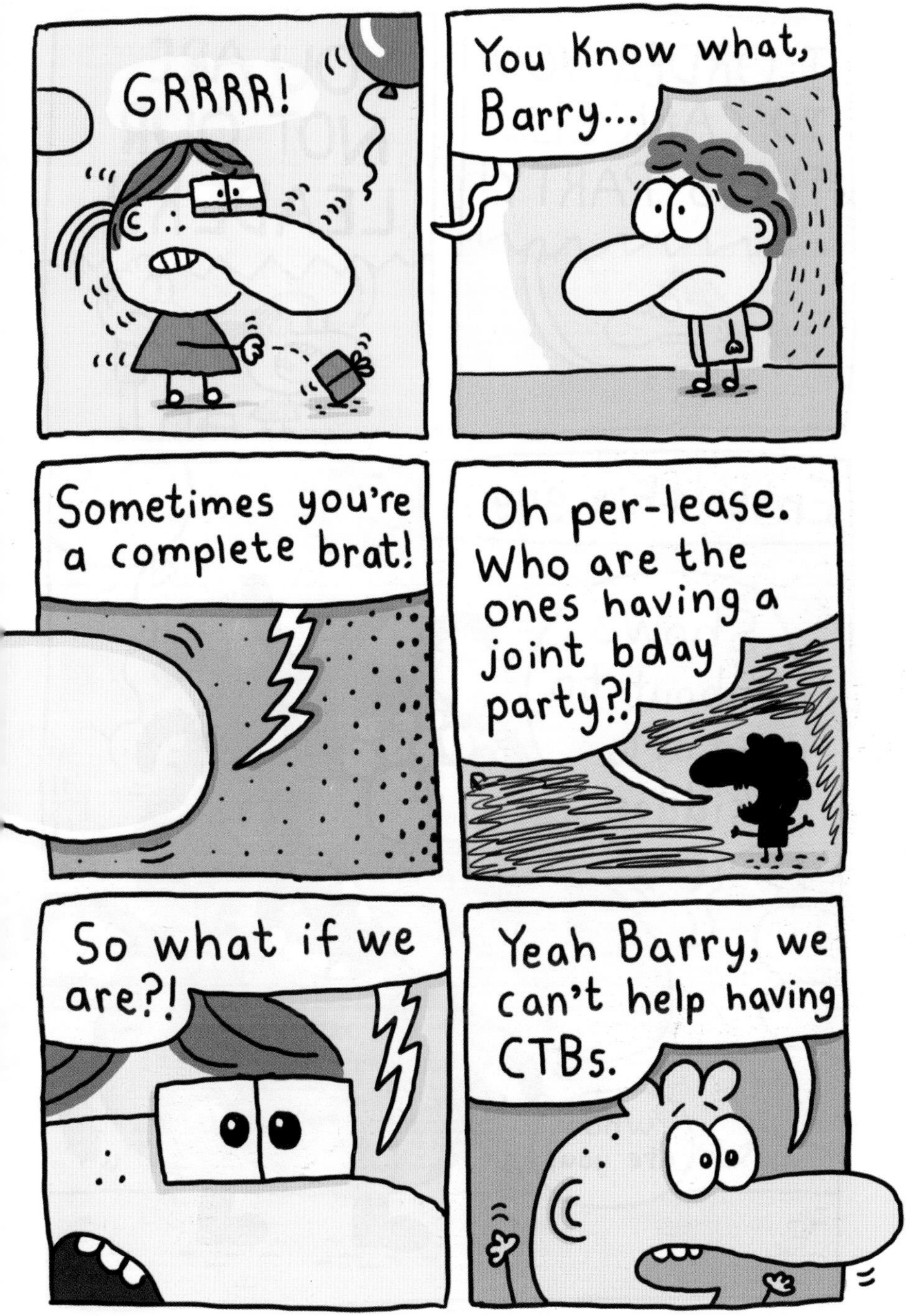
GRRRR!
You know what, Barry...
Sometimes you're a complete brat!
Oh per-lease. Who are the ones having a joint bday party?!
So what if we are?!
Yeah Barry, we can't help having CTBs.

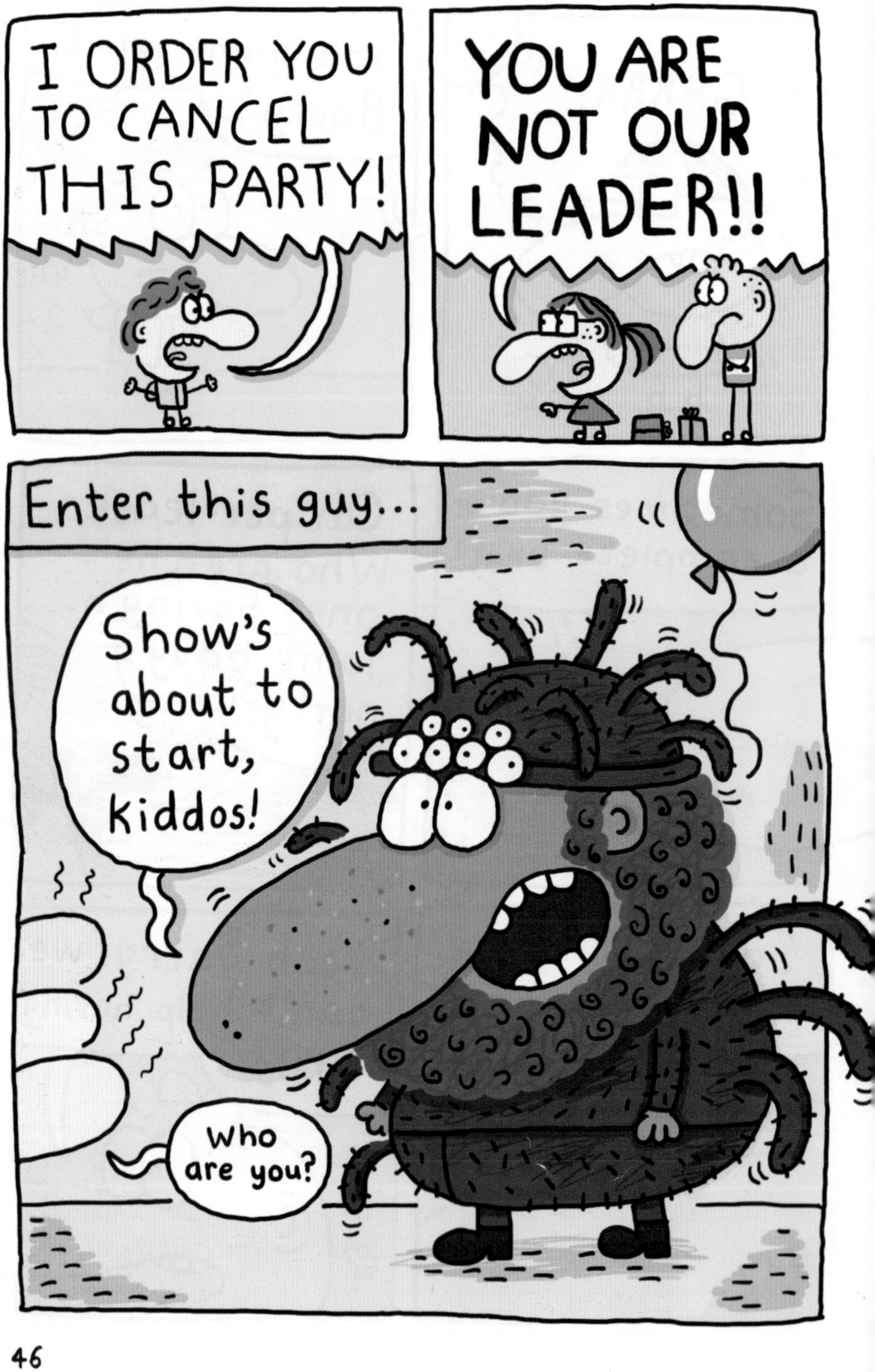
I ORDER YOU TO CANCEL THIS PARTY!
YOU ARE NOT OUR LEADER!!
Enter this guy...
Show's about to start, kiddos!
Who are you?

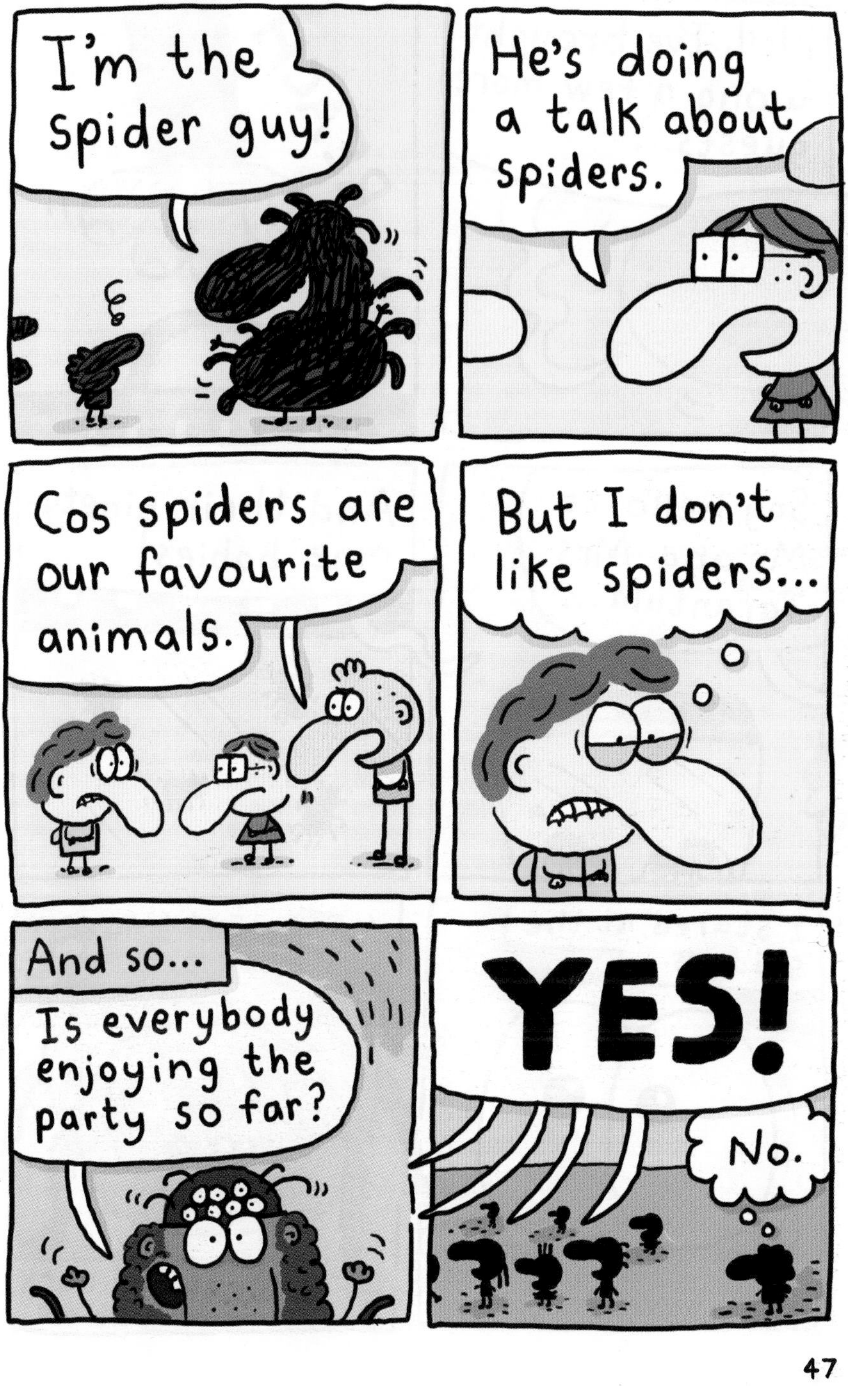
I'm the spider guy!
He's doing a talk about spiders.
Cos spiders are our favourite animals.
But I don't like spiders...
And so...
Is everybody enjoying the party so far?
YES!
No.

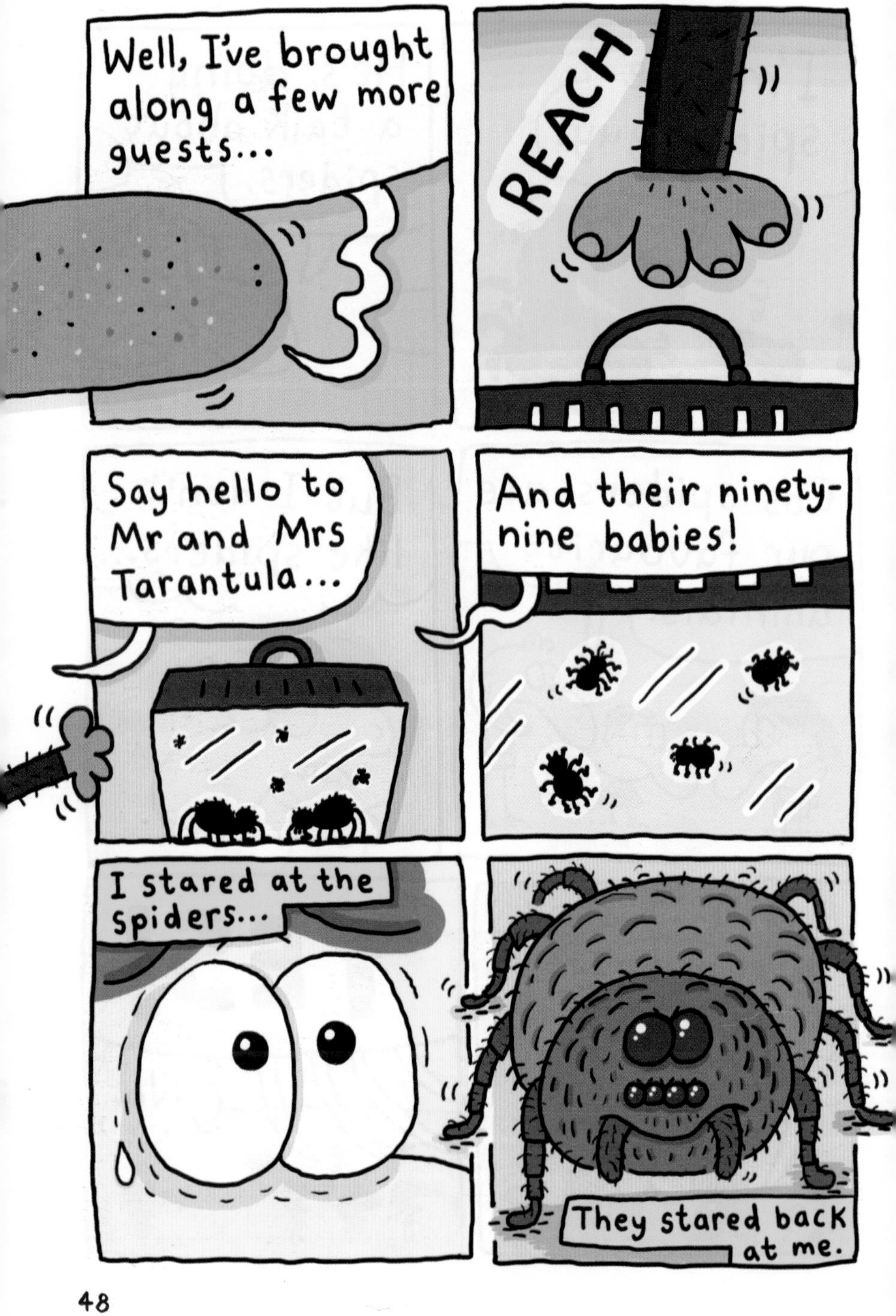
Well, I've brought along a few more guests...
REACH
Say hello to Mr and Mrs Tarantula...
And their ninety-nine babies!
I stared at the spiders...
They stared back at me.

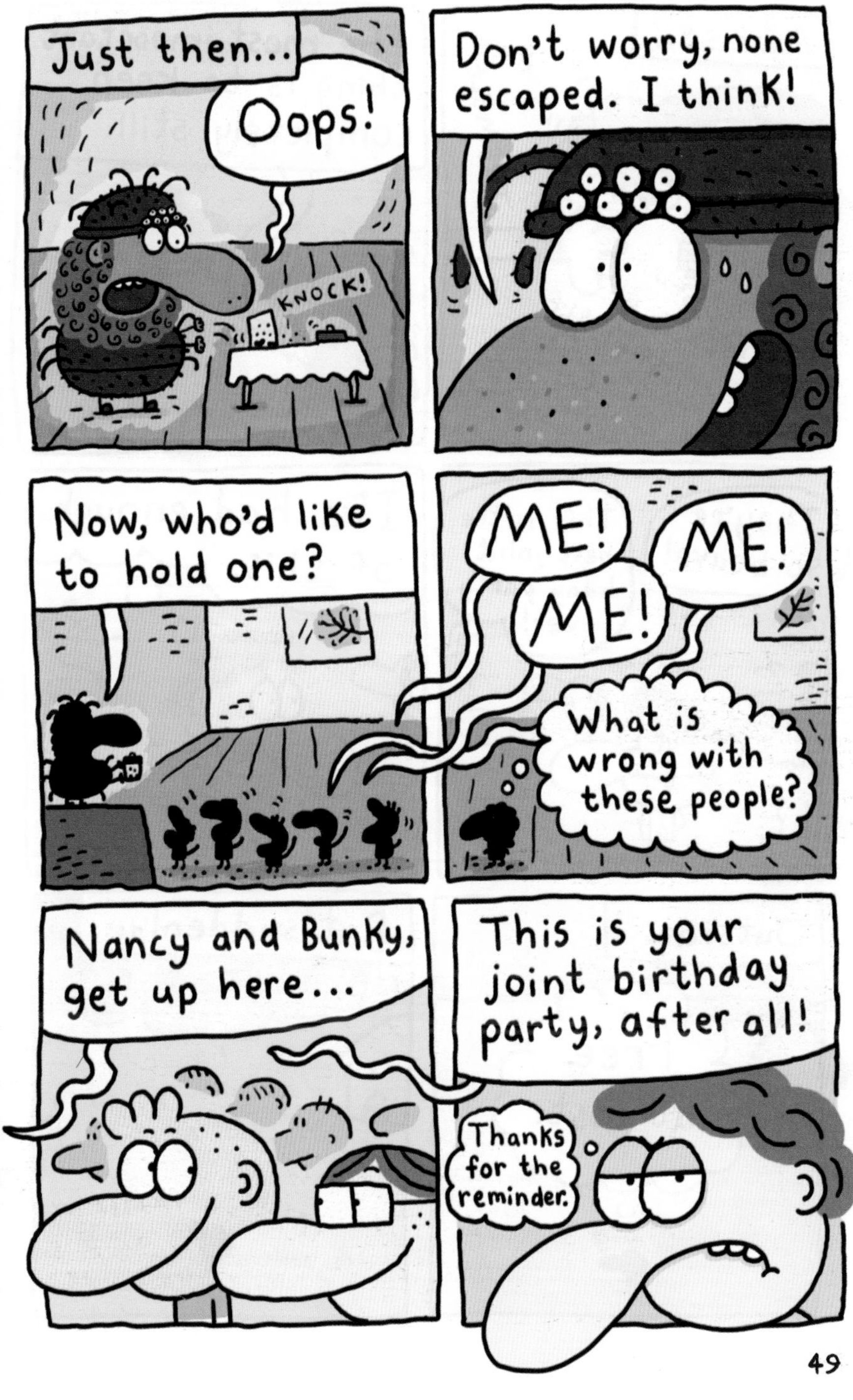
Just then...
Oops!
KNOCK!
Don't worry, none escaped. I think!
Now, who'd like to hold one?
ME!
ME!
ME!
What is wrong with these people?
Nancy and Bunky, get up here...
This is your joint birthday party, after all!
Thanks for the reminder.

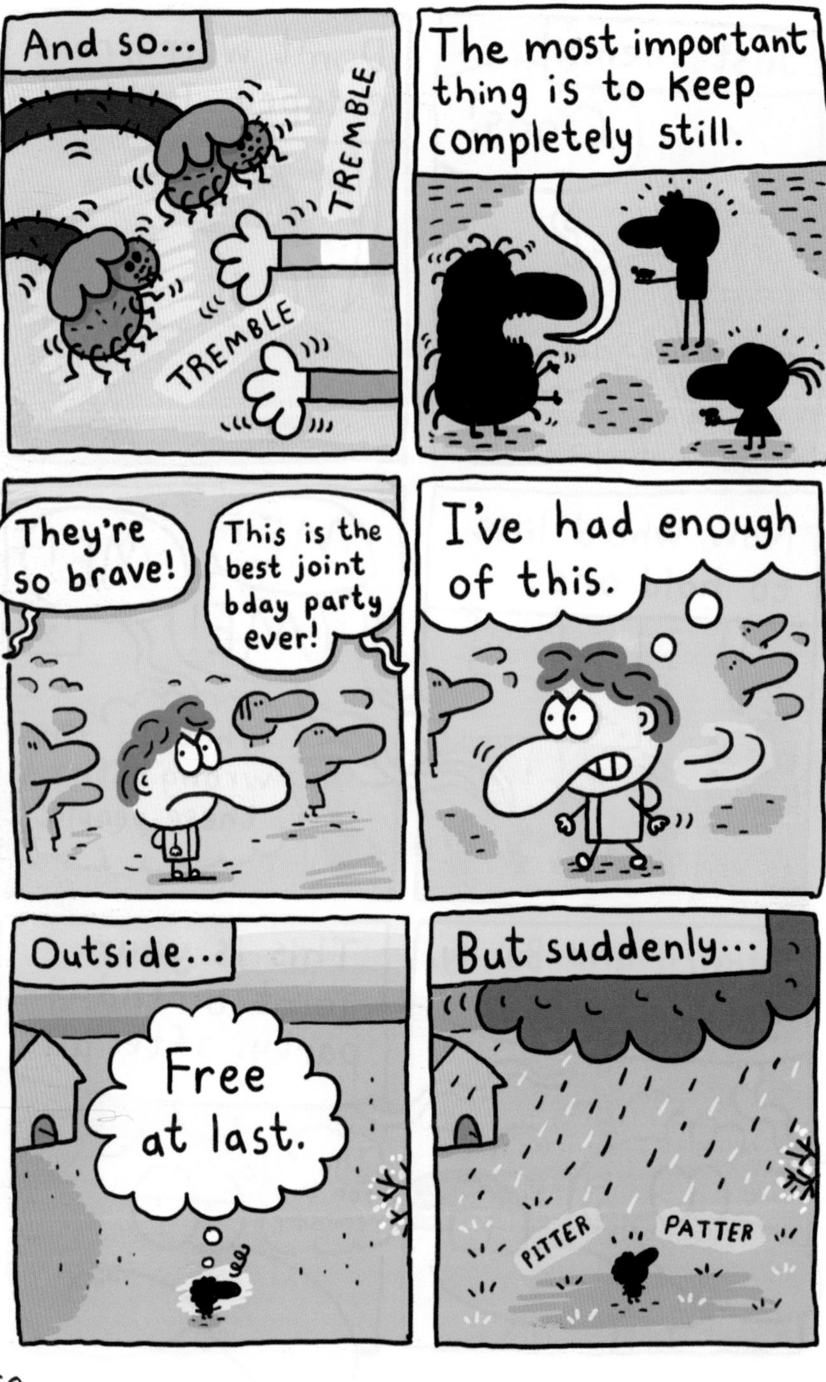
And so...
TREMBLE
TREMBLE
The most important thing is to keep completely still.
They're so brave!
This is the best joint bday party ever!
I've had enough of this.
Outside...
Free at last.
But suddenly...
PITTER
PATTER

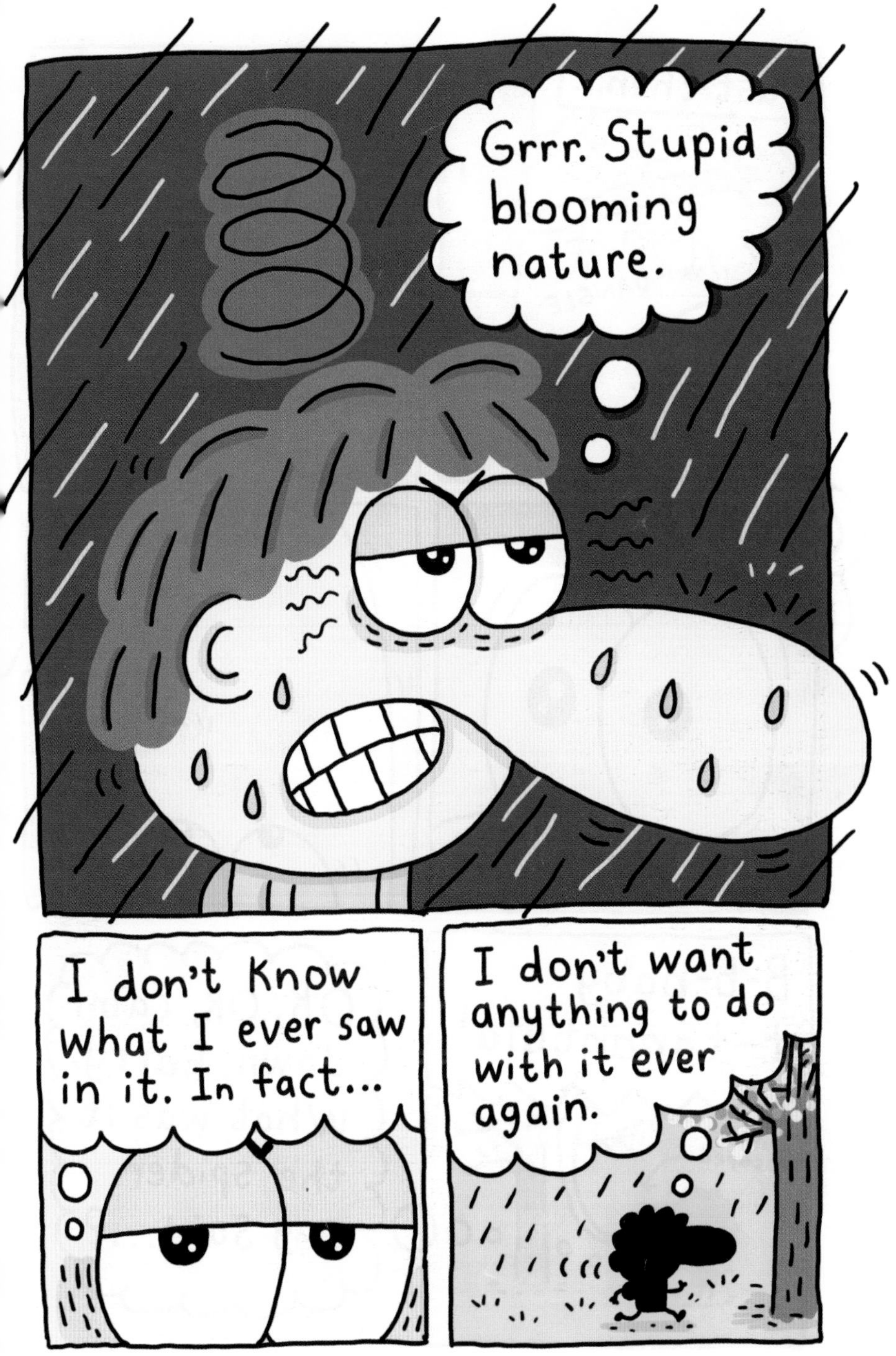

Grrr. Stupid blooming nature.
I don't know what I ever saw in it. In fact...
I don't want anything to do with it ever again.

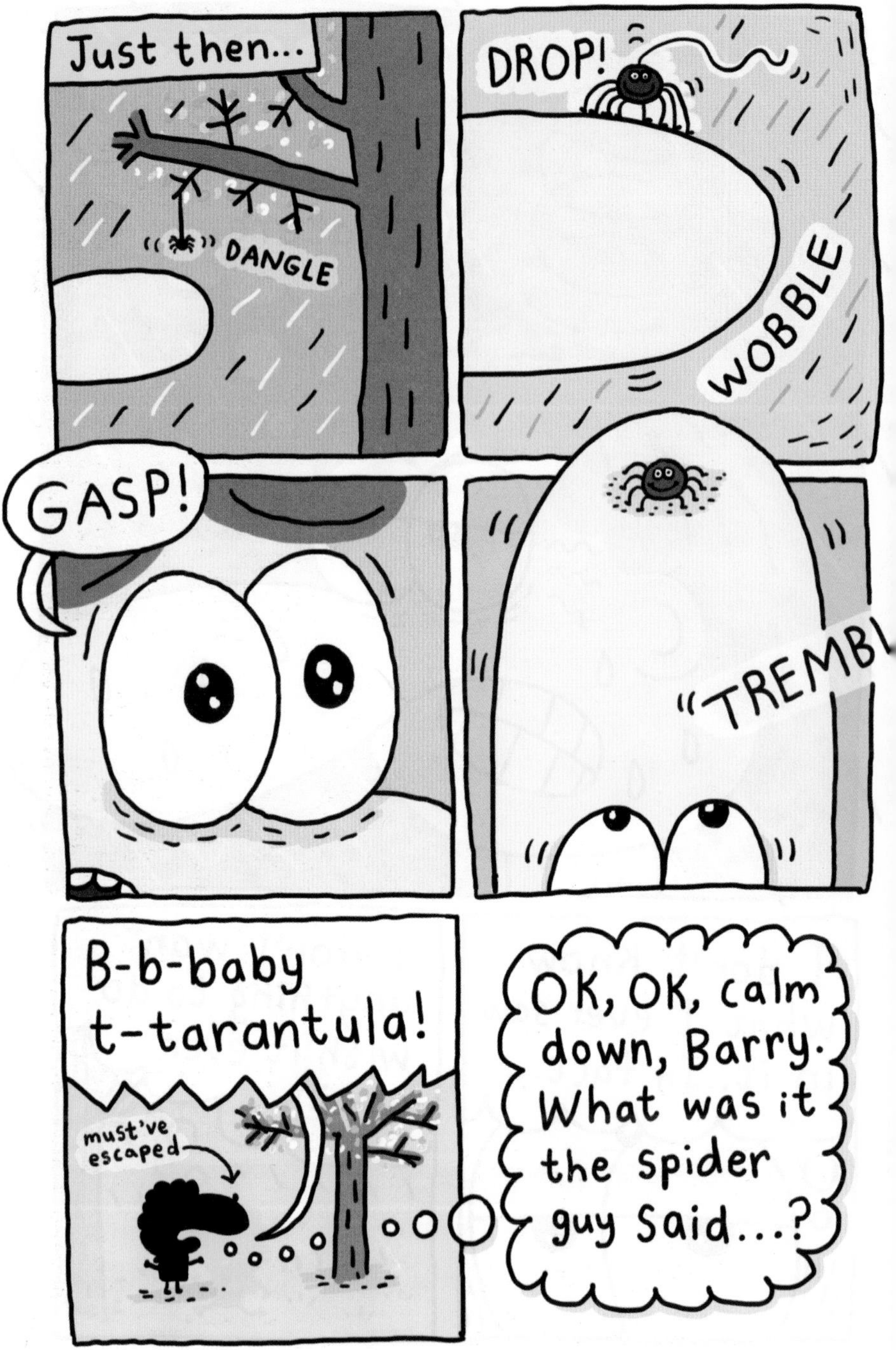
Just then...
DANGLE
DROP!
WOBBLE
GASP!
"TREMBL
B-b-baby
t-tarantula!
must've escaped
OK, OK, calm down, Barry. What was it the spider guy said...?

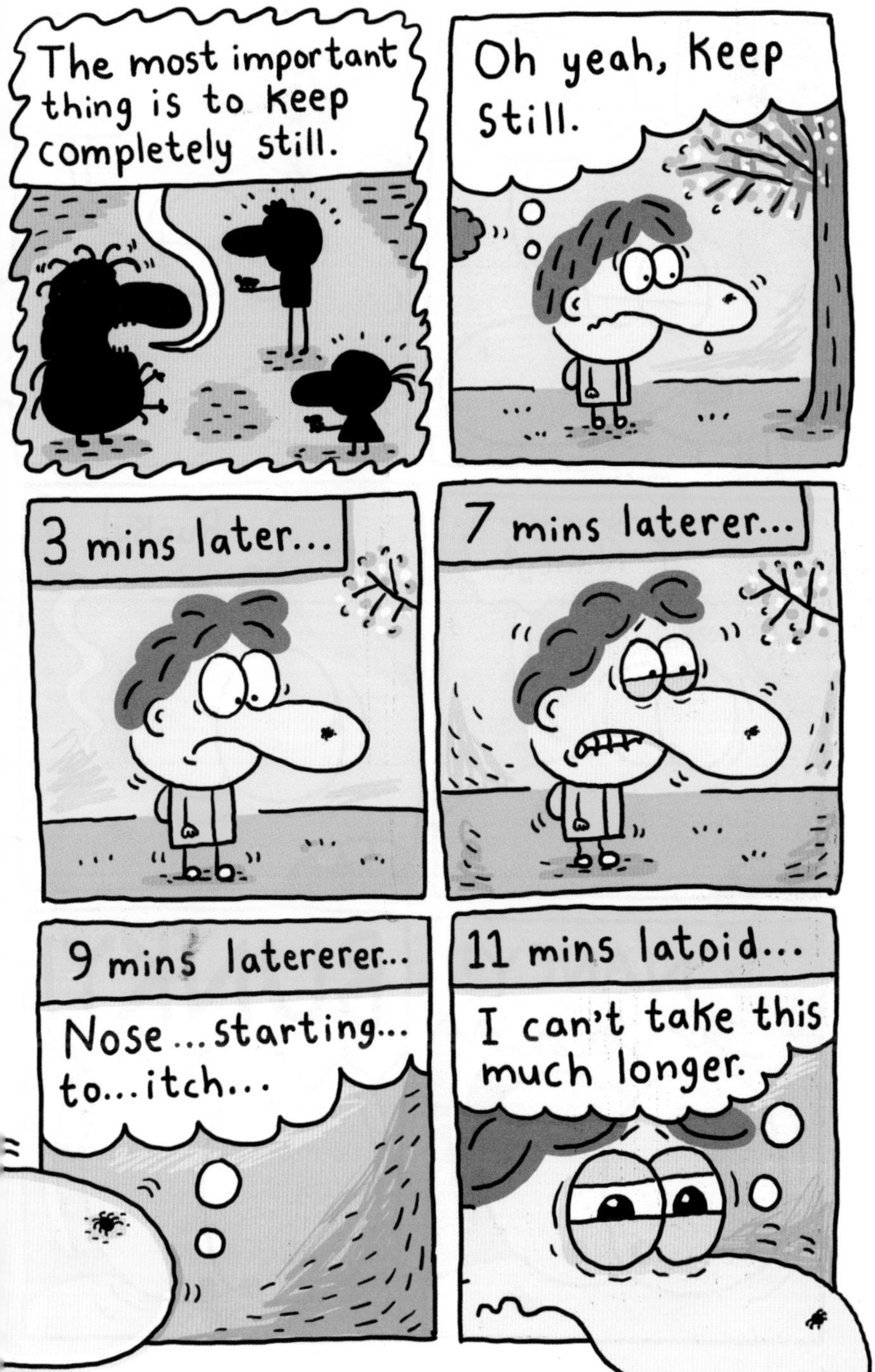

The most important thing is to keep completely still.
Oh yeah, keep still.
3 mins later...
7 mins laterer...
9 mins latererer...
Nose... starting... to... itch...
11 mins latoid...
I can't take this much longer.

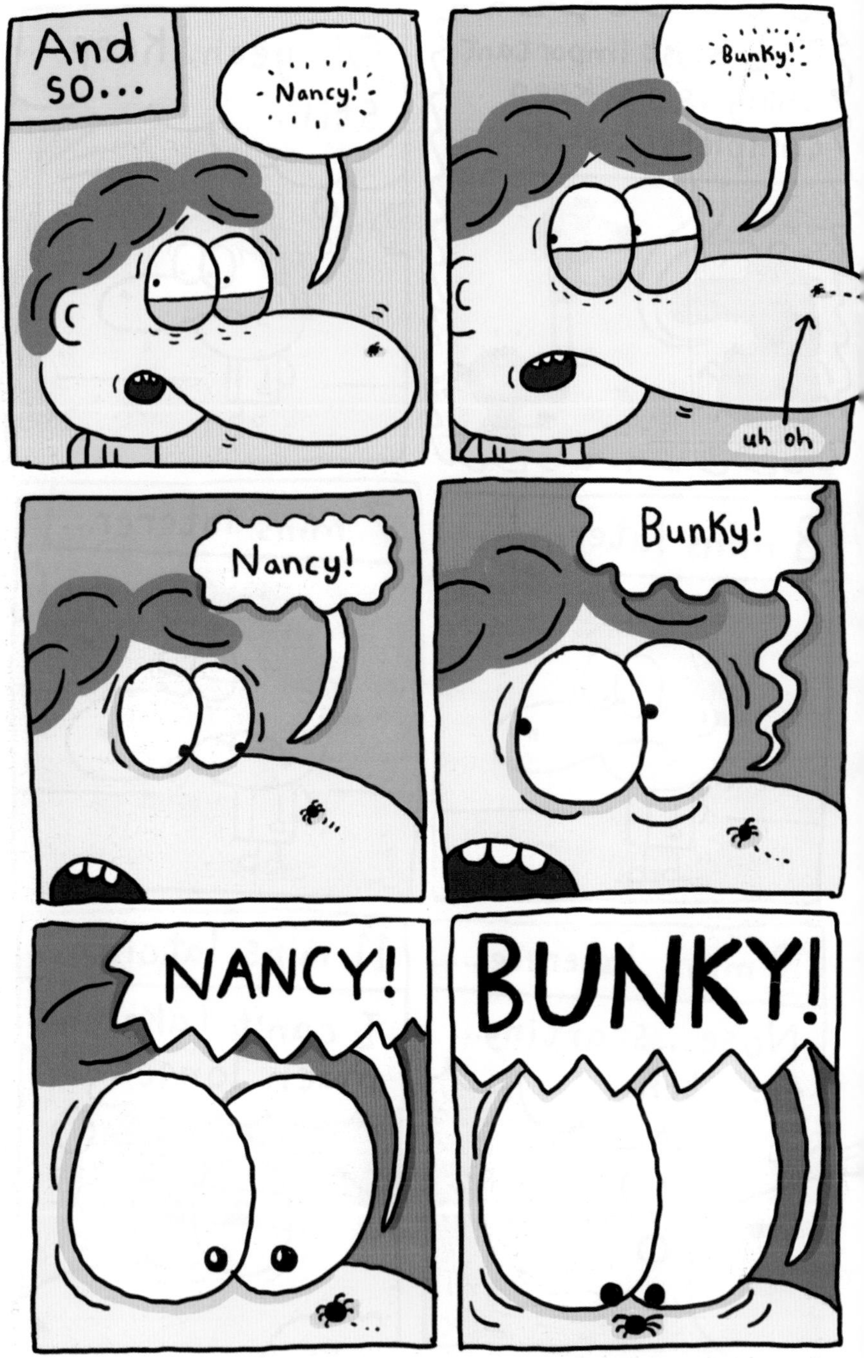

And so...
Nancy!
Bunky!
uh oh
Nancy!
Bunky!
NANCY!
BUNKY!

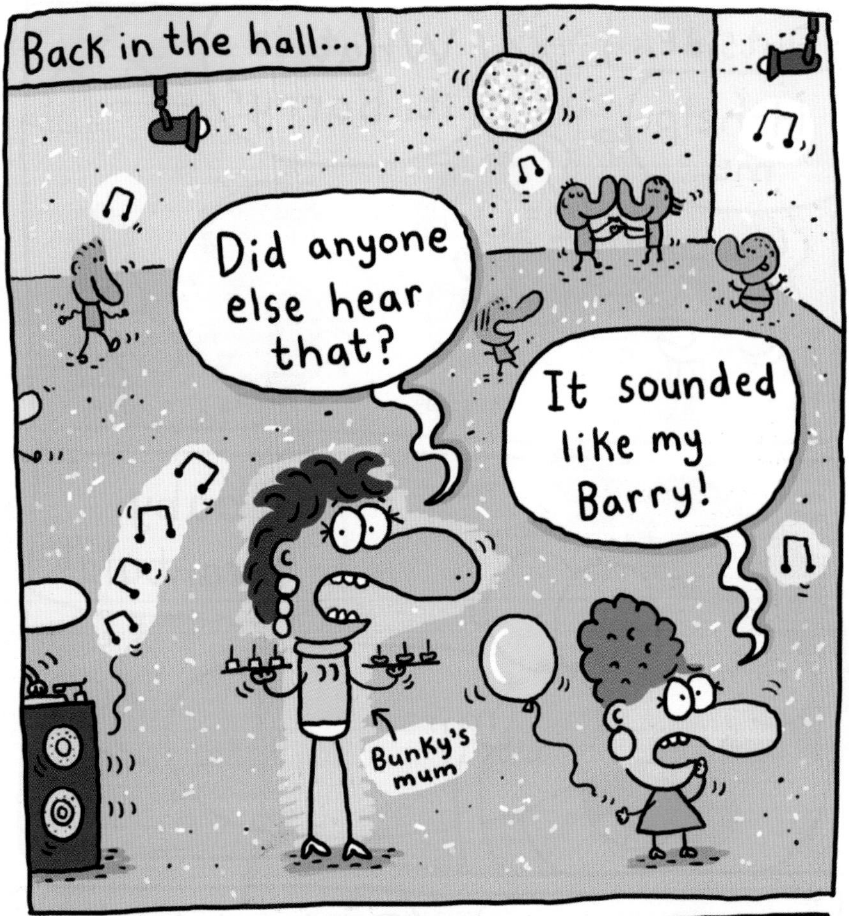
Back in the hall...
Did anyone else hear that?
It sounded like my Barry!
Bunky's mum

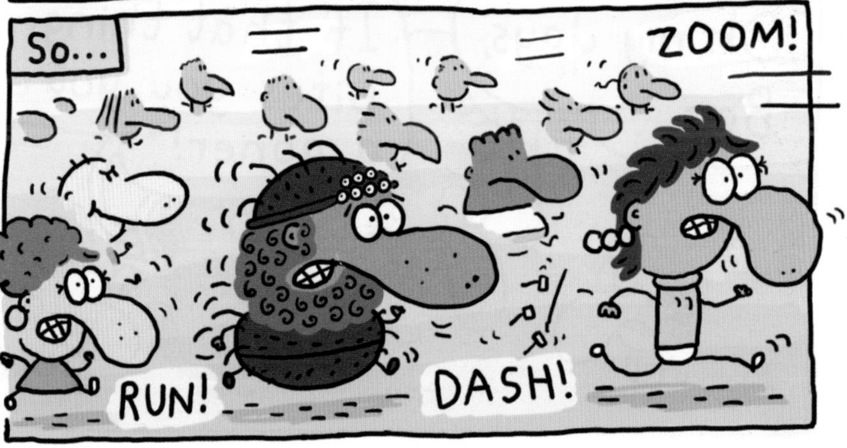
So...
ZOOM!
RUN!
DASH!

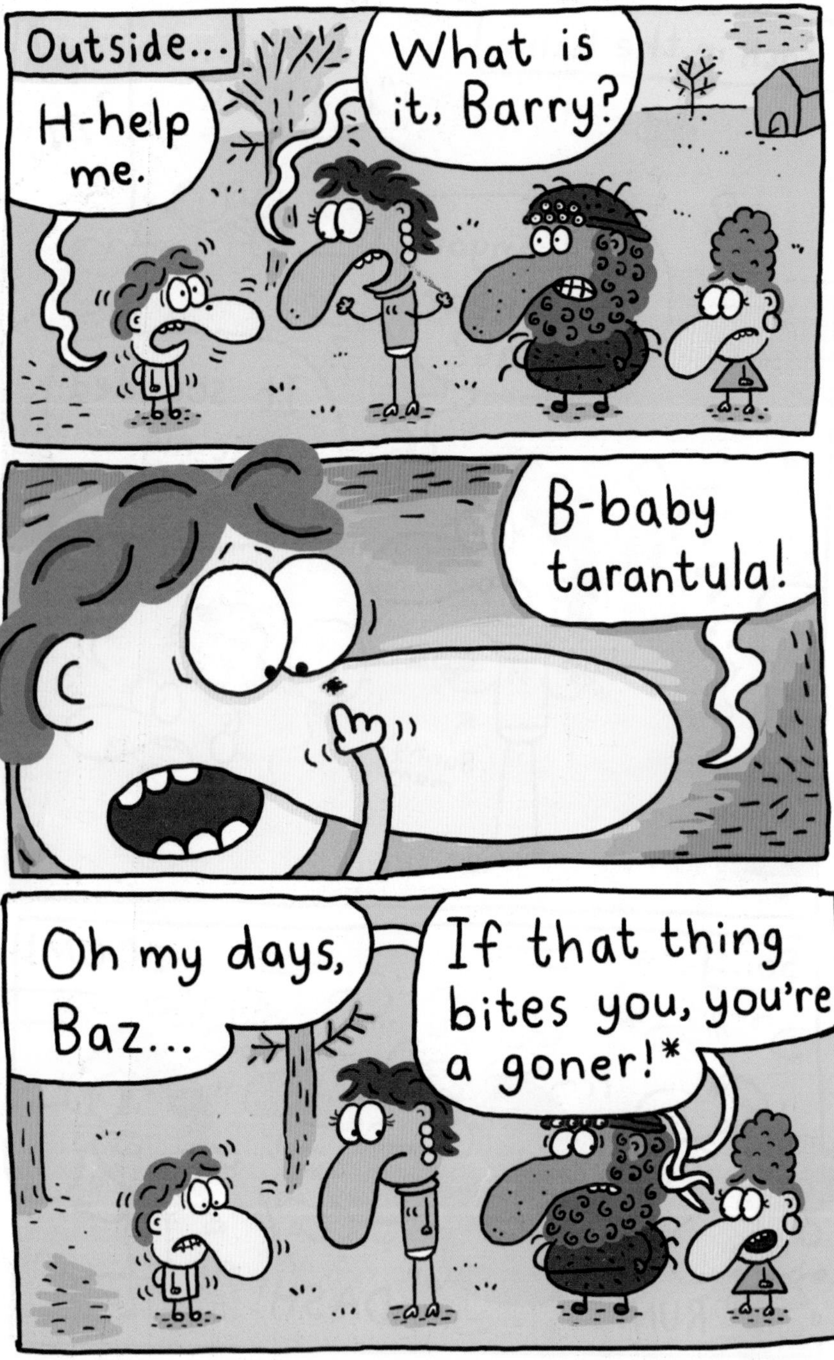
Outside...
H-help me.
What is it, Barry?
B-baby tarantula!
Oh my days, Baz...
If that thing bites you, you're a goner!*

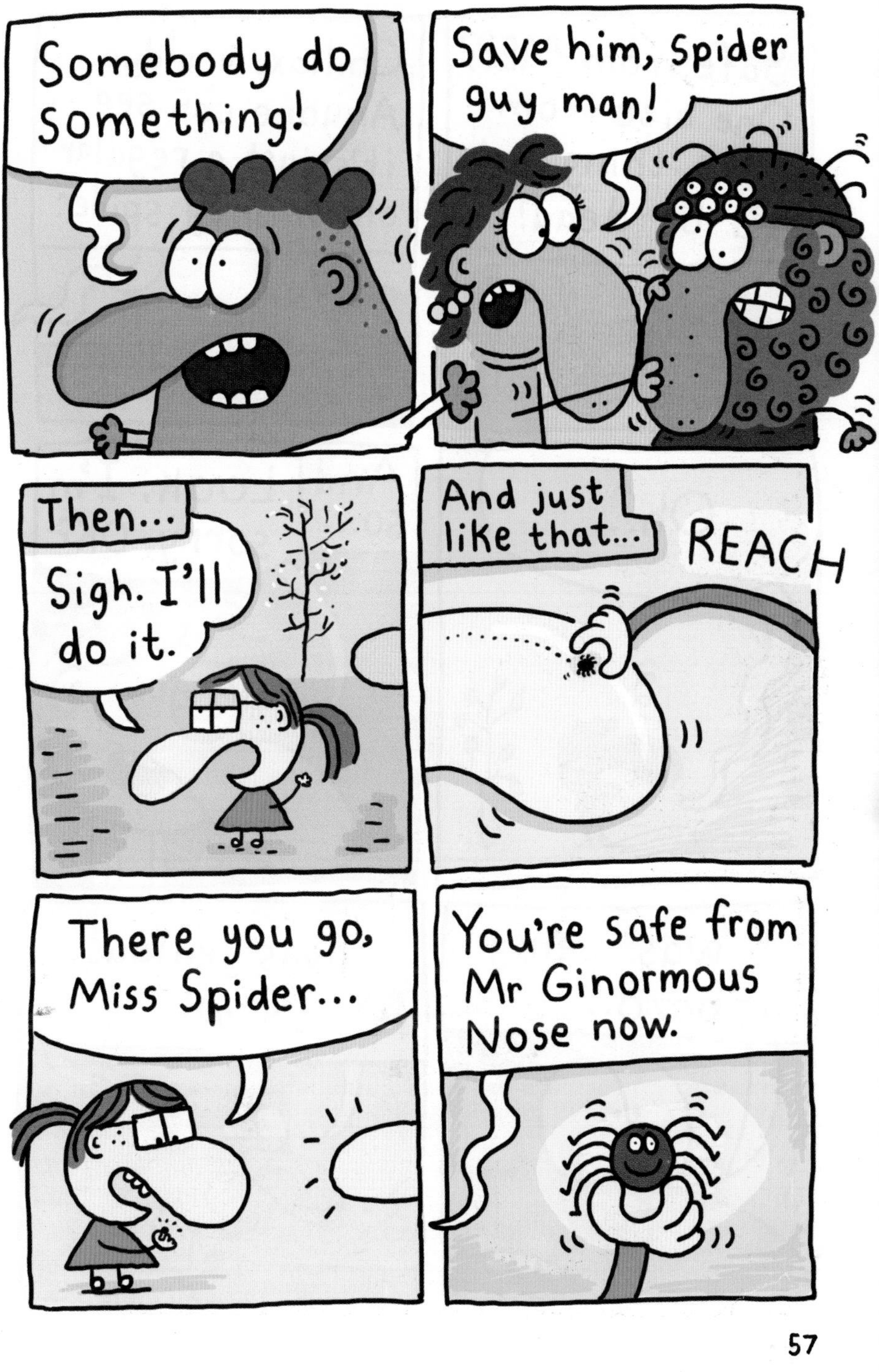
Somebody do something!
Save him, spider guy man!
Then...
Sigh. I'll do it.
And just like that...
REACH
There you go, Miss Spider...
You're safe from Mr Ginormous Nose now.

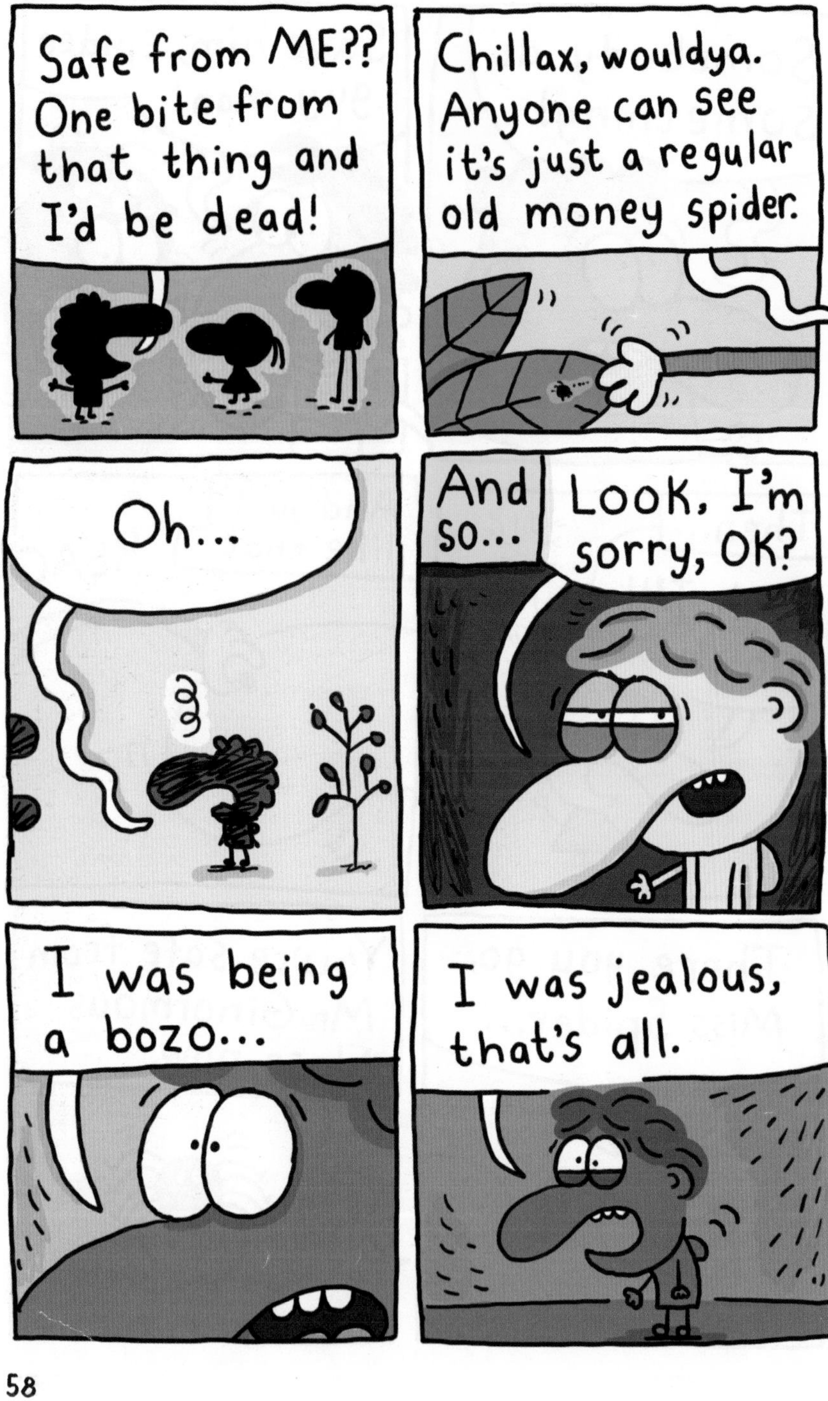

Safe from ME?? One bite from that thing and I'd be dead!
Chillax, wouldya. Anyone can see it's just a regular old money spider.
Oh...
And so...
Look, I'm sorry, OK?
I was being a bozo...
I was jealous, that's all.

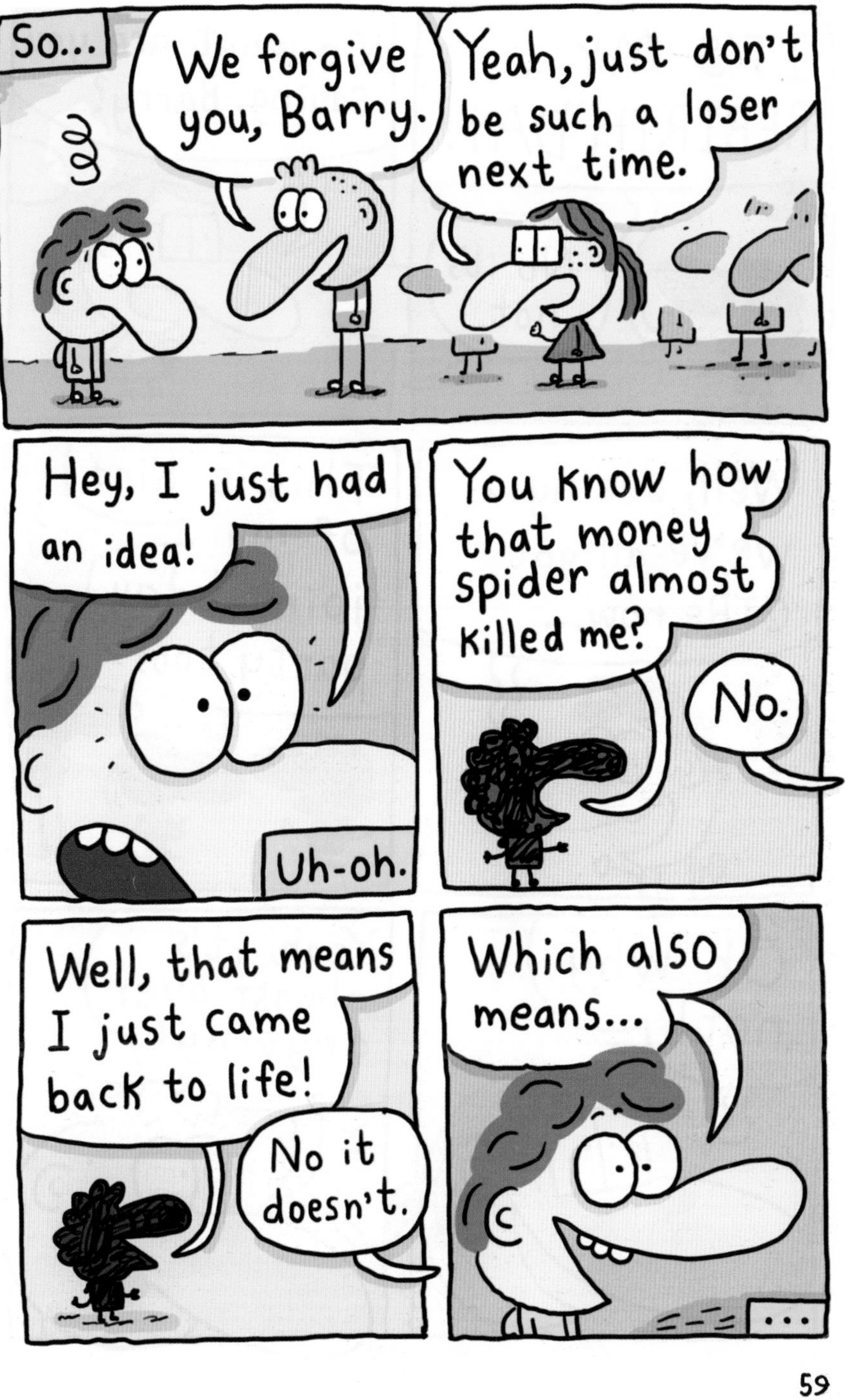
So...
We forgive you, Barry.
Yeah, just don't be such a loser next time.
Hey, I just had an idea!
Uh-oh.
You know how that money spider almost killed me?
No.
Well, that means I just came back to life!
No it doesn't.
Which also means...
...

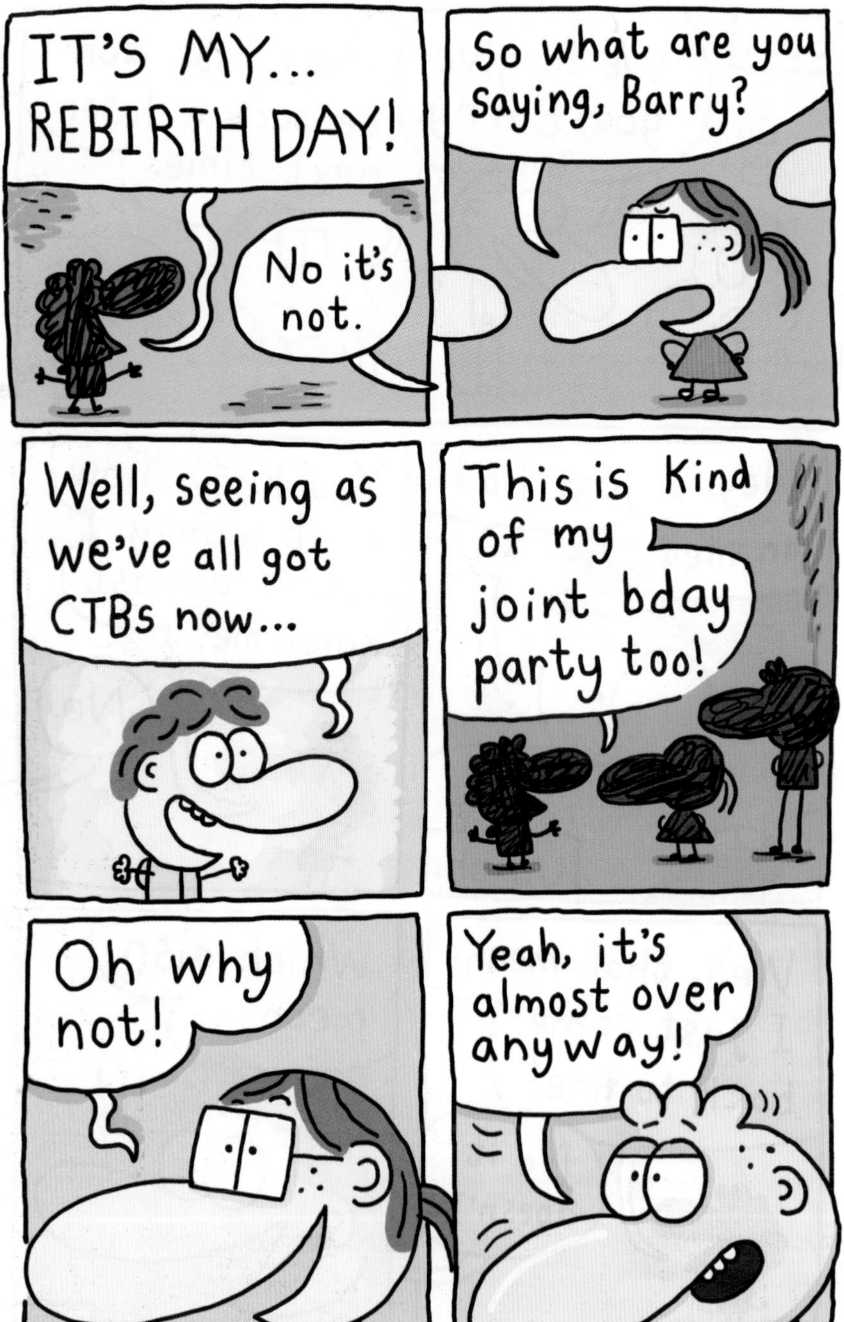
IT'S MY...
REBIRTH DAY!
No it's not.
So what are you saying, Barry?
Well, seeing as we've all got CTBs now...
This is kind of my joint bday party too!
Oh why not!
Yeah, it's almost over anyway!

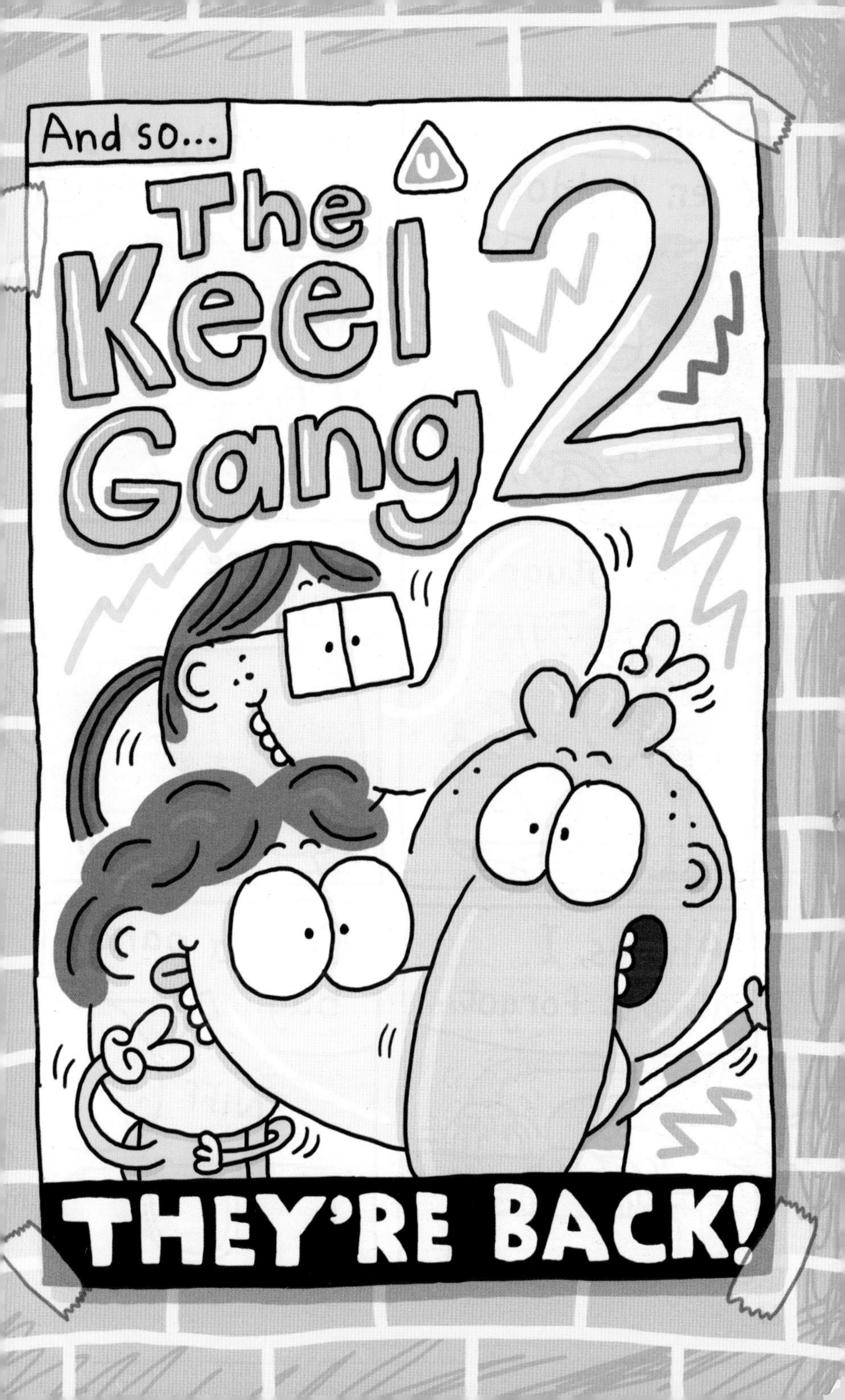
And so...
The Keel Gang 2
THEY'RE BACK!

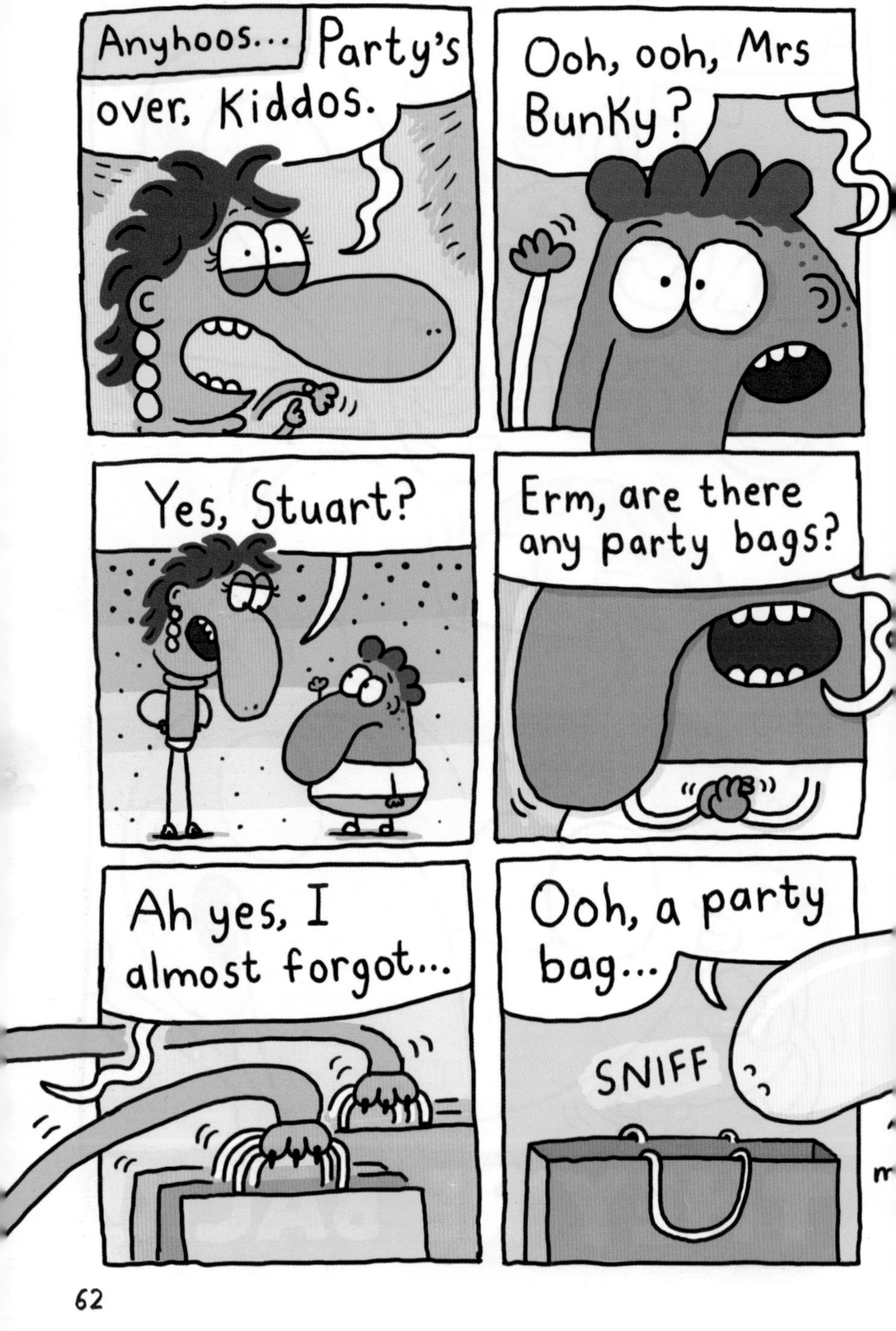
Anyhoos...
Party's over, Kiddos.
Ooh, ooh, Mrs Bunky?
Yes, Stuart?
Erm, are there any party bags?
Ah yes, I almost forgot...
Ooh, a party bag...
SNIFF

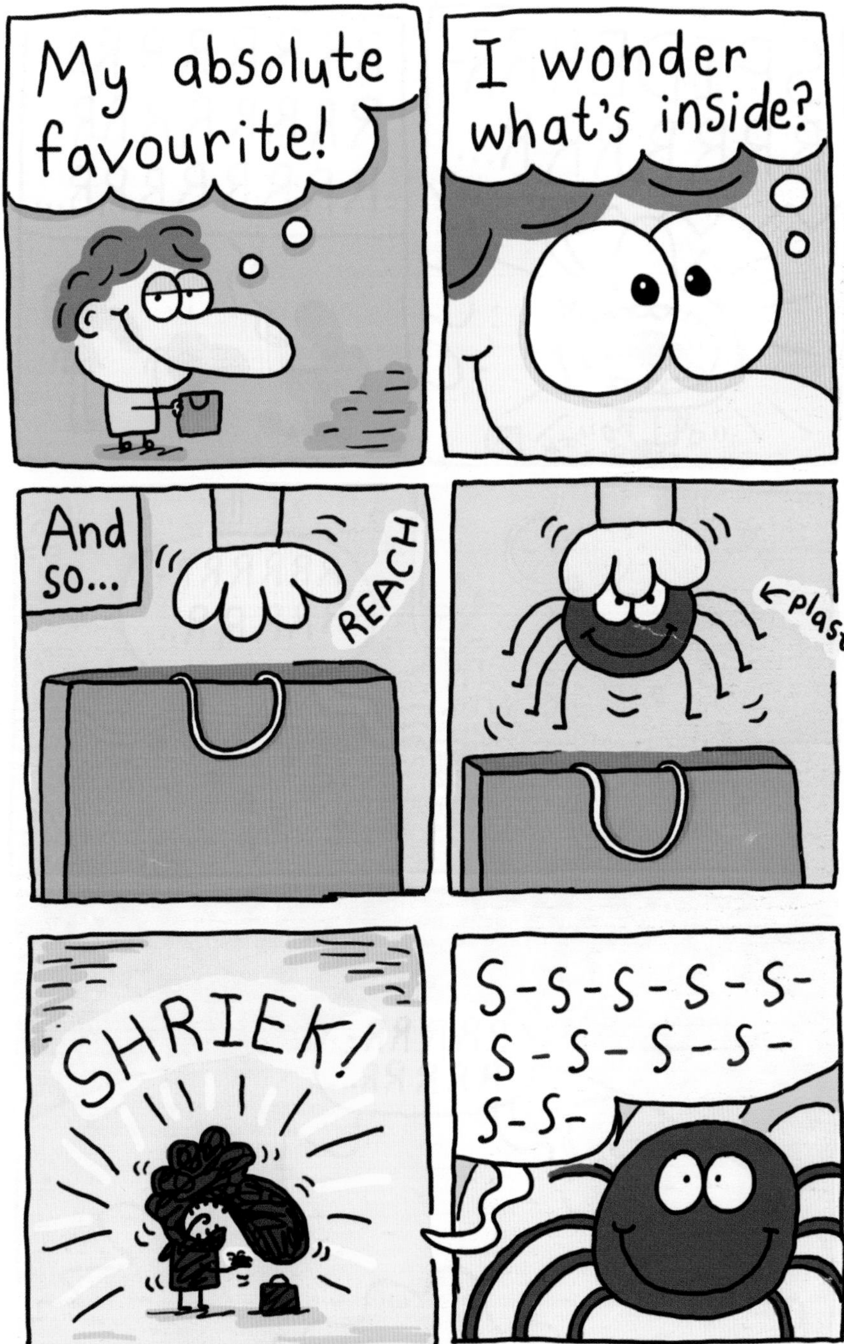
My absolute favourite!
I wonder what's inside?
And so...
REACH
←plastic
SHRIEK!
S-S-S-S-S-S-S-S-S-S-S-

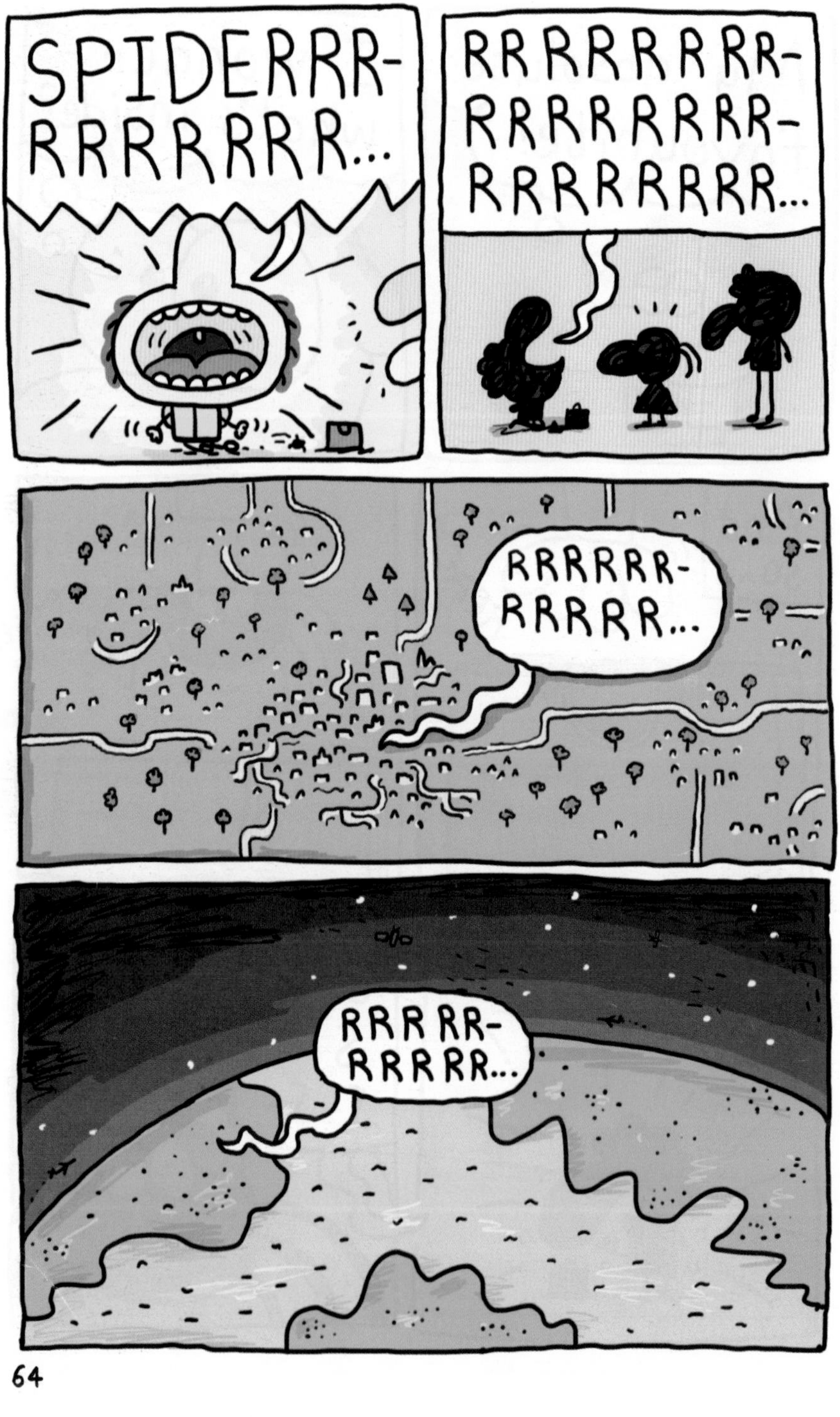
SPIDERRR-
RRRRRRRR...
RRRRRRRRR-
RRRRRRRRR-
RRRRRRRRR...
RRRRRR-
RRRRRR...
RRRRR-
RRRRR...

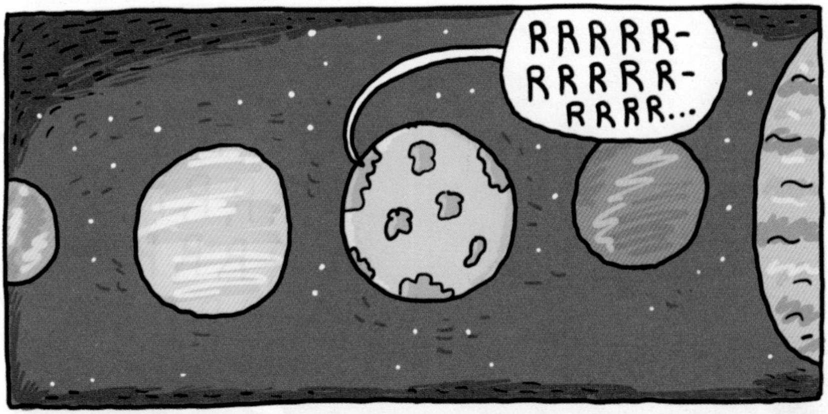
RRRRR-
RRRRR-
RRRR...

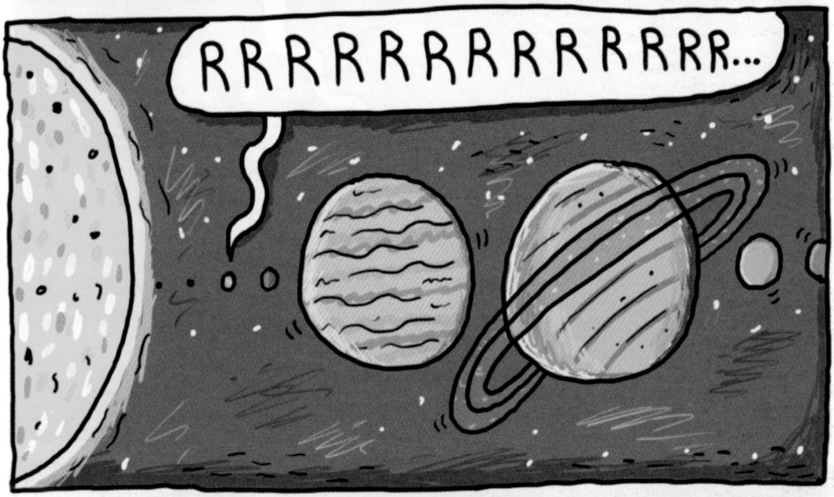
RRRRRRRRRRRR...

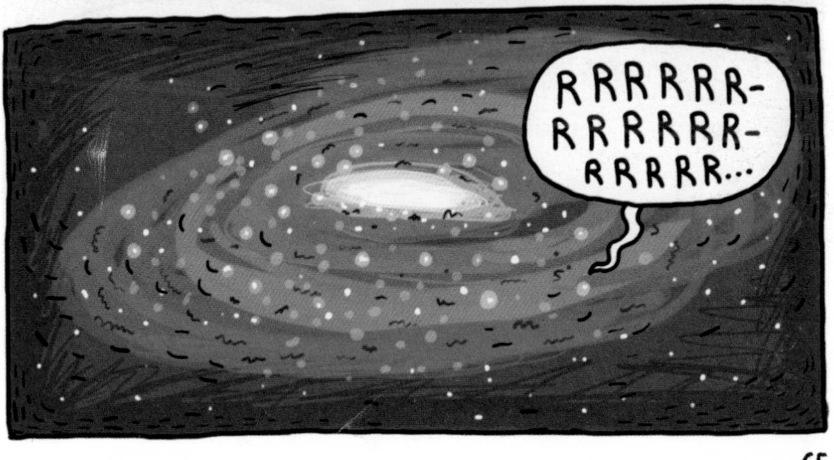
RRRRRR-
RRRRRR-
RRRRR...

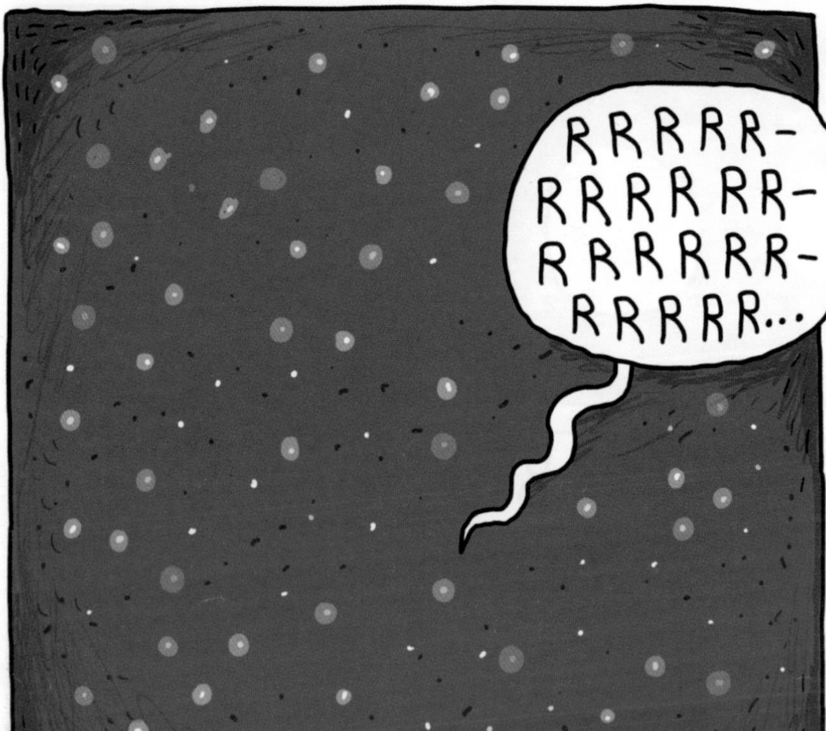
RRRRR-
RRRR RR-
RRRRRR-
RRRRR...

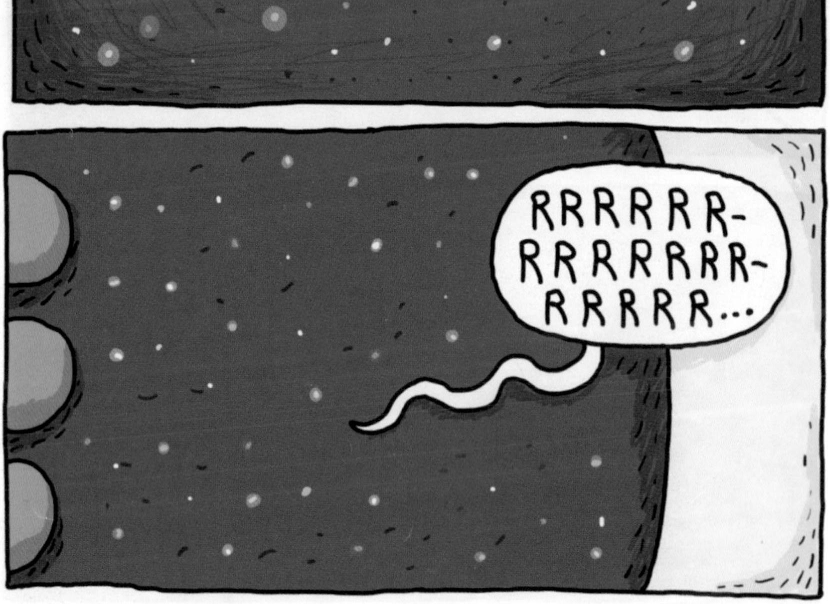
RRRRRR-
RRRRRRR-
RRRRR...

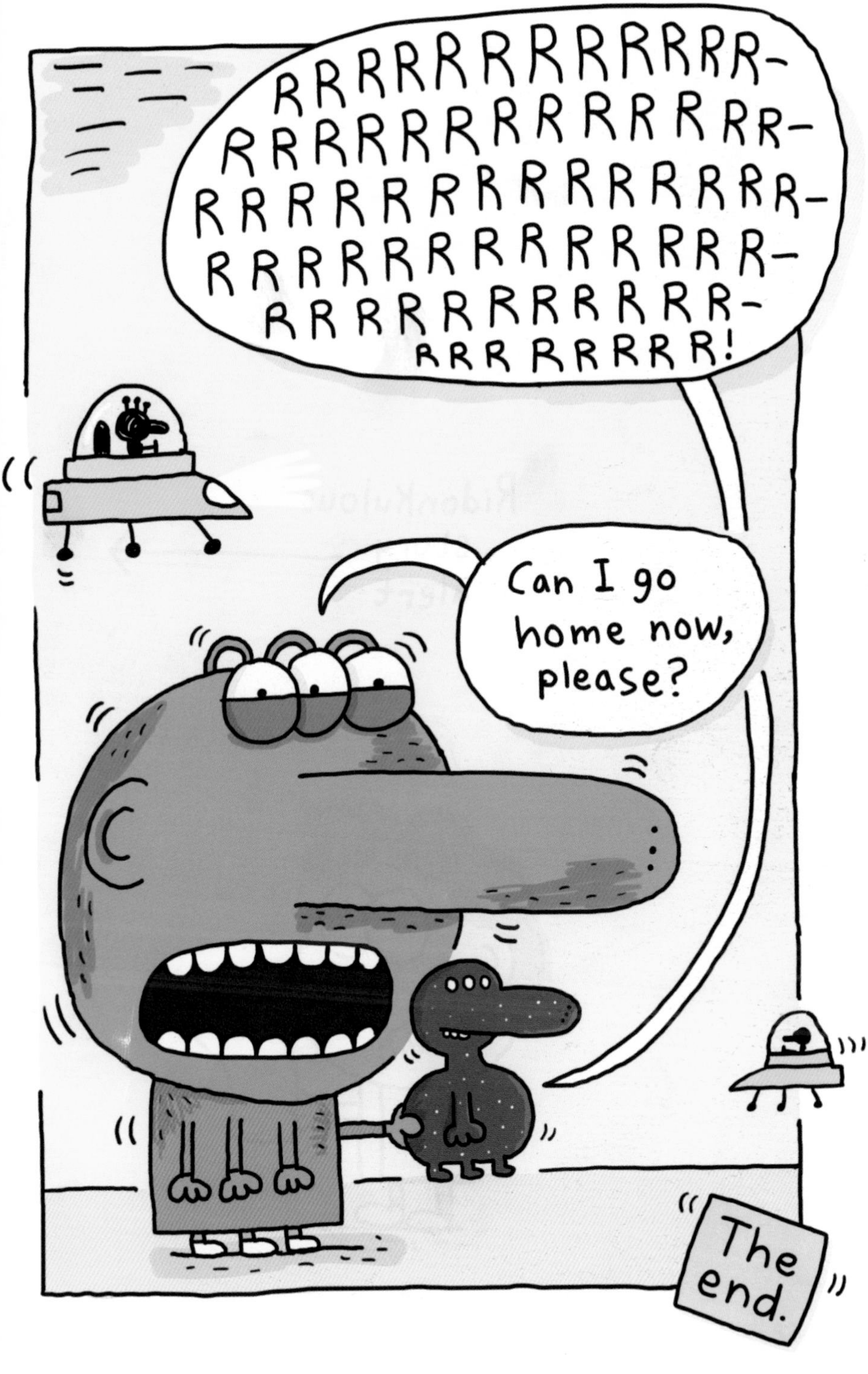
RRRRRRRRRRRR-
RRRRRRRRRRRRR-
RRRRRRRRRRRRRR-
RRRRRRRRRRRRR-
RRRRRRRRRRR-
RRR RRRRR!
Can I go home now, please?
The end.

Ridonkulous
story
alert $\longrightarrow$

Episode 2

CONTAINS SCENES OF NOSES FALLING COMPLETELY OFF

Snozzy the very naughty nose

Strolling home from school...
SHOES
De
BREAKING NEWS: I've renamed my nose 'Snozzy'!*

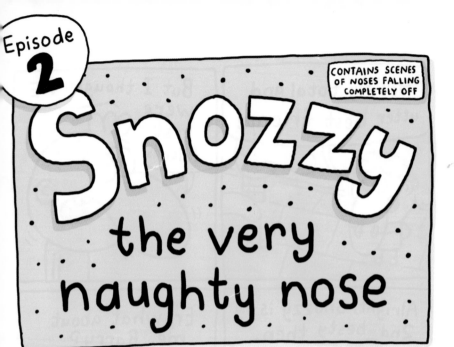

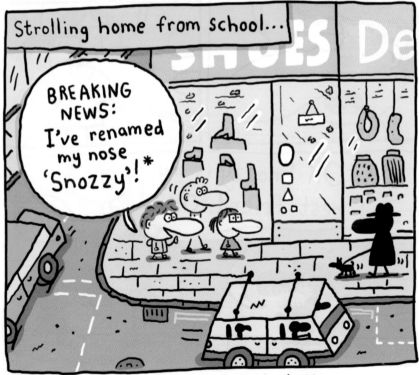

*Not that it had a name in the first place.

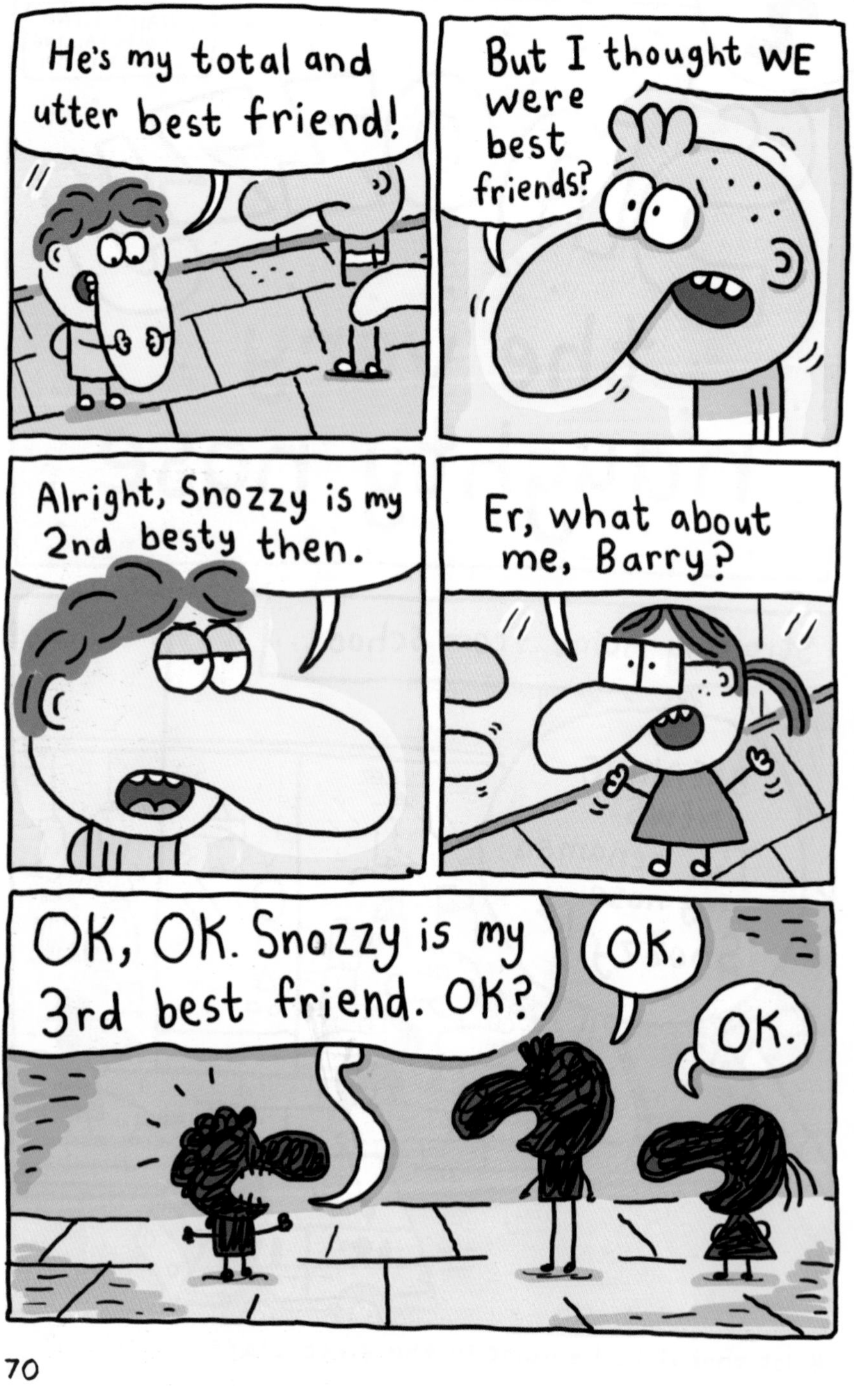
He's my total and utter best friend!
But I thought WE were best friends?
Alright, Snozzy is my 2nd besty then.
Er, what about me, Barry?
OK, OK. Snozzy is my 3rd best friend. OK?
OK.
OK.

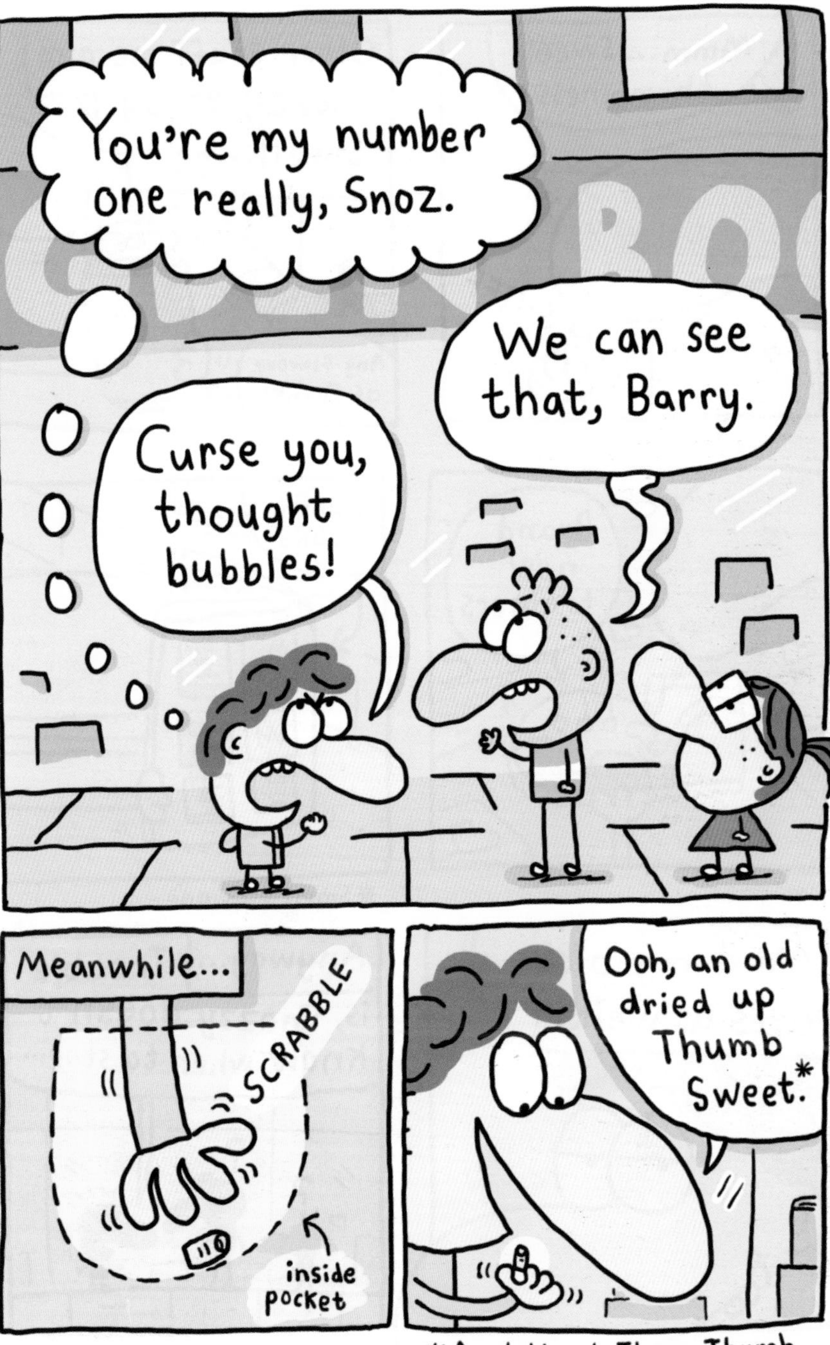
You're my number one really, Snoz.
Curse you, thought bubbles!
We can see that, Barry.
Meanwhile...
SCRABBLE
inside pocket
Ooh, an old dried up Thumb Sweet.*

*Available at Three Thumb Rita's Sweetshop.

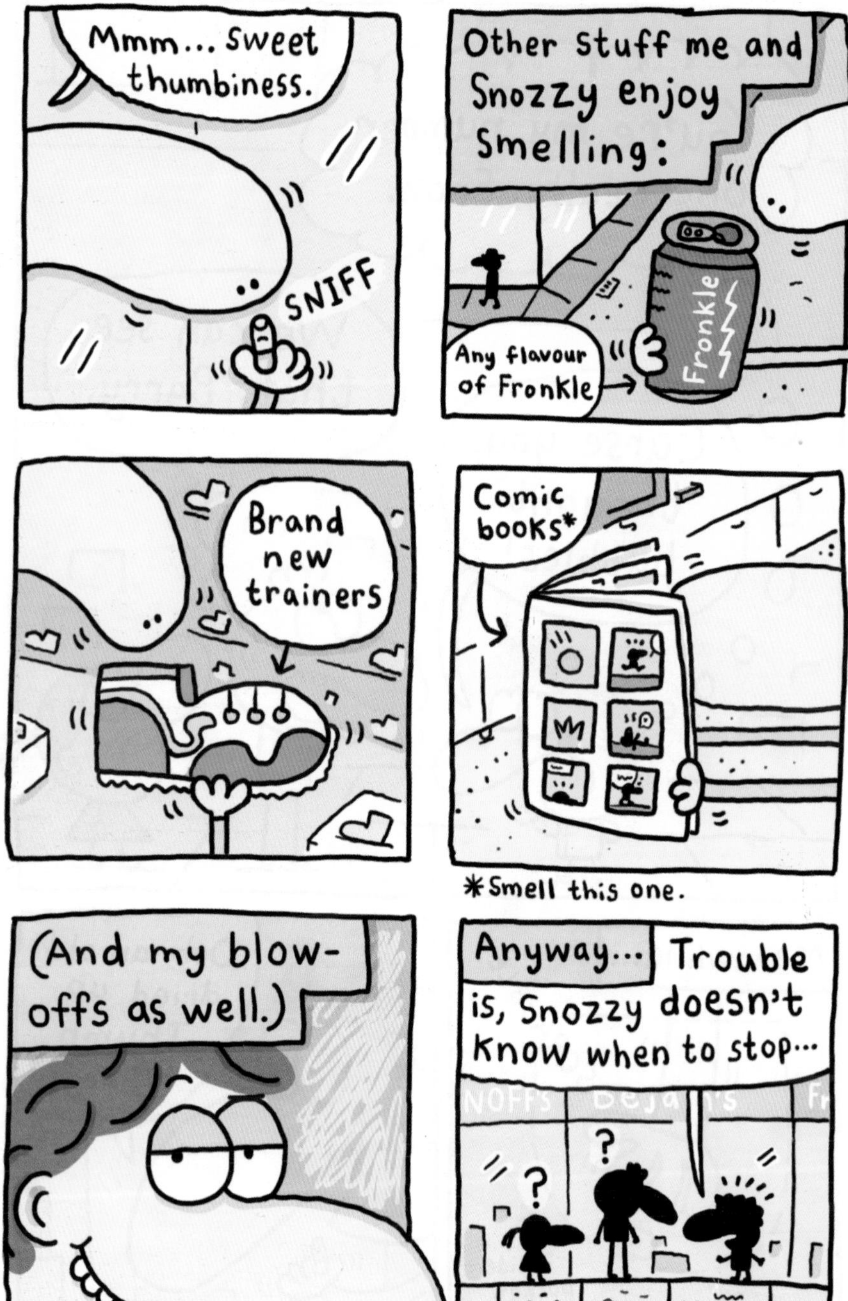
Mmm... sweet thumbiness.
SNIFF
Other stuff me and Snozzy enjoy smelling:
Any flavour of Fronkle
Fronkle
Brand new trainers
Comic books*
*Smell this one.
(And my blow-offs as well.)
Anyway...
Trouble is, Snozzy doesn't know when to stop...

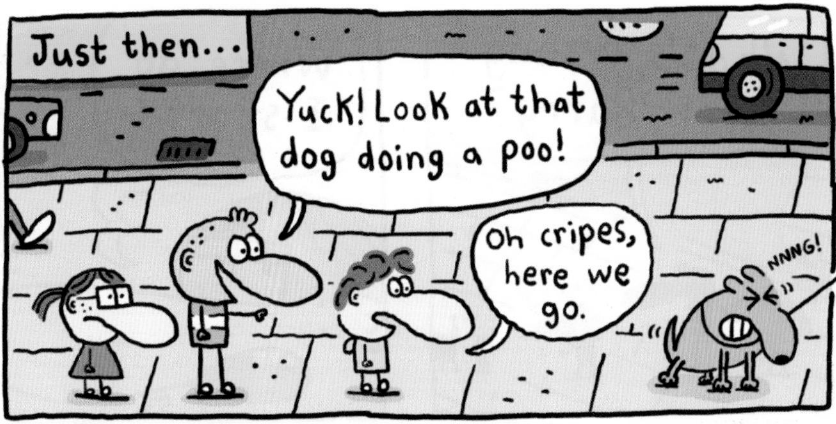
Just then...
Yuck! Look at that dog doing a poo!
Oh cripes, here we go.
NNNG!

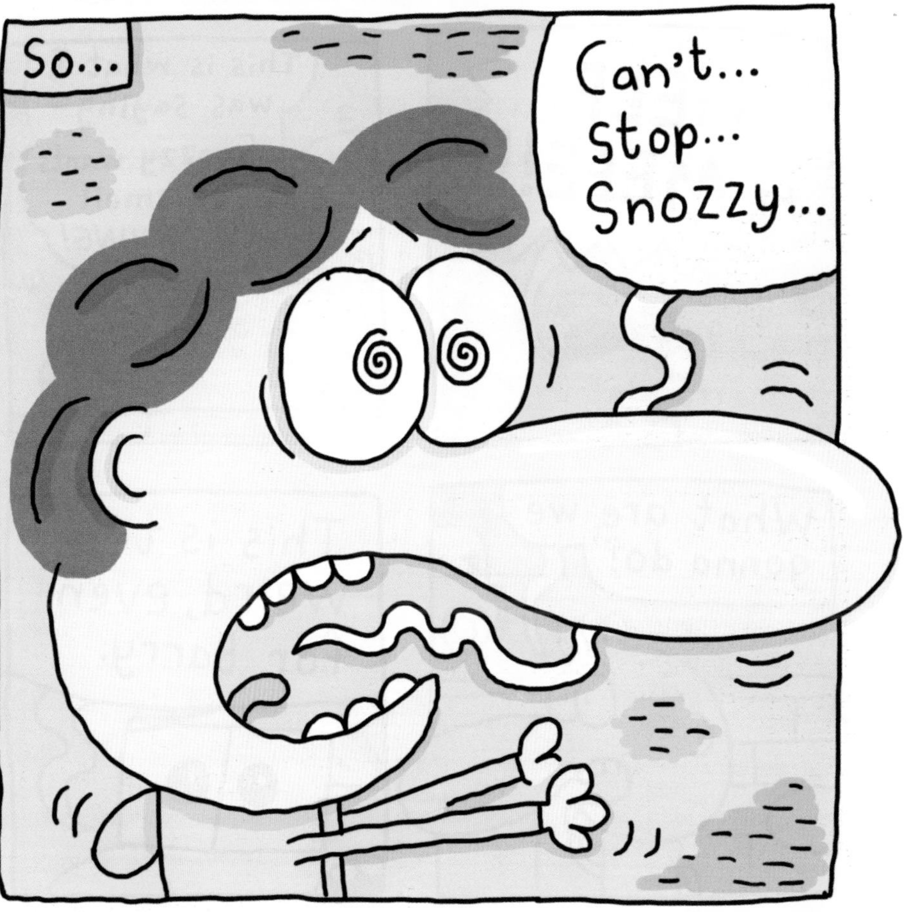
So...
Can't...
Stop...
Snozzy...

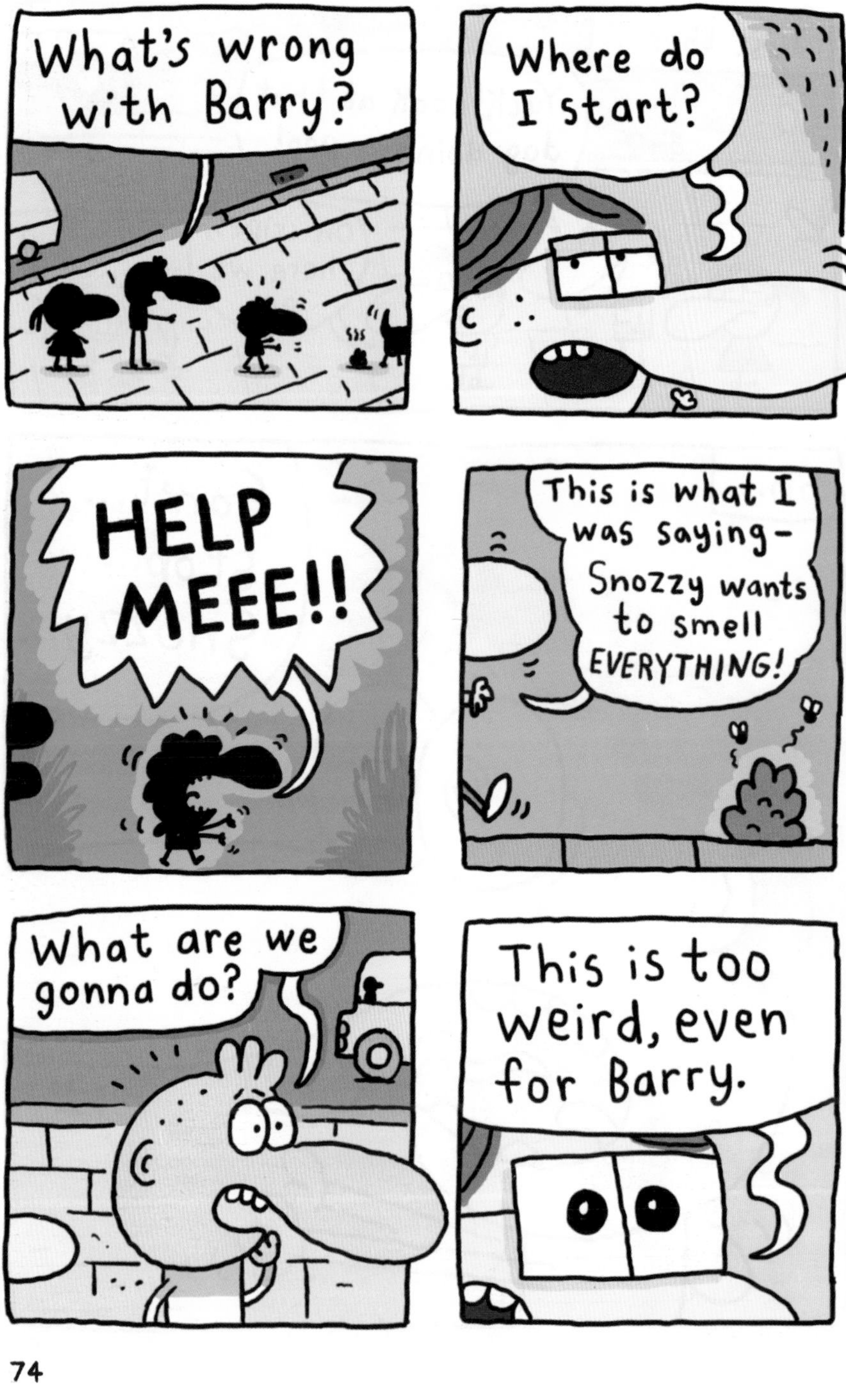
What's wrong with Barry?
Where do I start?
HELP MEEE!!
This is what I was saying- Snozzy wants to smell EVERYTHING!
What are we gonna do?
This is too weird, even for Barry.

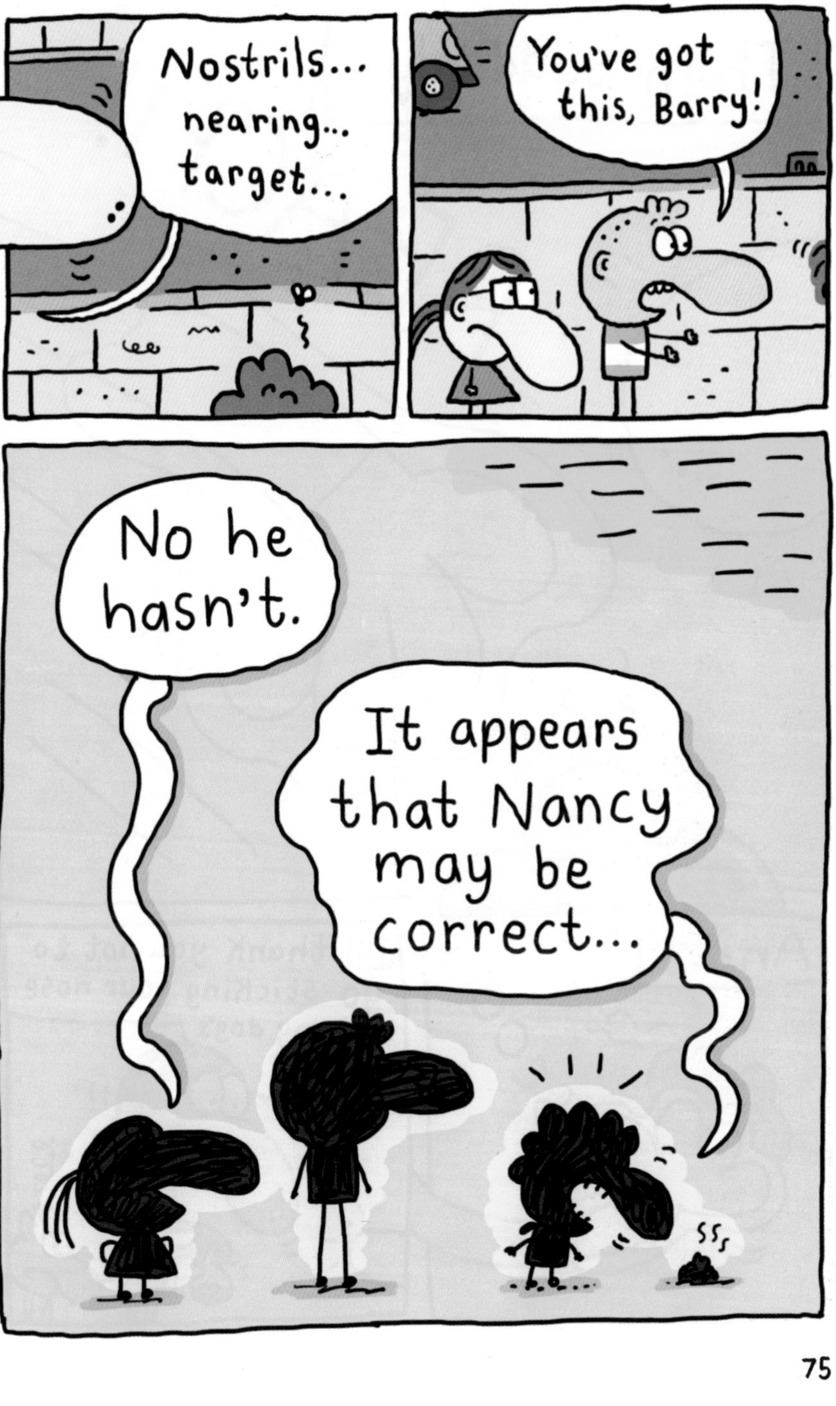
Nostrils... nearing... target...
You've got this, Barry!
No he hasn't.
It appears that Nancy may be correct...

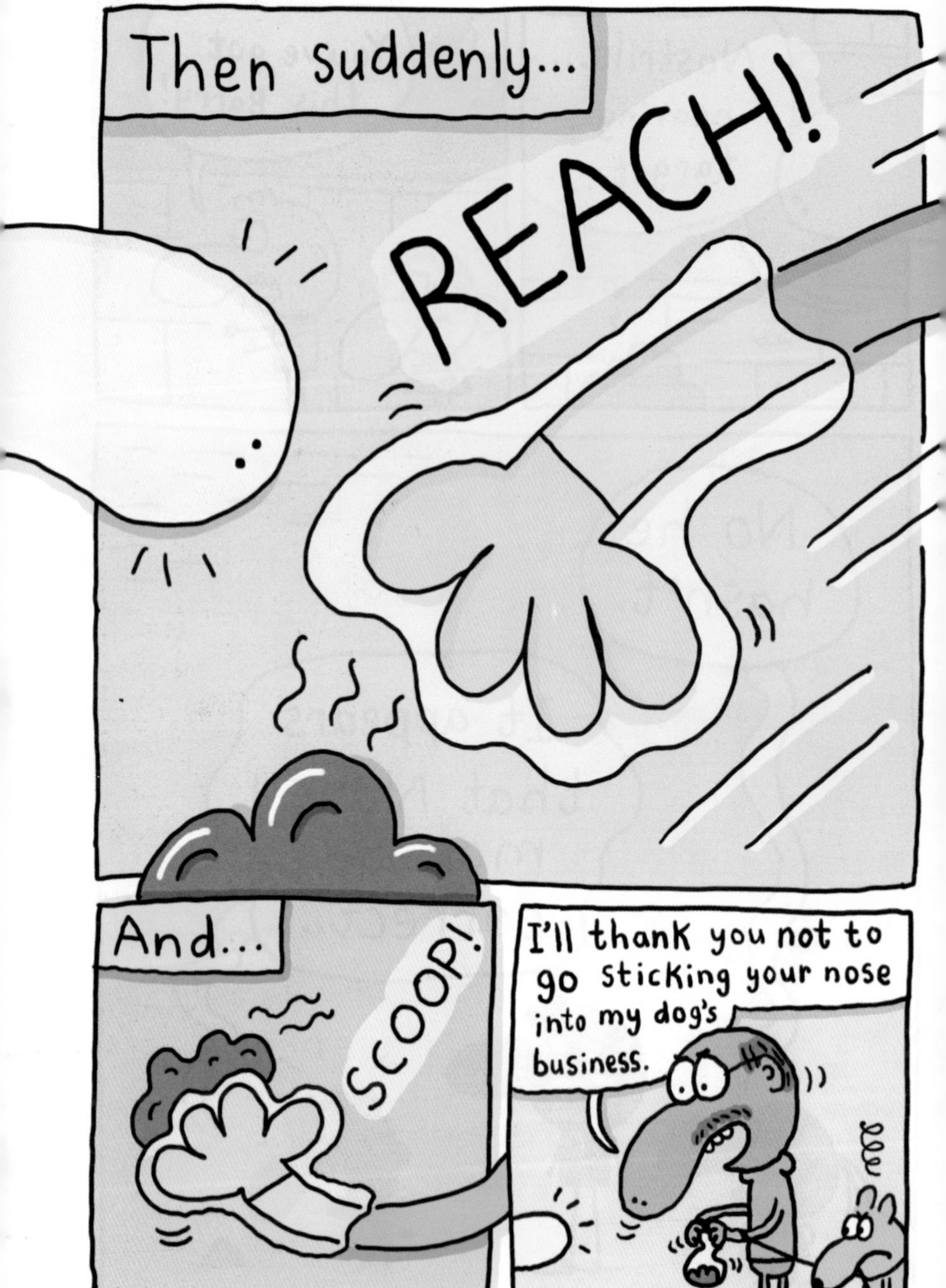
Then suddenly...
REACH!
And...
SCOOP!
I'll thank you not to go sticking your nose into my dog's business.

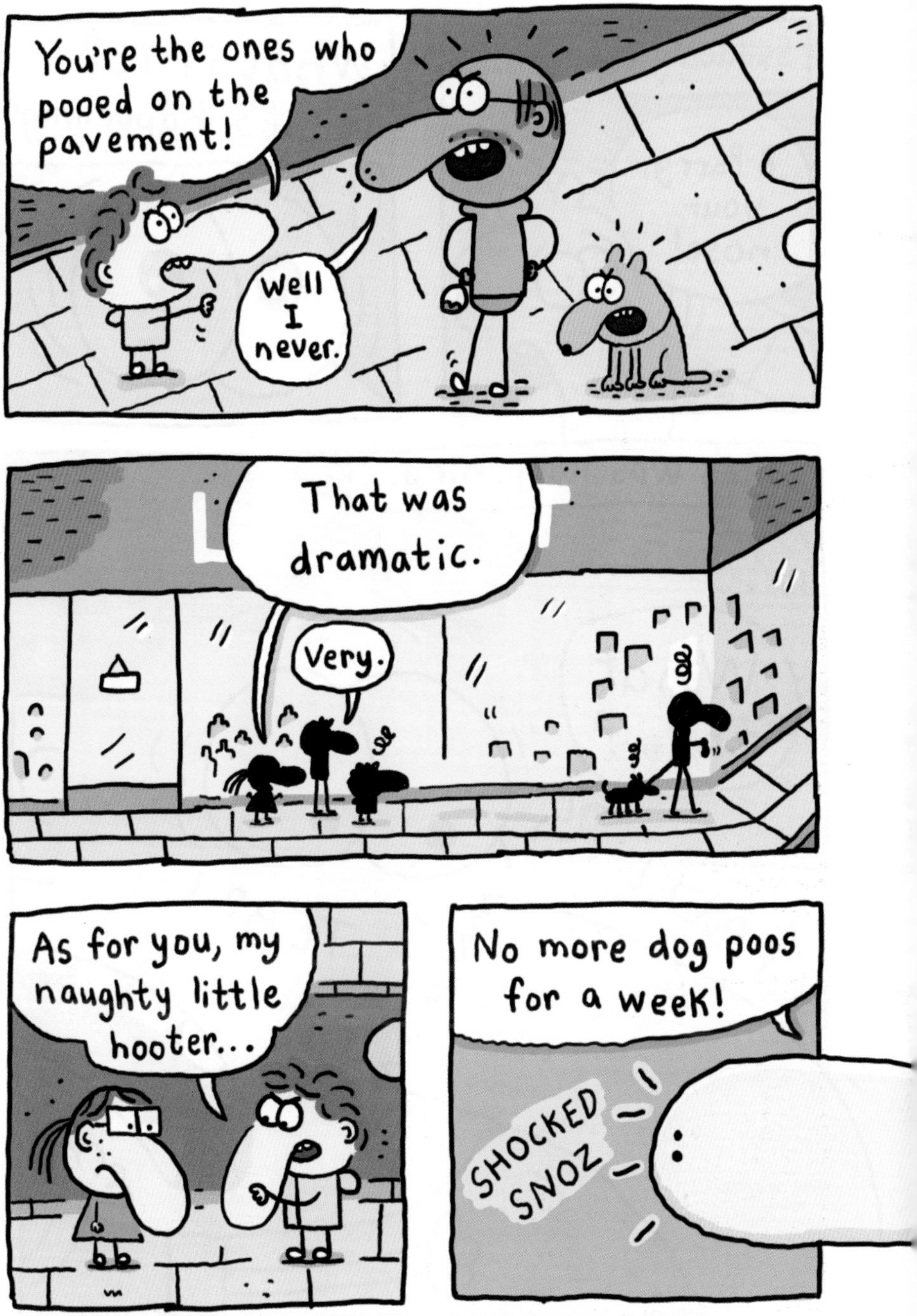
You're the ones who pooed on the pavement!
Well I never.
That was dramatic.
Very.
As for you, my naughty little hooter...
No more dog poos for a week!
SHOCKED SNOZ

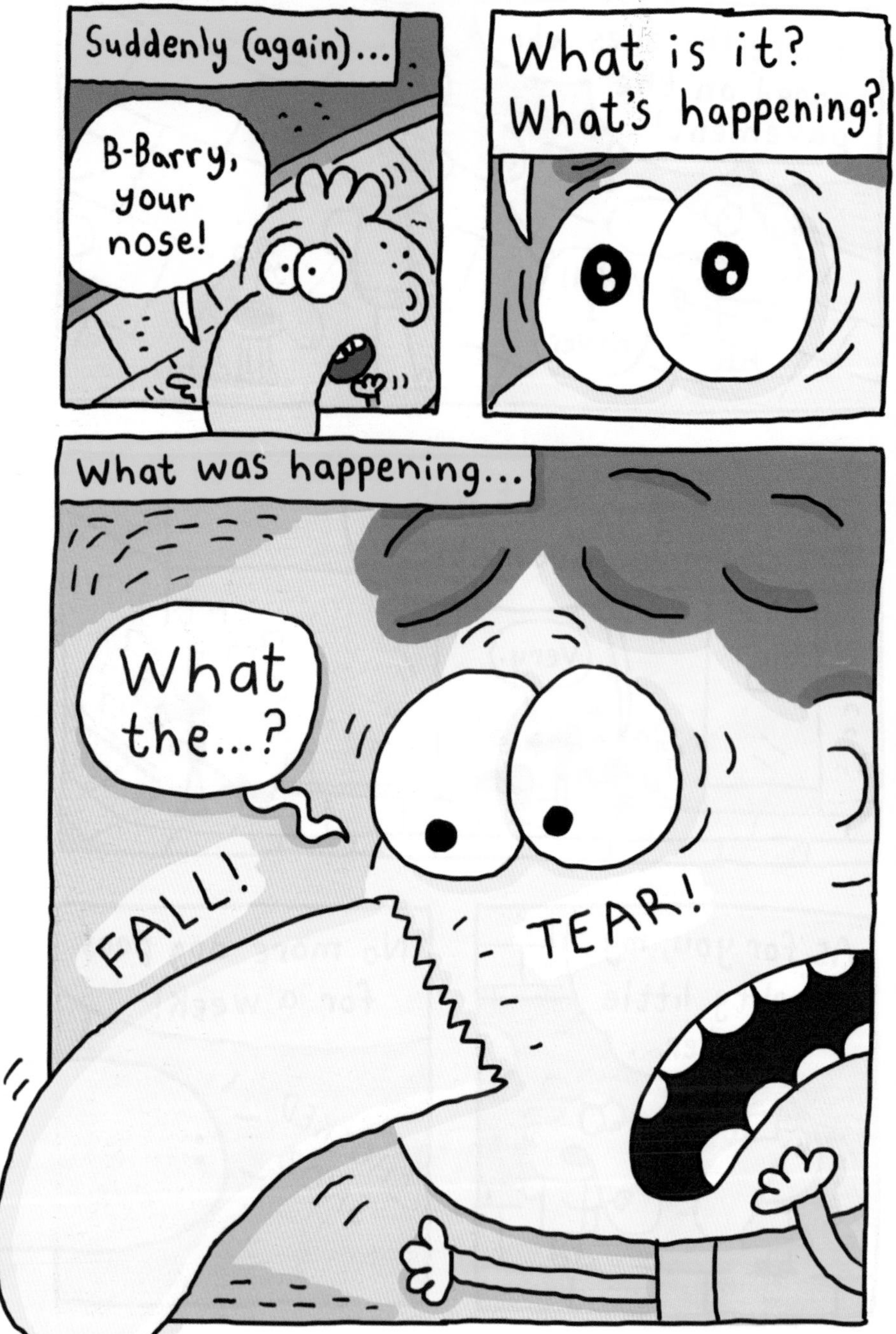
Suddenly (again)...
B-Barry, your nose!
What is it? What's happening?
What was happening...
What the...?
FALL!
TEAR!

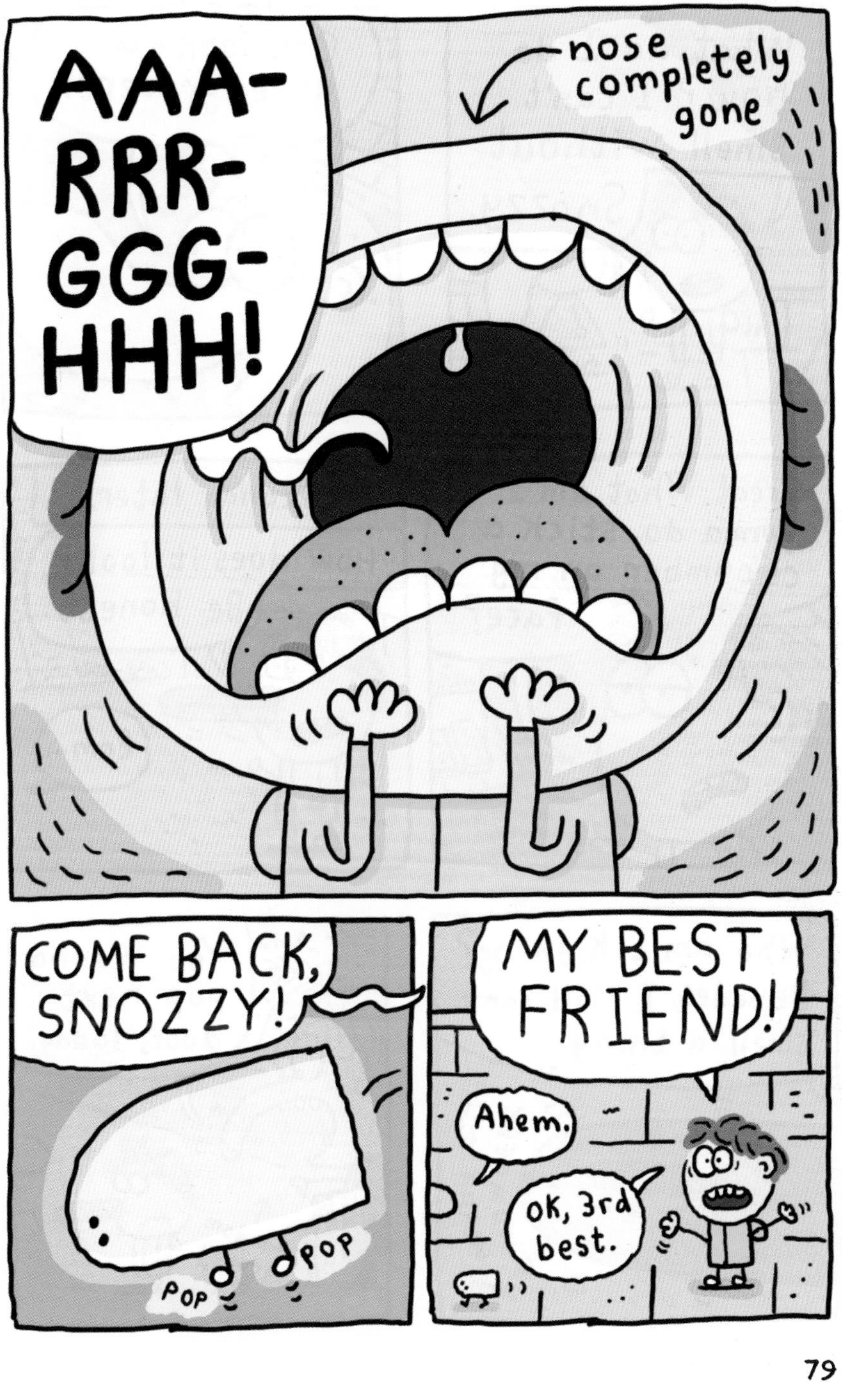
AAA-RRR-GGG-HHH!
nose completely gone
COME BACK, SNOZZY!
POP
POP
MY BEST FRIEND!
Ahem.
OK, 3rd best.

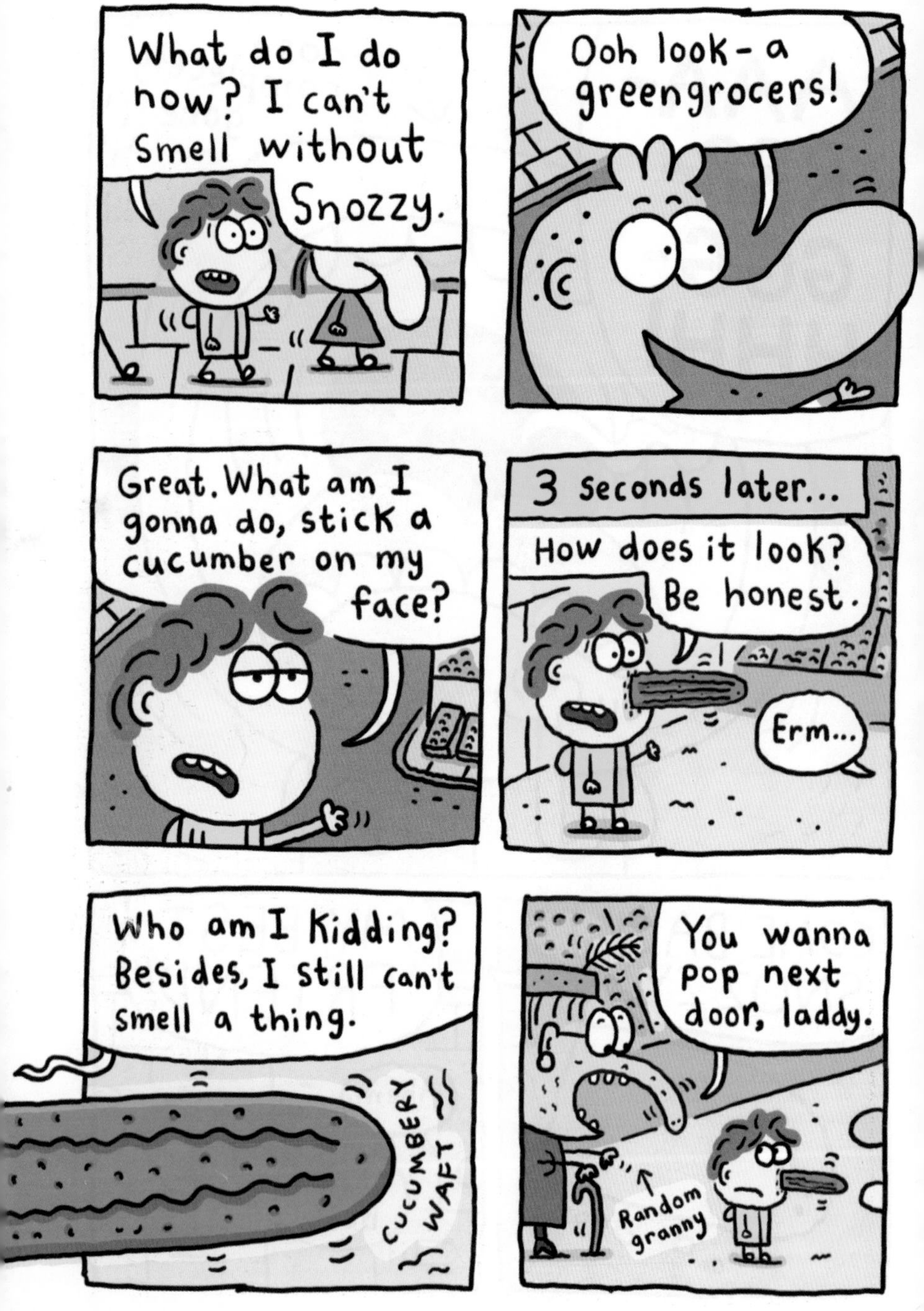
What do I do now? I can't smell without Snozzy.
Ooh look - a greengrocers!
Great. What am I gonna do, stick a cucumber on my face?
3 seconds later...
How does it look? Be honest.
Erm...
Who am I kidding? Besides, I still can't smell a thing.
CUCUMBERY WAFT
You wanna pop next door, laddy.
Random granny

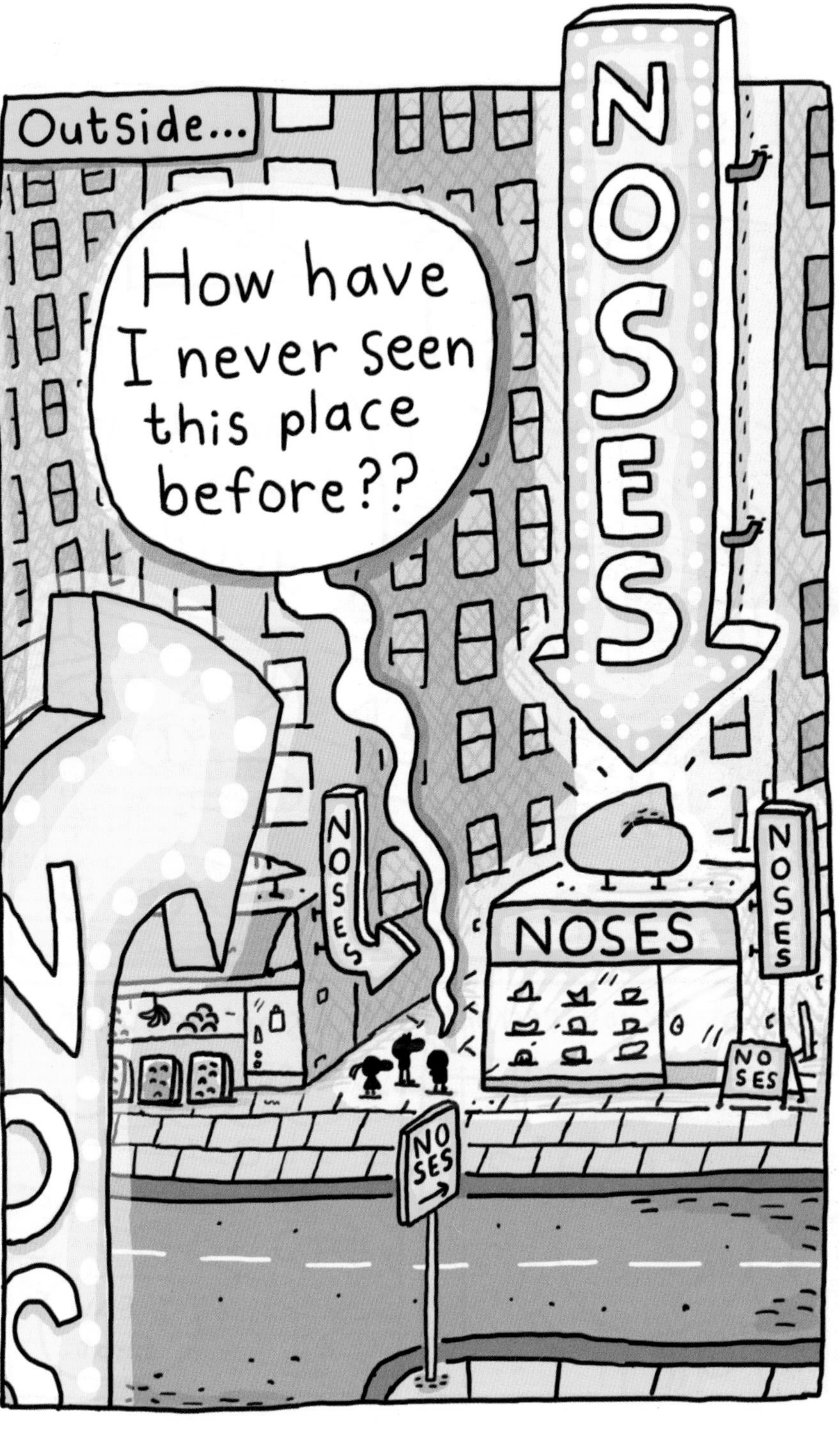
Outside...
How have I never seen this place before??
NOSES
NOSES
NOSES
NOSES
NO SES
NO SES

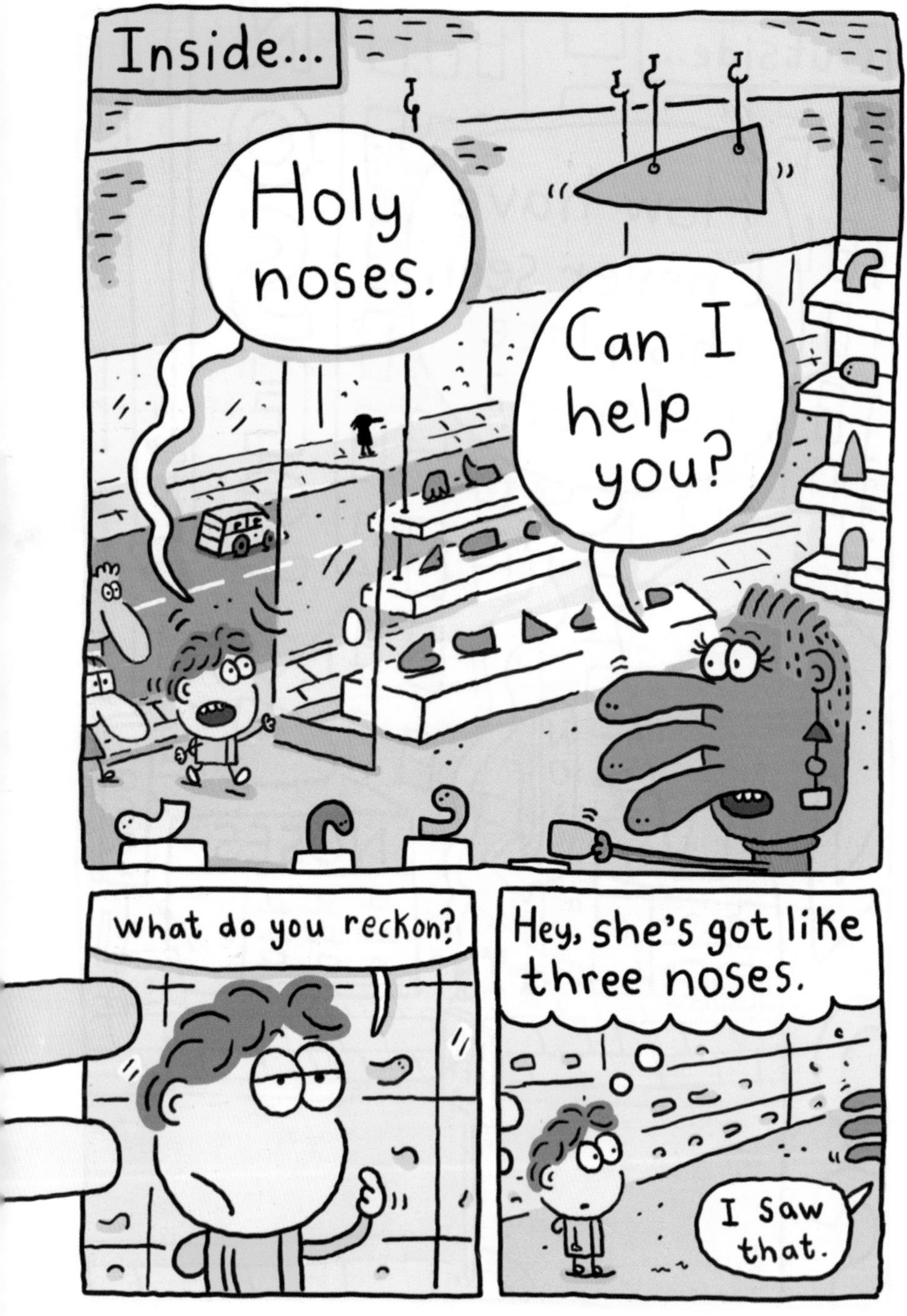
Inside...
Holy noses.
Can I help you?
What do you reckon?
Hey, she's got like three noses.
I saw that.

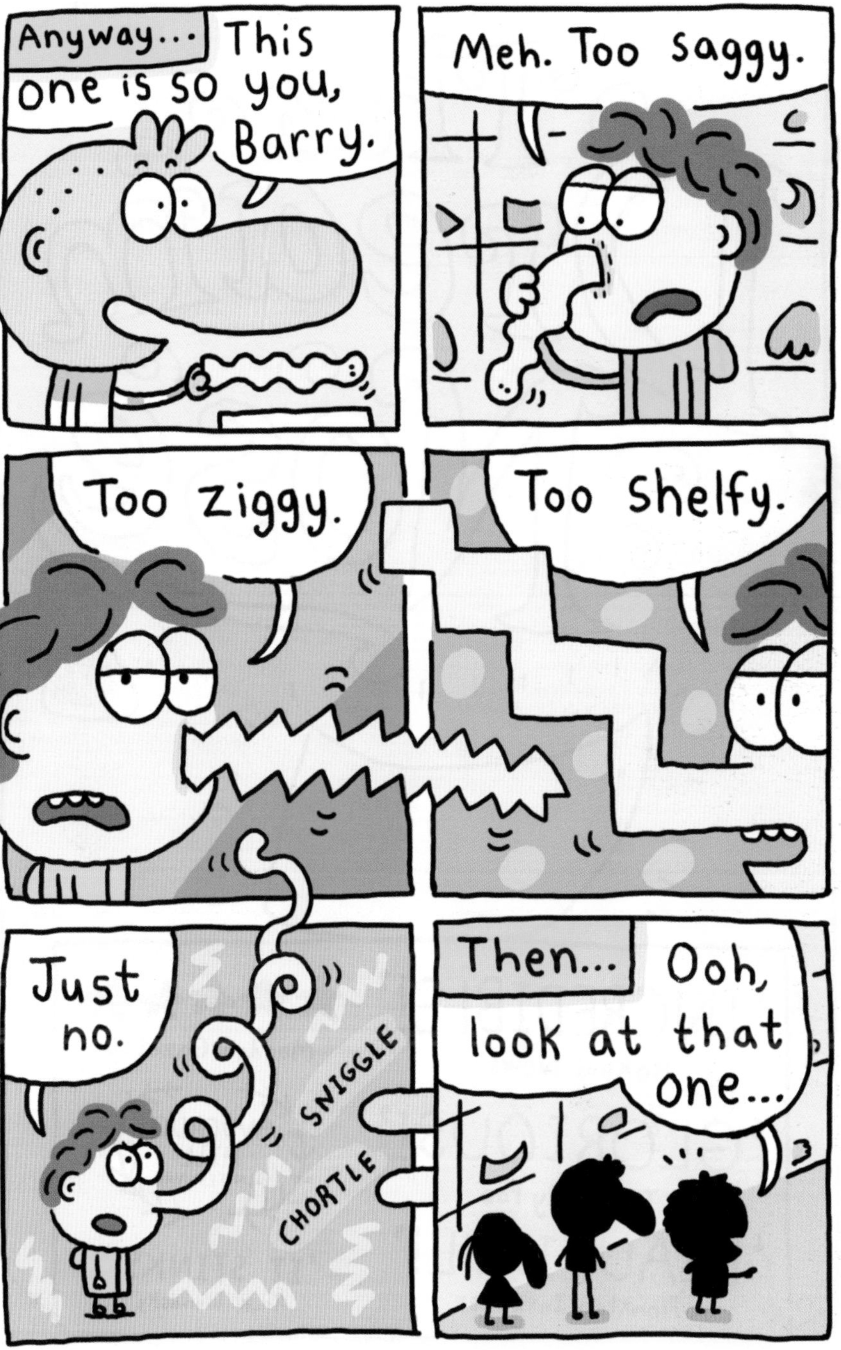
Anyway...
This one is so you, Barry.
Meh. Too saggy.
Too Ziggy.
Too Shelfy.
Just no.
SNIGGLE
CHORTLE
Then...
Ooh, look at that one...

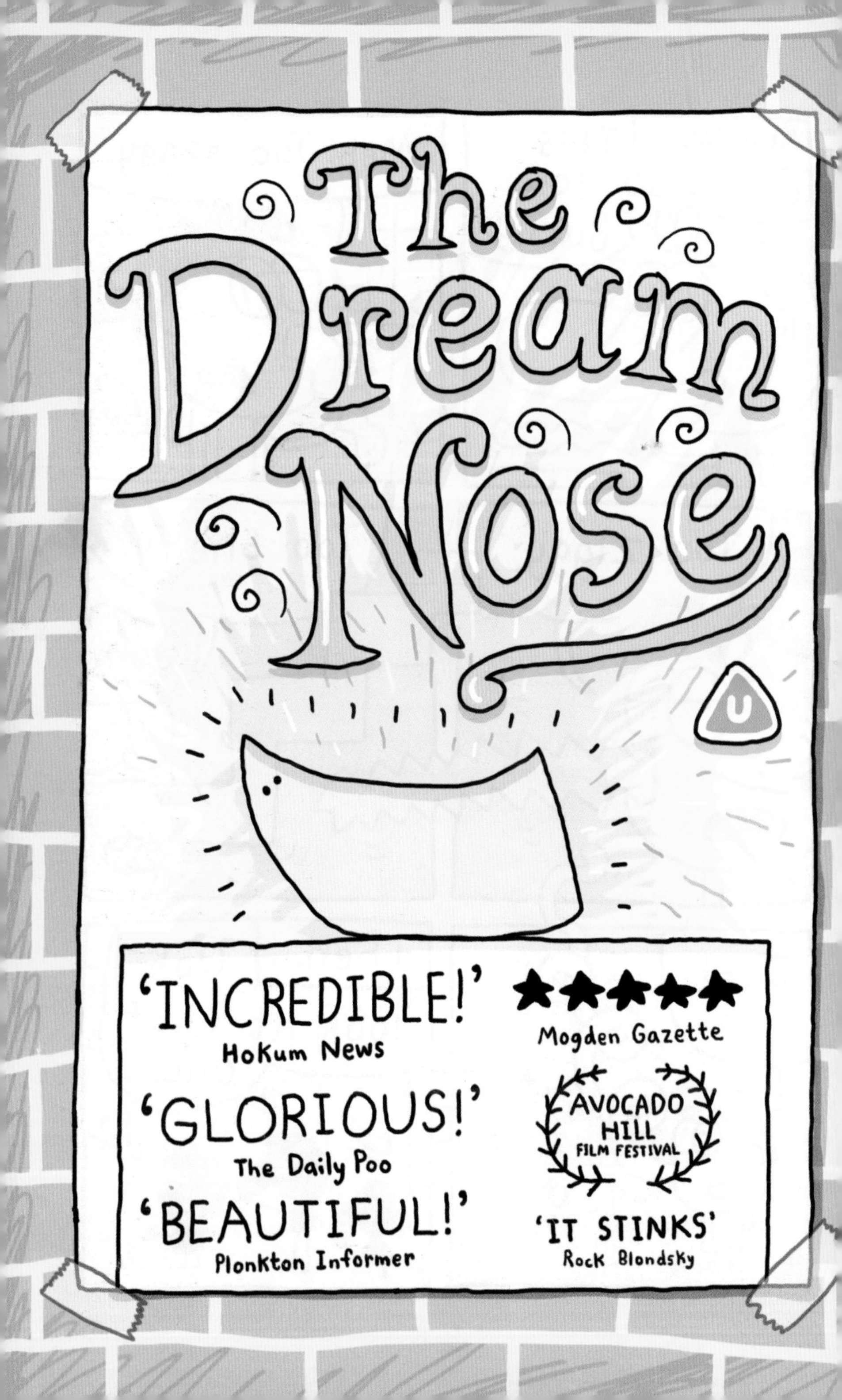
The Dream Nose
U
'INCREDIBLE!'
HoKum News
'GLORIOUS!'
The Daily Poo
'BEAUTIFUL!'
Plonkton Informer
★★★★★
Mogden Gazette
AVOCADO HILL FILM FESTIVAL
'IT STINKS'
Rock Blondsky

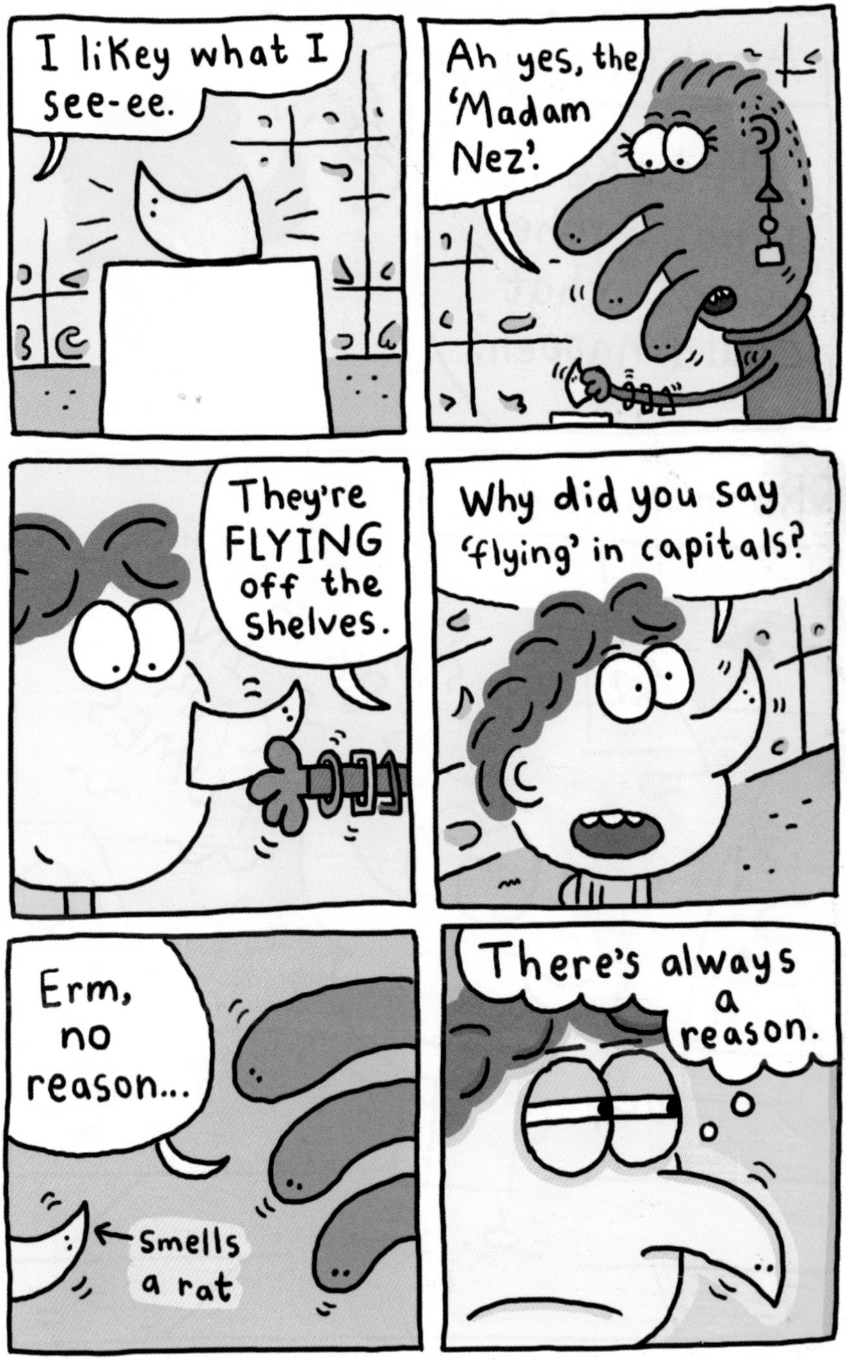
I likey what I see-ee.
Ah yes, the 'Madam Nez'.
They're FLYING off the shelves.
Why did you say 'flying' in capitals?
Erm, no reason...
Smells a rat
There's always a reason.

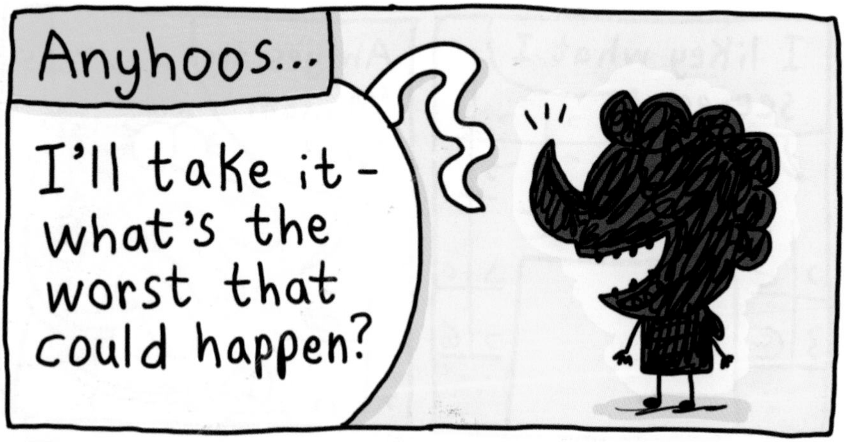
Anyhoos...
I'll take it - what's the worst that could happen?

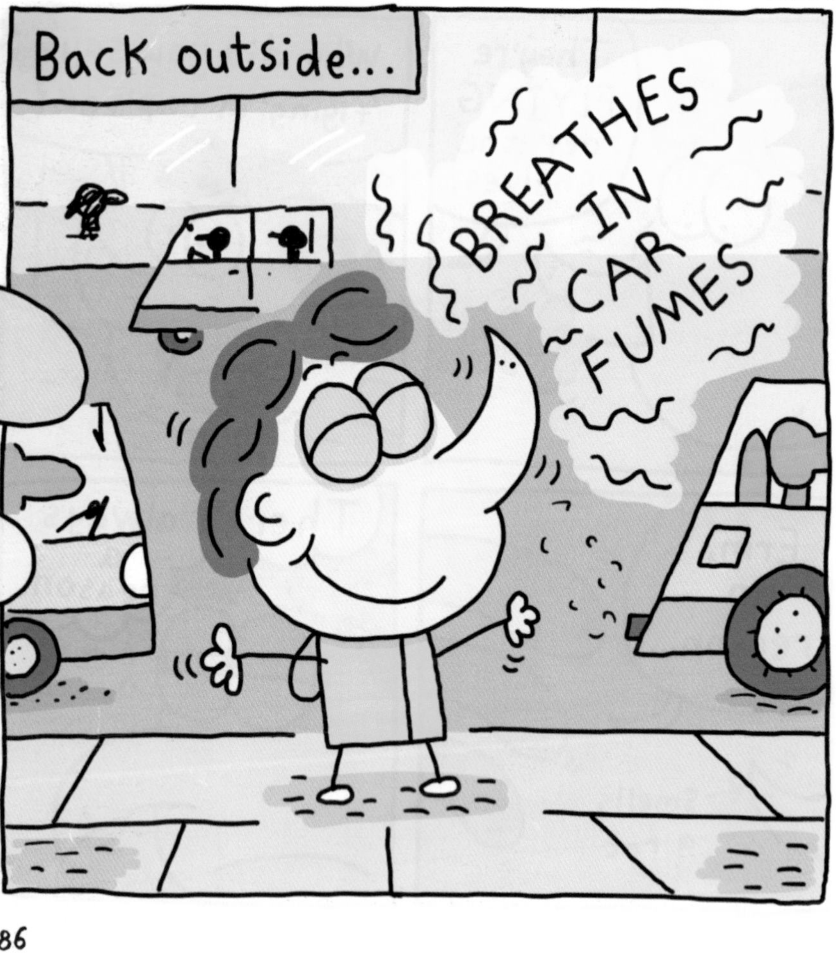
Back outside...
BREATHES IN CAR FUMES

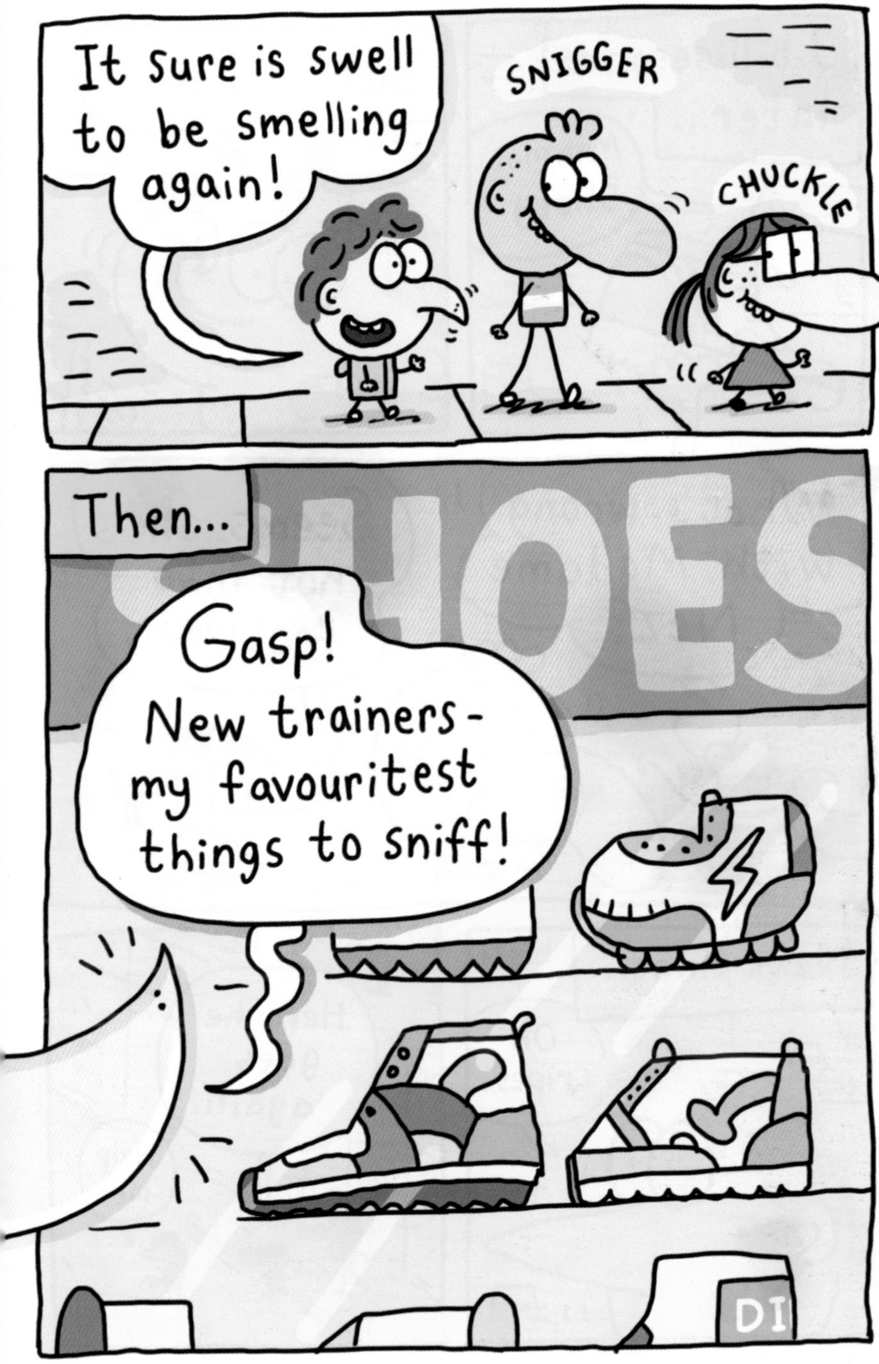
It sure is swell to be smelling again!
SNIGGER
CHUCKLE
Then...
SHOES
Gasp! New trainers- my favouritest things to sniff!

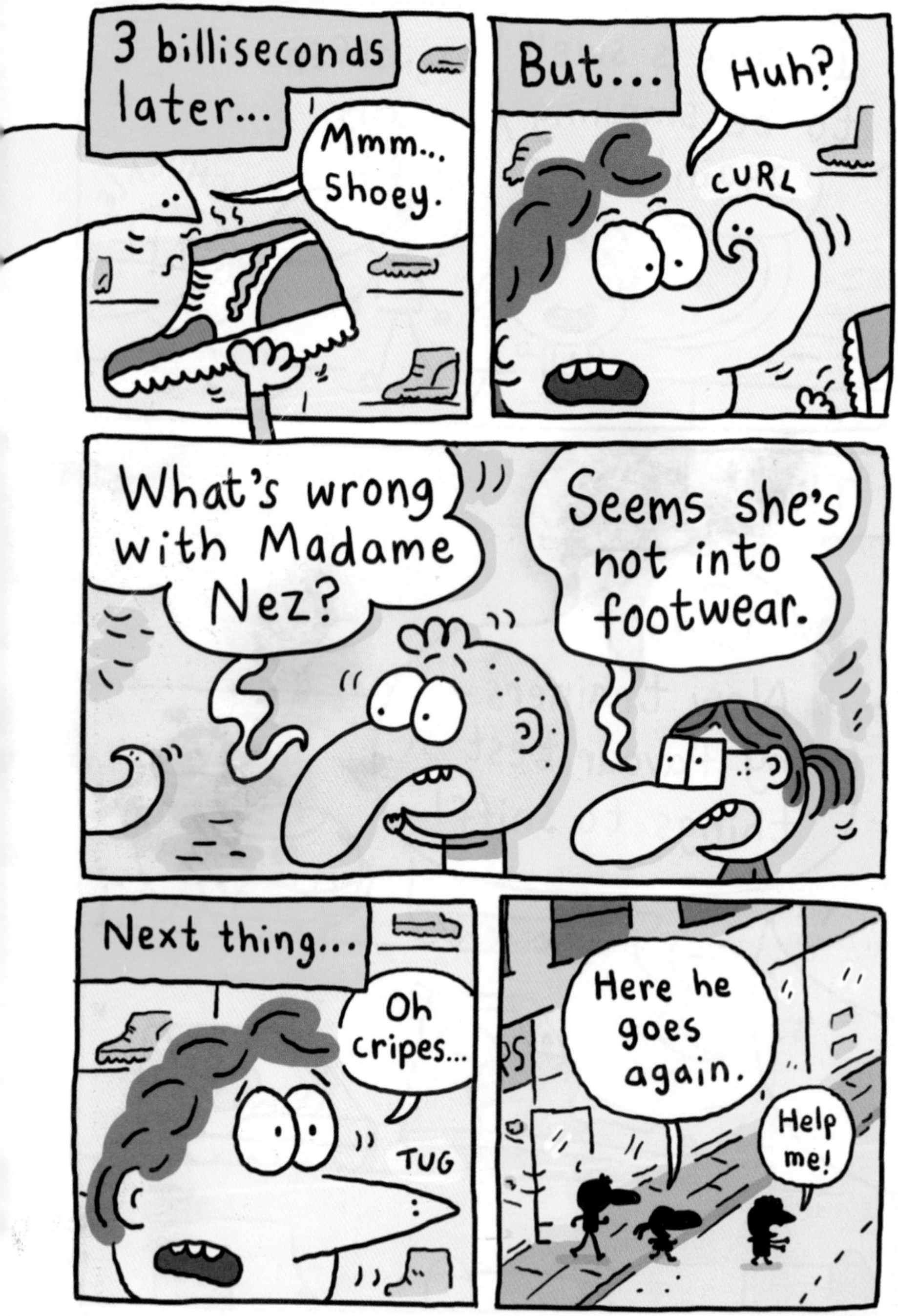
3 billiseconds later...
Mmm... Shoey.
But...
Huh?
CURL
What's wrong with Madame Nez?
Seems she's not into footwear.
Next thing...
Oh cripes...
TUG
Here he goes again.
Help me!

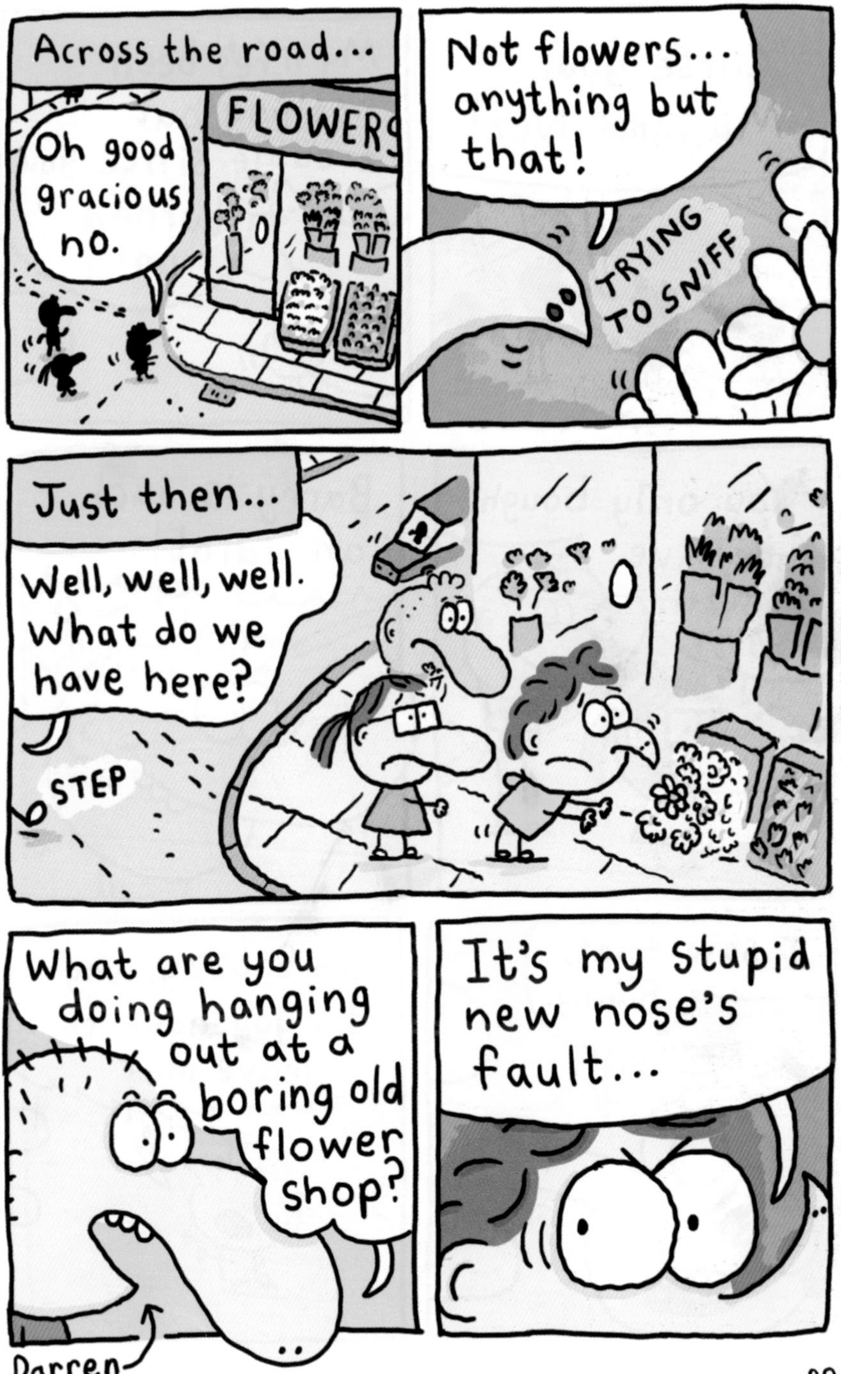
Across the road...
Oh good gracious no.
FLOWERS
Not flowers... anything but that!
TRYING TO SNIFF
Just then...
Well, well, well. What do we have here?
STEP
What are you doing hanging out at a boring old flower shop?
Darren
It's my stupid new nose's fault...

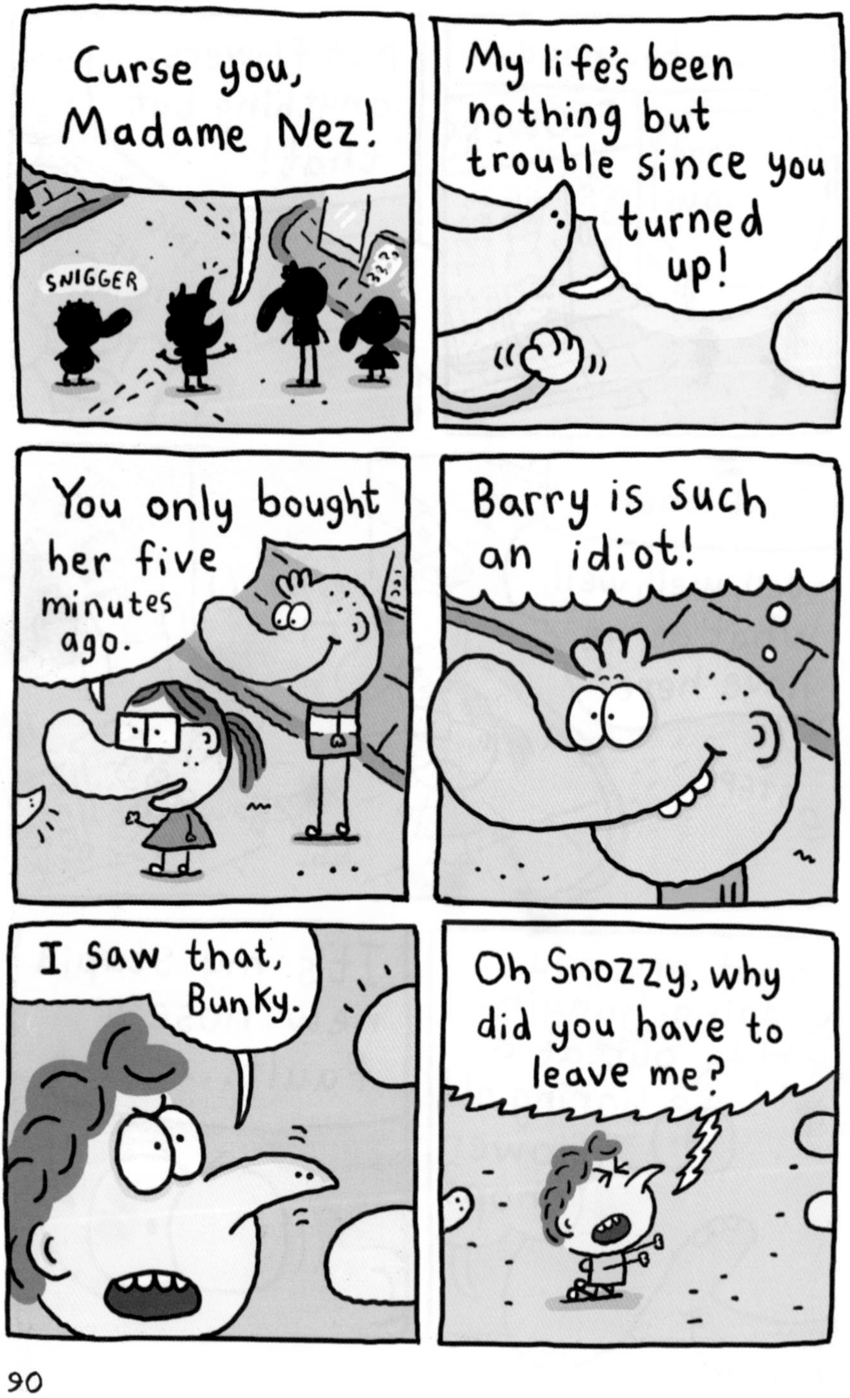
Curse you, Madame Nez!
SNIGGER
My life's been nothing but trouble since you turned up!
You only bought her five minutes ago.
Barry is such an idiot!
I saw that, Bunky.
Oh Snozzy, why did you have to leave me?

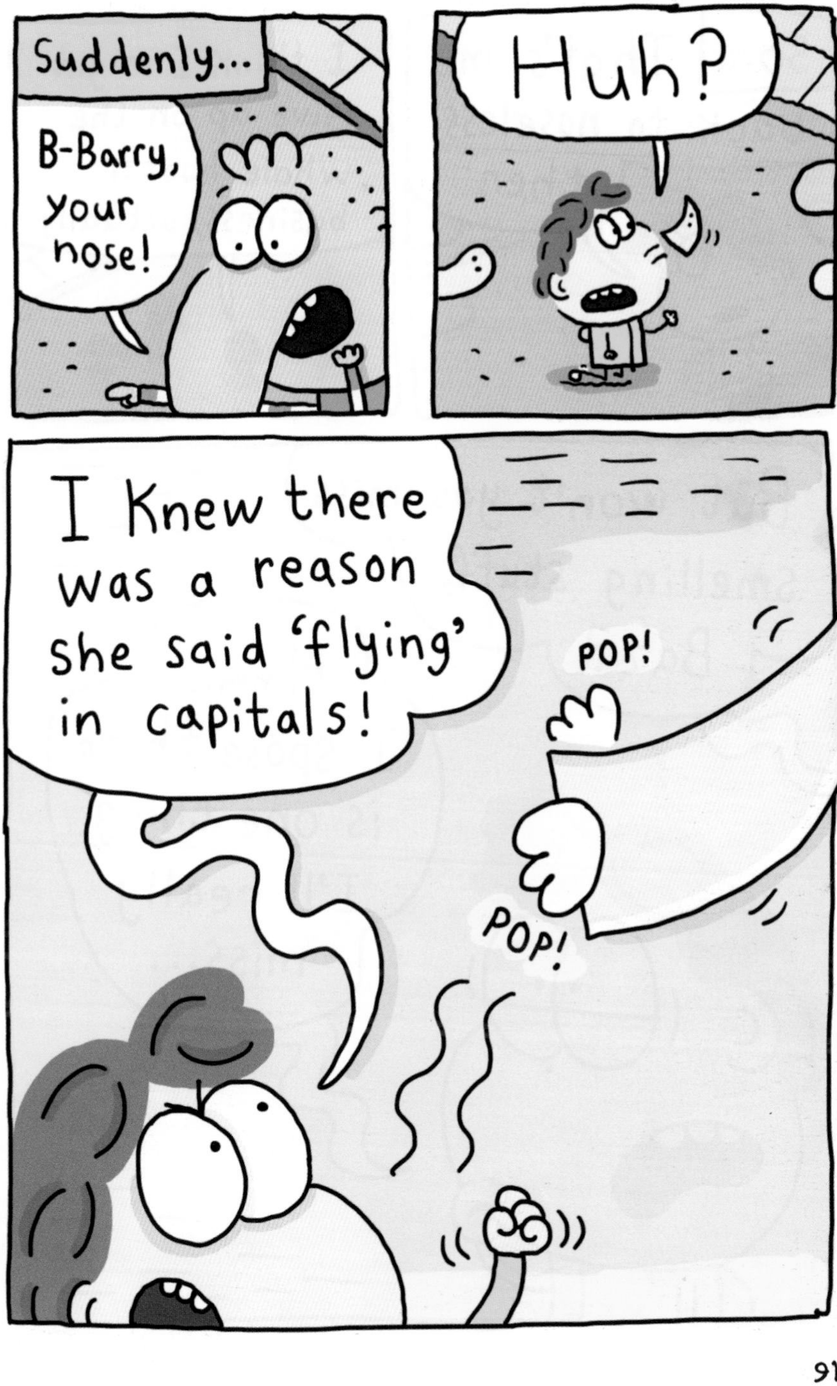
Suddenly...
B-Barry, your nose!
Huh?
I Knew there was a reason she said 'flying' in capitals!
POP!
POP!

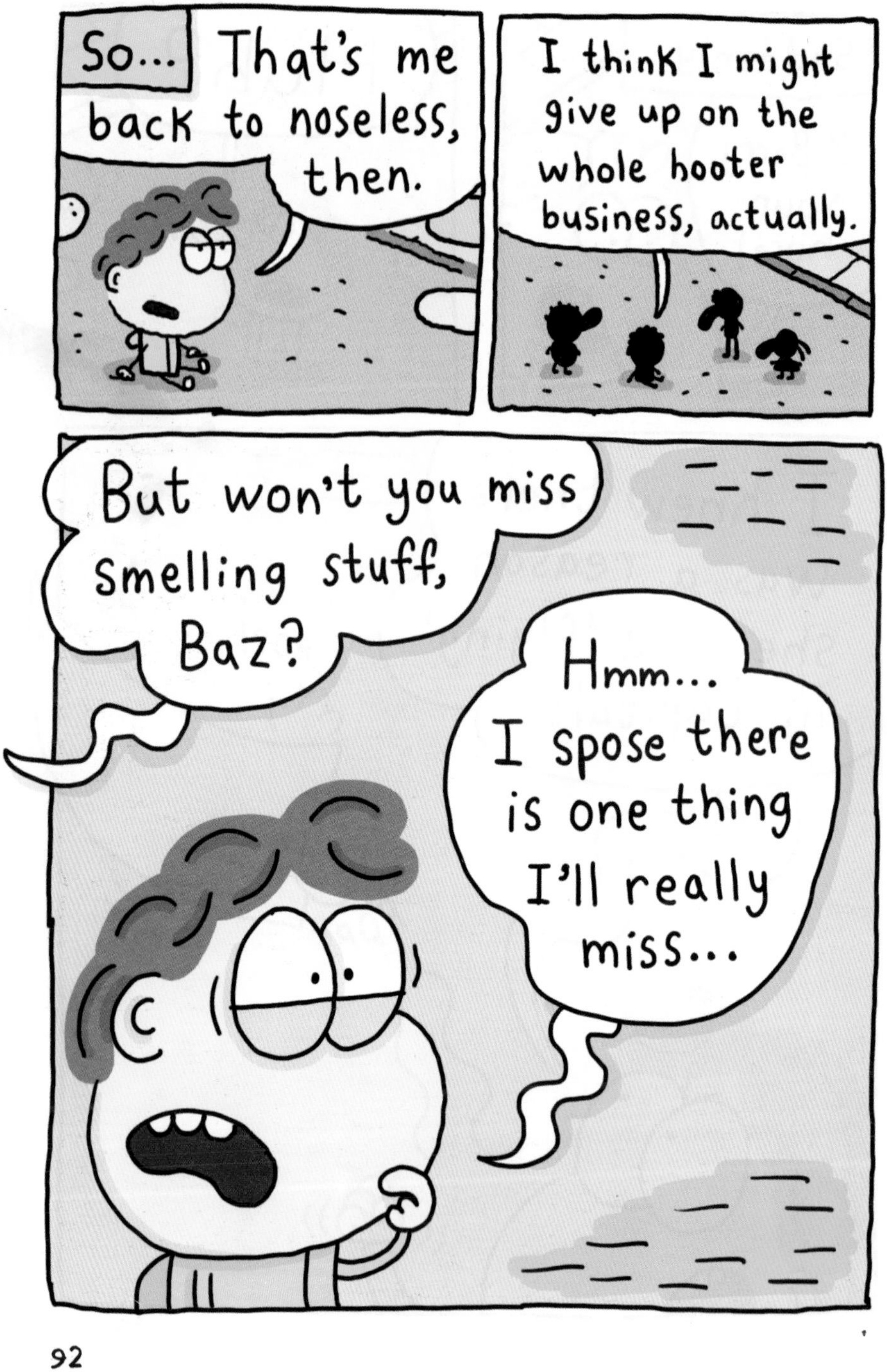
So...
That's me back to noseless, then.
I think I might give up on the whole hooter business, actually.
But won't you miss smelling stuff, Baz?
Hmm... I spose there is one thing I'll really miss...

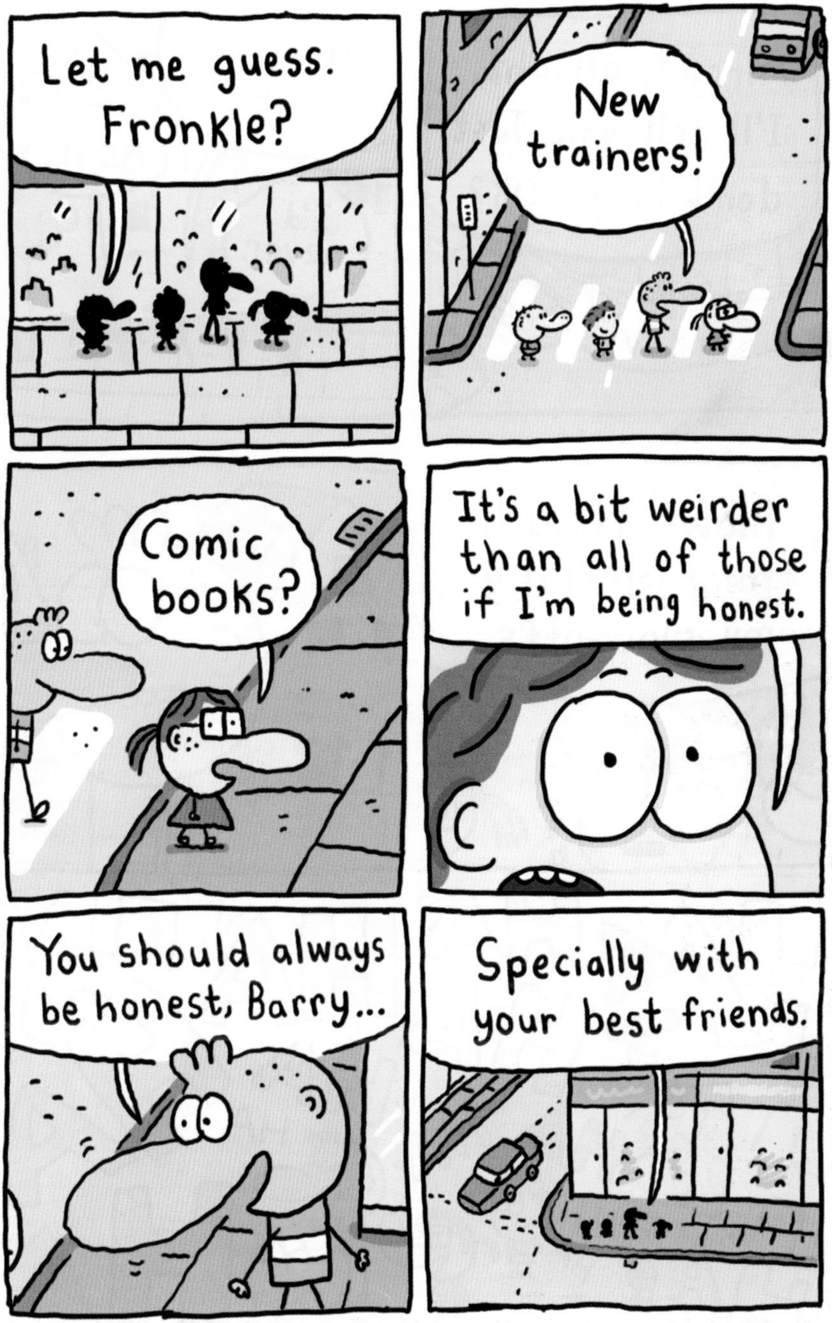
Let me guess. Fronkle?
New trainers!
Comic books?
It's a bit weirder than all of those if I'm being honest.
You should always be honest, Barry...
Specially with your best friends.

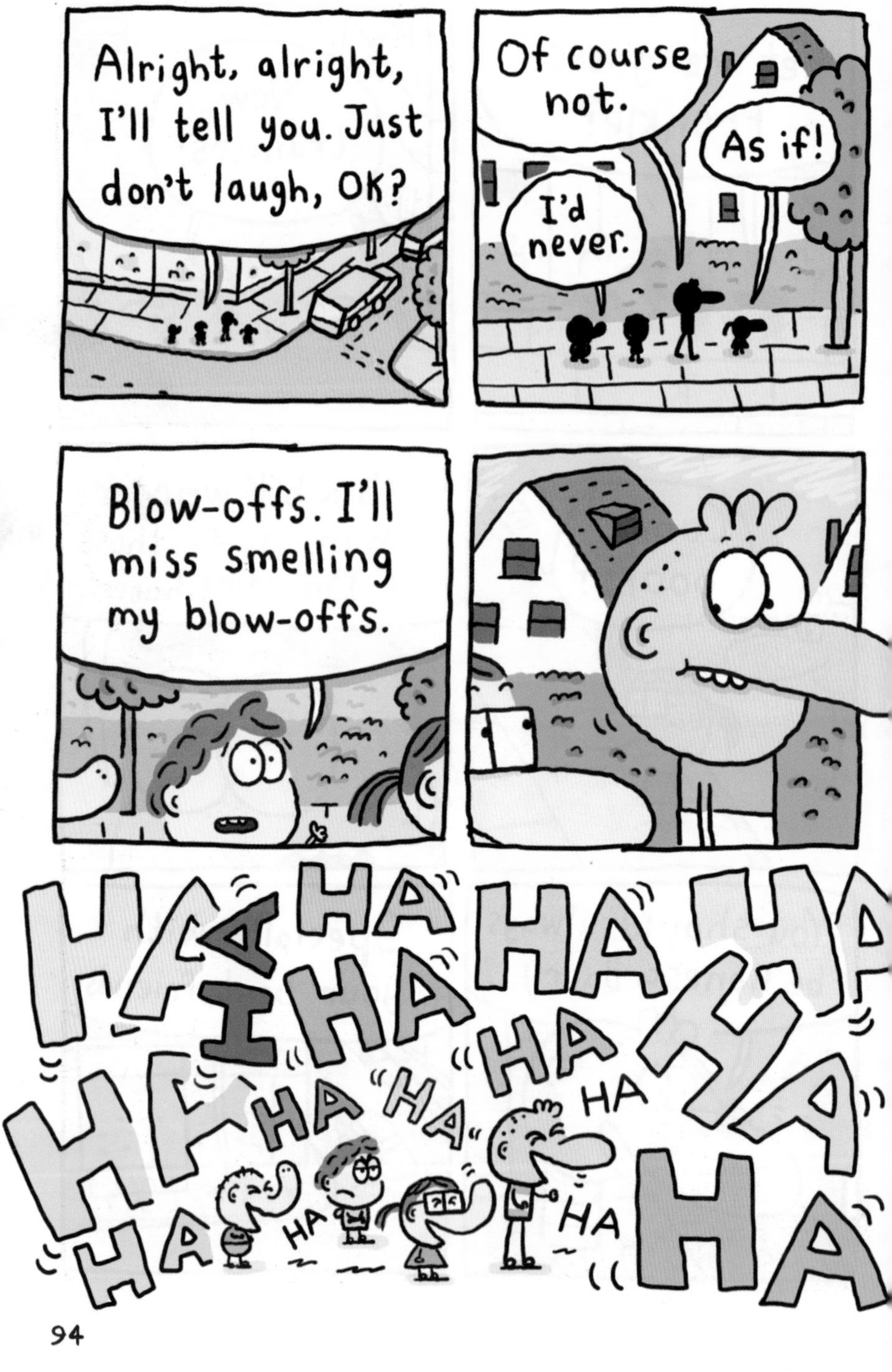
Alright, alright, I'll tell you. Just don't laugh, OK?
Of course not.
I'd never.
As if!
Blow-offs. I'll miss smelling my blow-offs.
HA HA HA HA HA HA HA HA HA HA HA HA HA HA HA HA HA HA HA HA

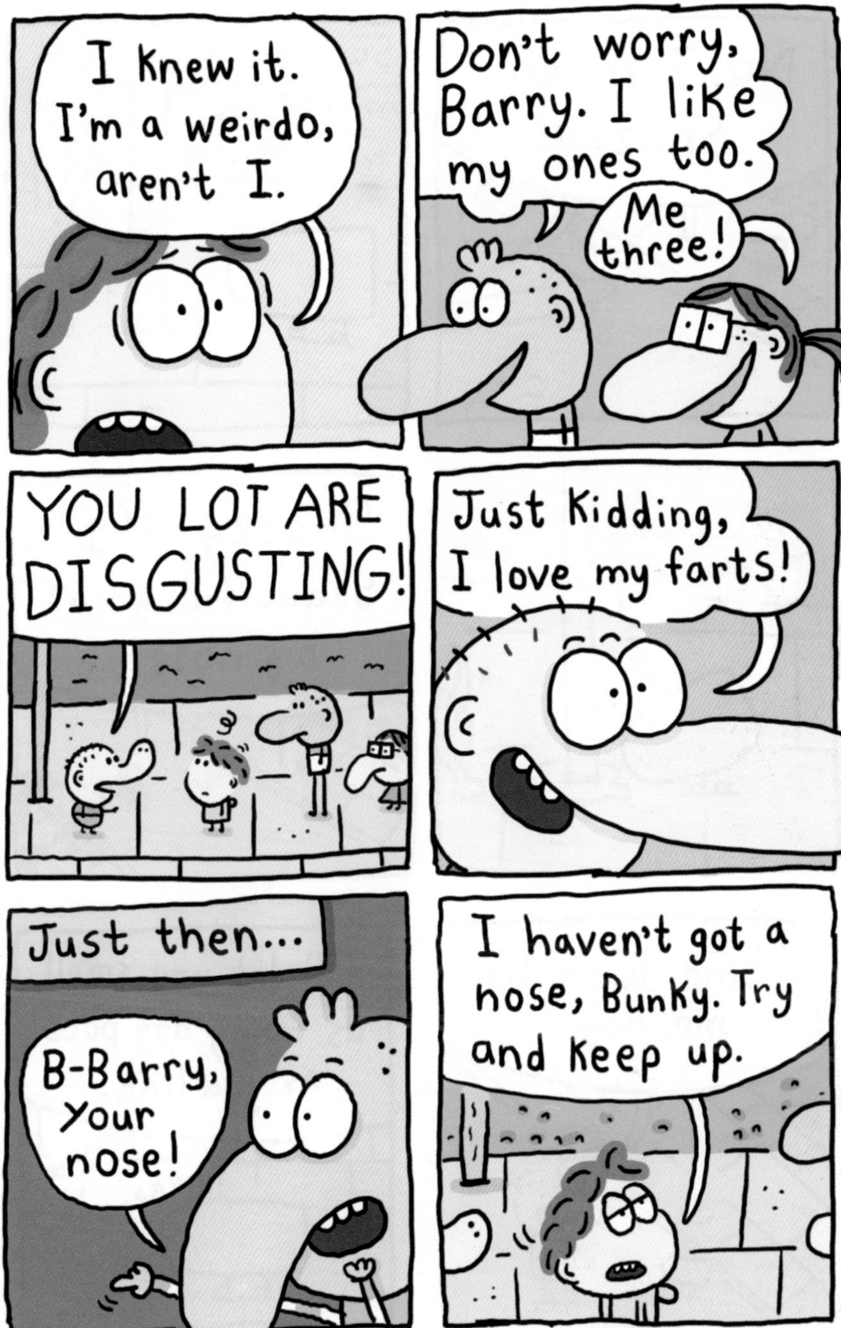
I knew it. I'm a weirdo, aren't I.
Don't worry, Barry. I like my ones too.
Me three!
YOU LOT ARE DISGUSTING!
Just kidding, I love my farts!
Just then...
B-Barry, your nose!
I haven't got a nose, Bunky. Try and keep up.

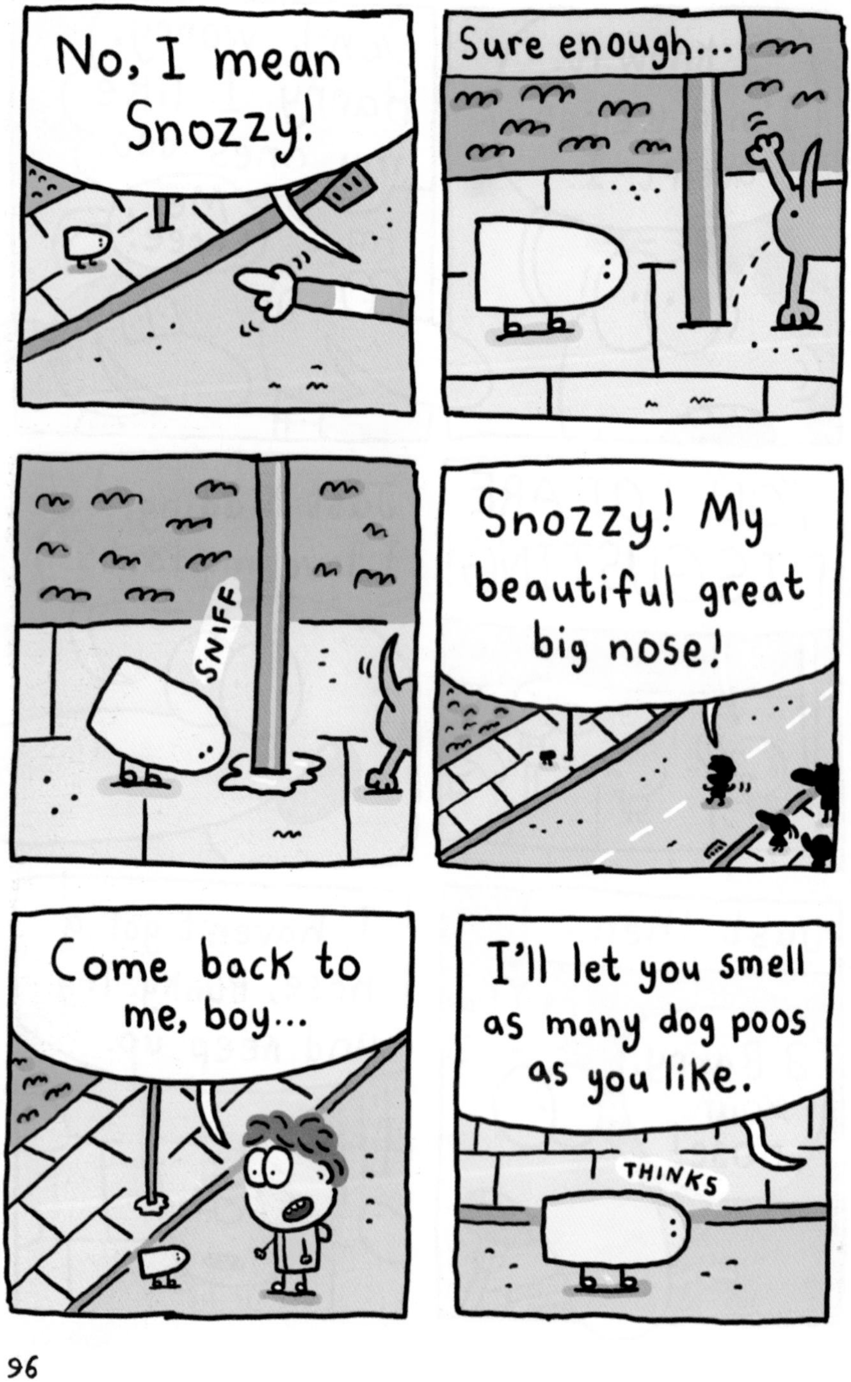
No, I mean Snozzy!
Sure enough...
SNIFF
Snozzy! My beautiful great big nose!
Come back to me, boy...
I'll let you smell as many dog poos as you like.
THINKS

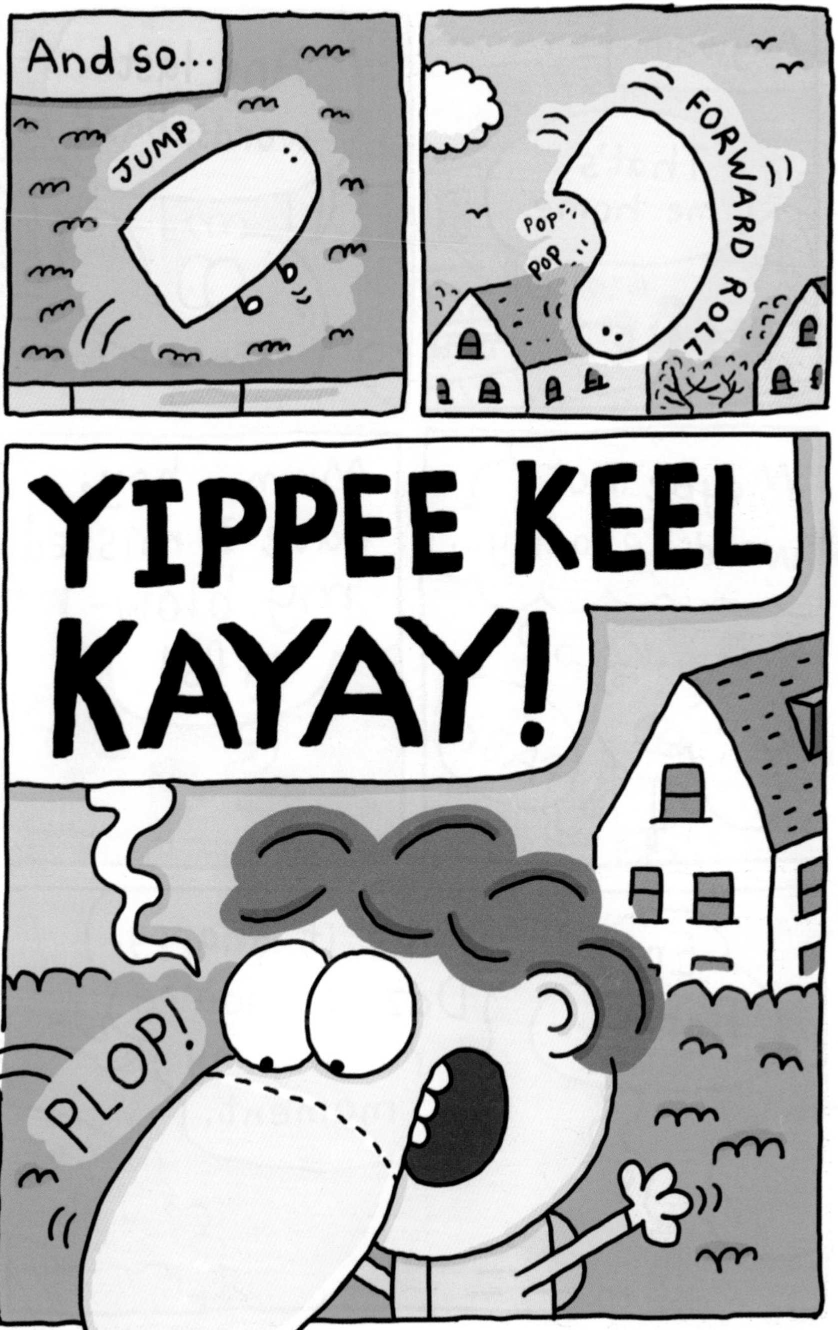

And so...
JUMP
FORWARD ROLL
POP
POP
YIPPEE KEEL KAYAY!
PLOP!

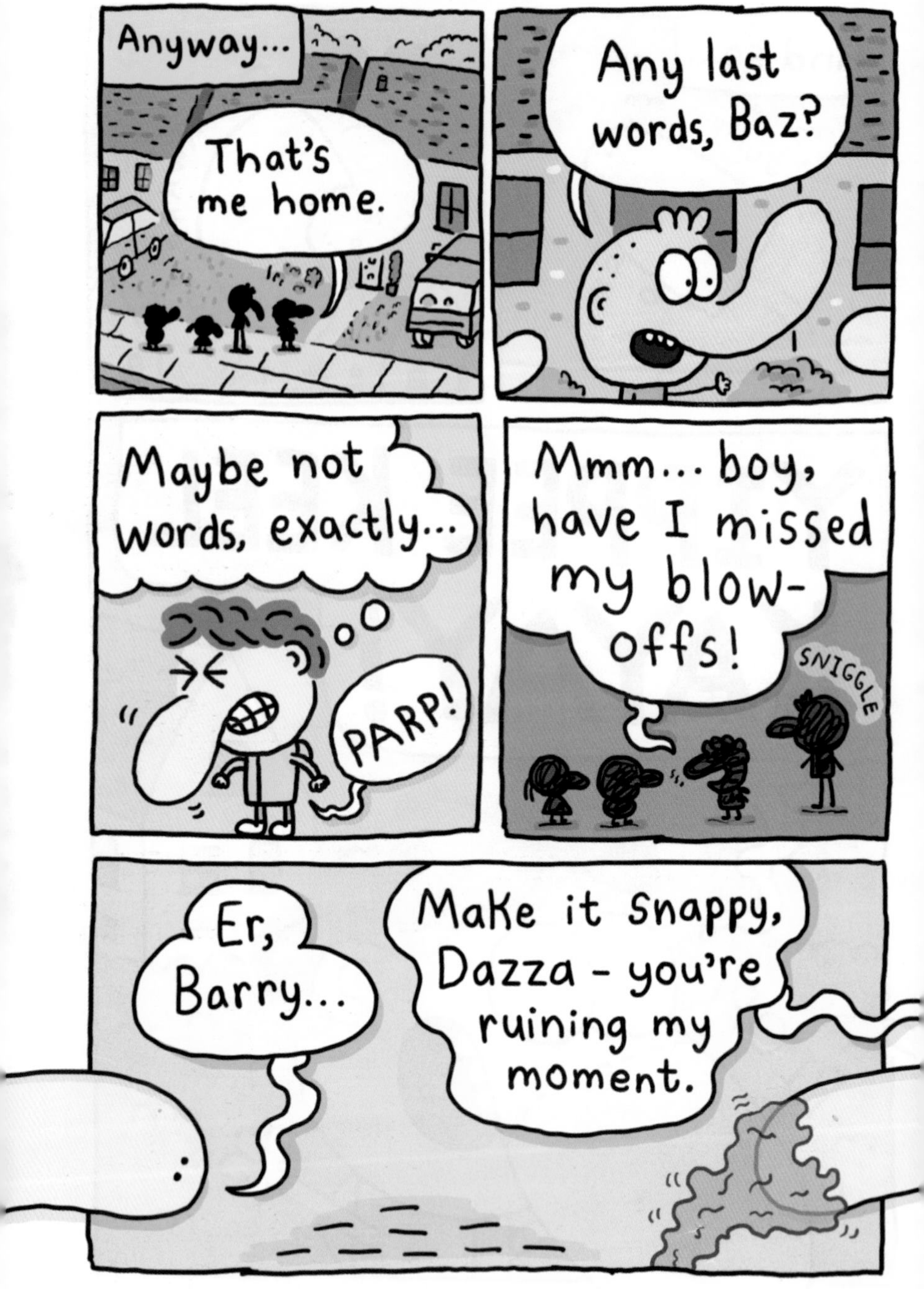
Anyway...
That's me home.
Any last words, Baz?
Maybe not words, exactly...
PARP!
Mmm... boy, have I missed my blow-offs!
SNIGGLE
Er, Barry...
Make it snappy, Dazza - you're ruining my moment.

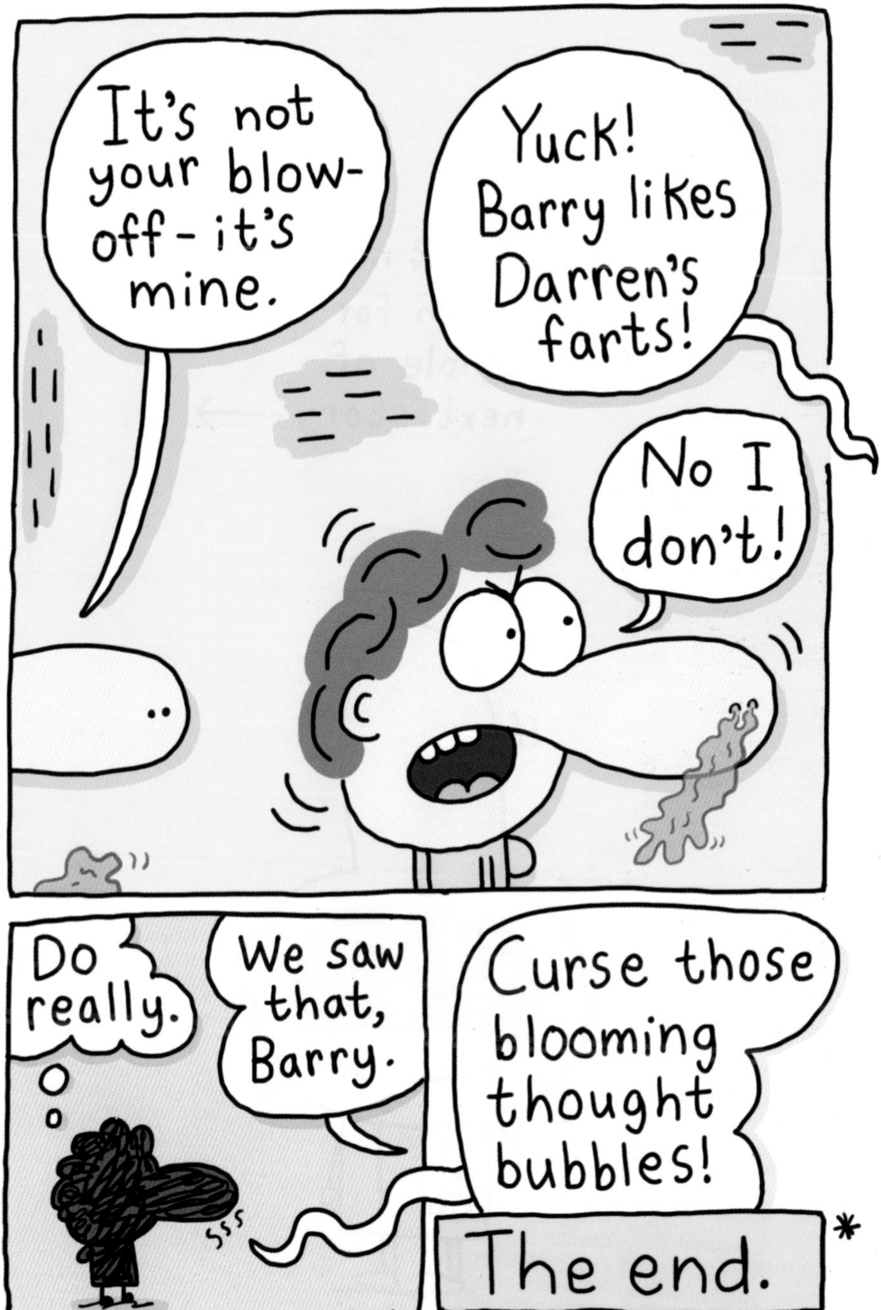
It's not your blow-off - it's mine.
Yuck! Barry likes Darren's farts!
No I don't!
Do really.
We saw that, Barry.
Curse those blooming thought bubbles!
The end.*

*Some of this might not have actukeely happened.

Try & not
yawn for
whole of
next story $\longrightarrow$

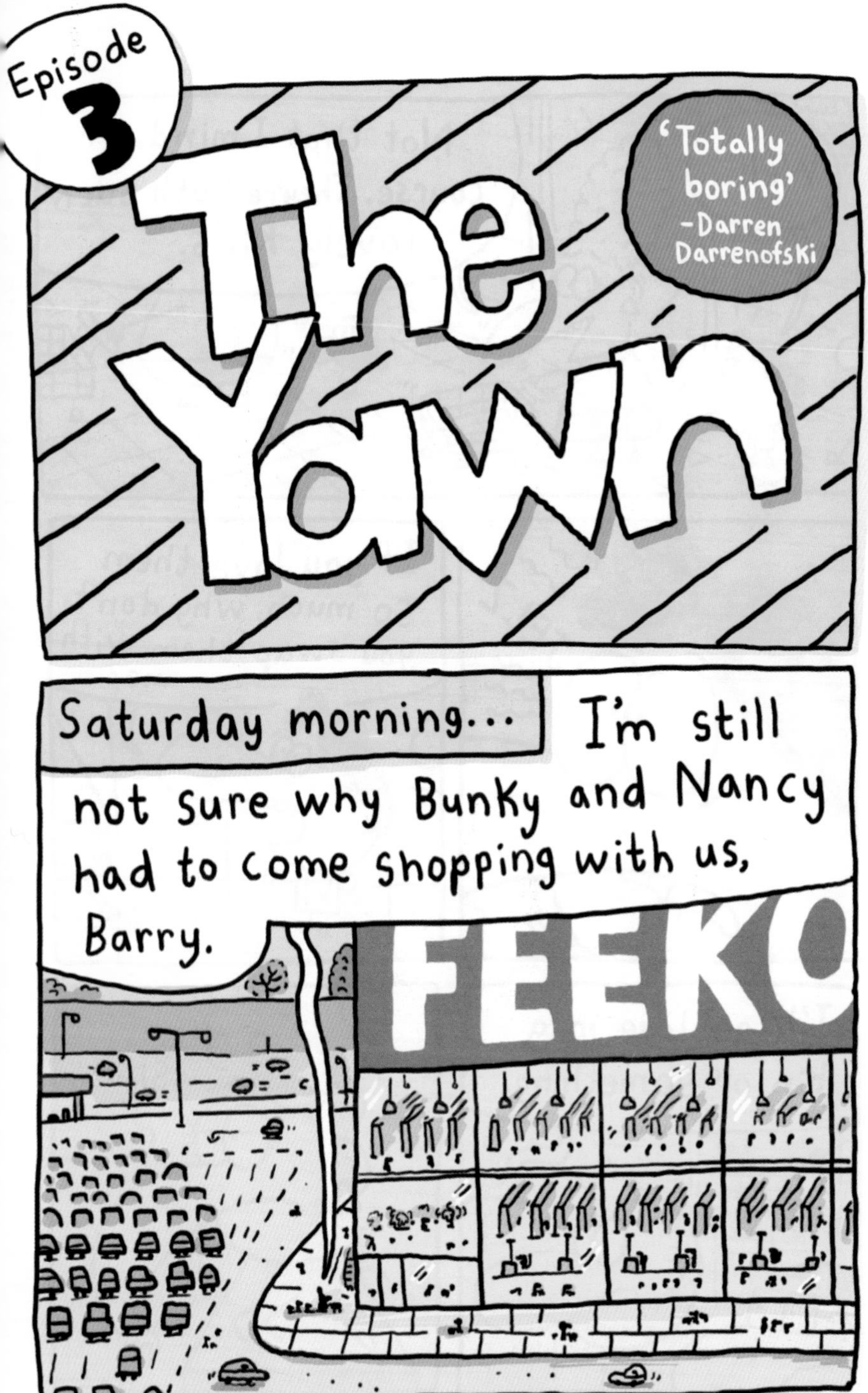

Episode 3
The Yawn
'Totally boring' -Darren Darrenofski
Saturday morning...
I'm still not sure why Bunky and Nancy had to come shopping with us, Barry.
FEEKO

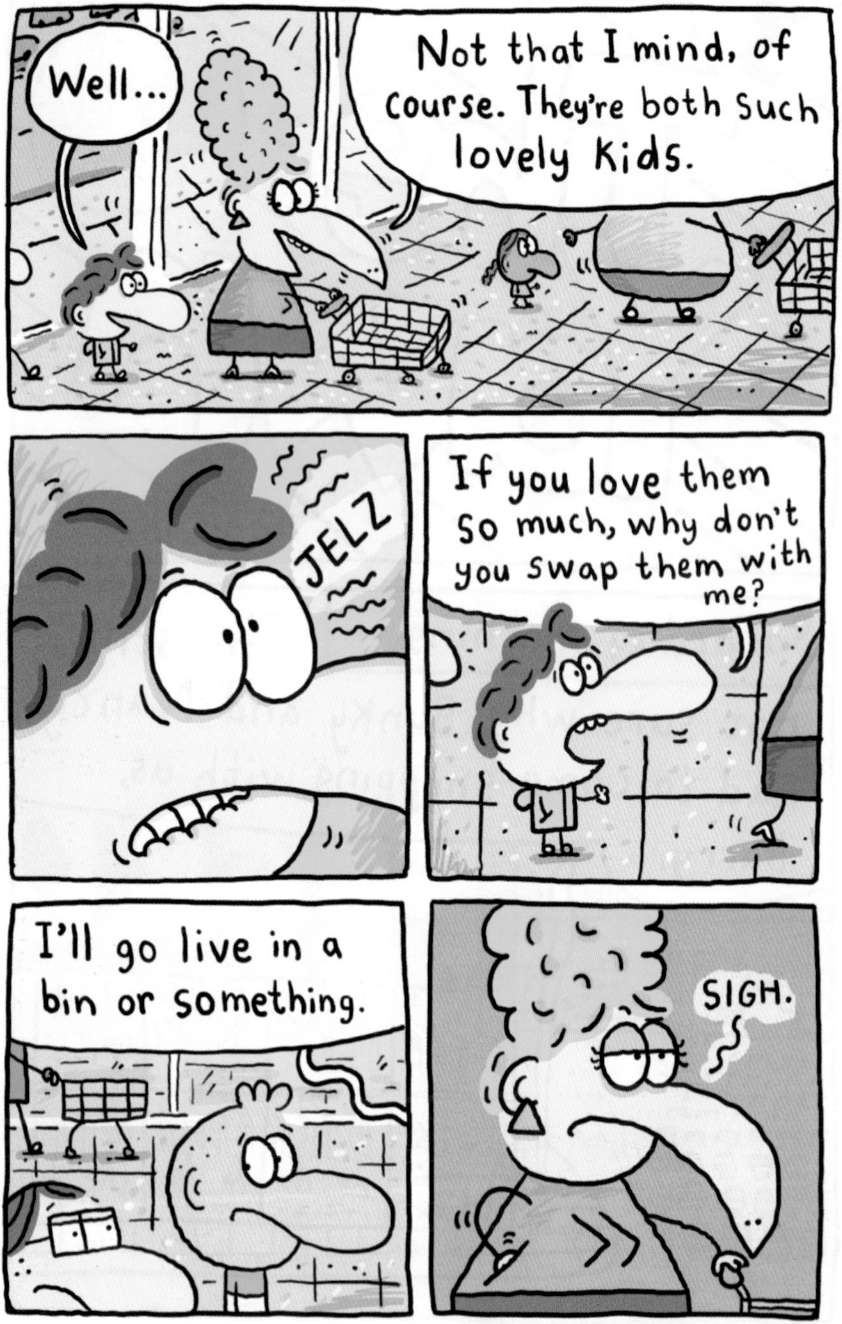

Well...
Not that I mind, of course. They're both such lovely kids.
JELZ
If you love them so much, why don't you swap them with me?
I'll go live in a bin or something.
SIGH.

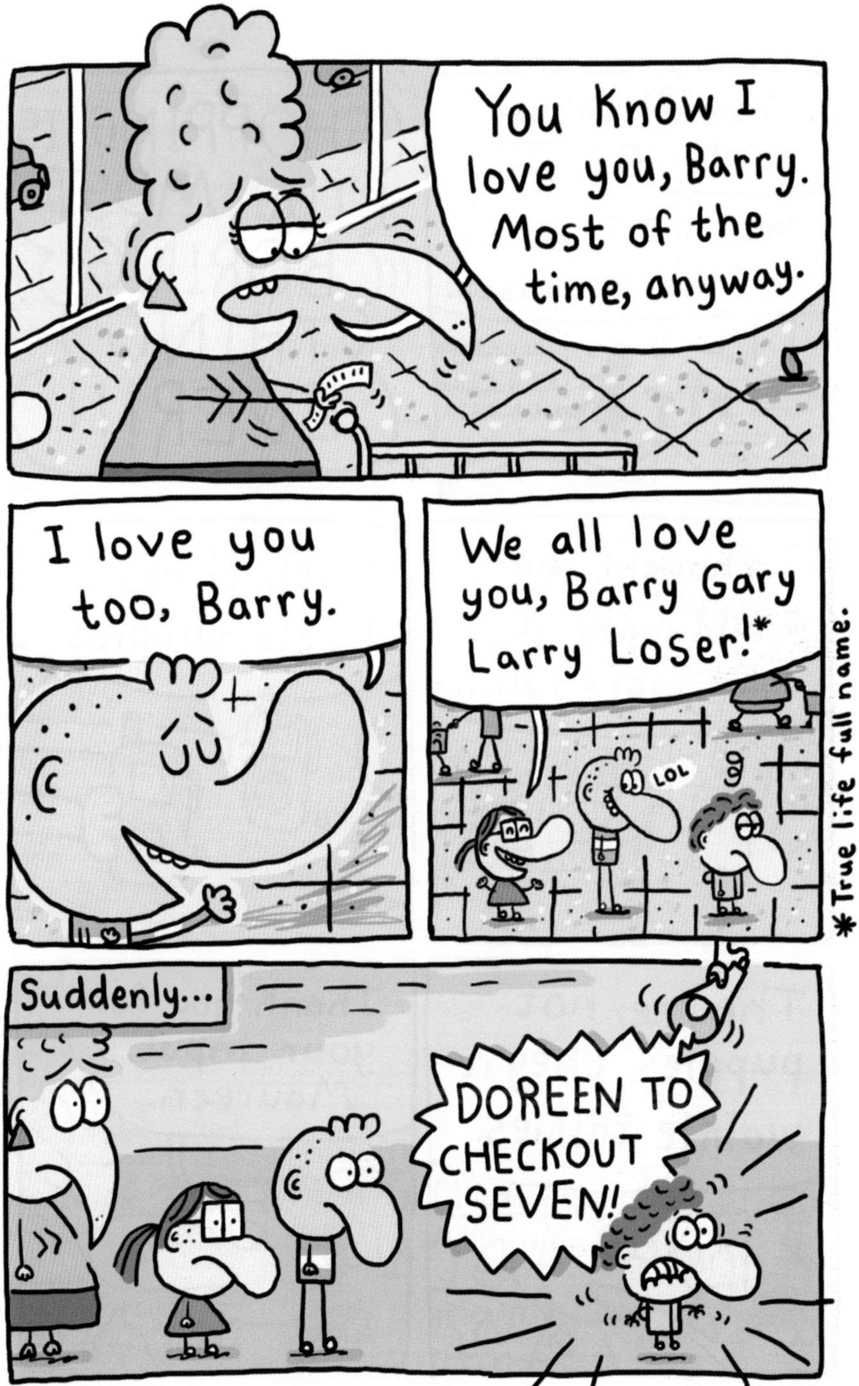
You Know I love you, Barry. Most of the time, anyway.
I love you too, Barry.
We all love you, Barry Gary Larry Loser!*
LOL
*True life full name.
Suddenly...
DOREEN TO CHECKOUT SEVEN!

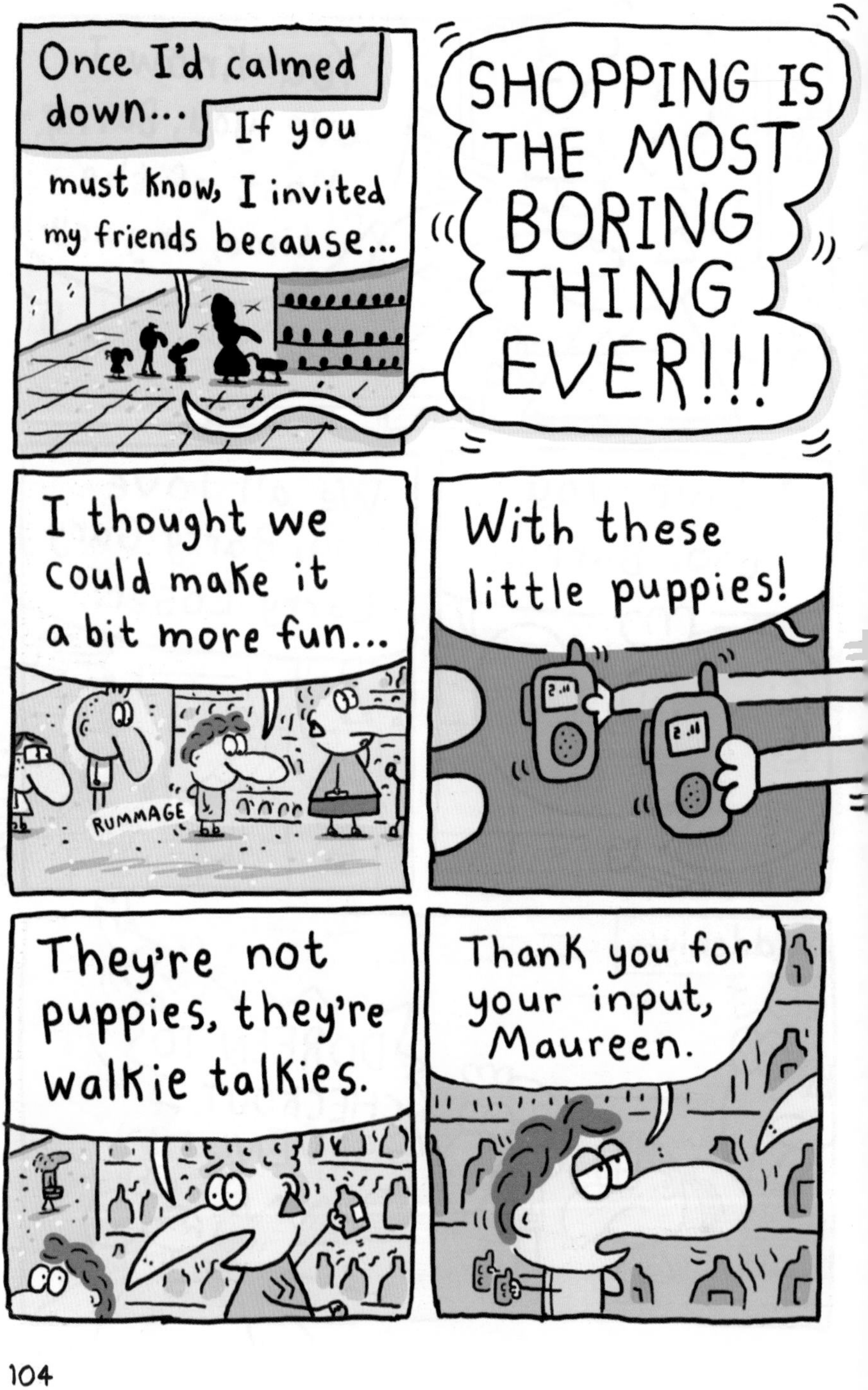
Once I'd calmed down...
If you must know, I invited my friends because...
SHOPPING IS THE MOST BORING THING EVER!!!
I thought we could make it a bit more fun...
RUMMAGE
With these little puppies!
They're not puppies, they're walkie talkies.
Thank you for your input, Maureen.

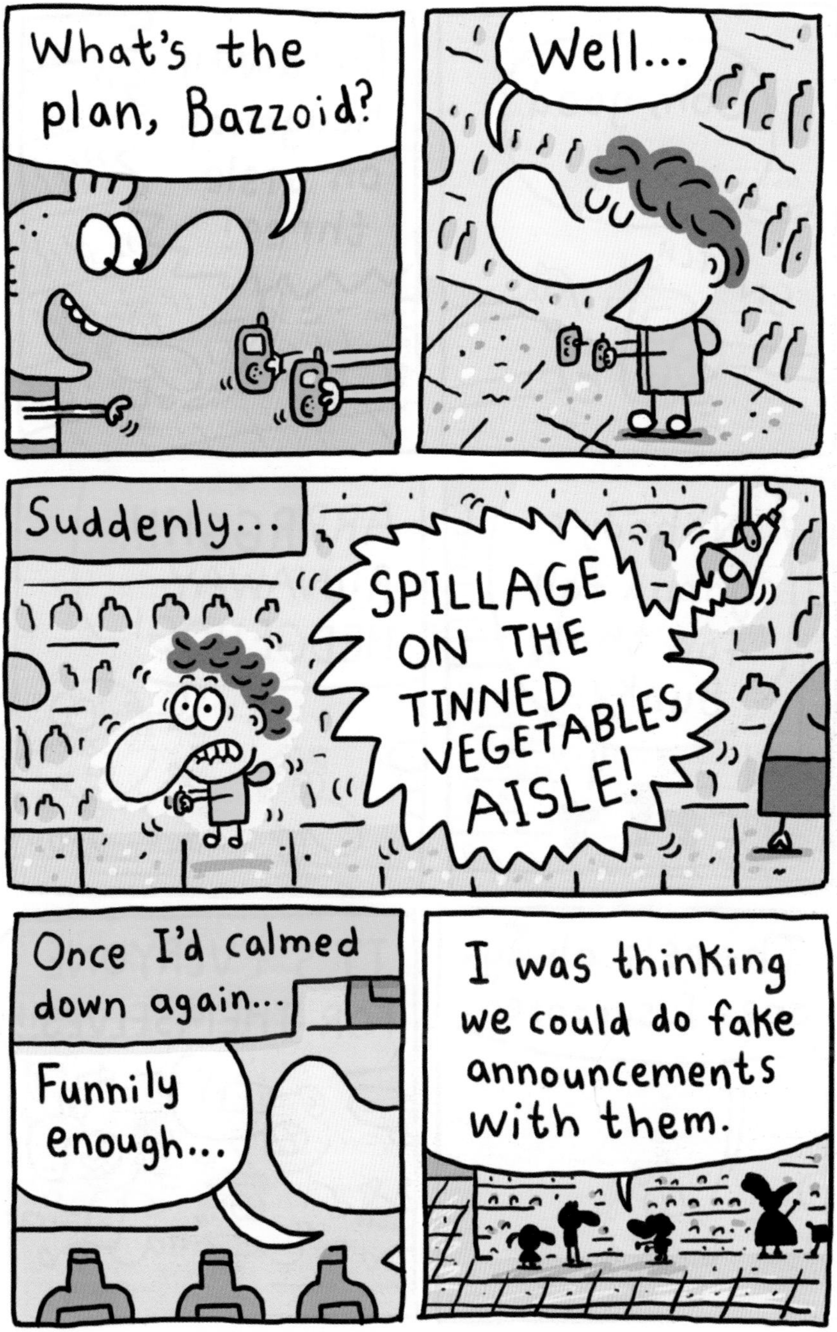
What's the plan, Bazzoid?
Well...
Suddenly...
SPILLAGE ON THE TINNED VEGETABLES AISLE!
Once I'd calmed down again...
Funnily enough...
I was thinking we could do fake announcements with them.

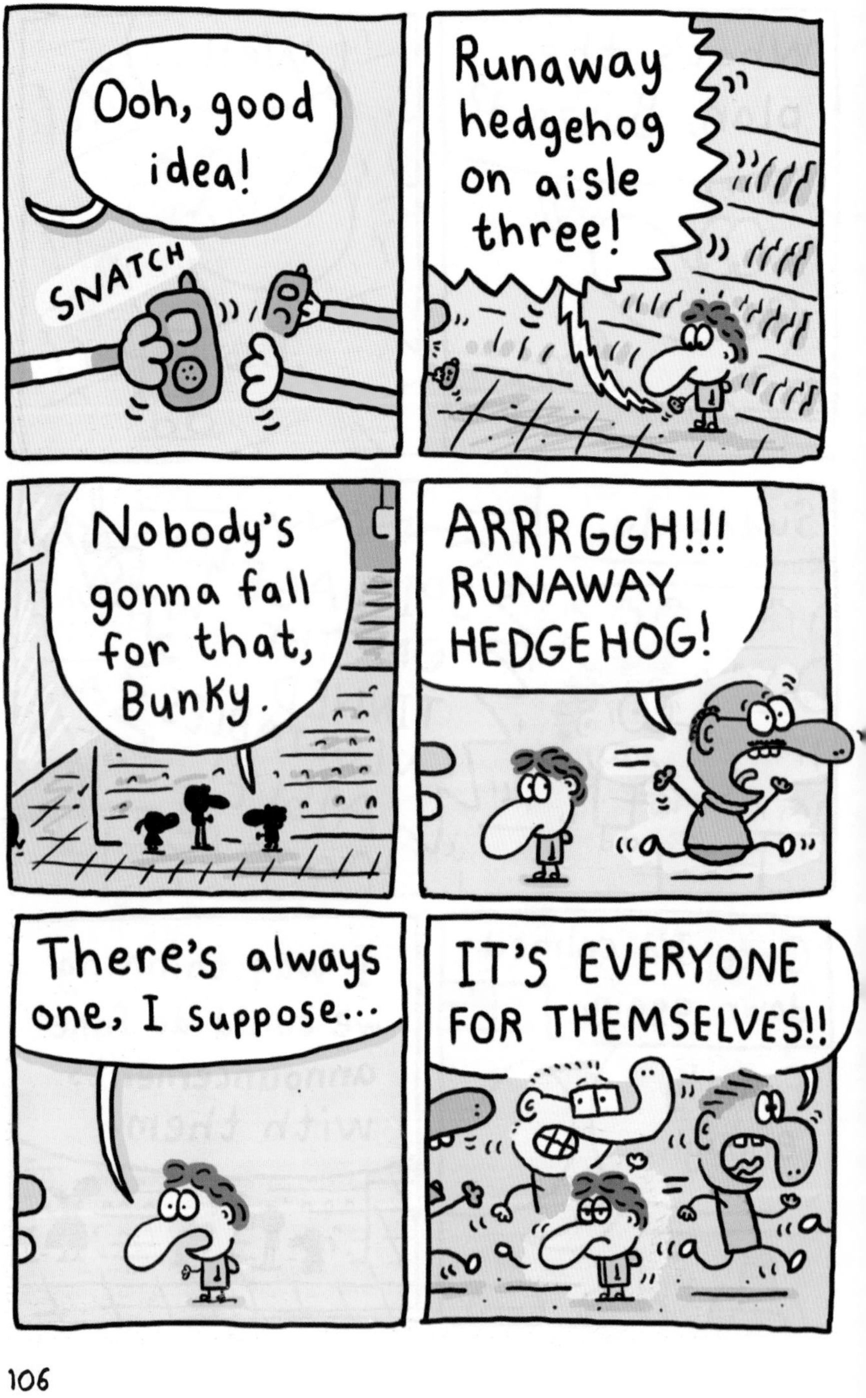
Ooh, good idea!
SNATCH
Runaway hedgehog on aisle three!
Nobody's gonna fall for that, Bunky.
ARRRGGH!!! RUNAWAY HEDGEHOG!
There's always one, I suppose...
IT'S EVERYONE FOR THEMSELVES!!

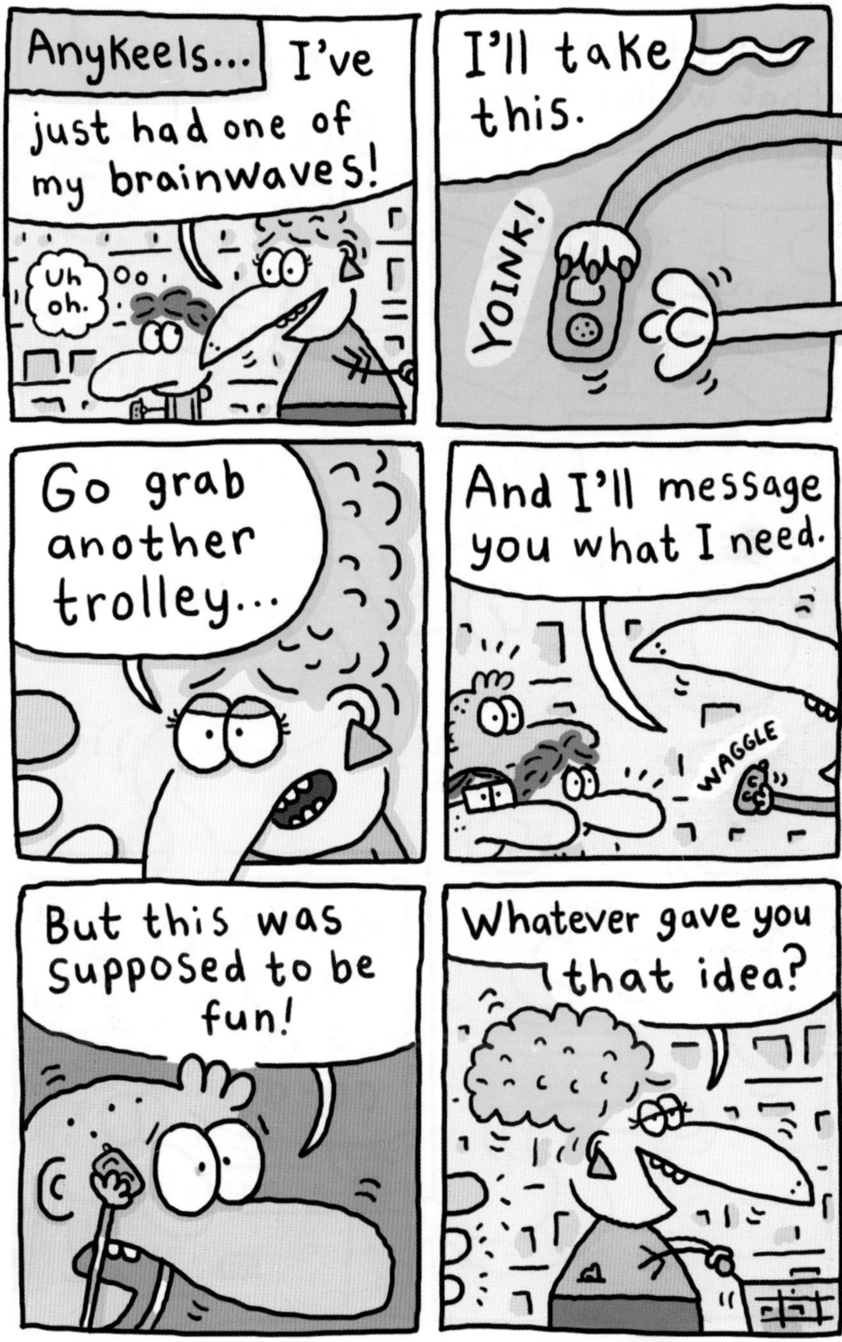
Anykeels...
I've just had one of my brainwaves!
Uh oh.
I'll take this.
YOINK!
Go grab another trolley...
And I'll message you what I need.
WAGGLE
But this was supposed to be fun!
Whatever gave you that idea?

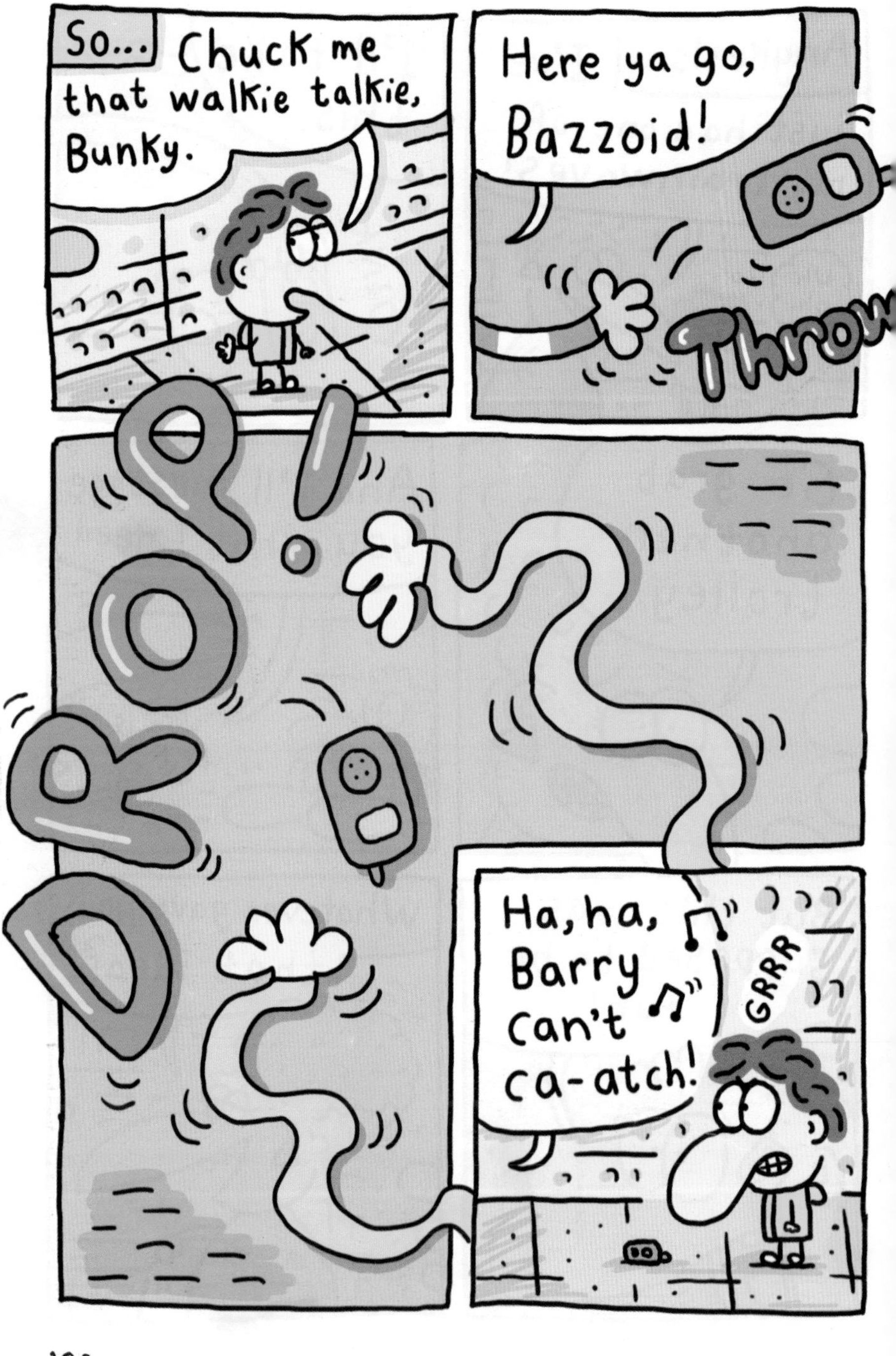
So...
Chuck me that walkie talkie, Bunky.
Here ya go, Bazzoid!
Throw
DROP!
Ha, ha, Barry can't ca-atch!
GRRR

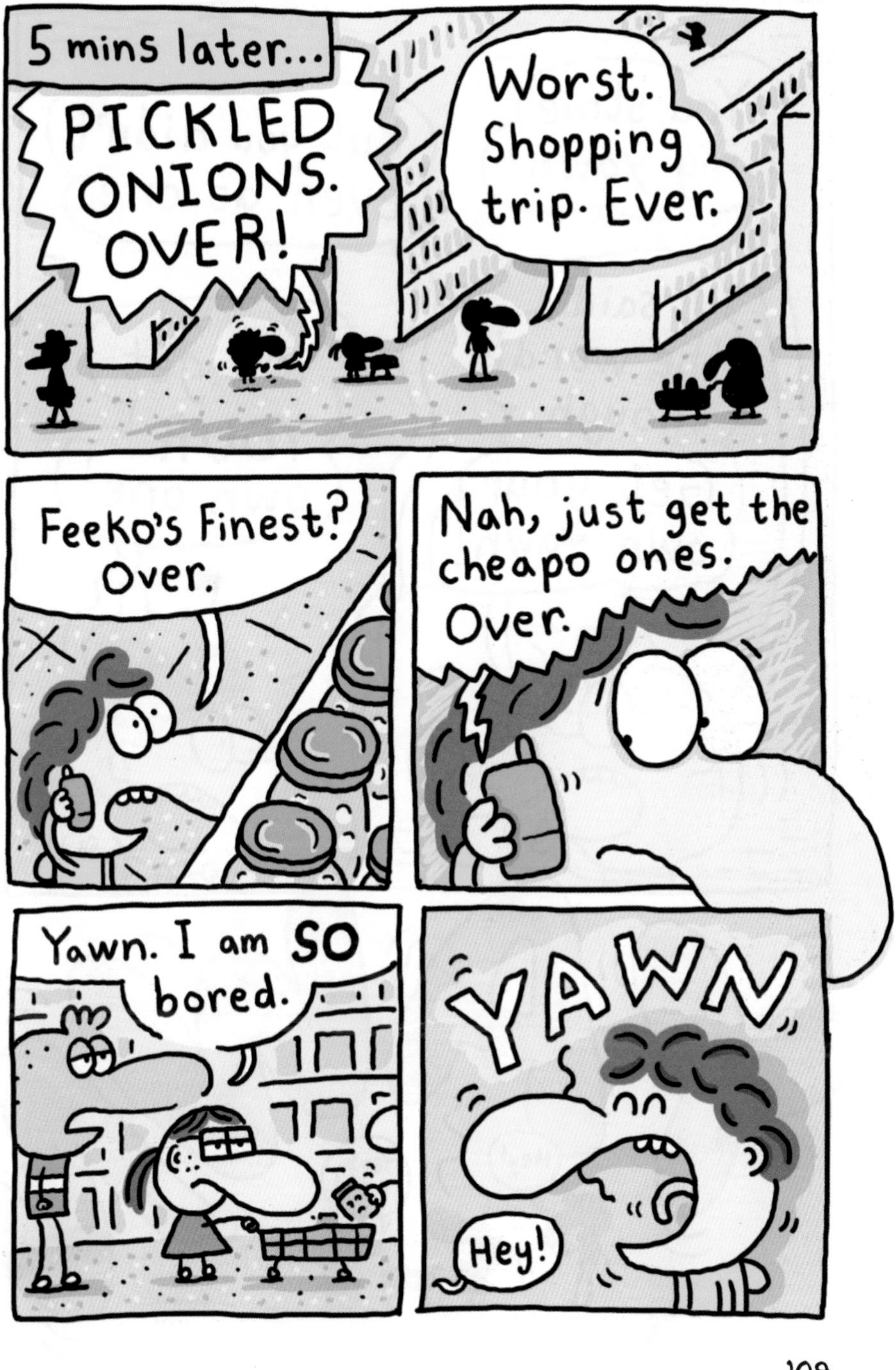
5 mins later...
PICKLED ONIONS. OVER!
Worst. Shopping trip. Ever.
Feeko's Finest? Over.
Nah, just get the cheapo ones. Over.
Yawn. I am SO bored.
YAWN
Hey!

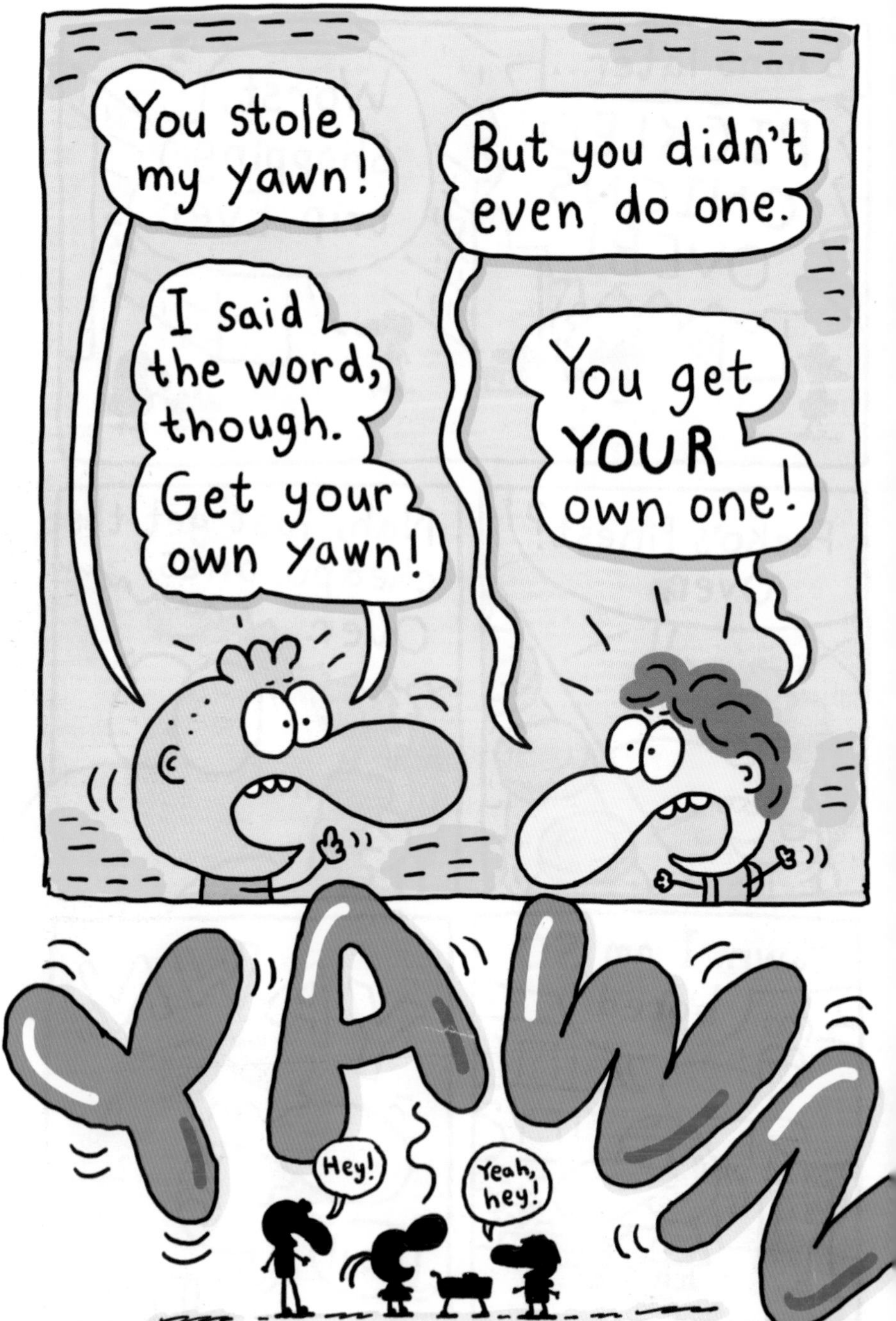
You stole my yawn!
I said the word, though. Get your own yawn!
But you didn't even do one.
You get YOUR own one!
YAWN
Hey!
Yeah, hey!

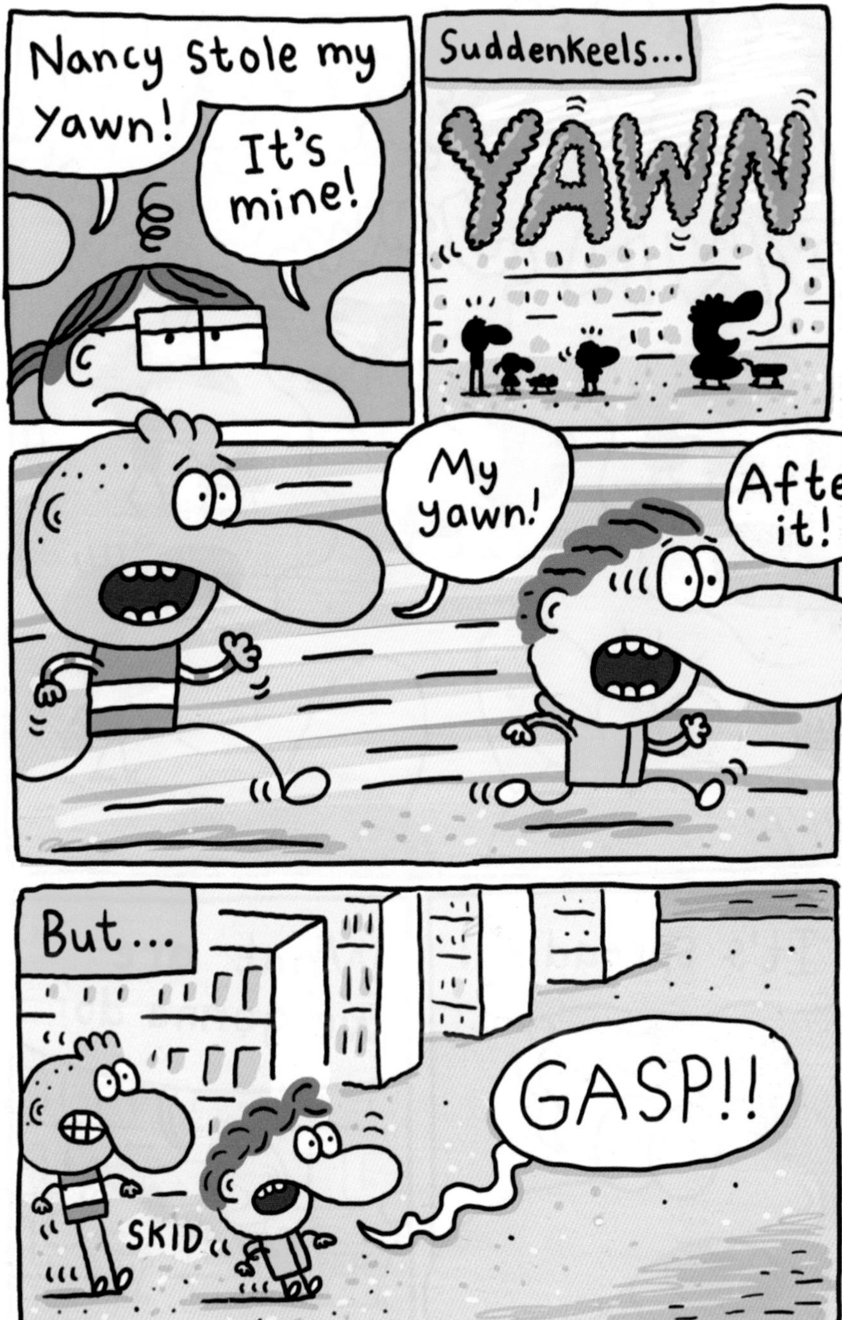
Nancy stole my yawn!
It's mine!
Suddenkeels...
YAWN
My yawn!
After it!
But...
GASP!!
SKID

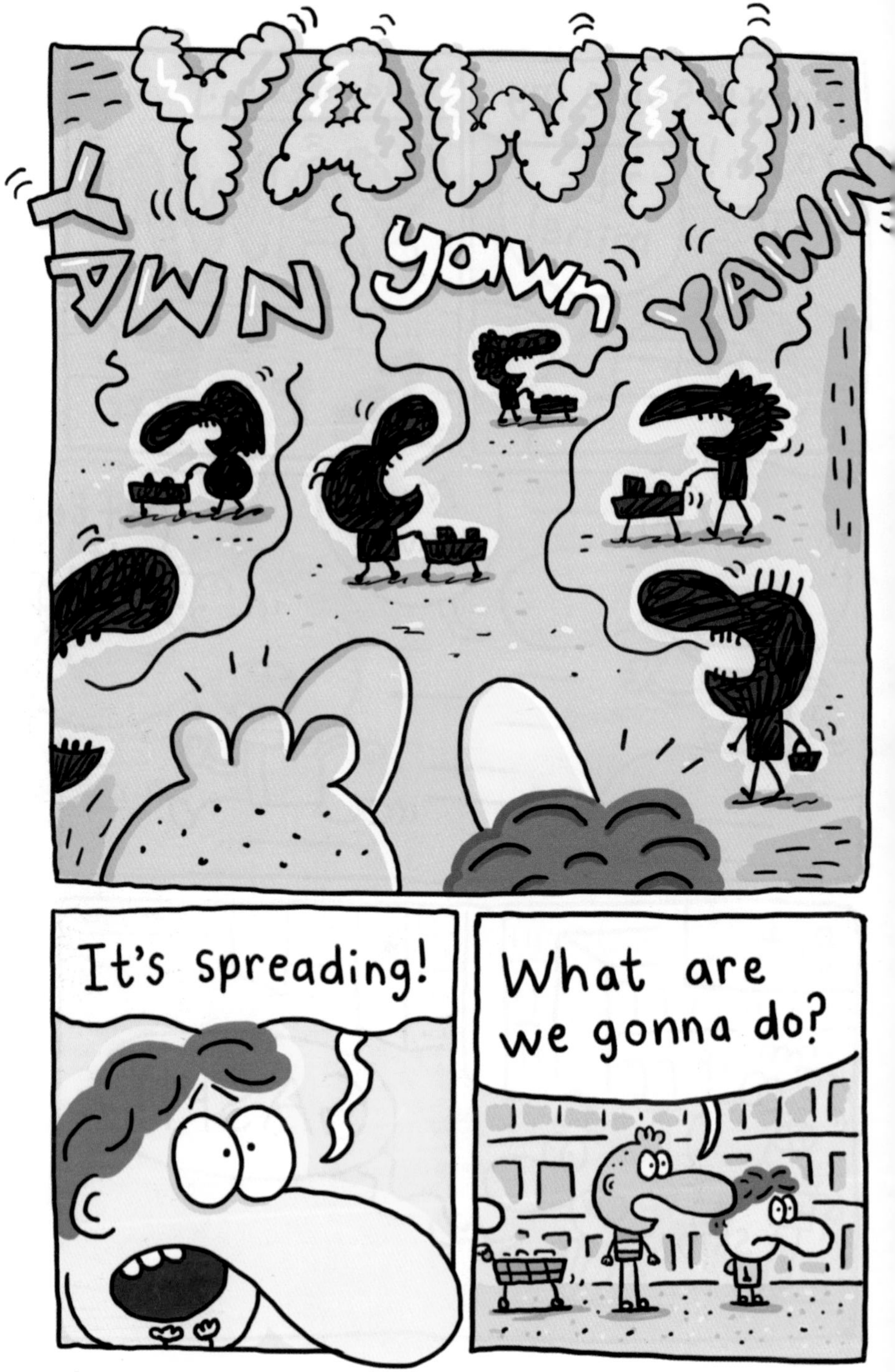
YAWN
YAWN
yawn
YAWN
YAWN
It's spreading!
What are we gonna do?

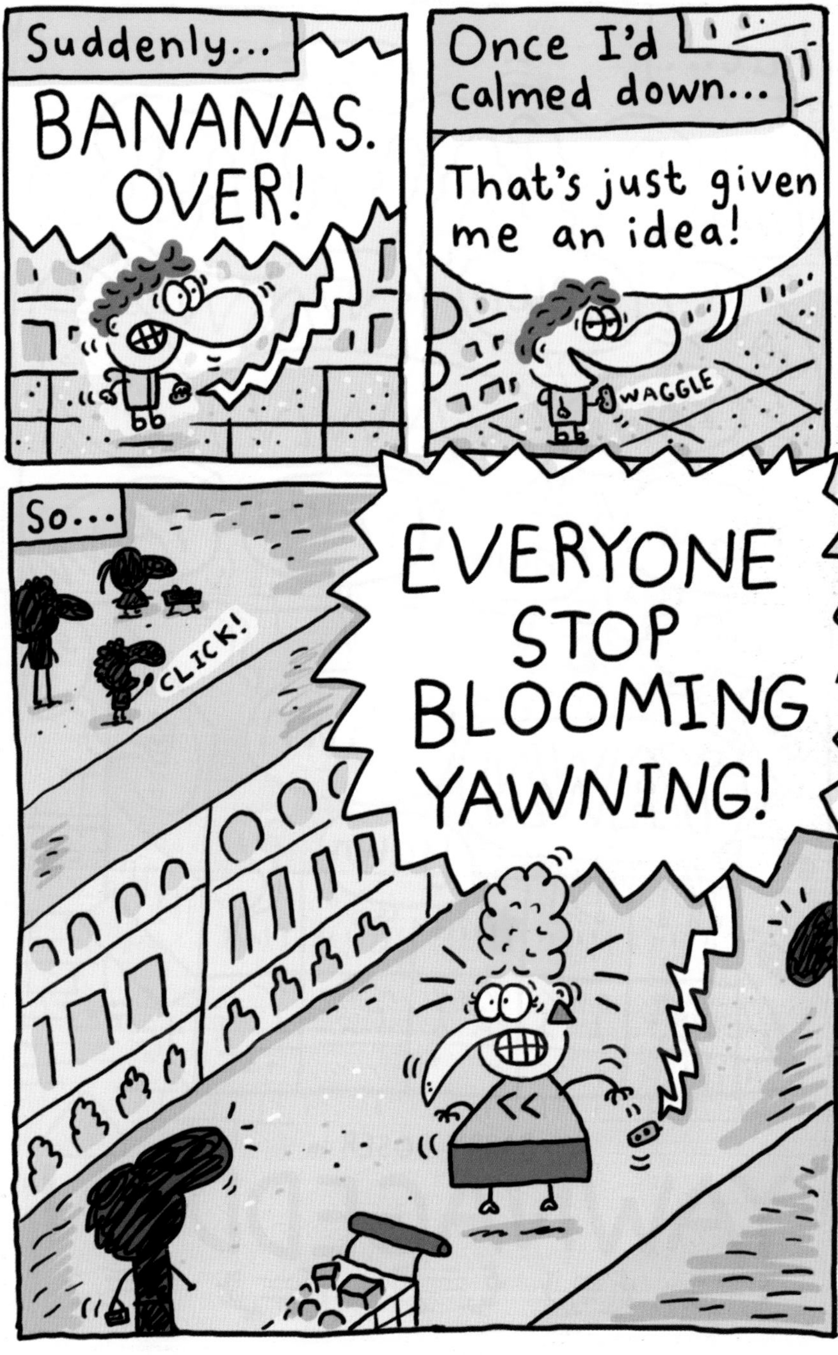
Suddenly...
BANANAS. OVER!
Once I'd calmed down...
That's just given me an idea!
WAGGLE
So...
CLICK!
EVERYONE STOP BLOOMING YAWNING!

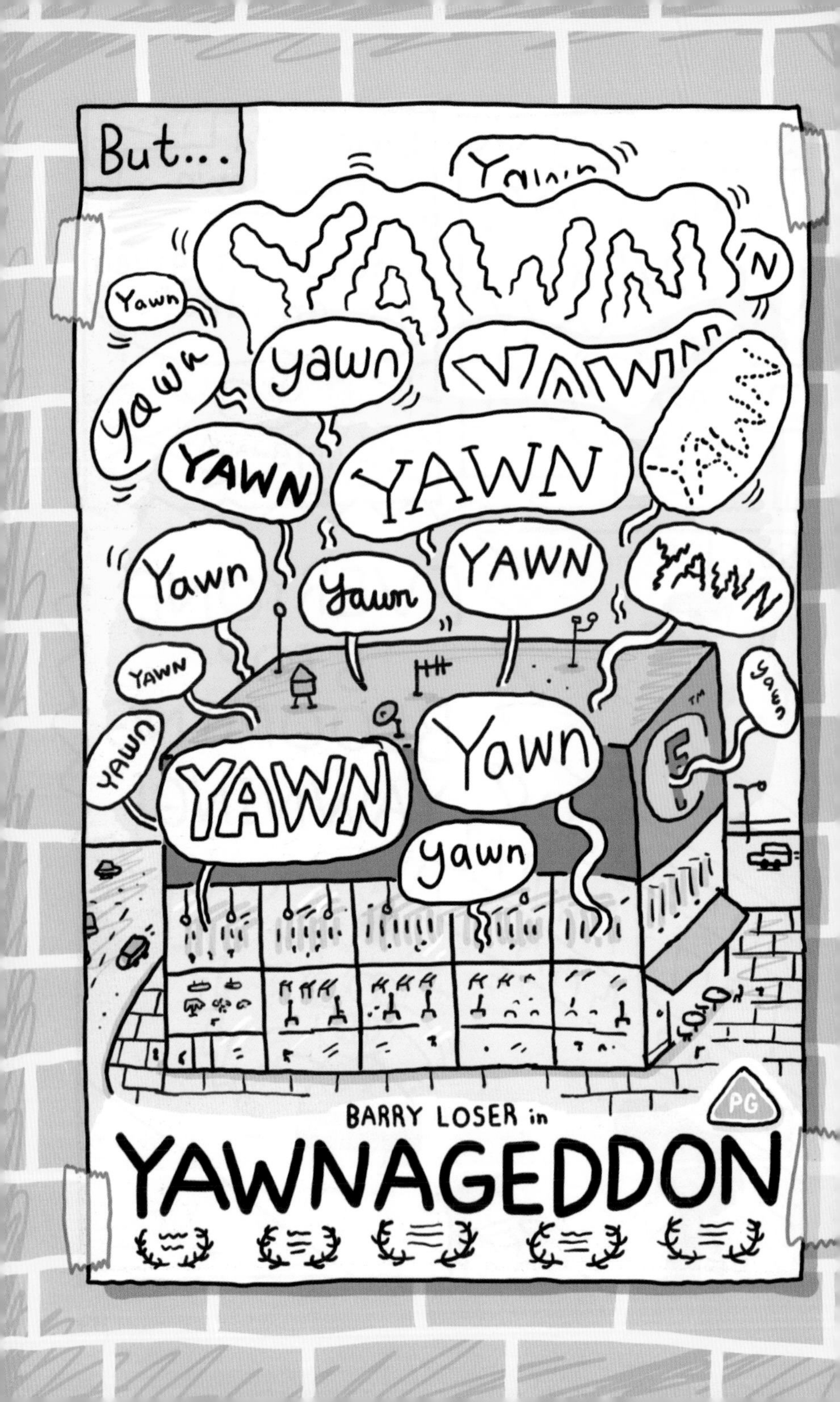

But...
YAWN
Yawn
yawn
yawn
YAWN
YAWN
YAWN
Yawn
Yawn
YAWN
YAWN
YAWN
yawn
YAWN
YAWN
Yawn
yawn
BARRY LOSER in
YAWNAGEDDON
PG

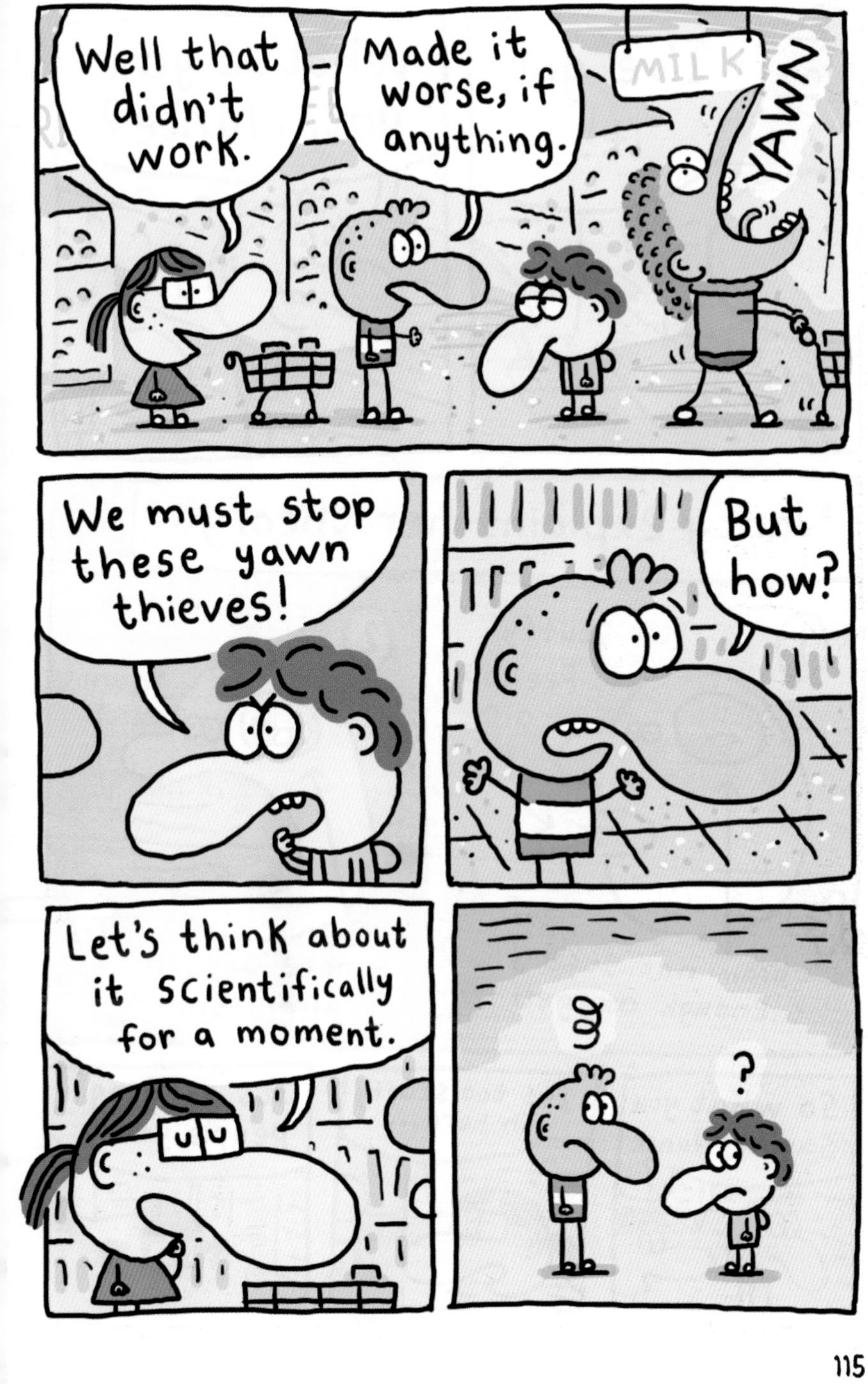
Well that didn't work.
Made it worse, if anything.
MILK
YAWN
We must stop these yawn thieves!
But how?
Let's think about it scientifically for a moment.
?

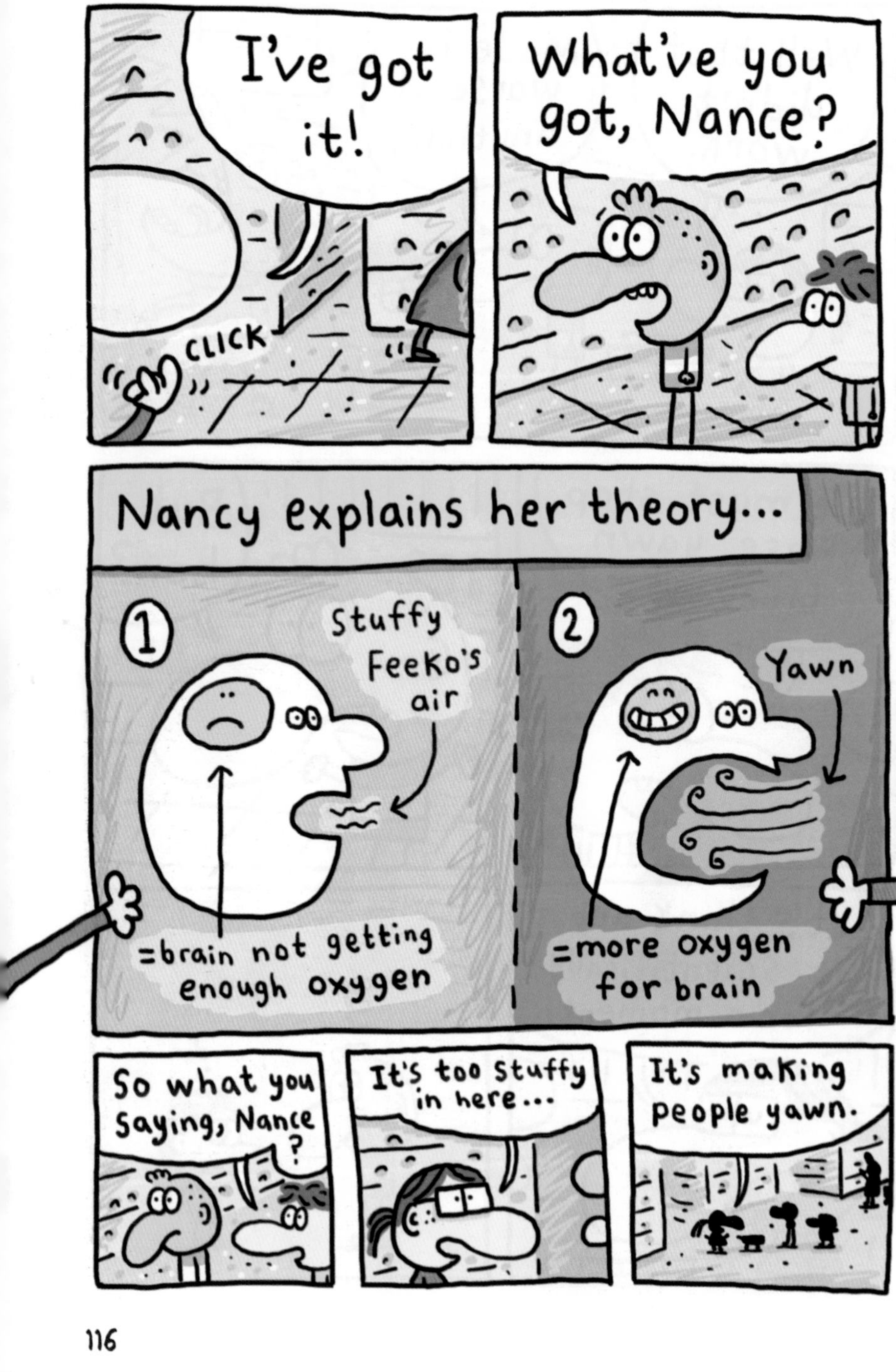
I've got it!
CLICK
What've you got, Nance?
Nancy explains her theory...
1
Stuffy Feeko's air
=brain not getting enough oxygen
2
Yawn
=more oxygen for brain
So what you saying, Nance?
It's too stuffy in here...
It's making people yawn.

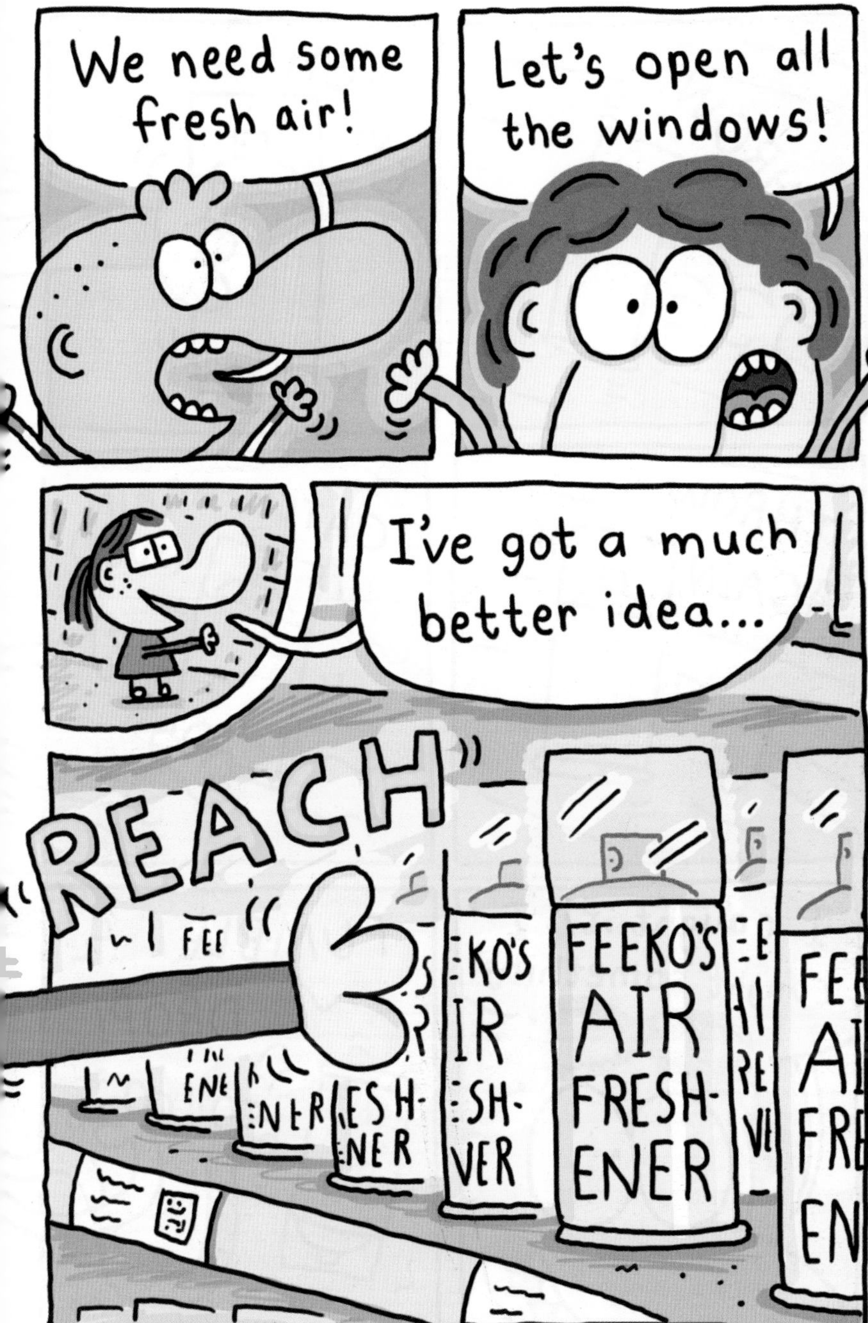

We need some fresh air!
Let's open all the windows!
I've got a much better idea...
REACH
FEEKO'S AIR FRESH-ENER

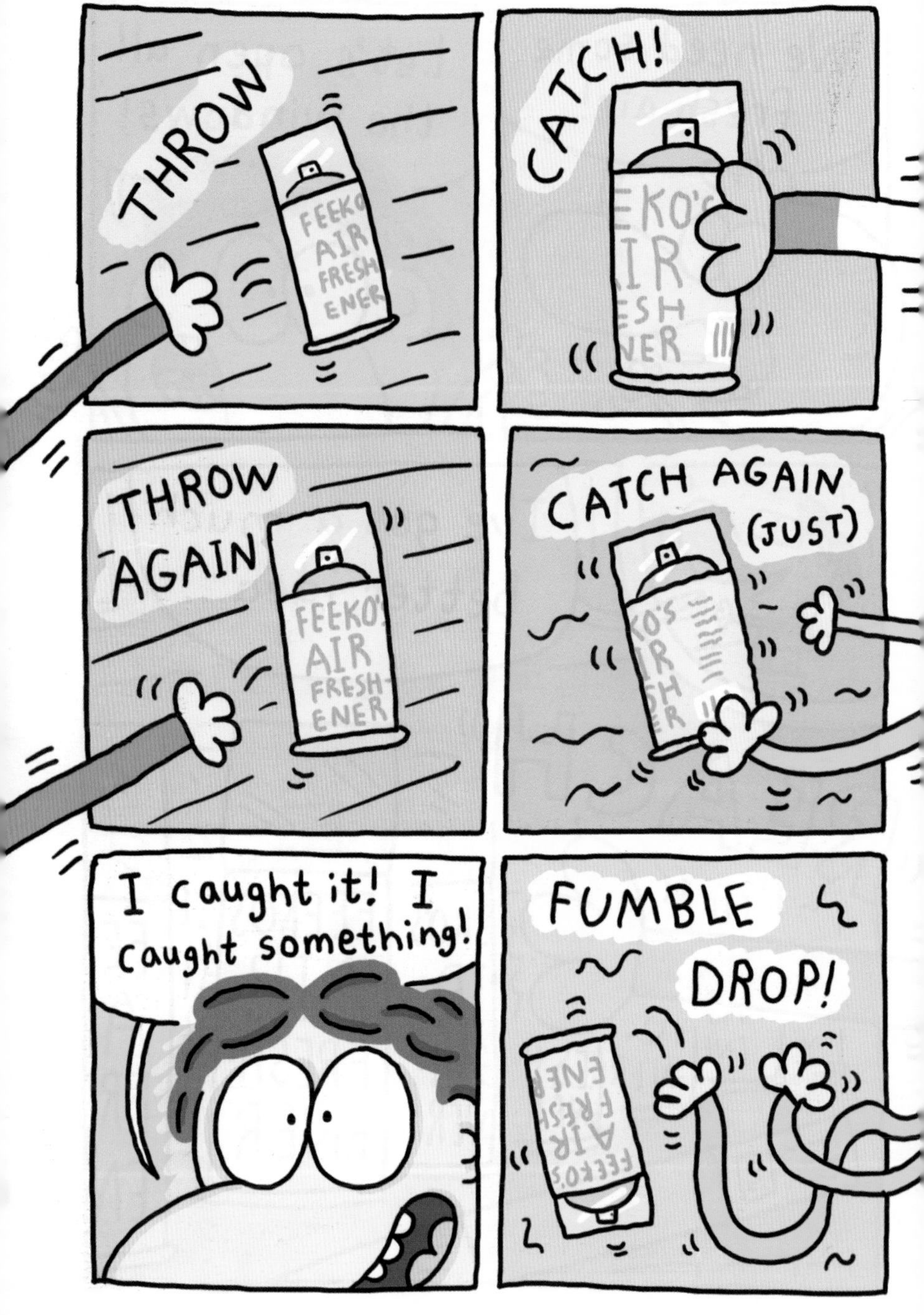
THROW
FEEKO AIR FRESHENER
CATCH!
THROW AGAIN
FEEKO'S AIR FRESHENER
CATCH AGAIN
(JUST)
I caught it! I caught something!
FUMBLE
DROP!
FEEKO'S AIR FRESHENER

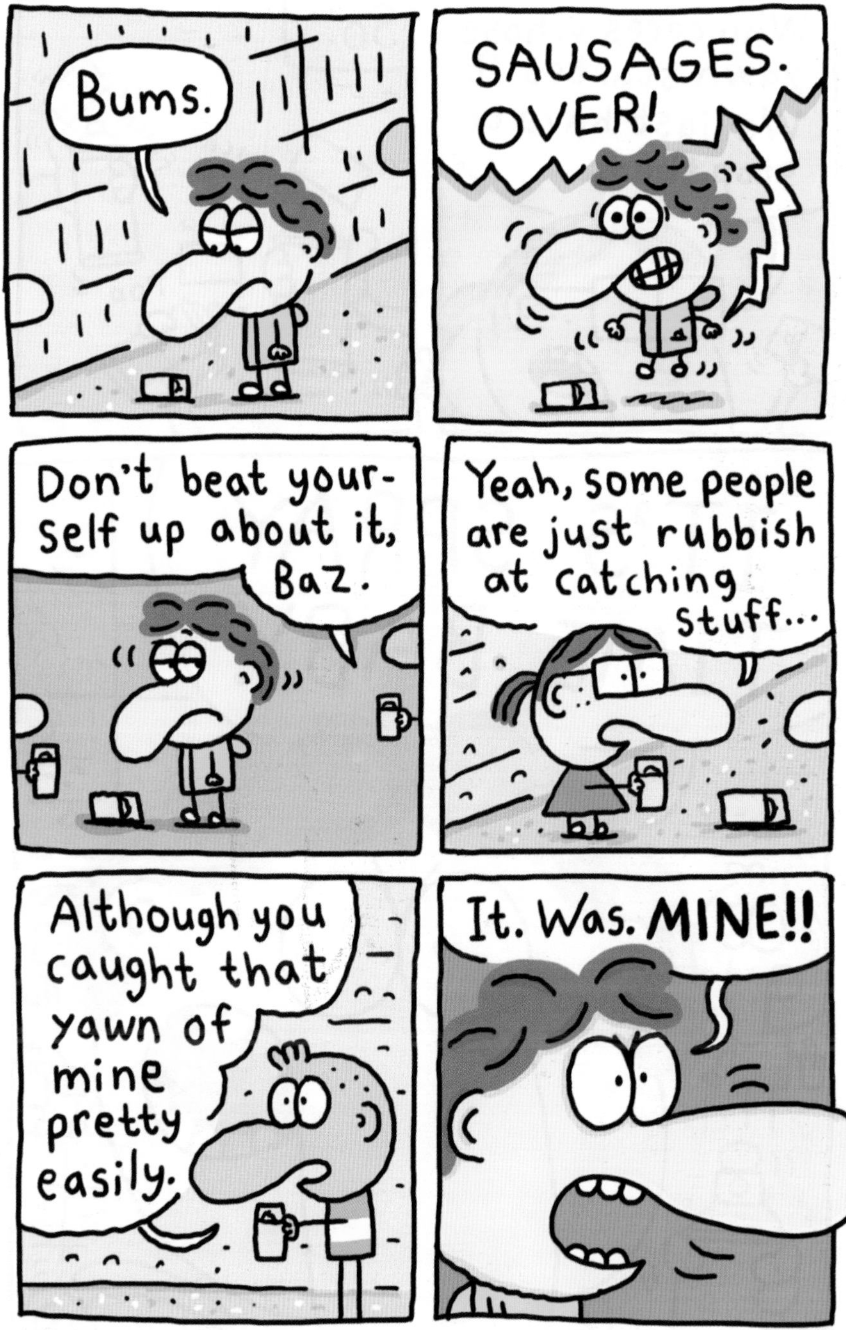
Bums.
SAUSAGES. OVER!
Don't beat yourself up about it, Baz.
Yeah, some people are just rubbish at catching stuff...
Although you caught that yawn of mine pretty easily.
It. Was. MINE!!

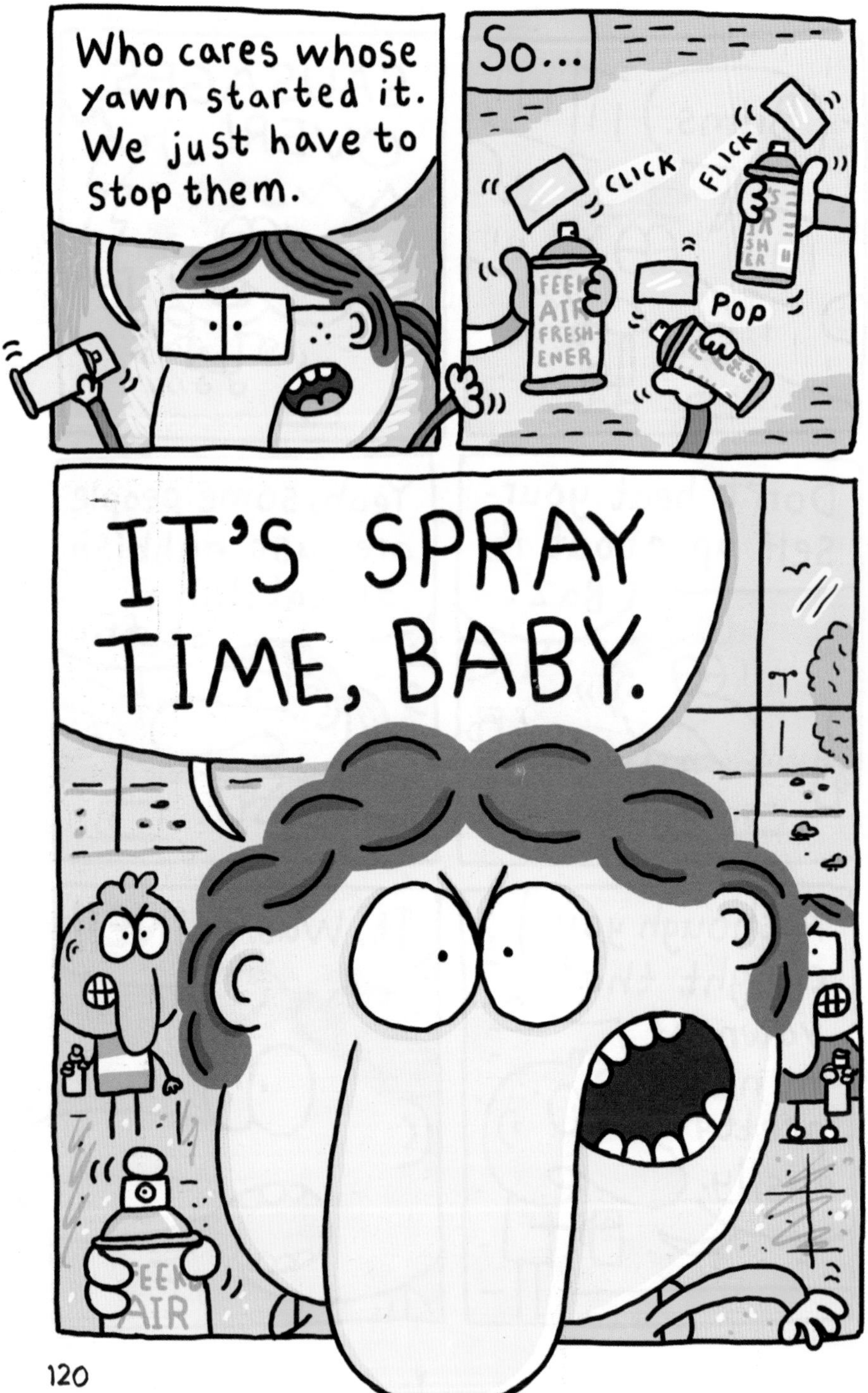
Who cares whose yawn started it. We just have to stop them.
So...
CLICK
FLICK
POP
FEEK AIR FRESHENER
IT'S SPRAY TIME, BABY.
FEEK AIR

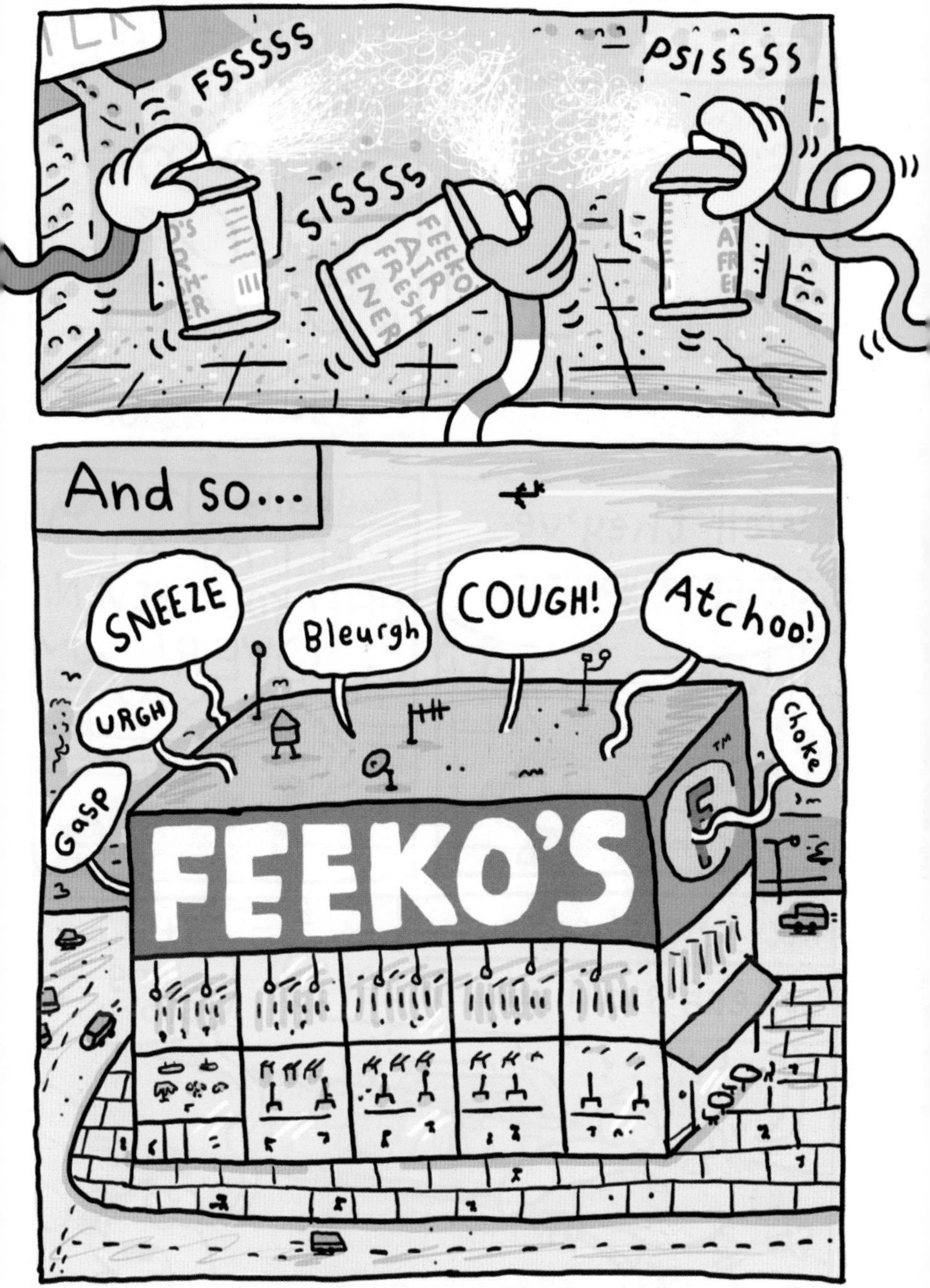
FSSSSS
SISSSS
PSISSSS
FEEKO AIR FRESHENER
And so...
SNEEZE
Bleurgh
COUGH!
Atchoo!
URGH
Choke
Gasp
FEEKO'S

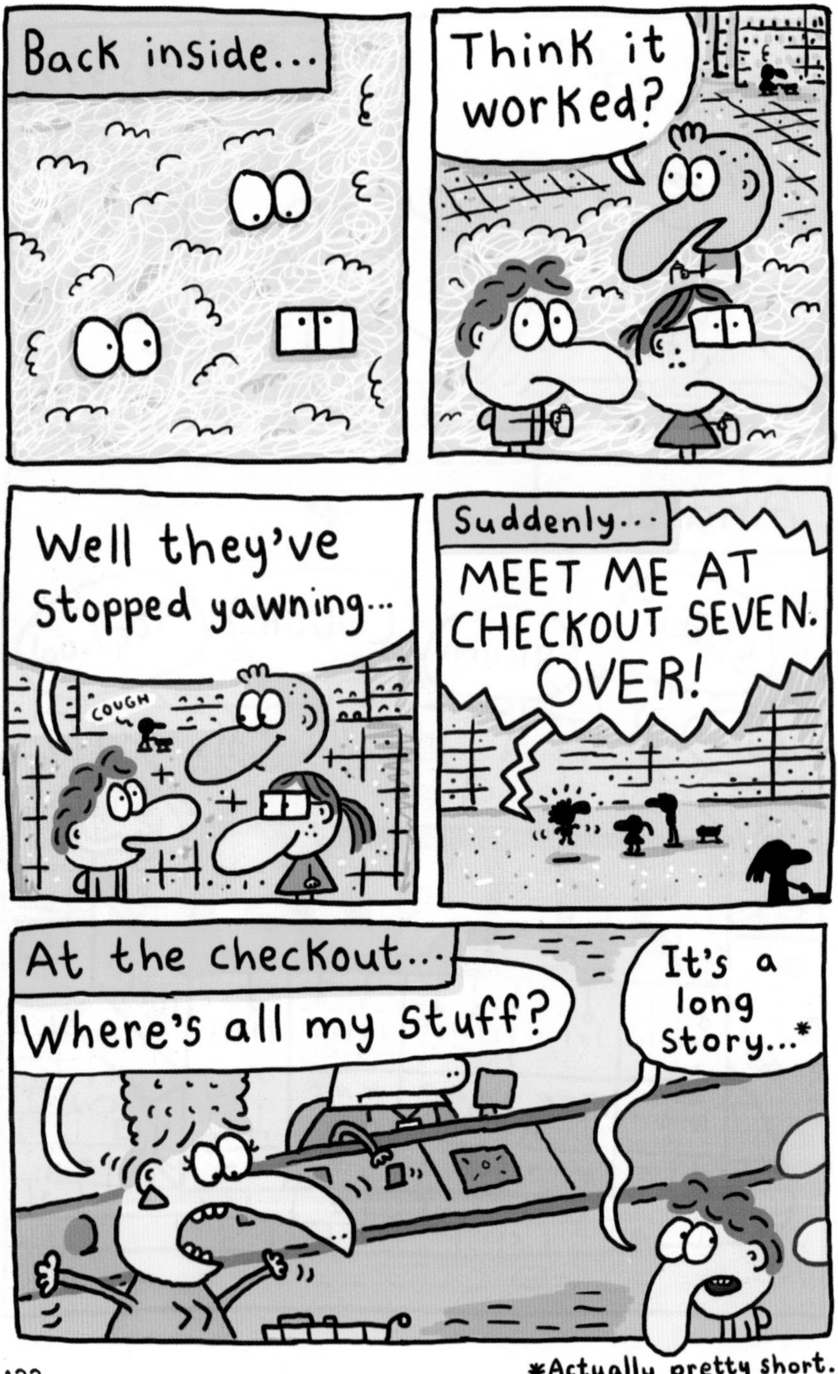
Back inside...
Think it worked?
Well they've stopped yawning...
COUGH
Suddenly...
MEET ME AT CHECKOUT SEVEN. OVER!
At the checkout...
Where's all my stuff?
It's a long story...*

*Actually pretty short.

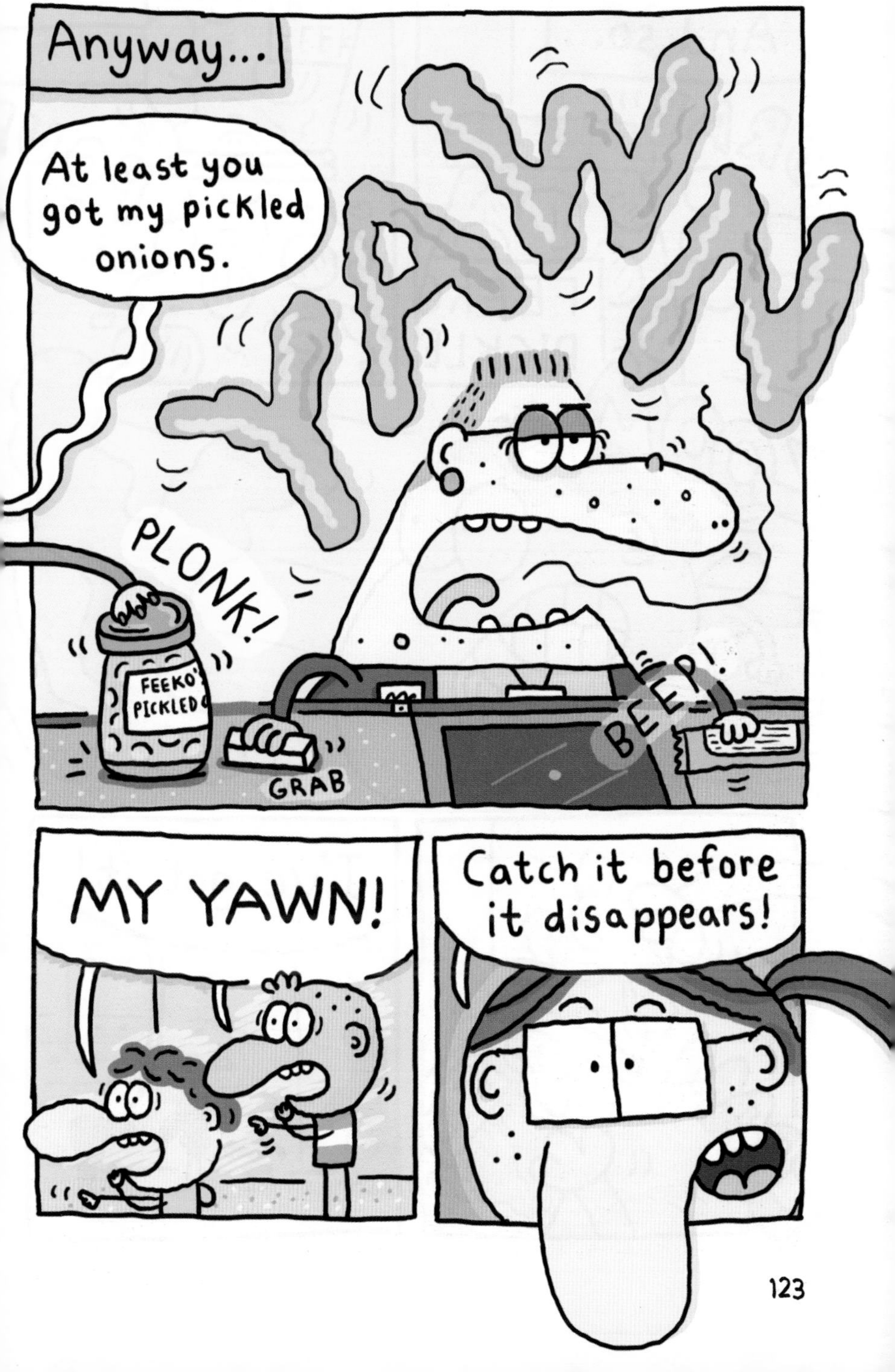

Anyway...
At least you got my pickled onions.
YAWN
PLONK!
FEEKO'S PICKLED
GRAB
BEEP!
MY YAWN!
Catch it before it disappears!

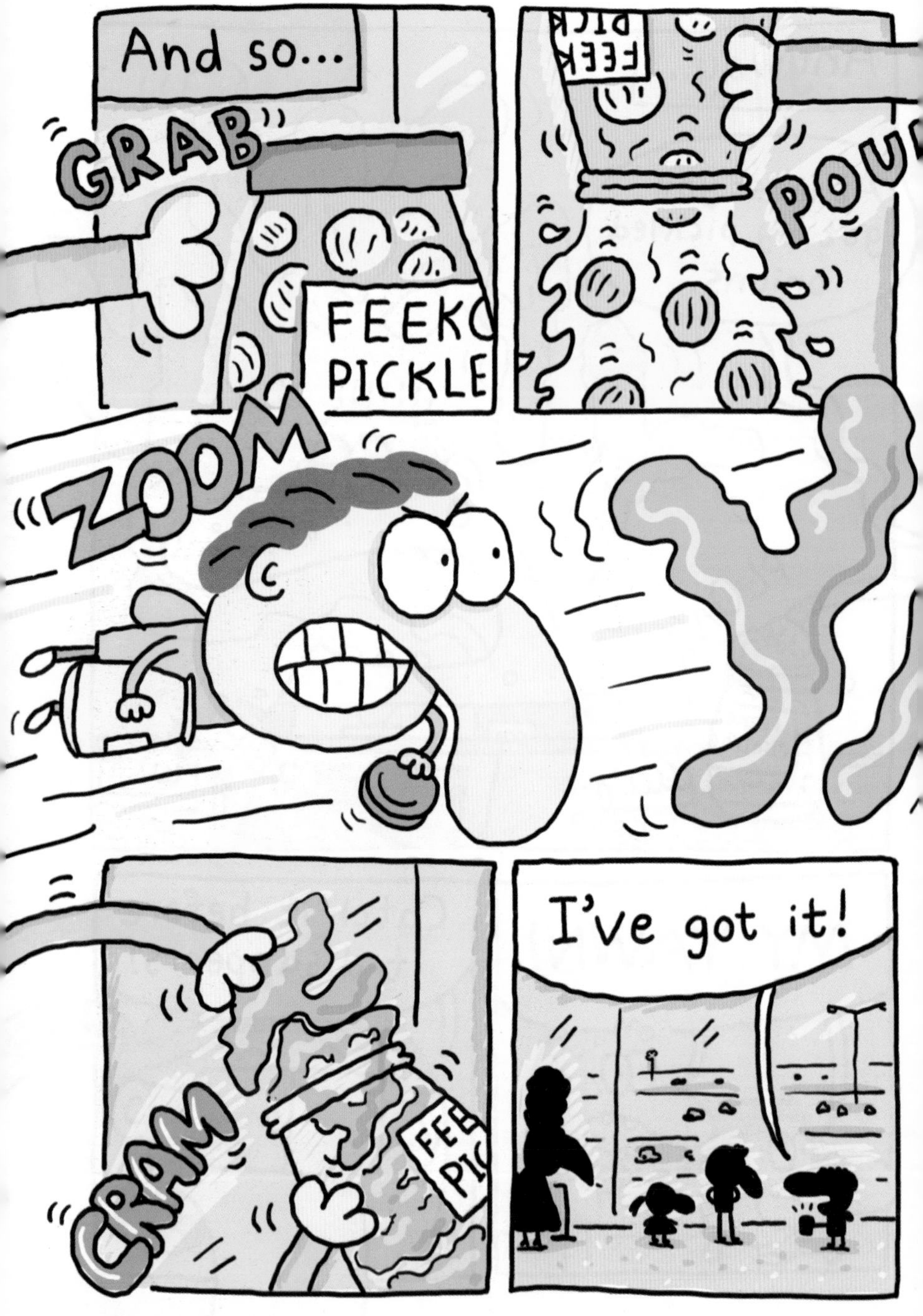
And so...
GRAB
FEEKO
PICKLE
POU
ZOOM
CRAM
I've got it!

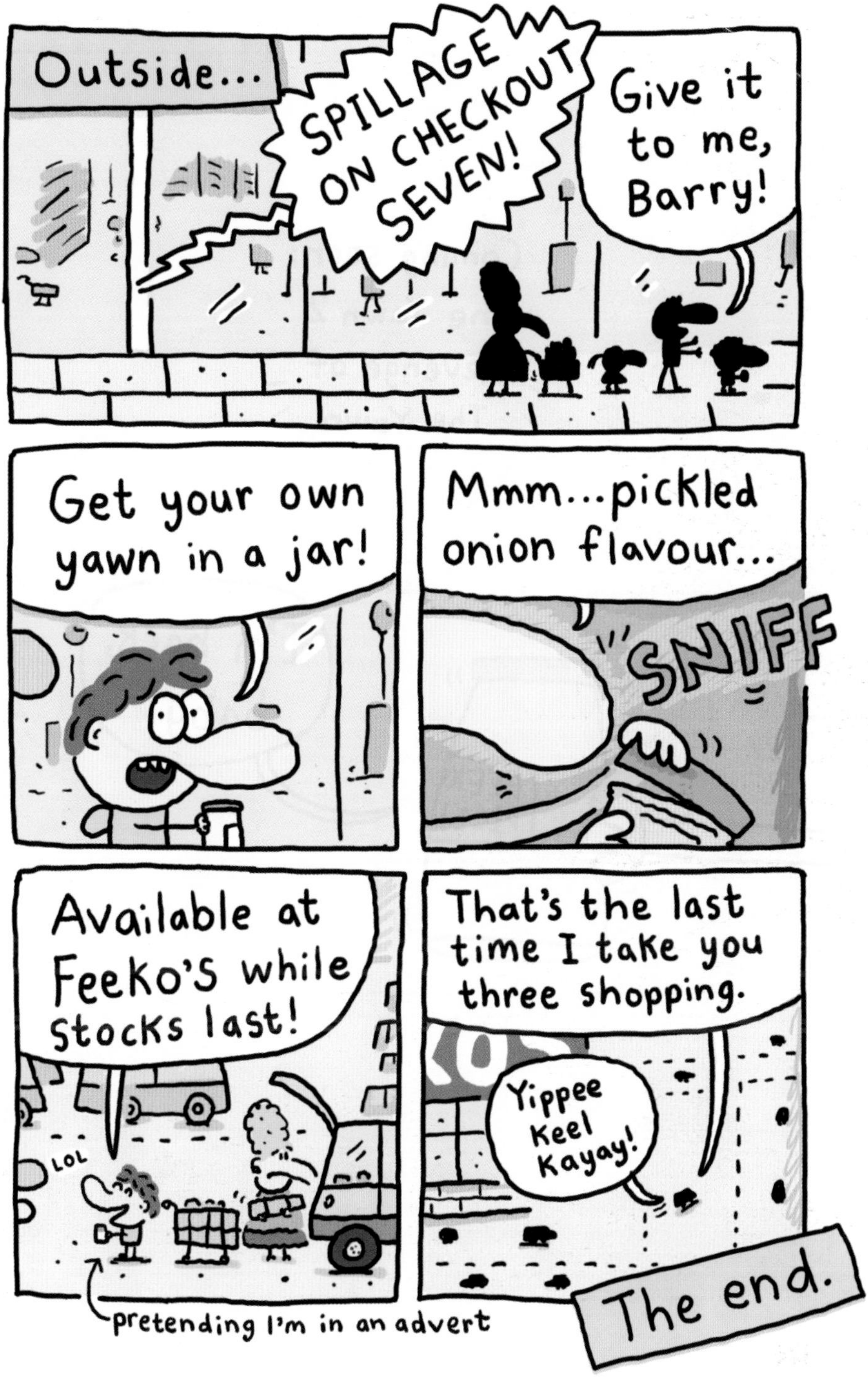
Outside...
SPILLAGE ON CHECKOUT SEVEN!
Give it to me, Barry!
Get your own yawn in a jar!
Mmm...pickled onion flavour...
SNIFF
Available at Feeko's while stocks last!
LOL
pretending I'm in an advert
That's the last time I take you three shopping.
Yippee Keel Kayay!
The end.

Coming soon:
The Yawn 2
Revenge of
The Yawn

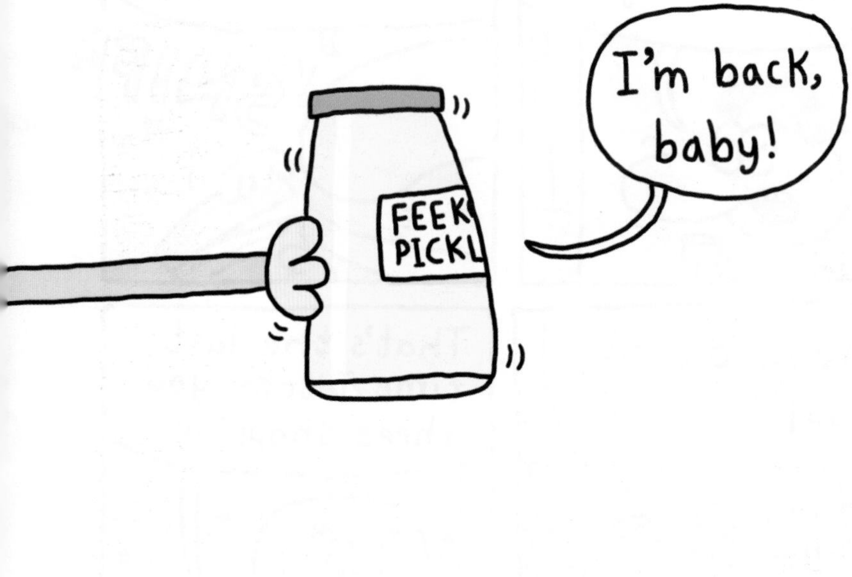

I'm back, baby!
FEEK
PICKL

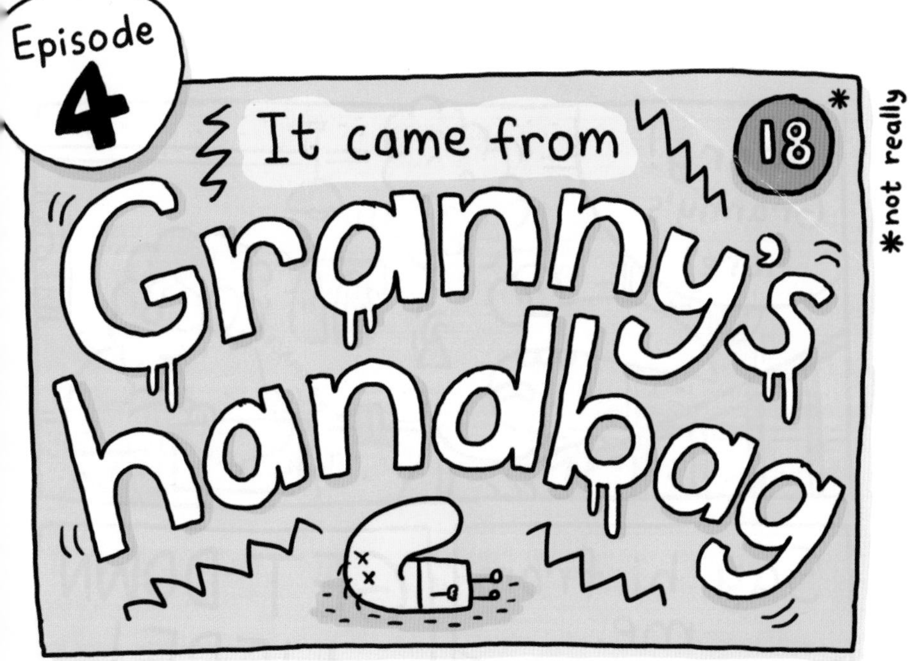
Episode 4
It came from
18*
Granny's handbag
*not really

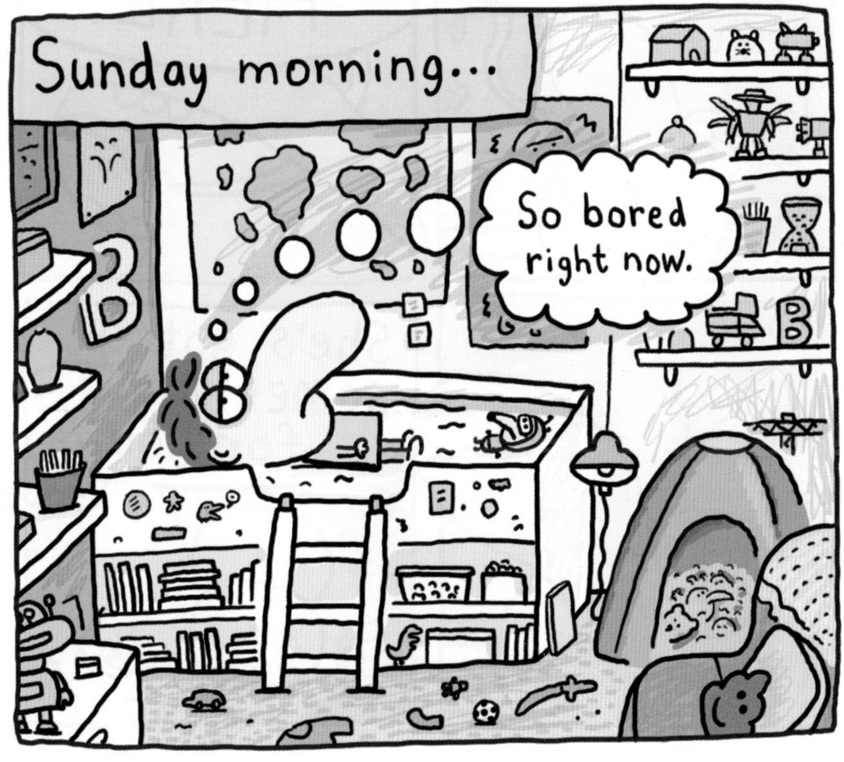
Sunday morning...
So bored right now.

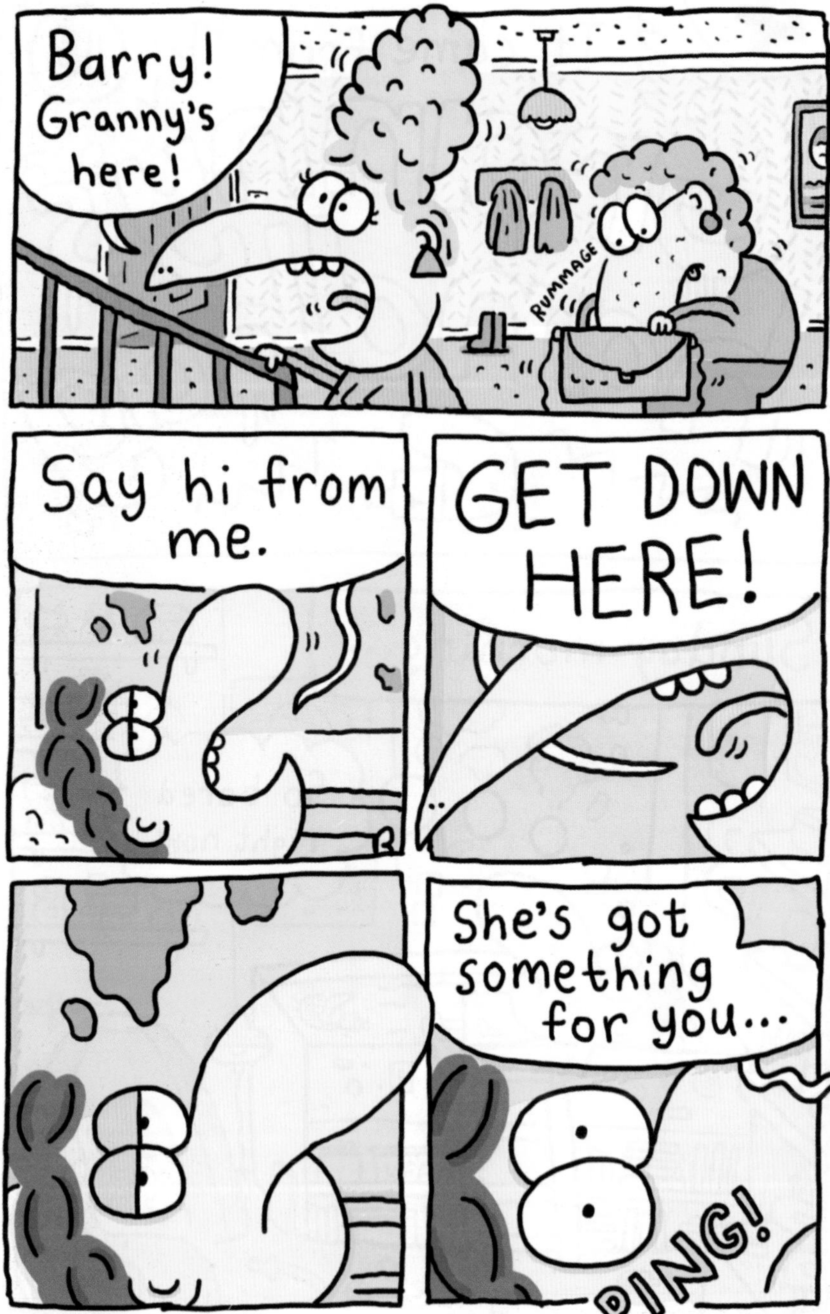
Barry! Granny's here!
RUMMAGE
Say hi from me.
GET DOWN HERE!
She's got something for you...
PING!

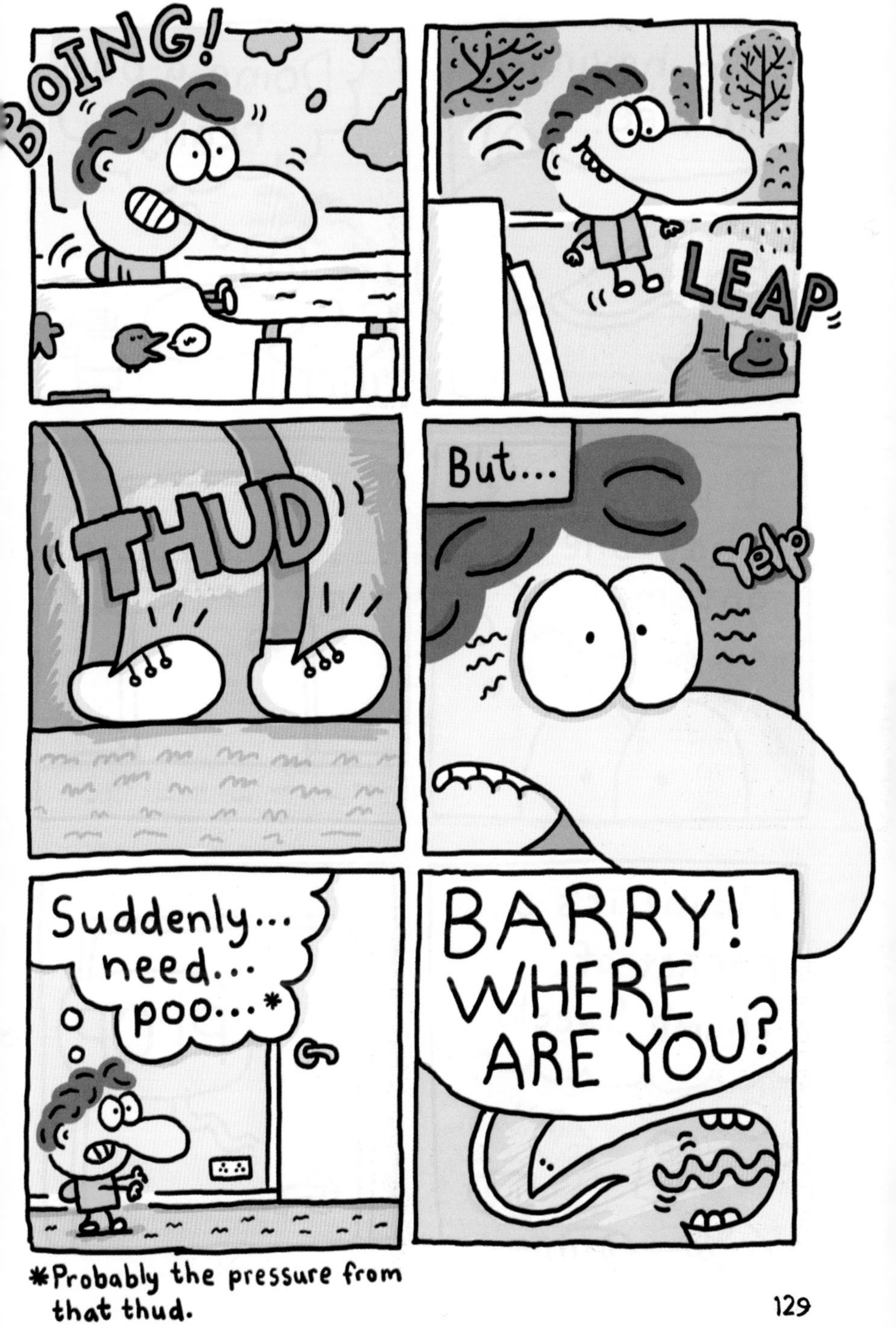
BOING!
LEAP
THUD
But...
Yelp
Suddenly... need... poo...*
BARRY! WHERE ARE YOU?

*Probably the pressure from that thud.

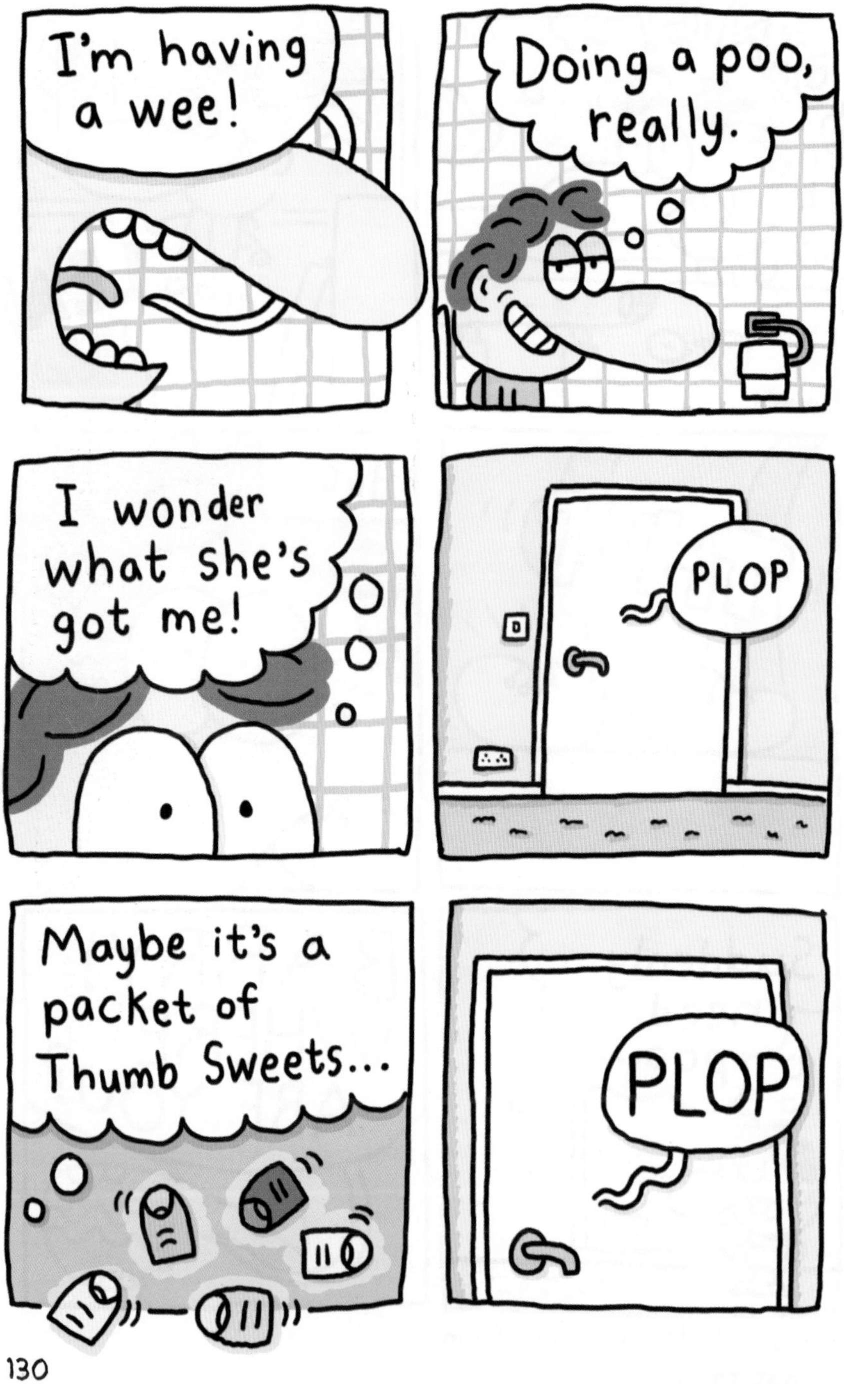
I'm having a wee!
Doing a poo, really.
I wonder what she's got me!
PLOP
Maybe it's a packet of Thumb Sweets...
PLOP

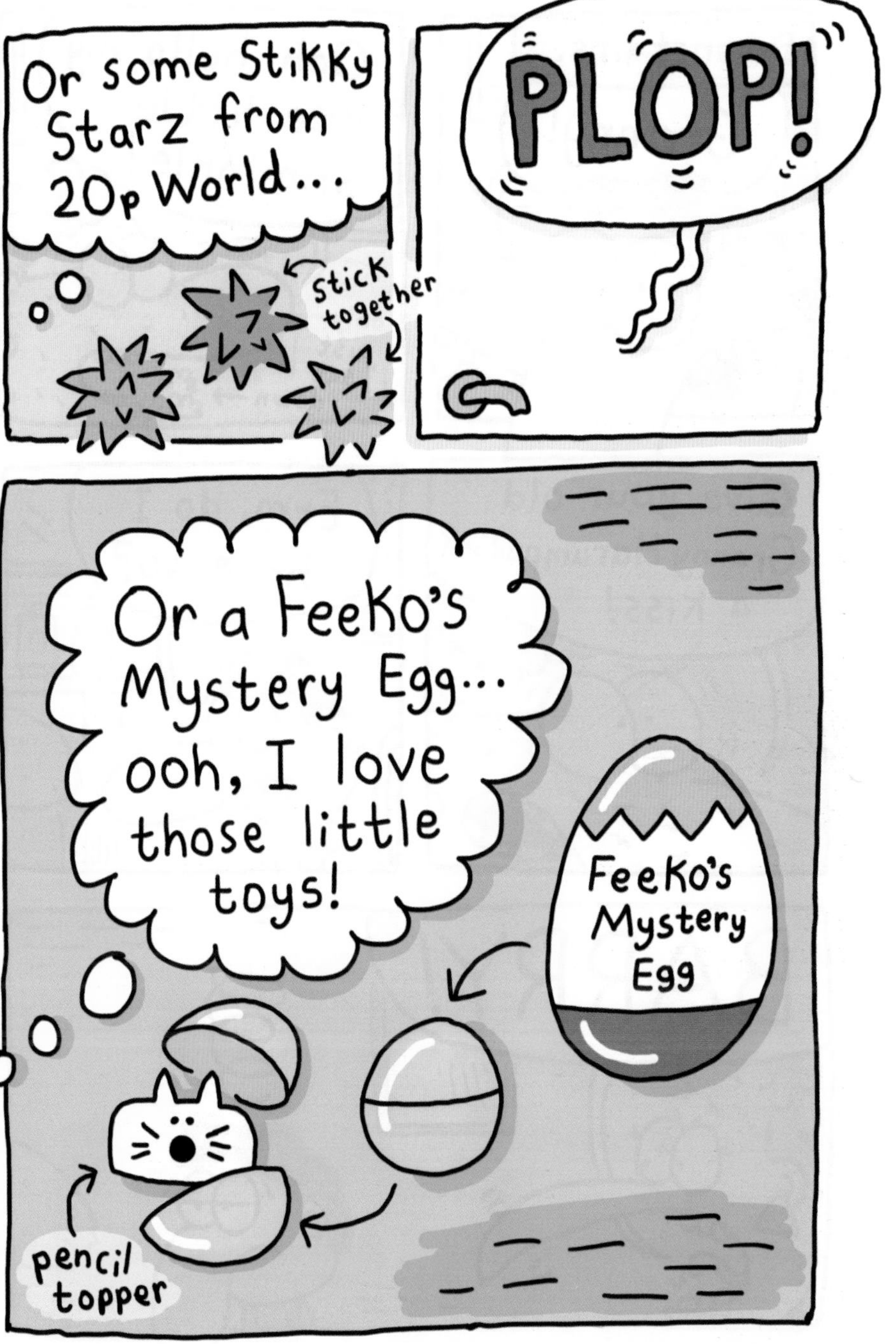
Or some StiKKy Starz from 20p World...
stick together
PLOP!
Or a FeeKo's Mystery Egg... ooh, I love those little toys!
FeeKo's Mystery Egg
pencil topper

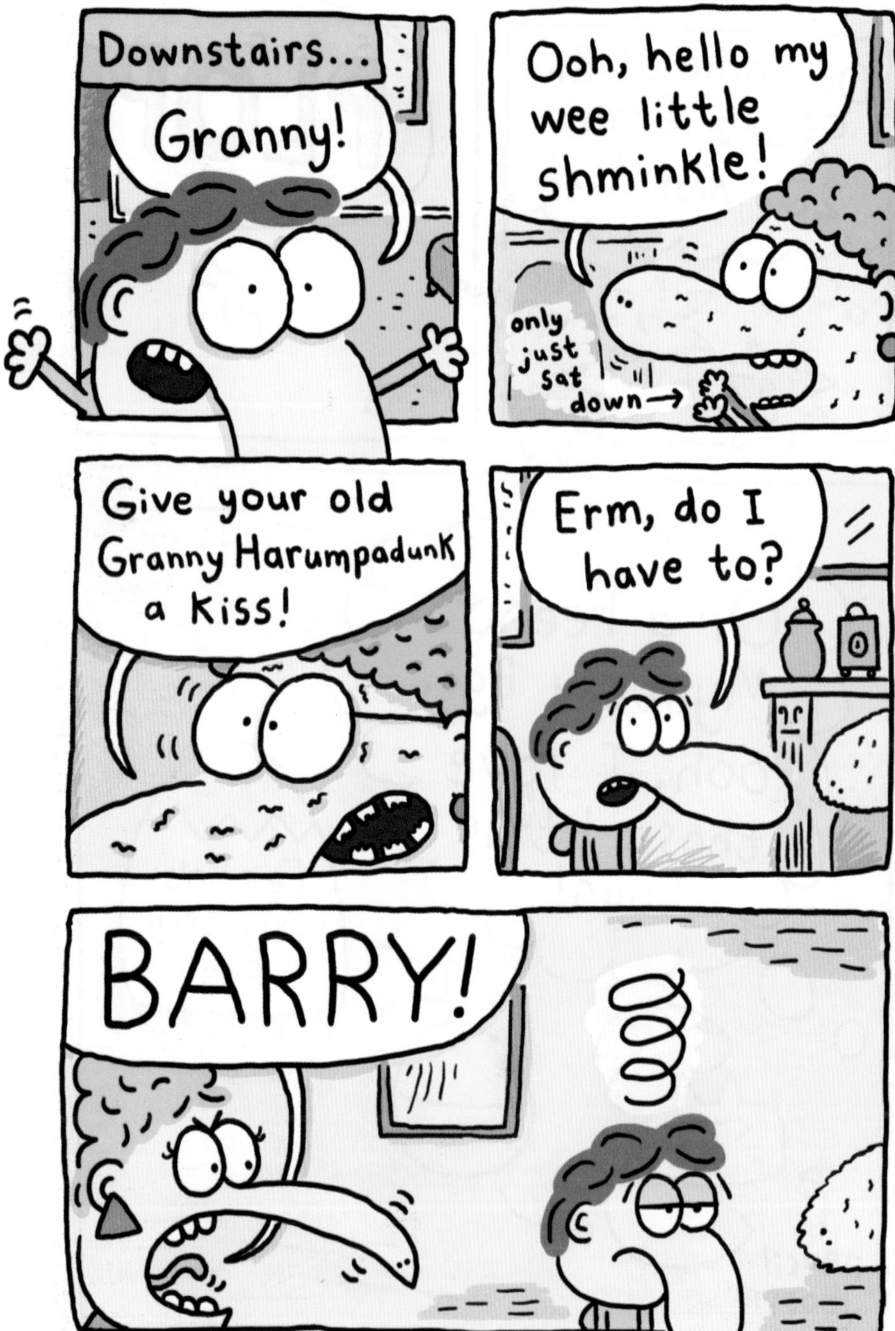
Downstairs...
Granny!
Ooh, hello my wee little shminkle!
only just sat down
Give your old Granny Harumpadunk a kiss!
Erm, do I have to?
BARRY!

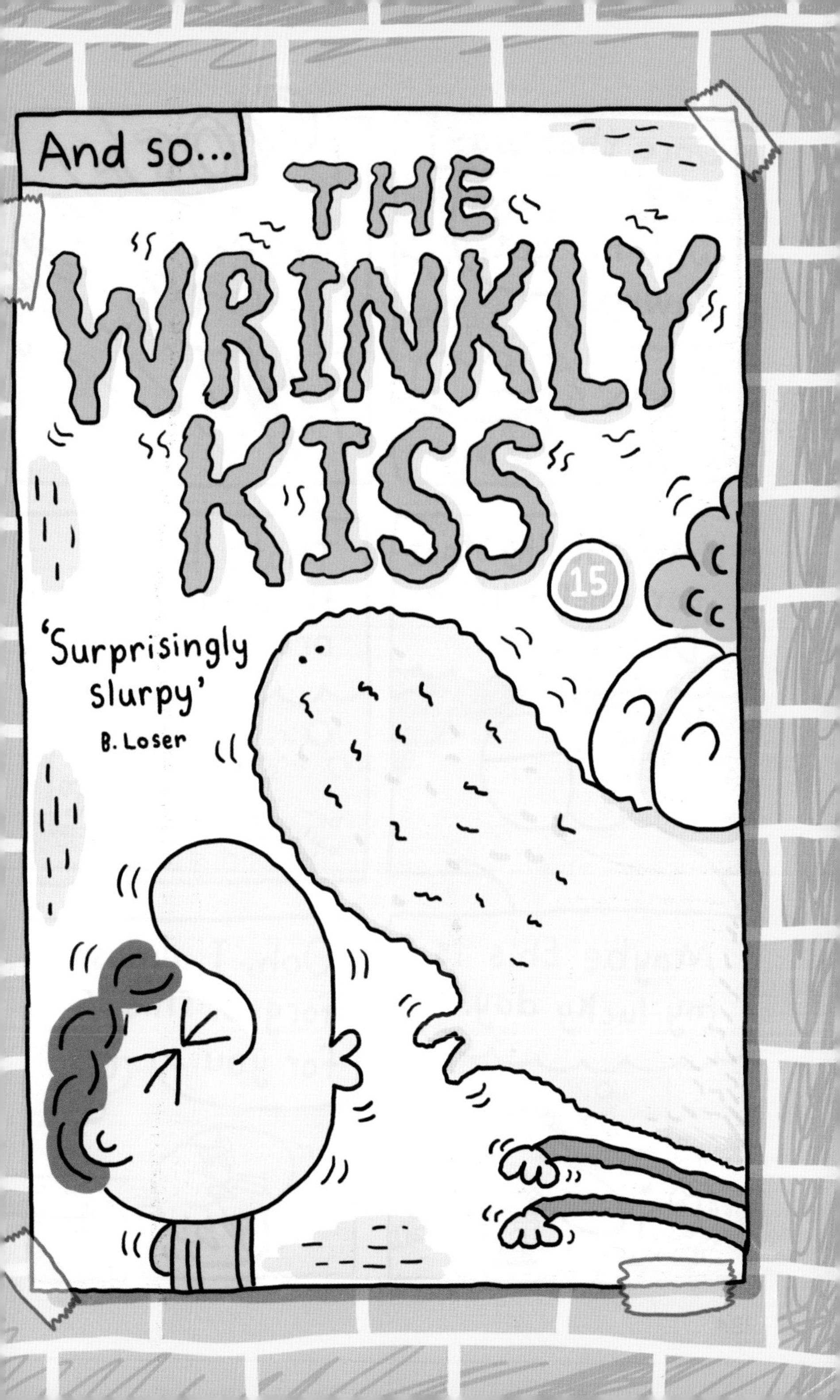
And so...
THE WRINKLY KISS
15
'Surprisingly slurpy'
B. Loser

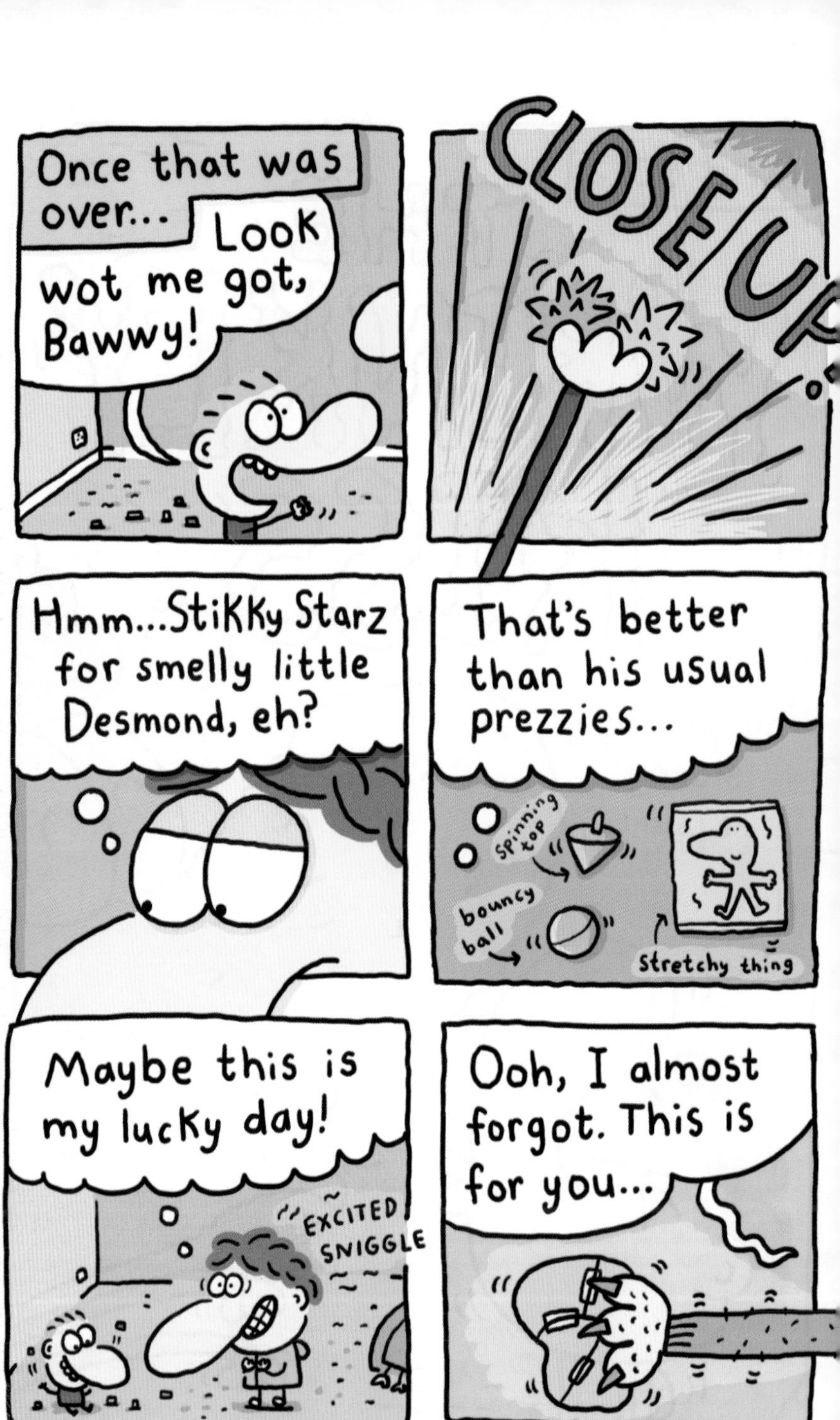
Once that was over...
Look wot me got, Bawwy!
CLOSE UP!
Hmm...StiKKy Starz for smelly little Desmond, eh?
That's better than his usual prezzies...
Spinning top
bouncy ball
Stretchy thing
Maybe this is my lucky day!
EXCITED SNIGGLE
Ooh, I almost forgot. This is for you...

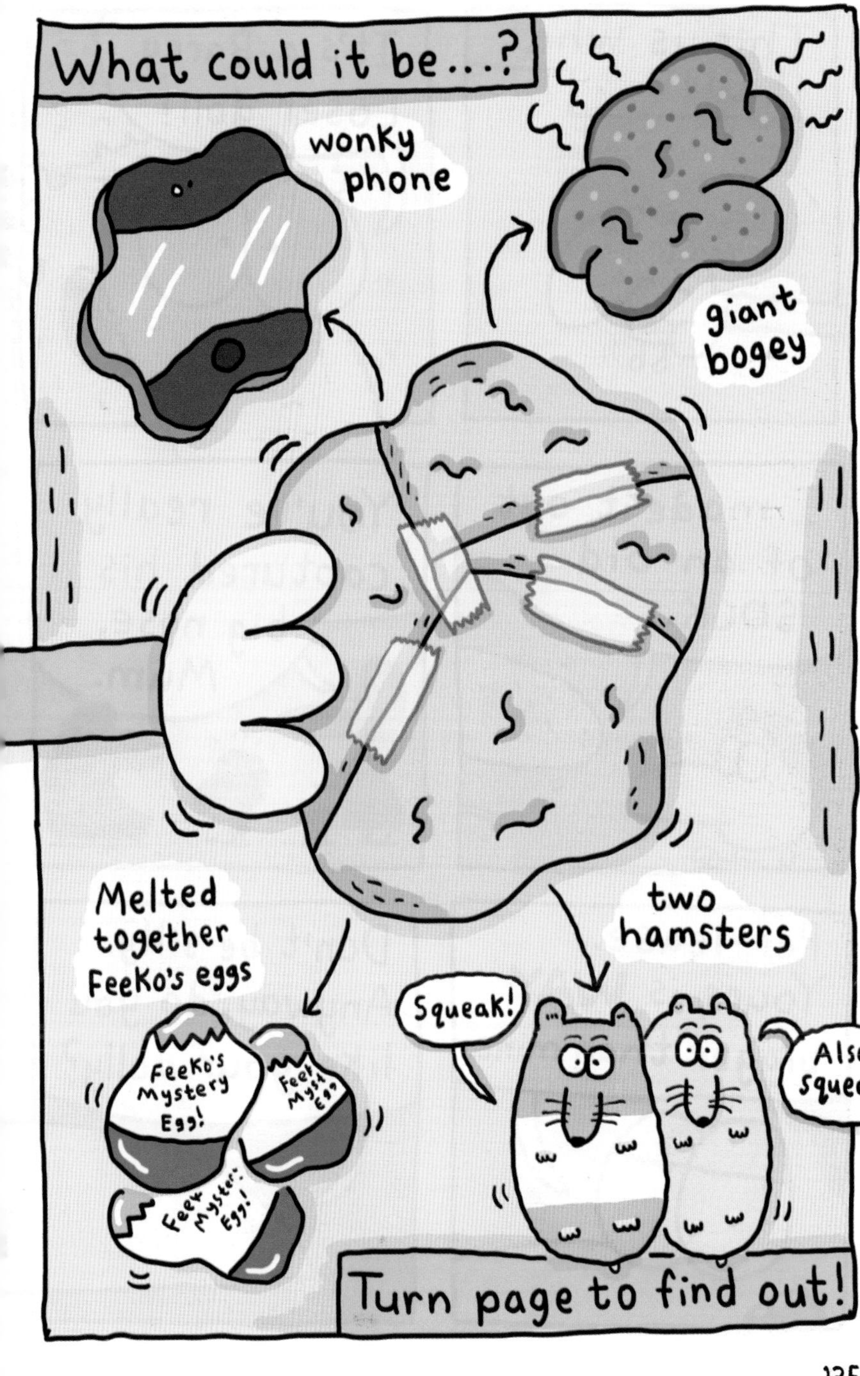
What could it be...?
wonky phone
giant bogey
Melted together FeeKo's eggs
FeeKo's Mystery Egg!
two hamsters
Squeak!
Also squeak!
Turn page to find out!

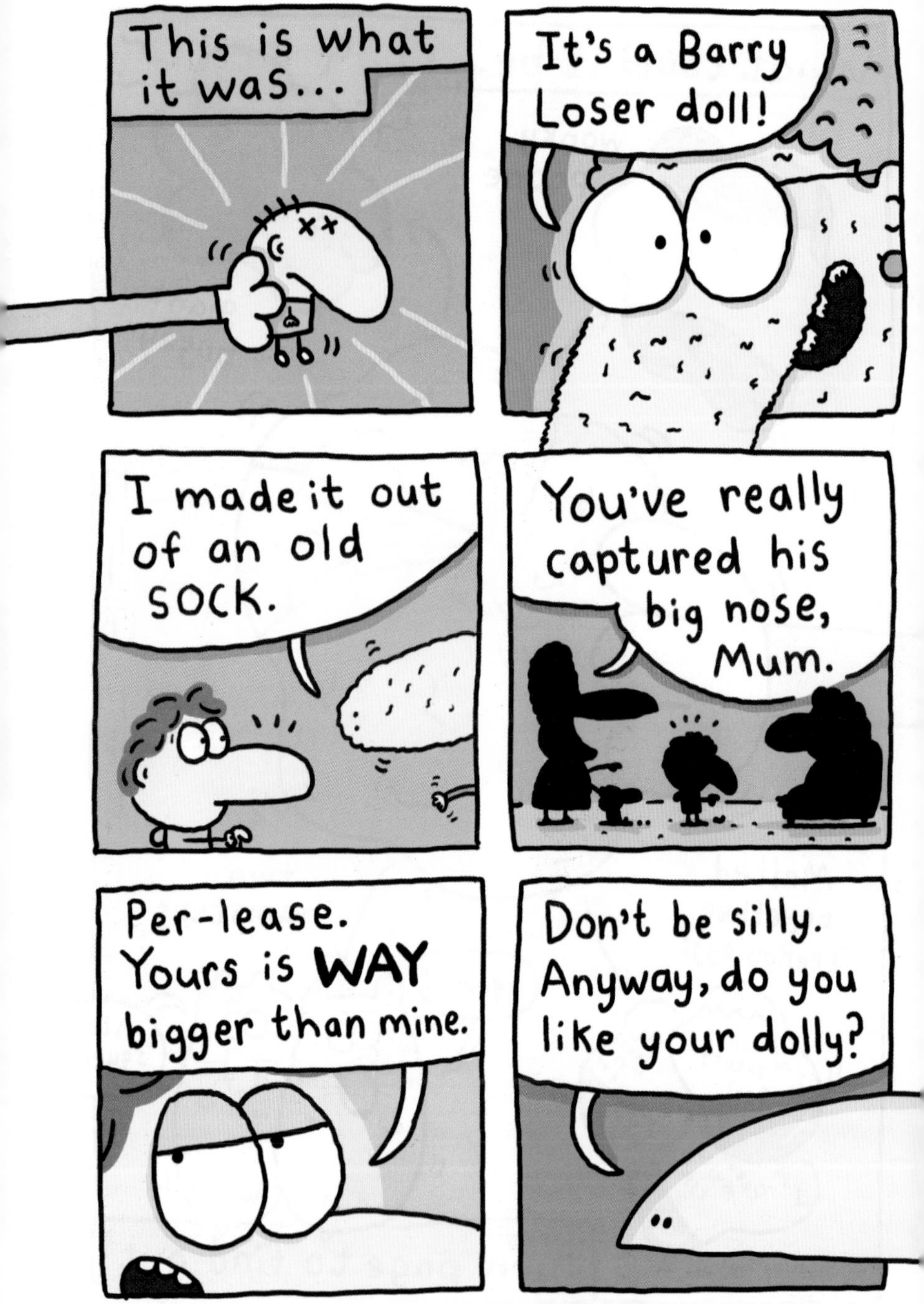

This is what it was...
It's a Barry Loser doll!
I made it out of an old SOCK.
You've really captured his big nose, Mum.
Per-lease. Yours is **WAY** bigger than mine.
Don't be silly. Anyway, do you like your dolly?

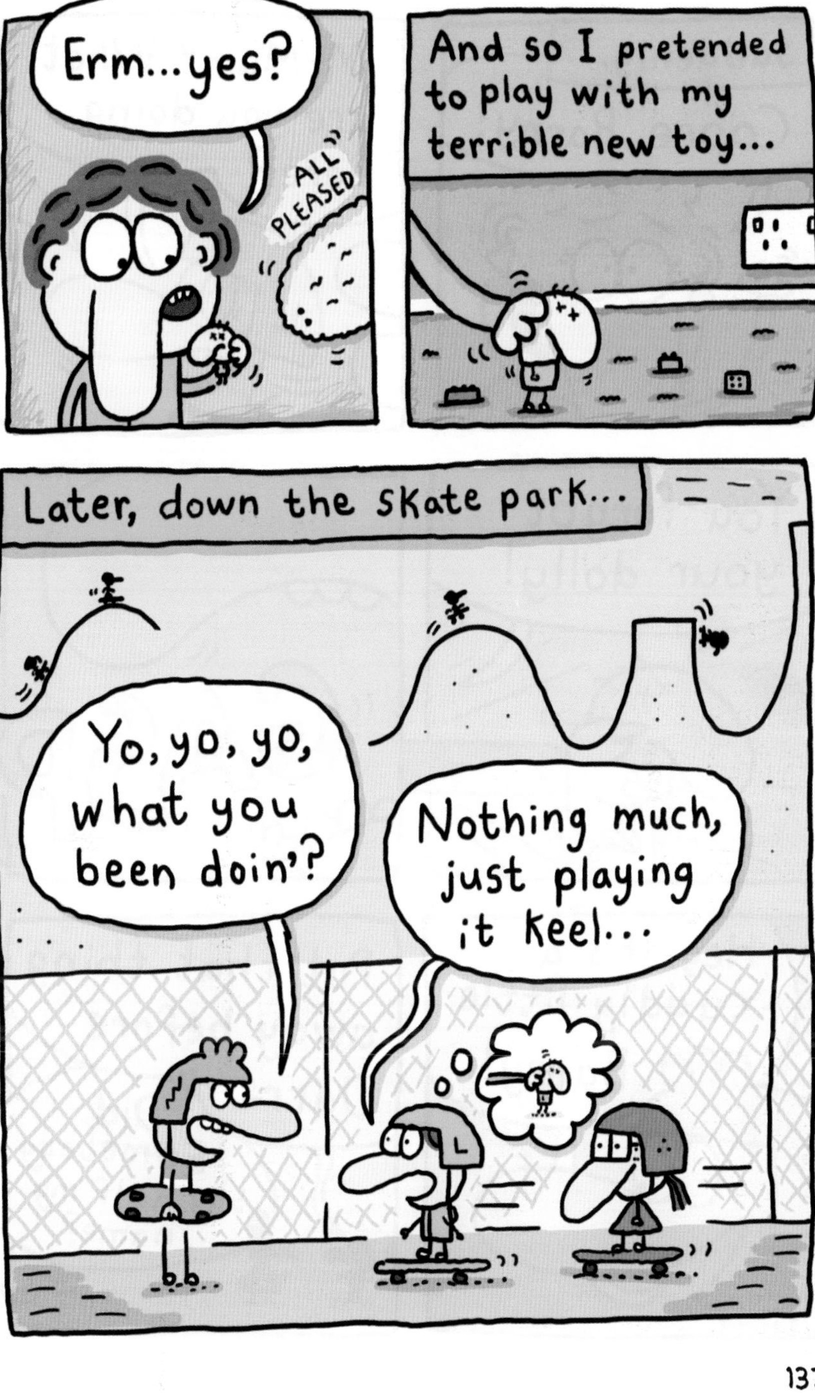

Erm...yes?
ALL PLEASED
And so I pretended to play with my terrible new toy...
Later, down the skate park...
Yo, yo, yo, what you been doin'?
Nothing much, just playing it keel...

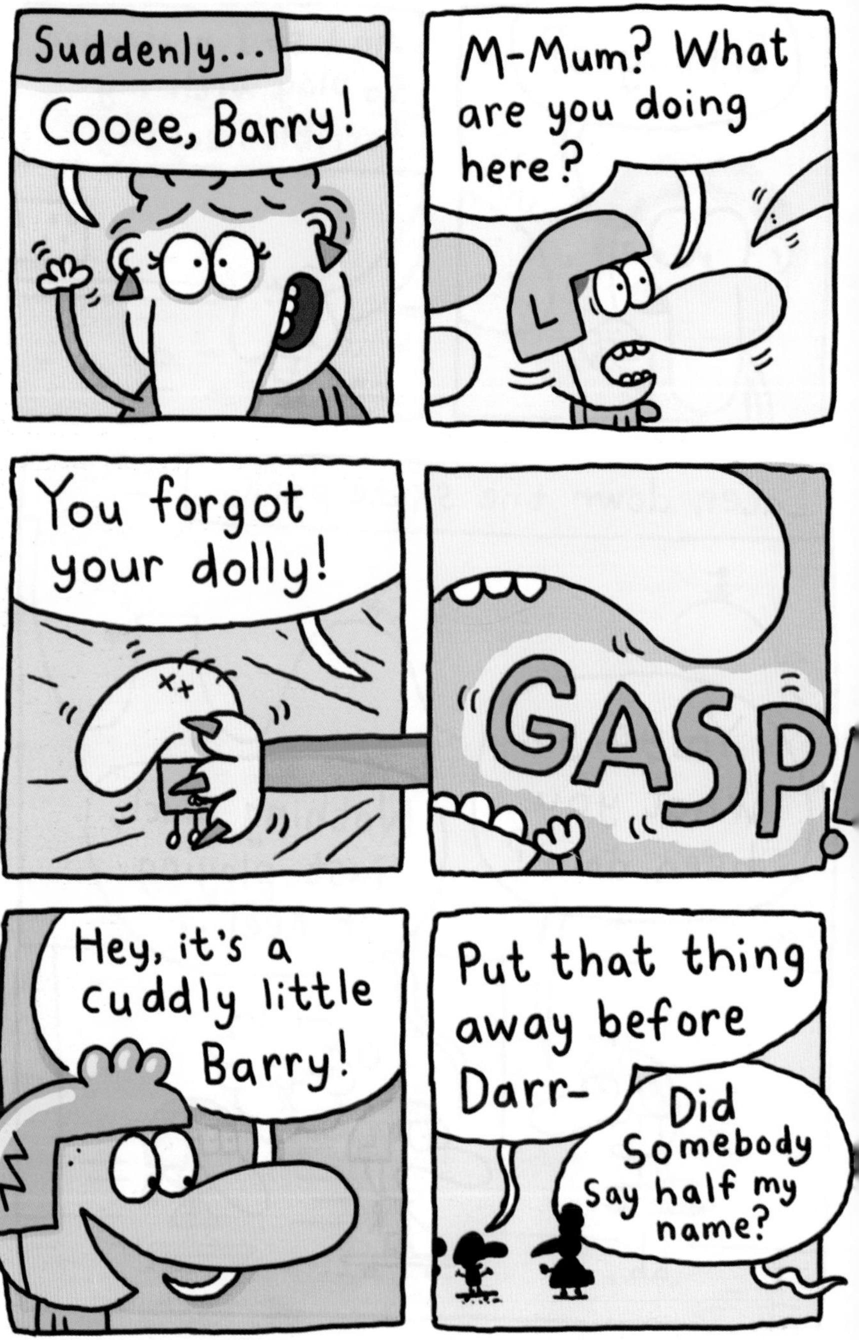
Suddenly...
Cooee, Barry!
M-Mum? What are you doing here?
You forgot your dolly!
GASP!
Hey, it's a cuddly little Barry!
Put that thing away before Darr-
Did Somebody Say half my name?

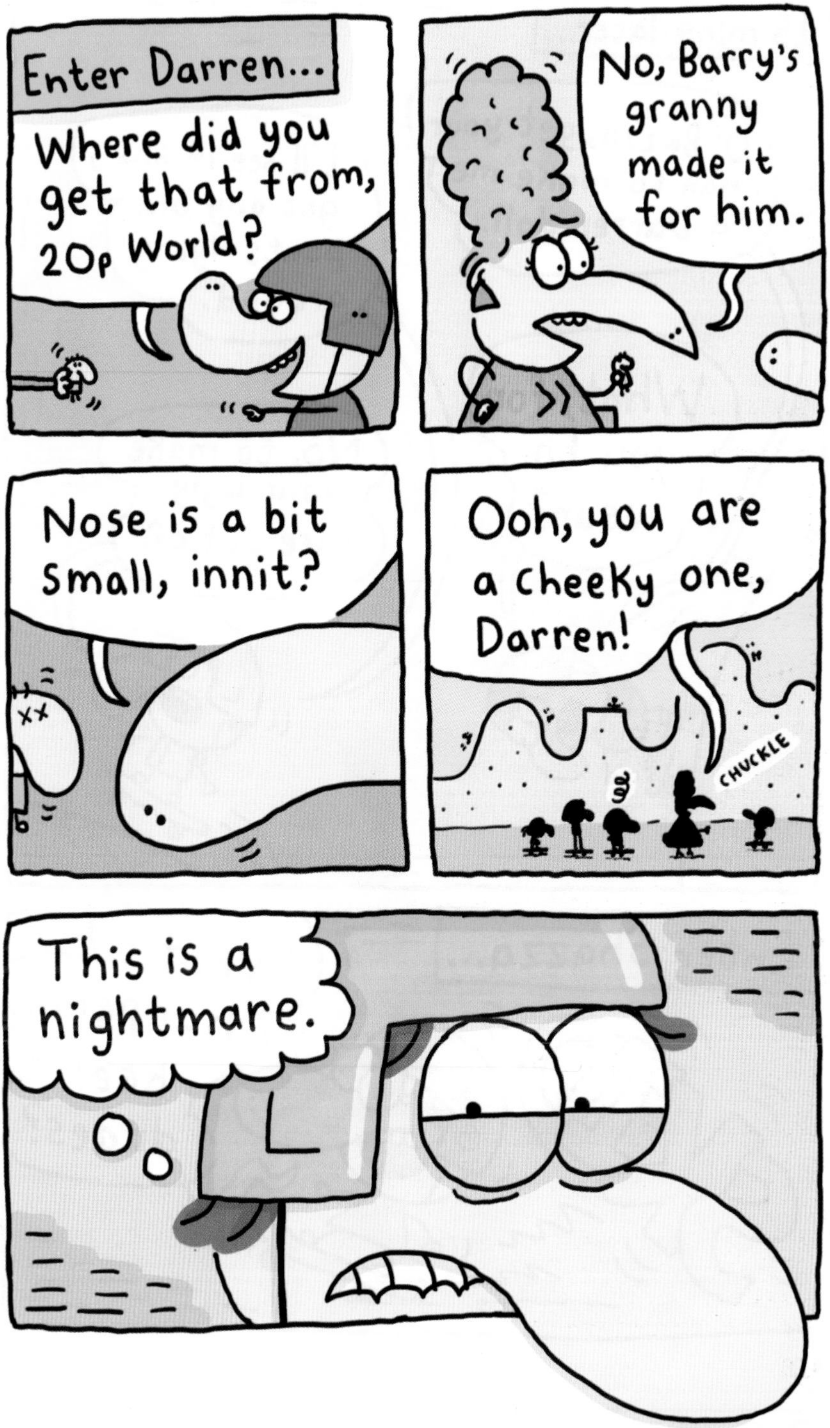
Enter Darren...
Where did you get that from, 20p World?
No, Barry's granny made it for him.
Nose is a bit small, innit?
Ooh, you are a cheeky one, Darren!
CHUCKLE
This is a nightmare.

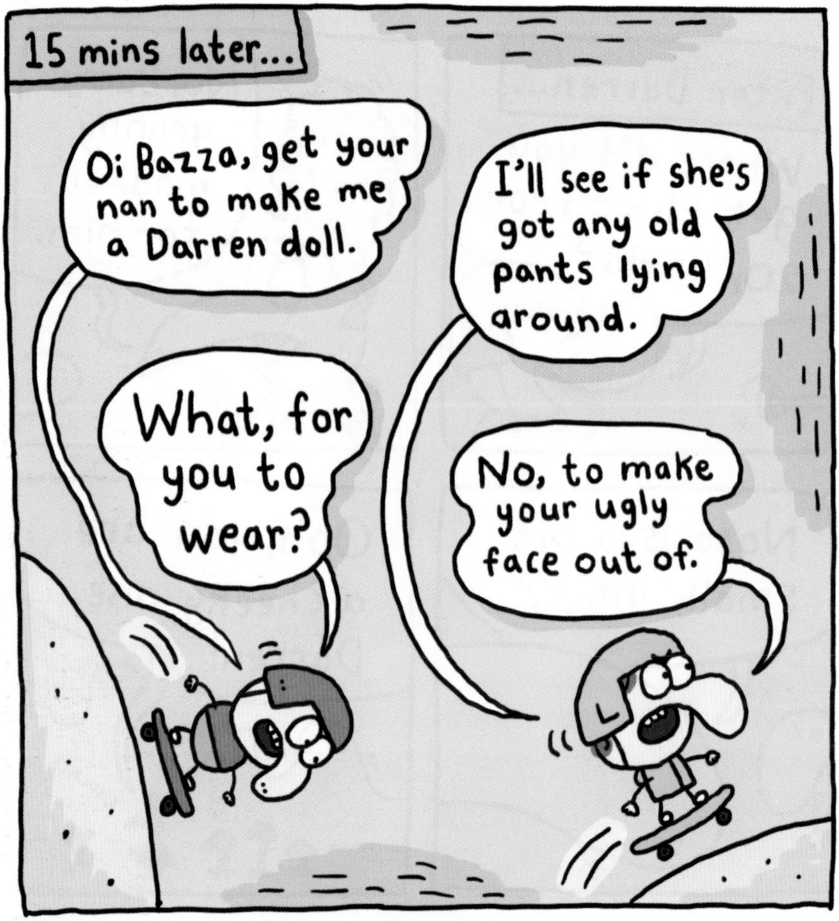
15 mins later...
Oi Bazza, get your nan to make me a Darren doll.
I'll see if she's got any old pants lying around.
What, for you to wear?
No, to make your ugly face out of.

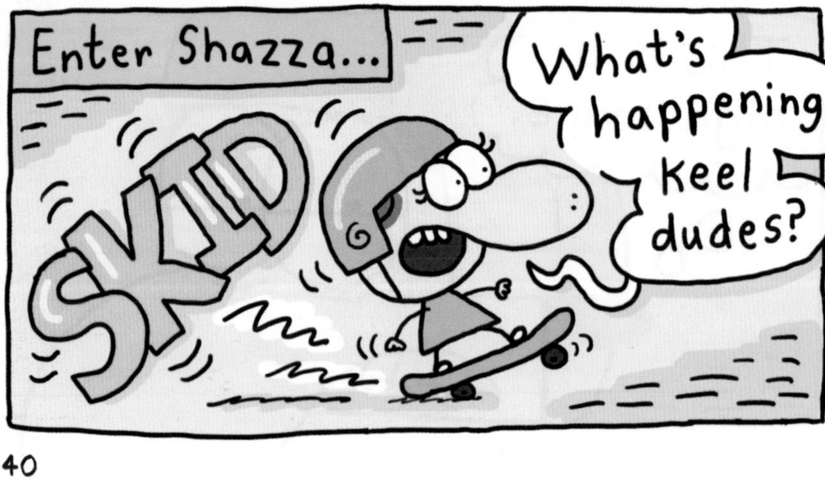
Enter Shazza...
SKID
What's happening, keel dudes?

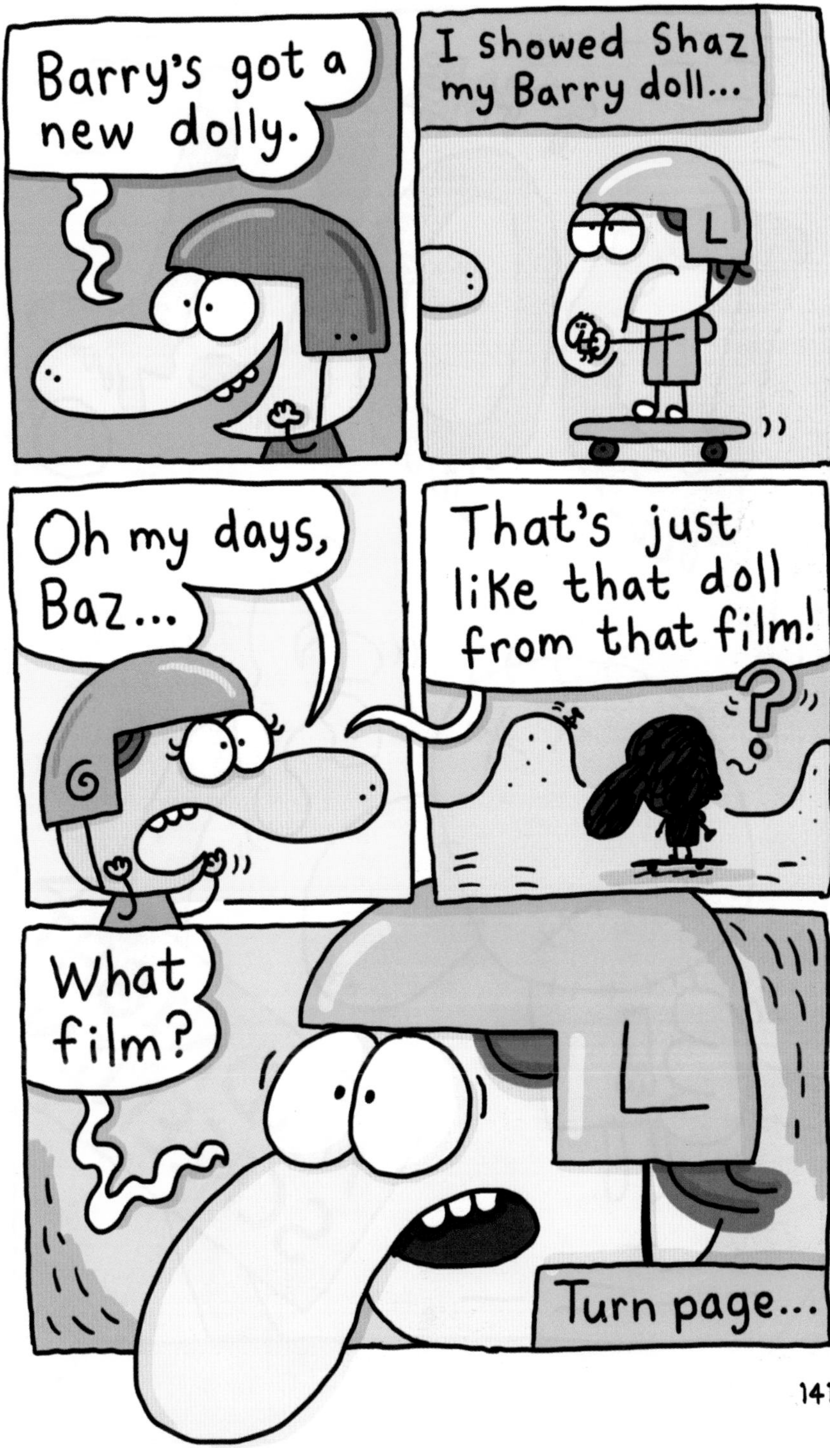
Barry's got a new dolly.
I showed Shaz my Barry doll...
Oh my days, Baz...
That's just like that doll from that film!
What film?
Turn page...

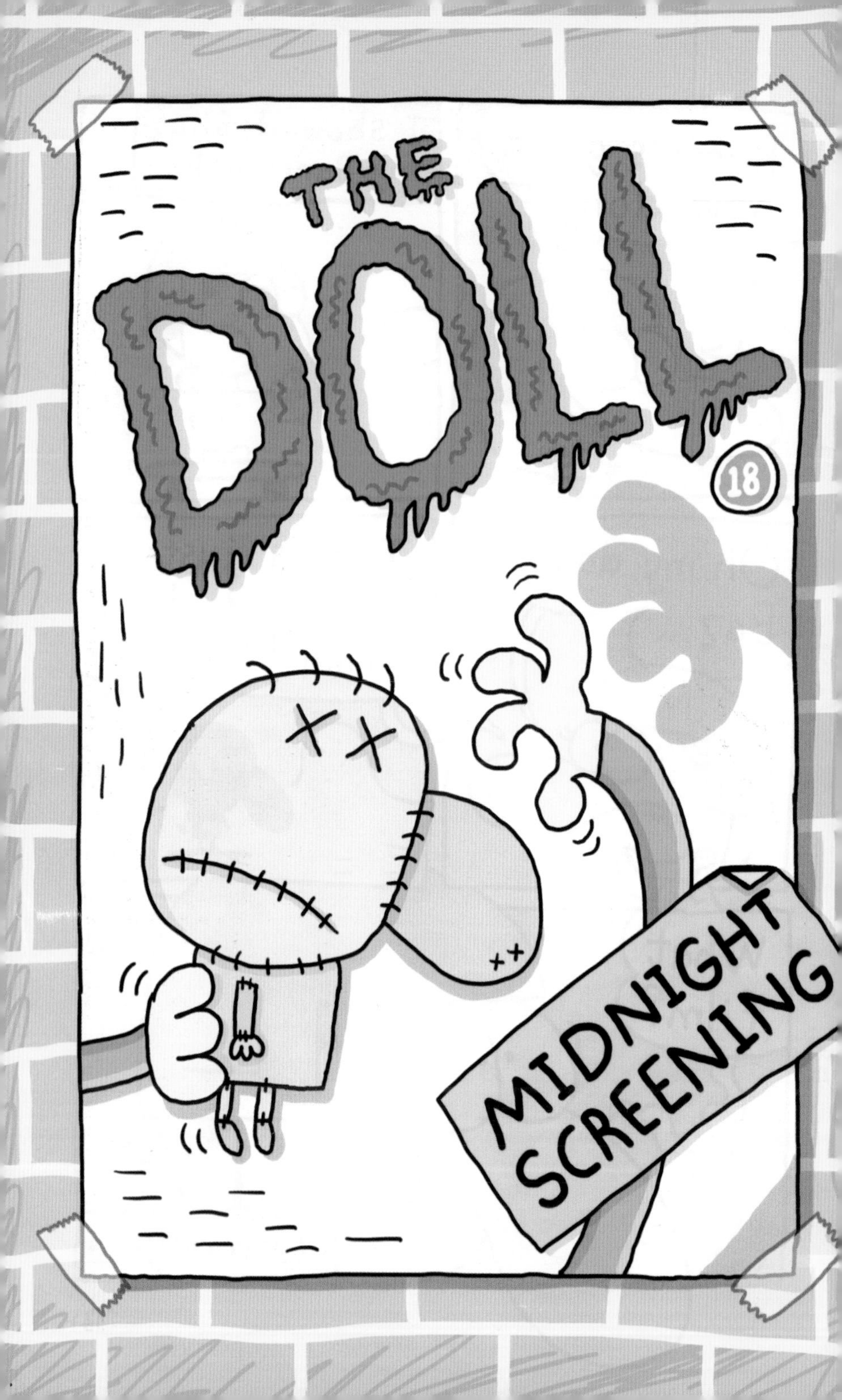
THE DOLL
18
MIDNIGHT SCREENING

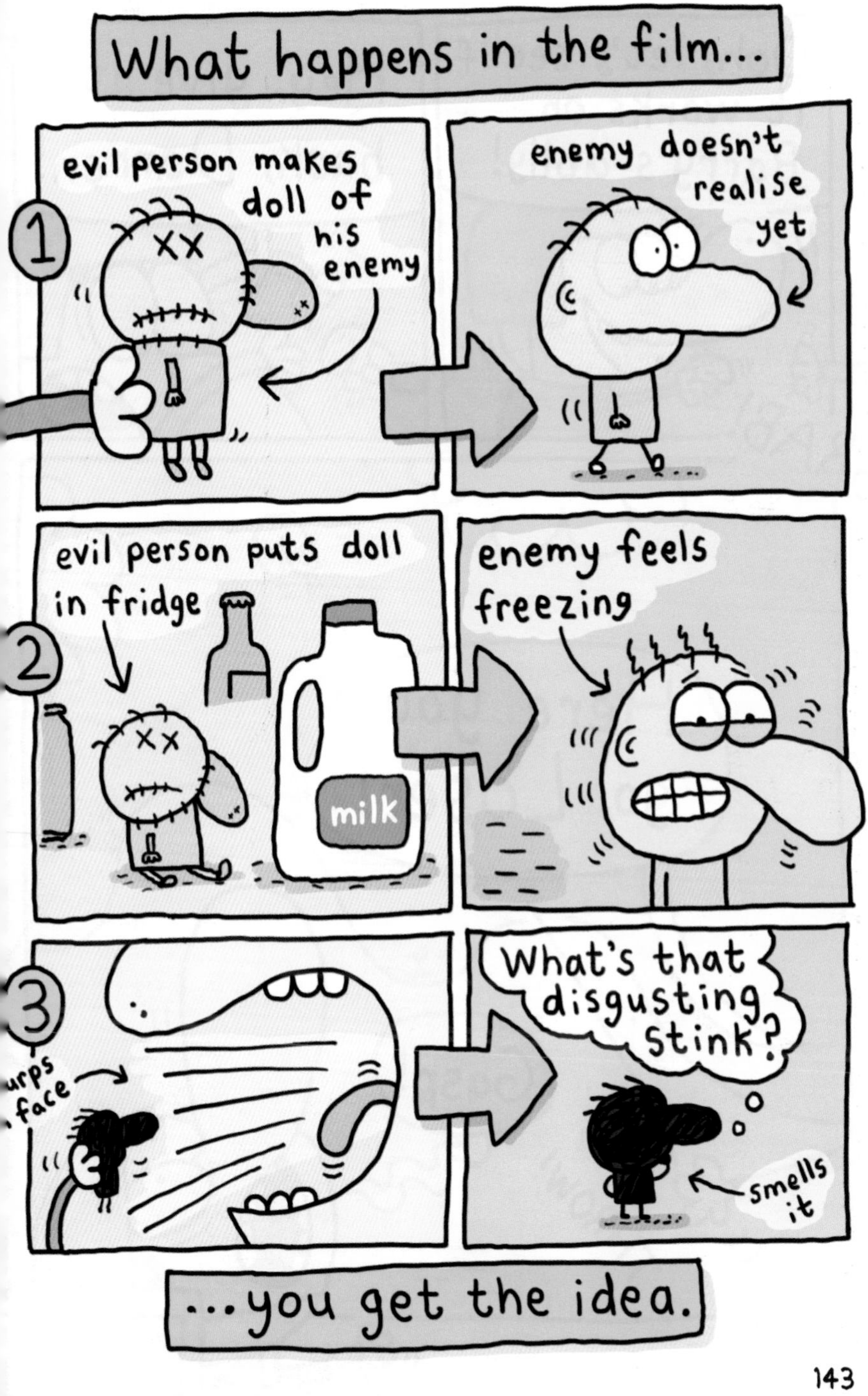
What happens in the film...
1
evil person makes doll of his enemy
enemy doesn't realise yet
2
evil person puts doll in fridge
milk
enemy feels freezing
3
What's that disgusting stink?
smells it
...you get the idea.

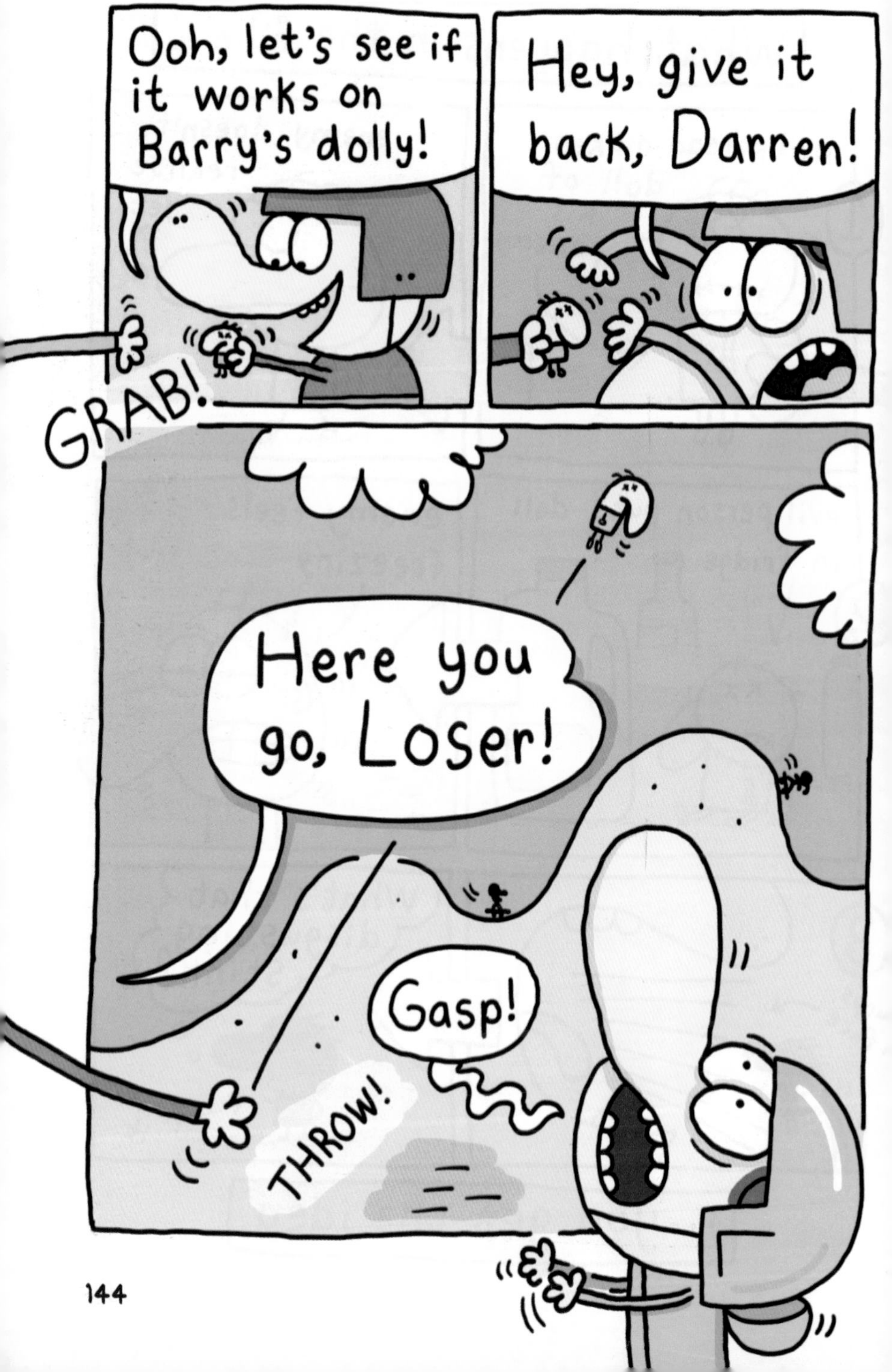

Ooh, let's see if it works on Barry's dolly!
GRAB!
Hey, give it back, Darren!
Here you go, Loser!
Gasp!
THROW!

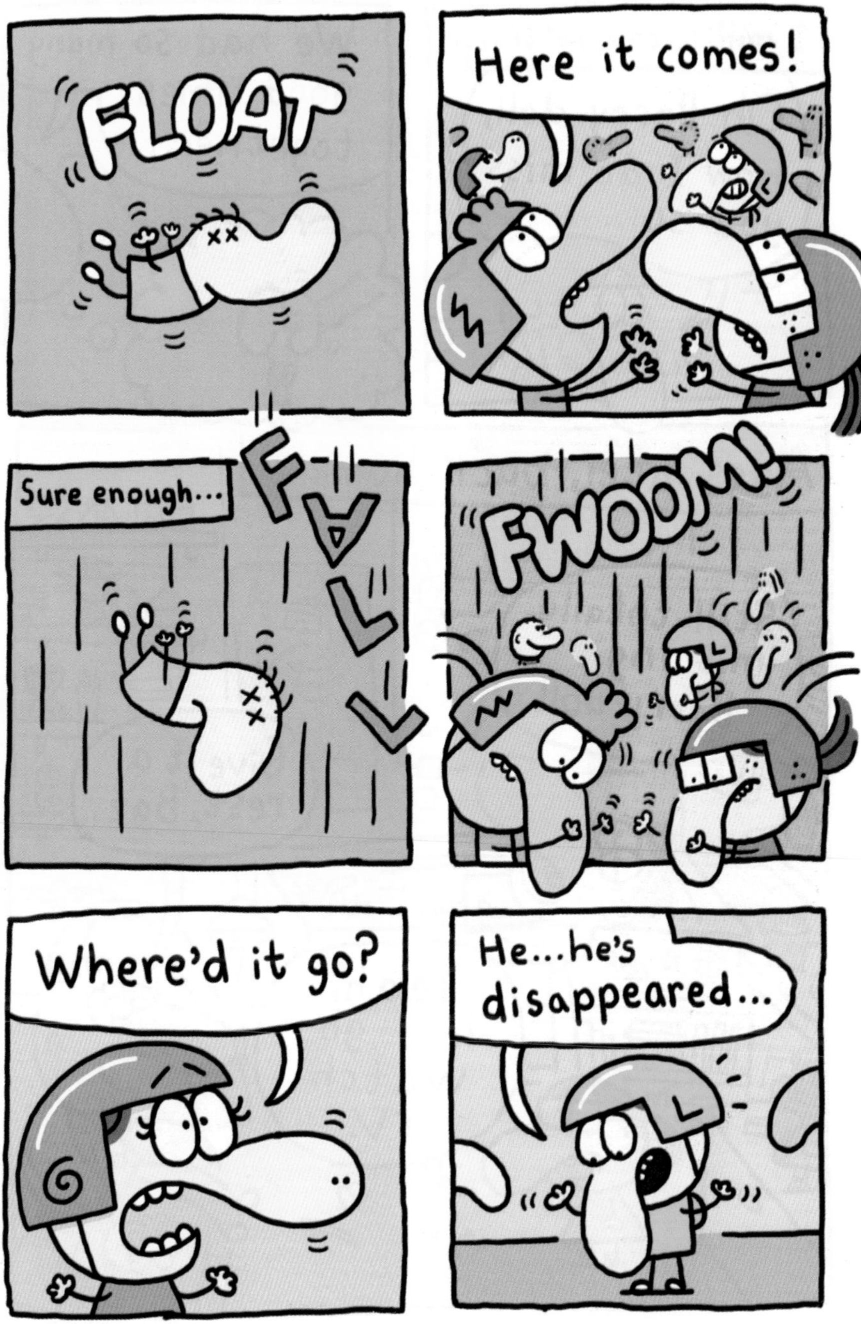
FLOAT
Here it comes!
Sure enough...
FALL
FWOOM!
Where'd it go?
He...he's disappeared...

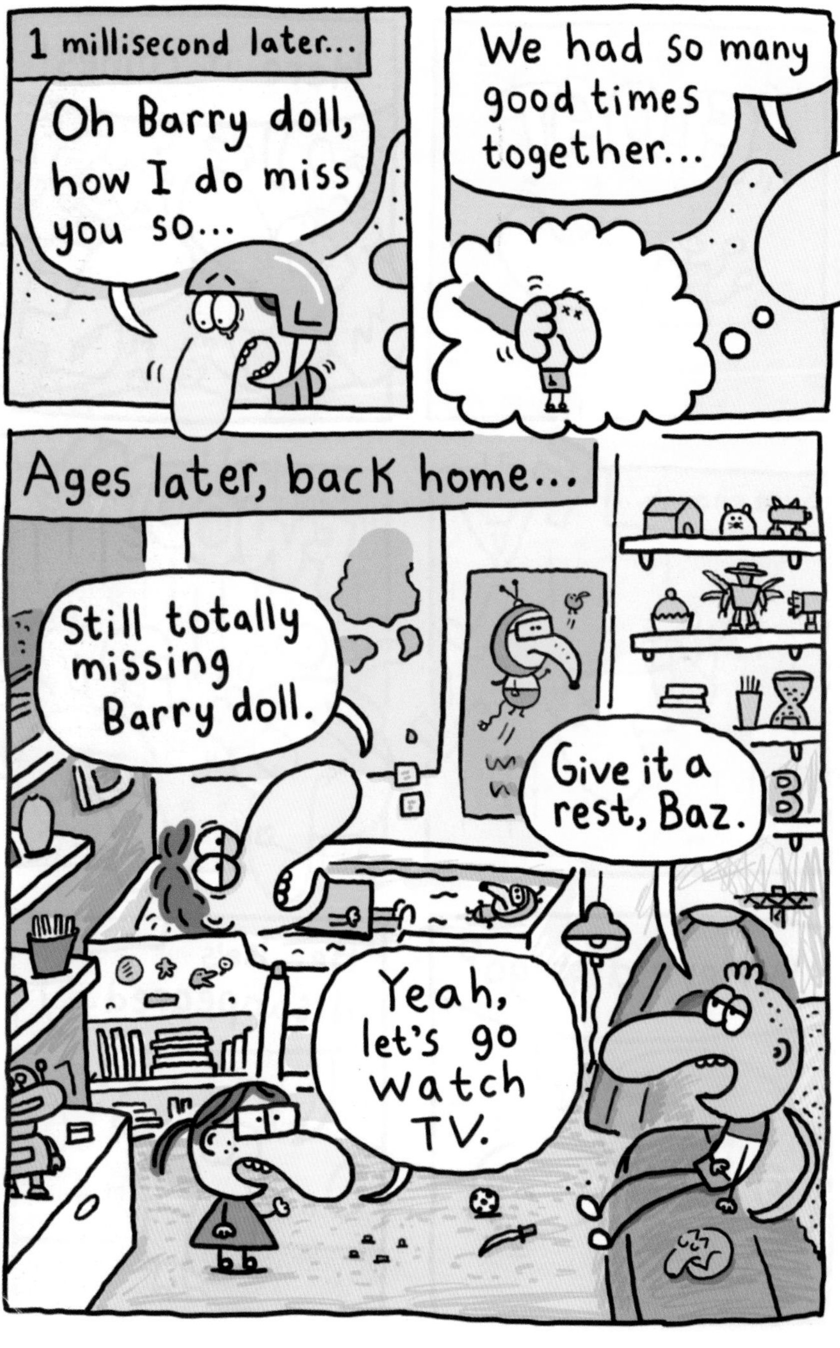
1 millisecond later...
Oh Barry doll, how I do miss you so...
We had so many good times together...
Ages later, back home...
Still totally missing Barry doll.
Give it a rest, Baz.
Yeah, let's go watch TV.

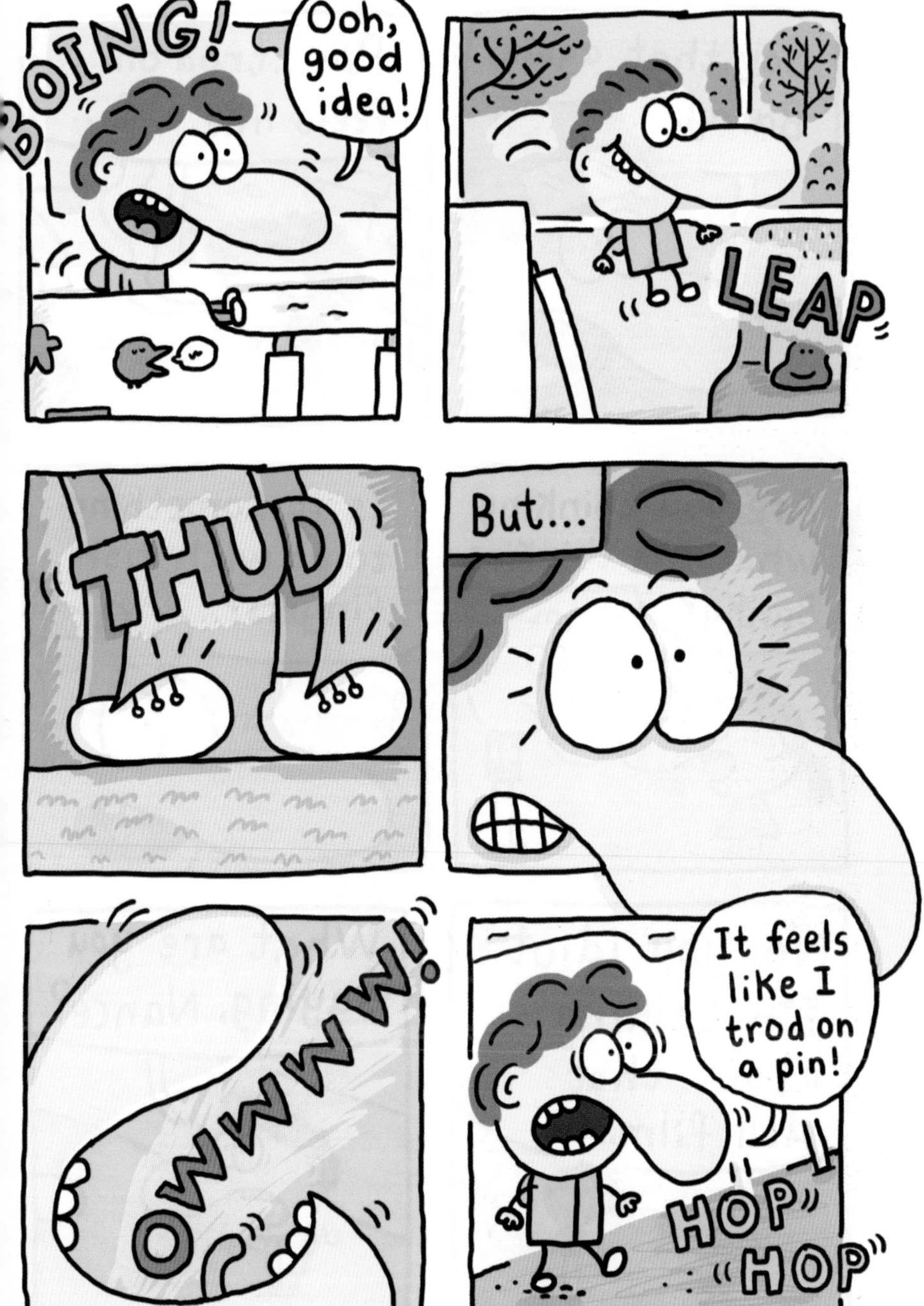
BOING!
Ooh, good idea!
LEAP
THUD
But...
OWWWWW!
It feels like I trod on a pin!
HOP
HOP

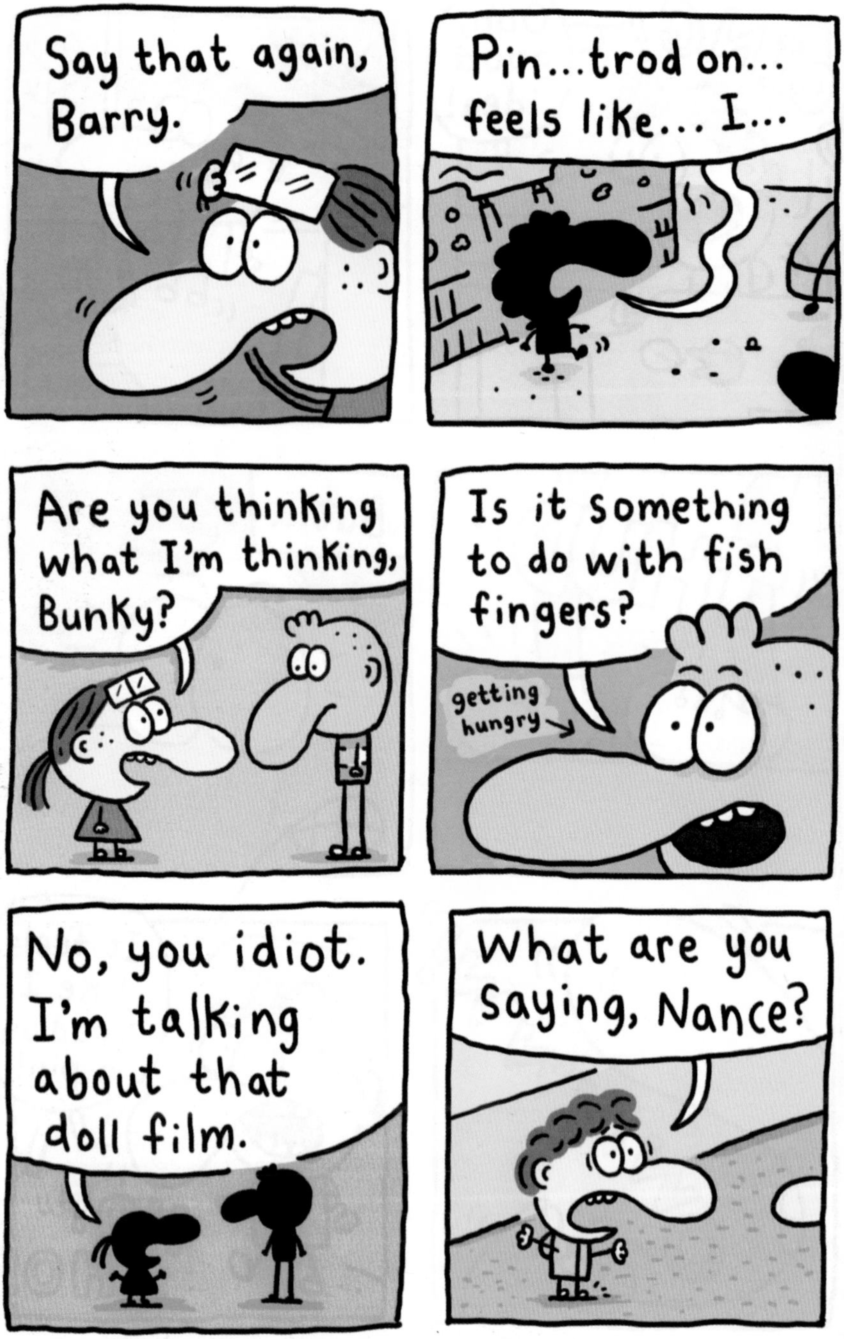
Say that again, Barry.
Pin...trod on... feels like... I...
Are you thinking what I'm thinking, Bunky?
Is it something to do with fish fingers?
getting hungry
No, you idiot. I'm talking about that doll film.
What are you saying, Nance?

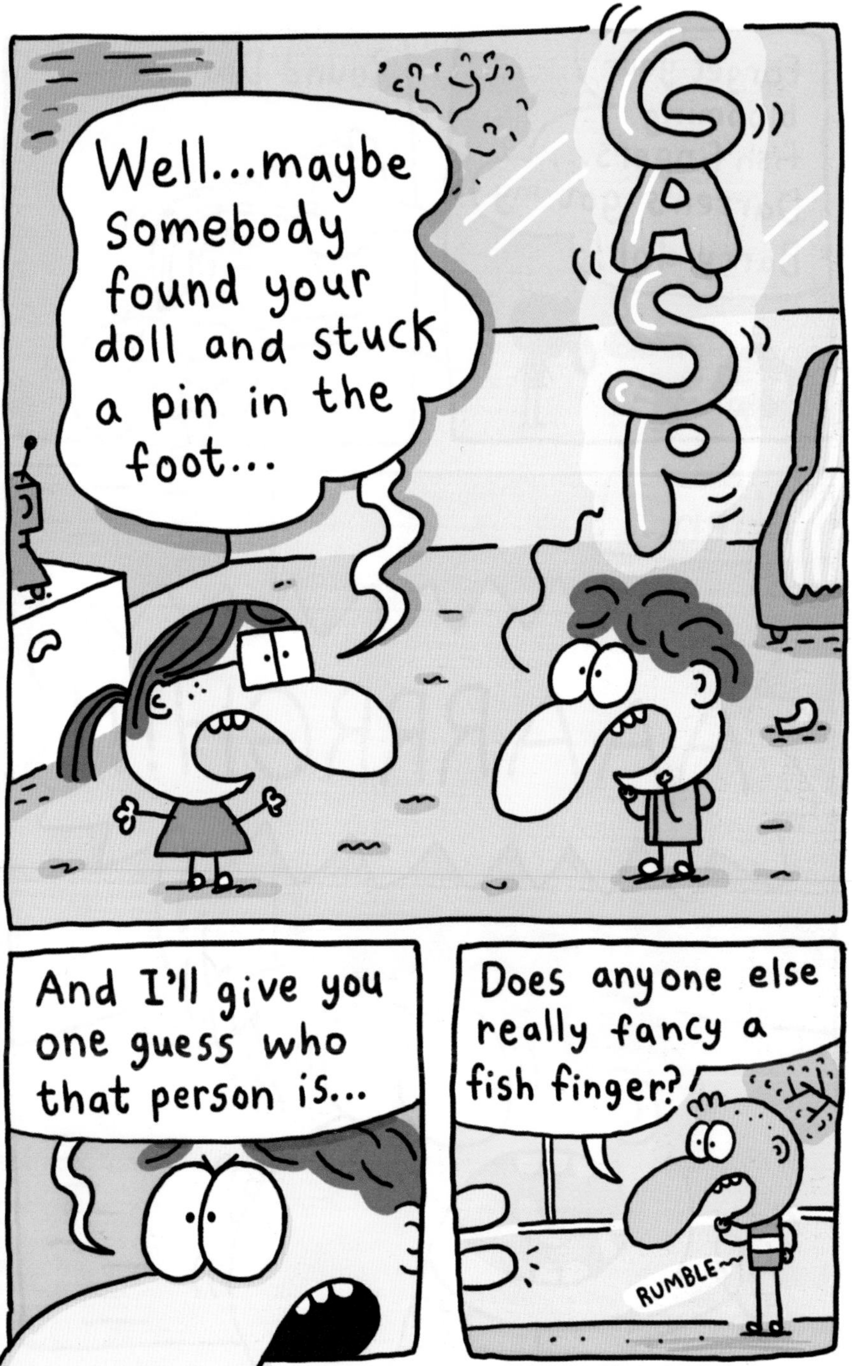
Well...maybe somebody found your doll and stuck a pin in the foot...
GASP
And I'll give you one guess who that person is...
Does anyone else really fancy a fish finger?
RUMBLE~~

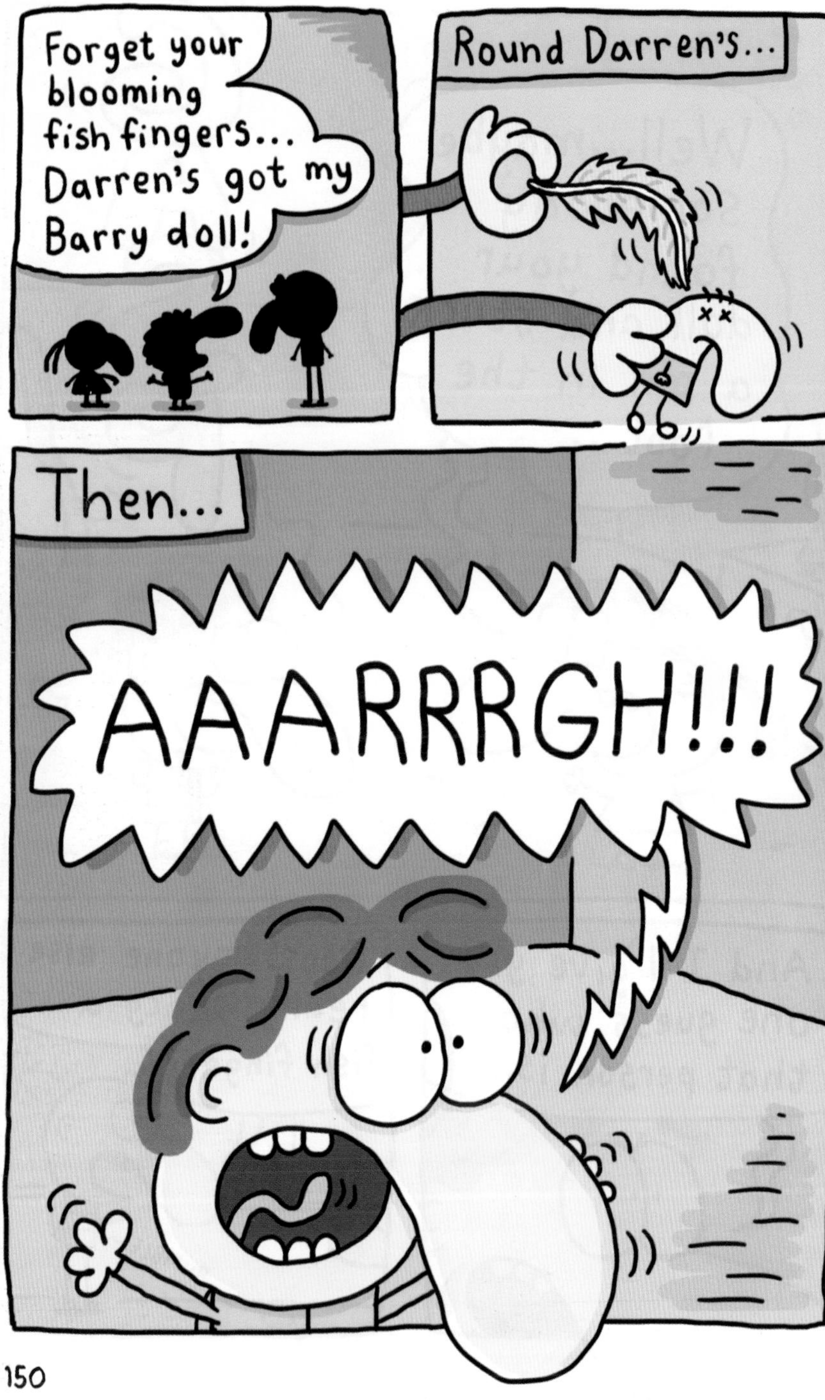
Forget your blooming fish fingers... Darren's got my Barry doll!
Round Darren's...
Then...
AAARRRGH!!!

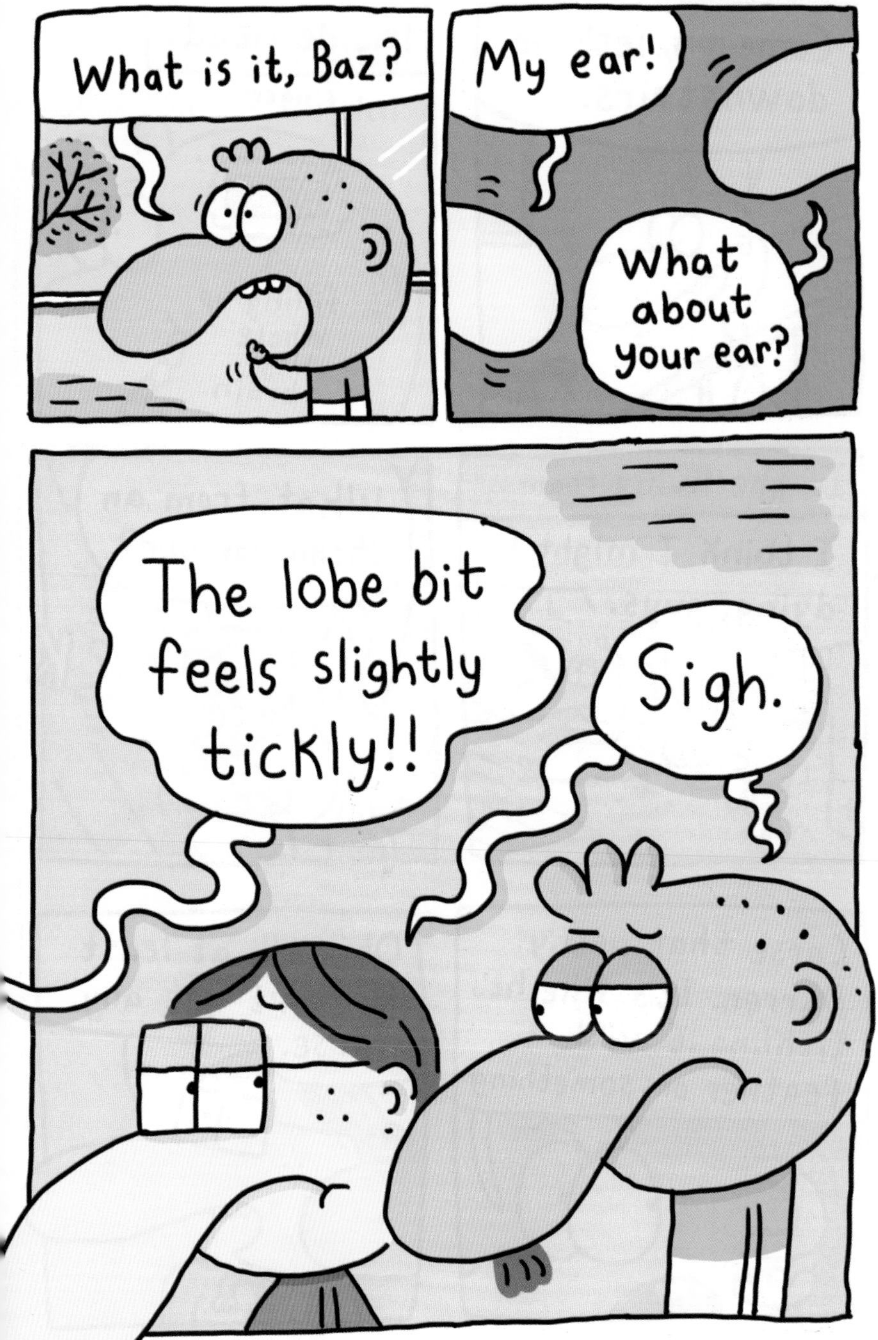
What is it, Baz?
My ear!
What about your ear?
The lobe bit feels slightly tickly!!
Sigh.

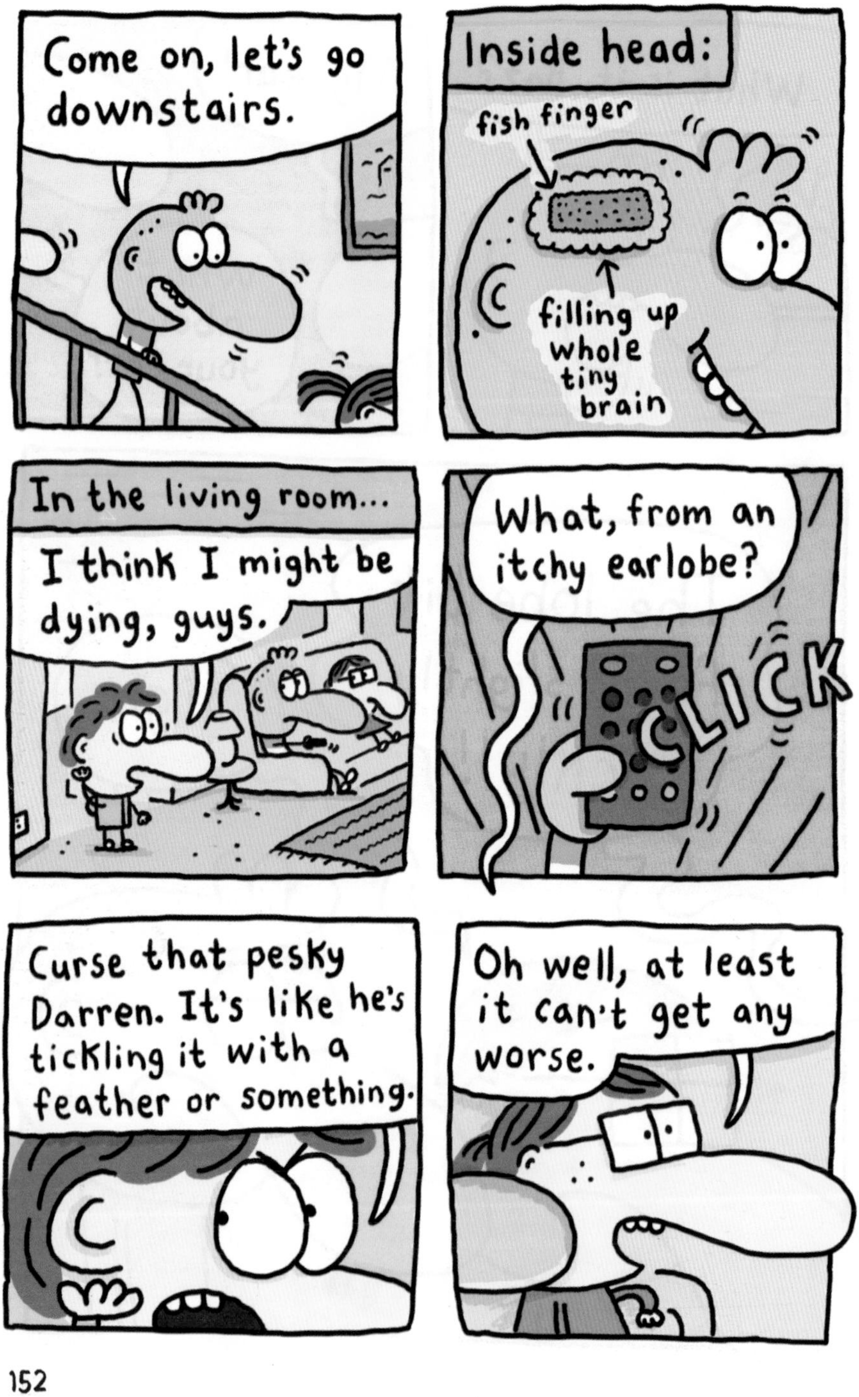

Come on, let's go downstairs.
Inside head:
fish finger
filling up whole tiny brain
In the living room...
I think I might be dying, guys.
What, from an itchy earlobe?
CLICK
Curse that pesky Darren. It's like he's tickling it with a feather or something.
Oh well, at least it can't get any worse.

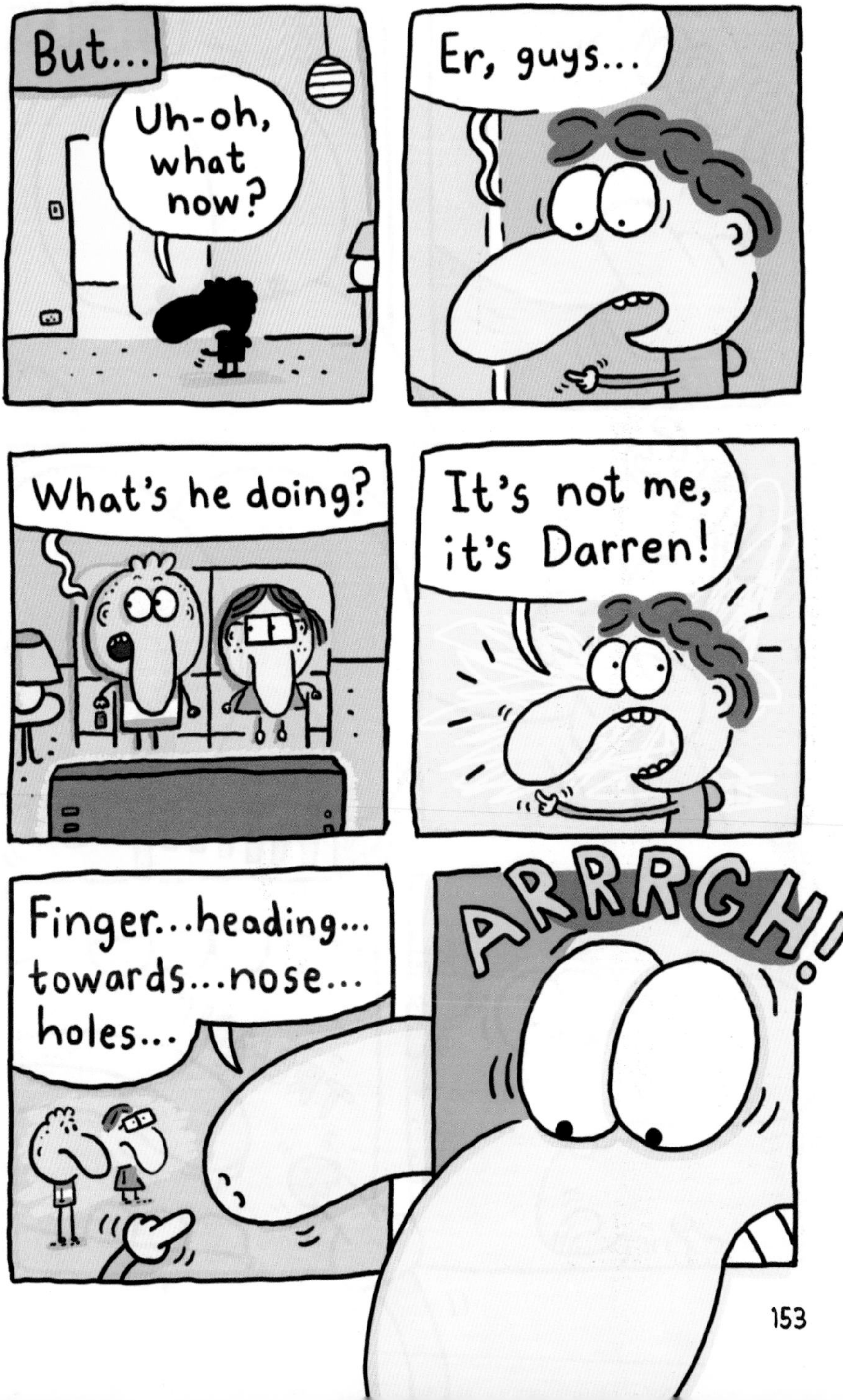
But...
Uh-oh, what now?
Er, guys...
What's he doing?
It's not me, it's Darren!
Finger...heading... towards...nose... holes...
ARRRGH!

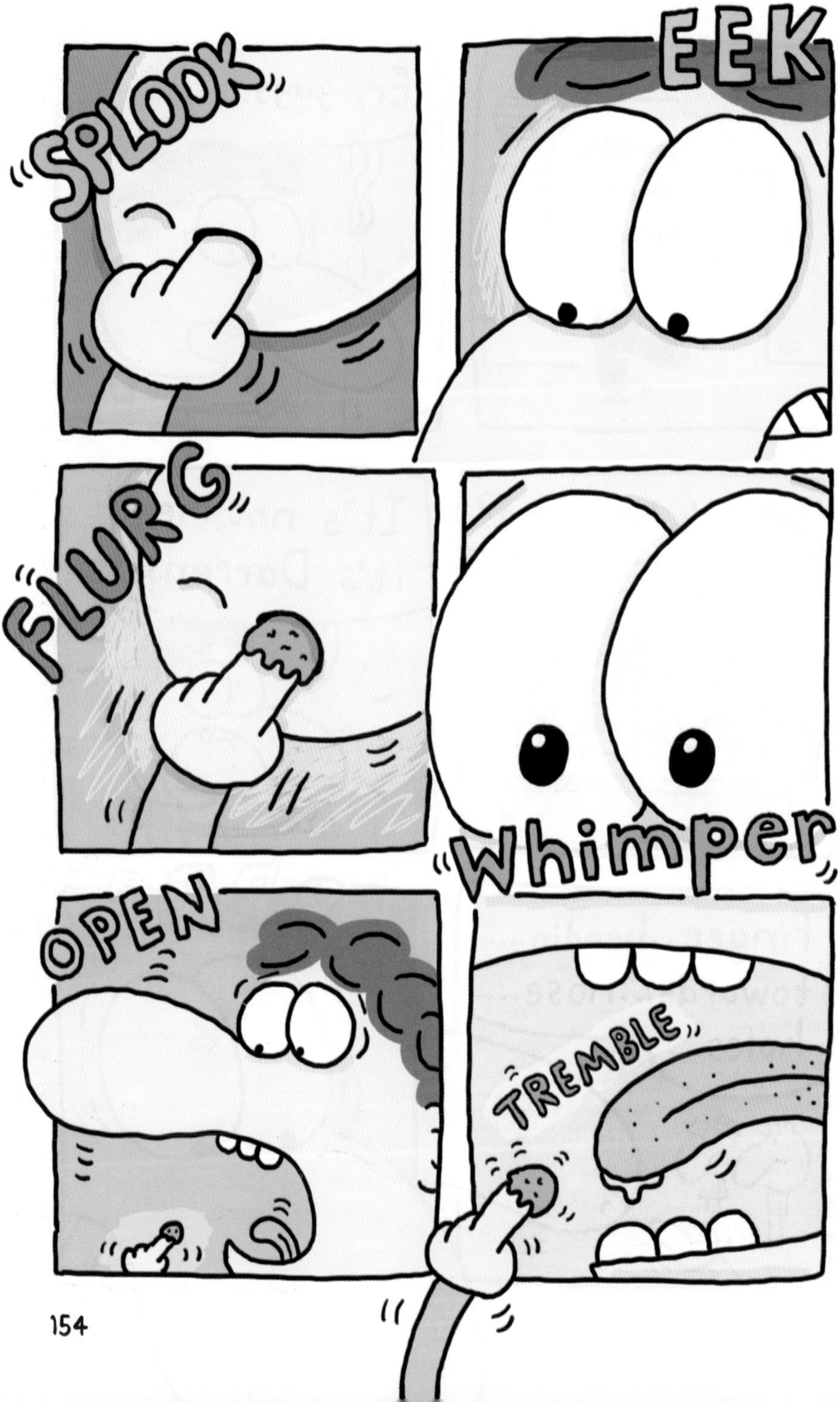
SPLOOK
EEK
FLURG
Whimper
OPEN
TREMBLE

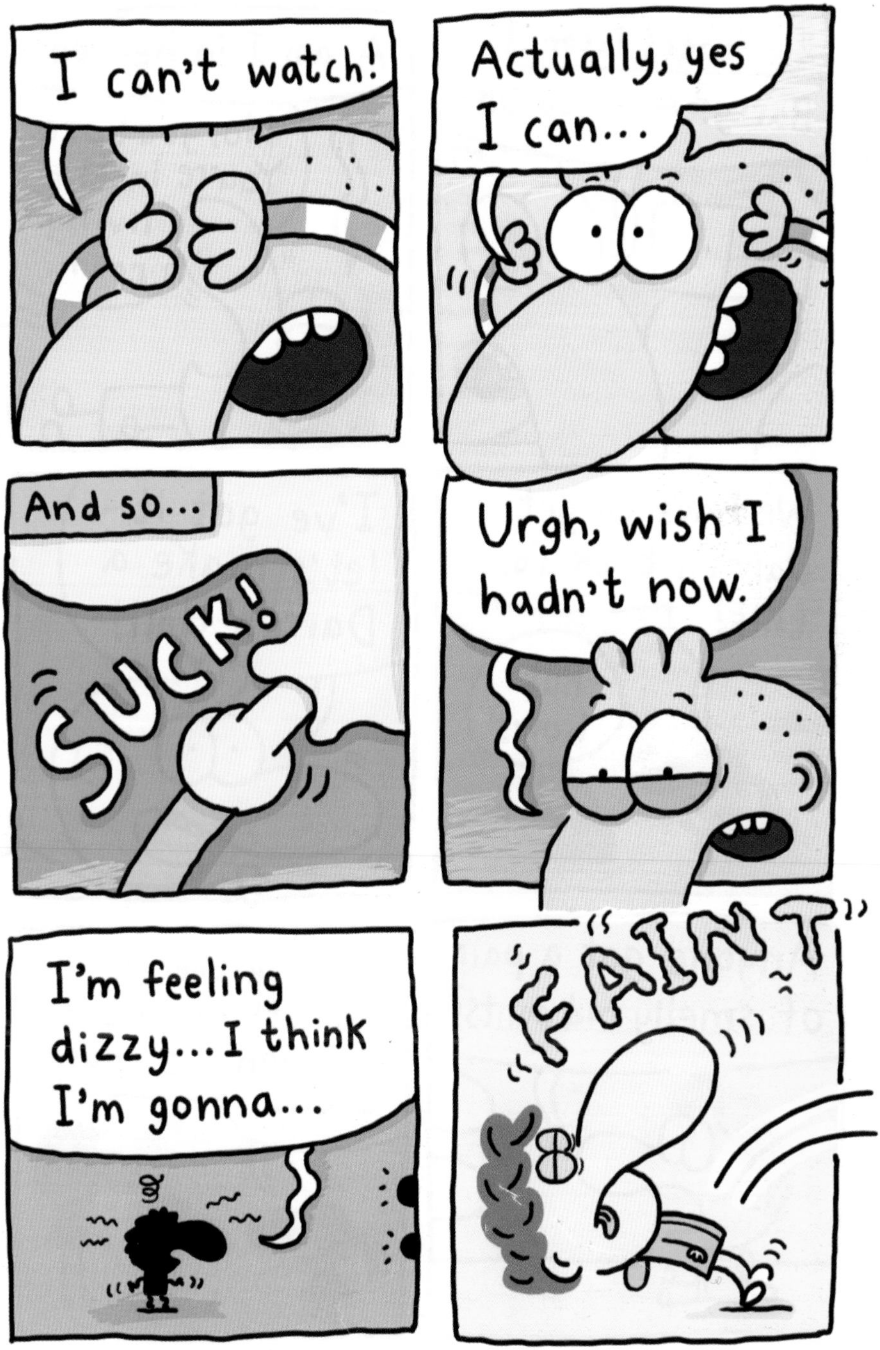
I can't watch!
Actually, yes I can...
And so...
SUCK!
Urgh, wish I hadn't now.
I'm feeling dizzy... I think I'm gonna...
FAINT

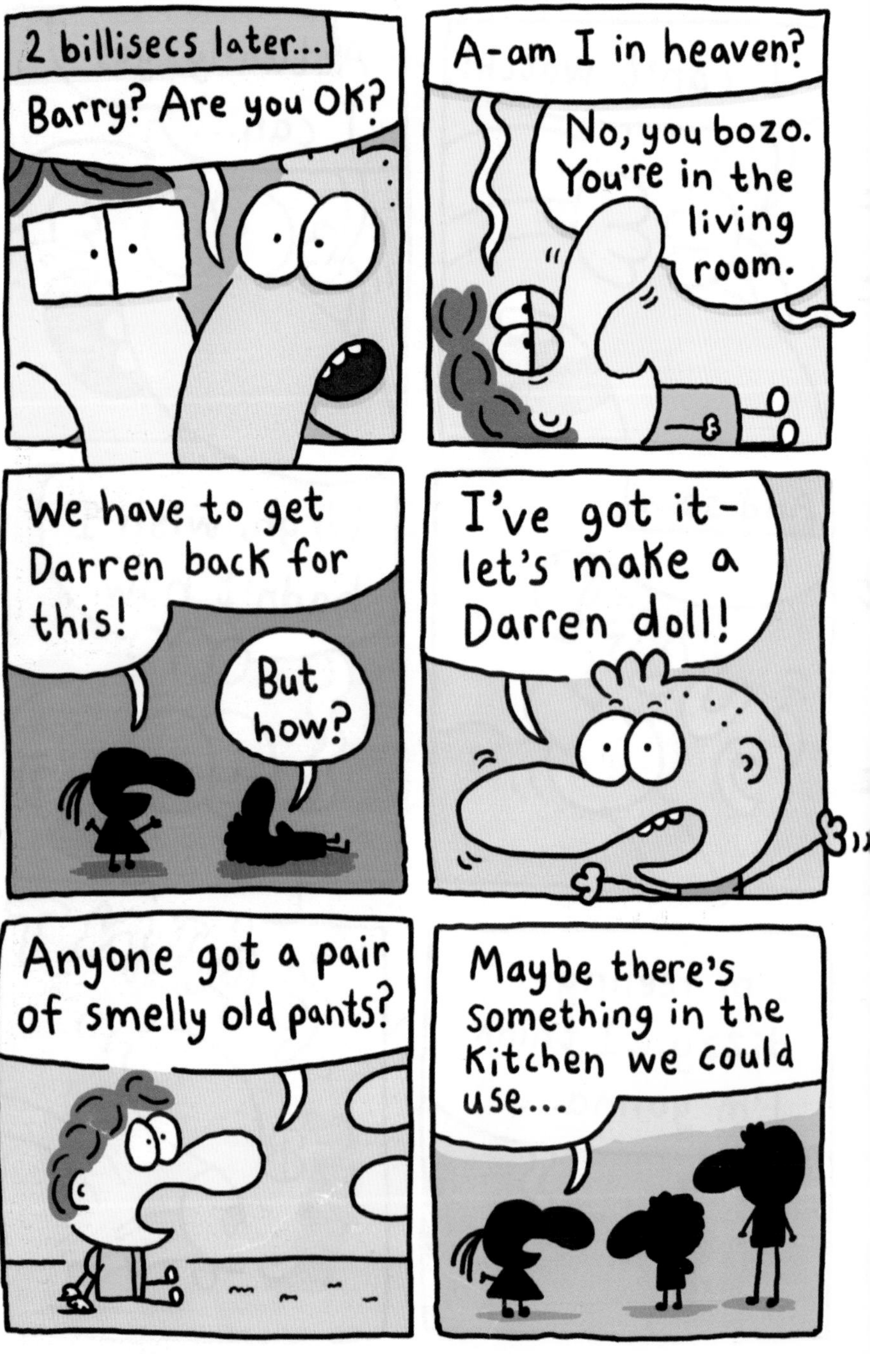
2 billisecs later...
Barry? Are you OK?
A-am I in heaven?
No, you bozo. You're in the living room.
We have to get Darren back for this!
But how?
I've got it - let's make a Darren doll!
Anyone got a pair of smelly old pants?
Maybe there's something in the kitchen we could use...

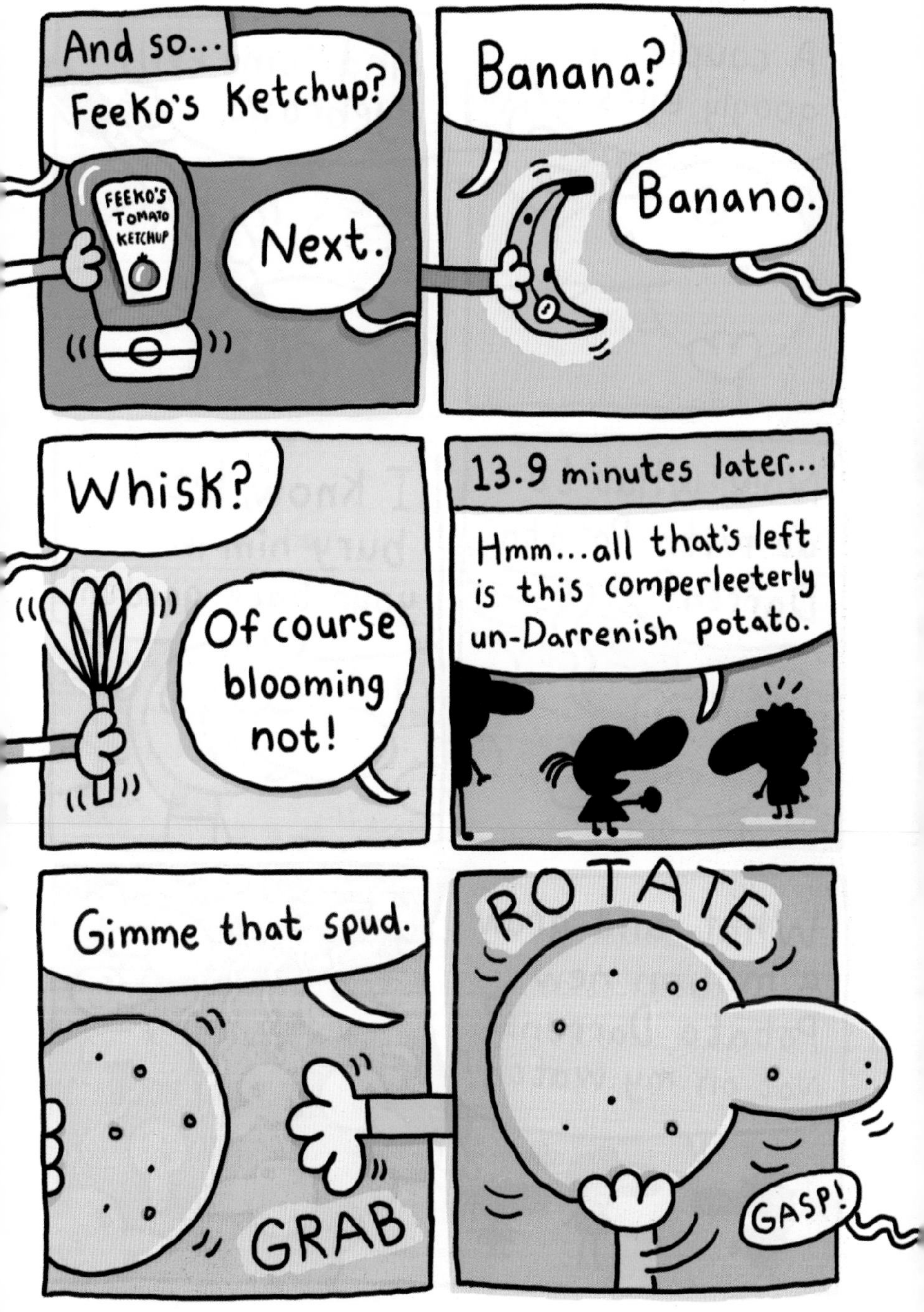
And so...
Feeko's Ketchup?
FEEKO'S TOMATO KETCHUP
Next.
Banana?
Banano.
Whisk?
Of course blooming not!
13.9 minutes later...
Hmm...all that's left is this comperleeterly un-Darrenish potato.
Gimme that spud.
GRAB
ROTATE
GASP!

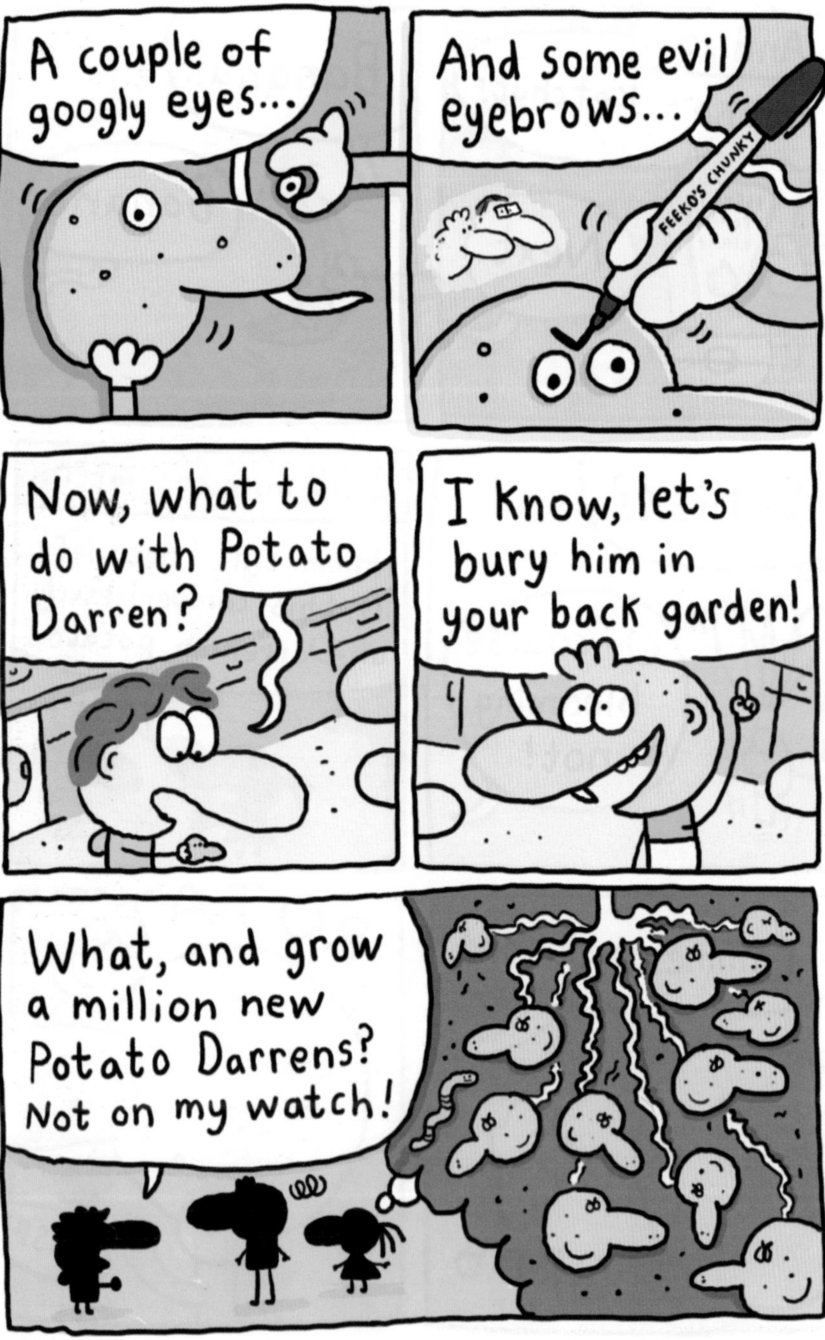
A couple of googly eyes...
And some evil eyebrows...
FEEKO'S CHUNKY
Now, what to do with Potato Darren?
I know, let's bury him in your back garden!
What, and grow a million new Potato Darrens? Not on my watch!

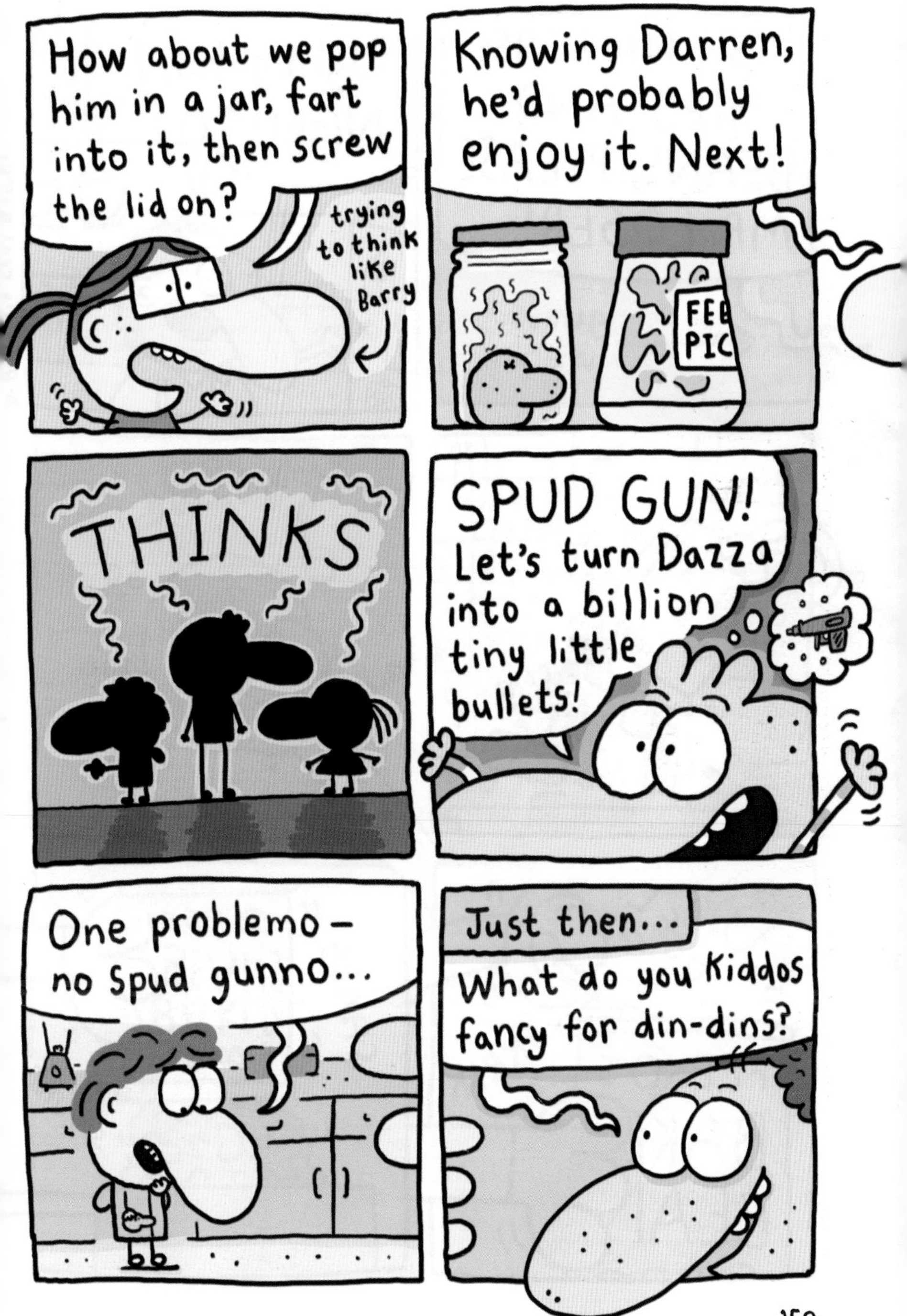
How about we pop him in a jar, fart into it, then screw the lid on?
trying to think like Barry
Knowing Darren, he'd probably enjoy it. Next!
FEE PIC
THINKS
SPUD GUN! Let's turn Dazza into a billion tiny little bullets!
One problemo – no spud gunno...
Just then...
What do you kiddos fancy for din-dins?

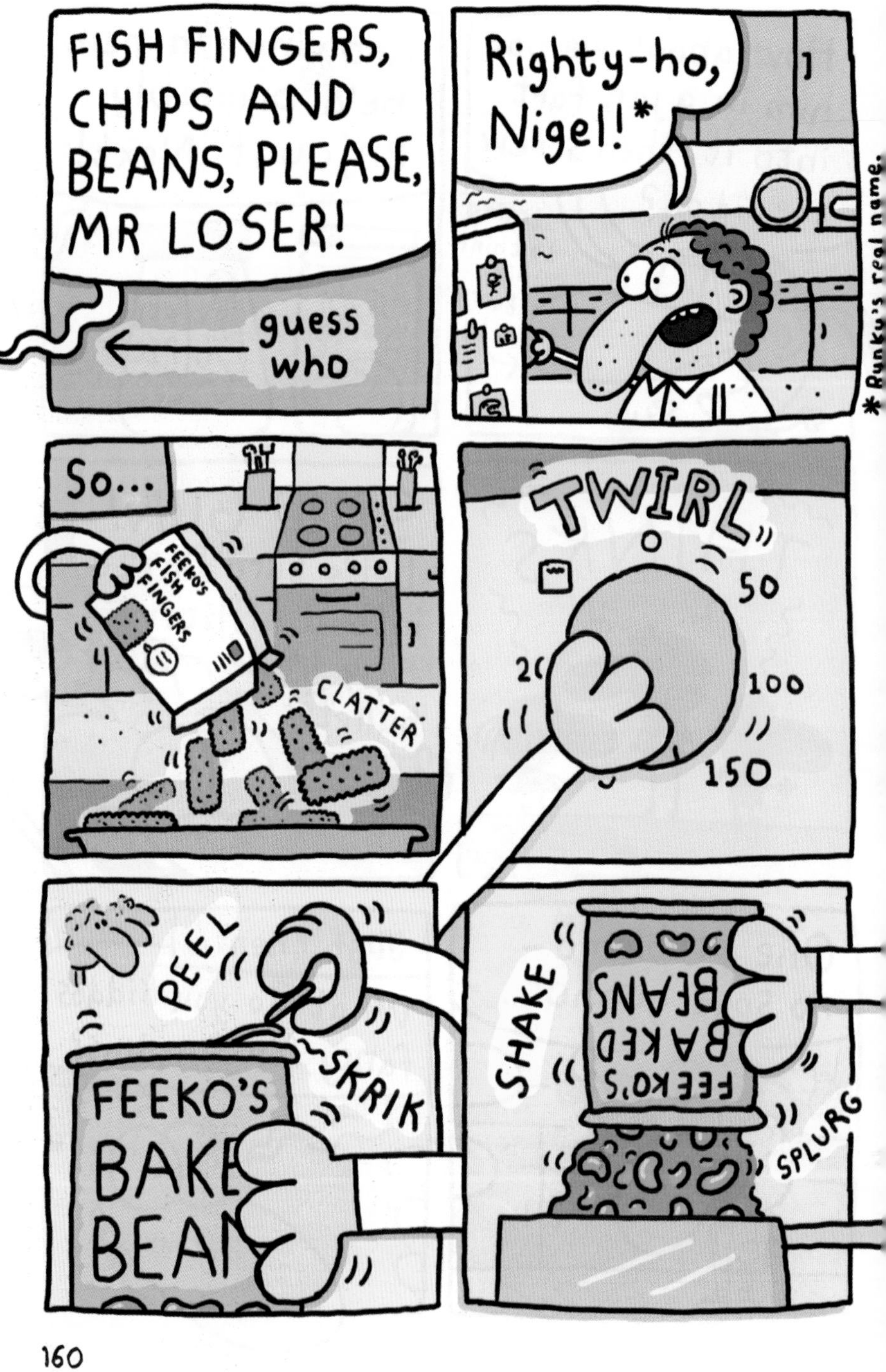
FISH FINGERS, CHIPS AND BEANS, PLEASE, MR LOSER!
guess who
Righty-ho, Nigel!*
* Runku's real name.
So...
FEEKO'S FISH FINGERS
CLATTER
TWIRL
50
100
150
PEEL
SKRIK
FEEKO'S BAKE BEA
SHAKE
FEEKO'S BAKED BEANS
SPLURG

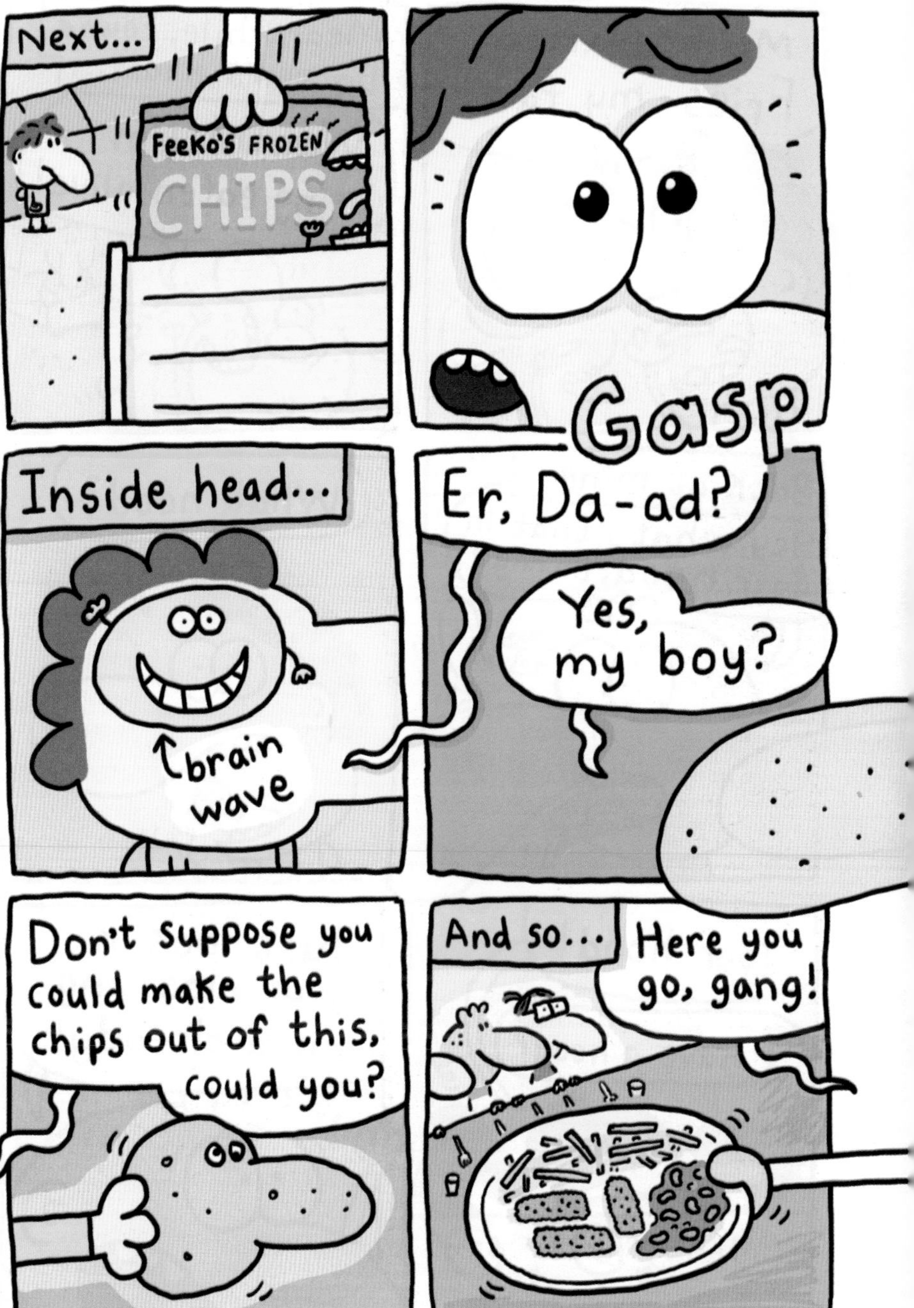
Next...
FeeKo'S FROZEN
CHIPS
Gasp
Inside head...
brain wave
Er, Da-ad?
Yes, my boy?
Don't suppose you could make the chips out of this, could you?
And so...
Here you go, gang!

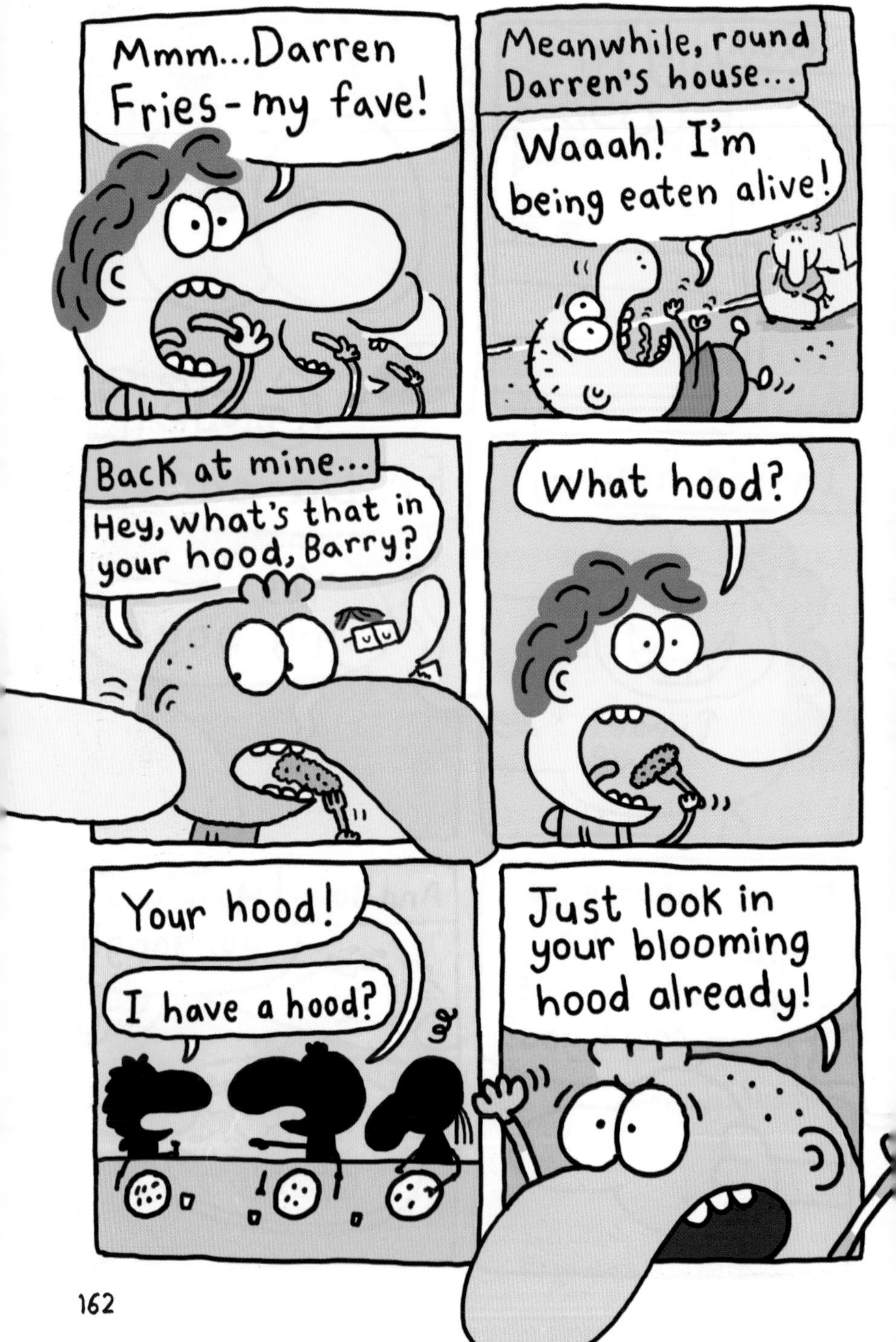
Mmm...Darren Fries-my fave!
Meanwhile, round Darren's house...
Waaah! I'm being eaten alive!
Back at mine...
Hey, what's that in your hood, Barry?
What hood?
Your hood!
I have a hood?
Just look in your blooming hood already!

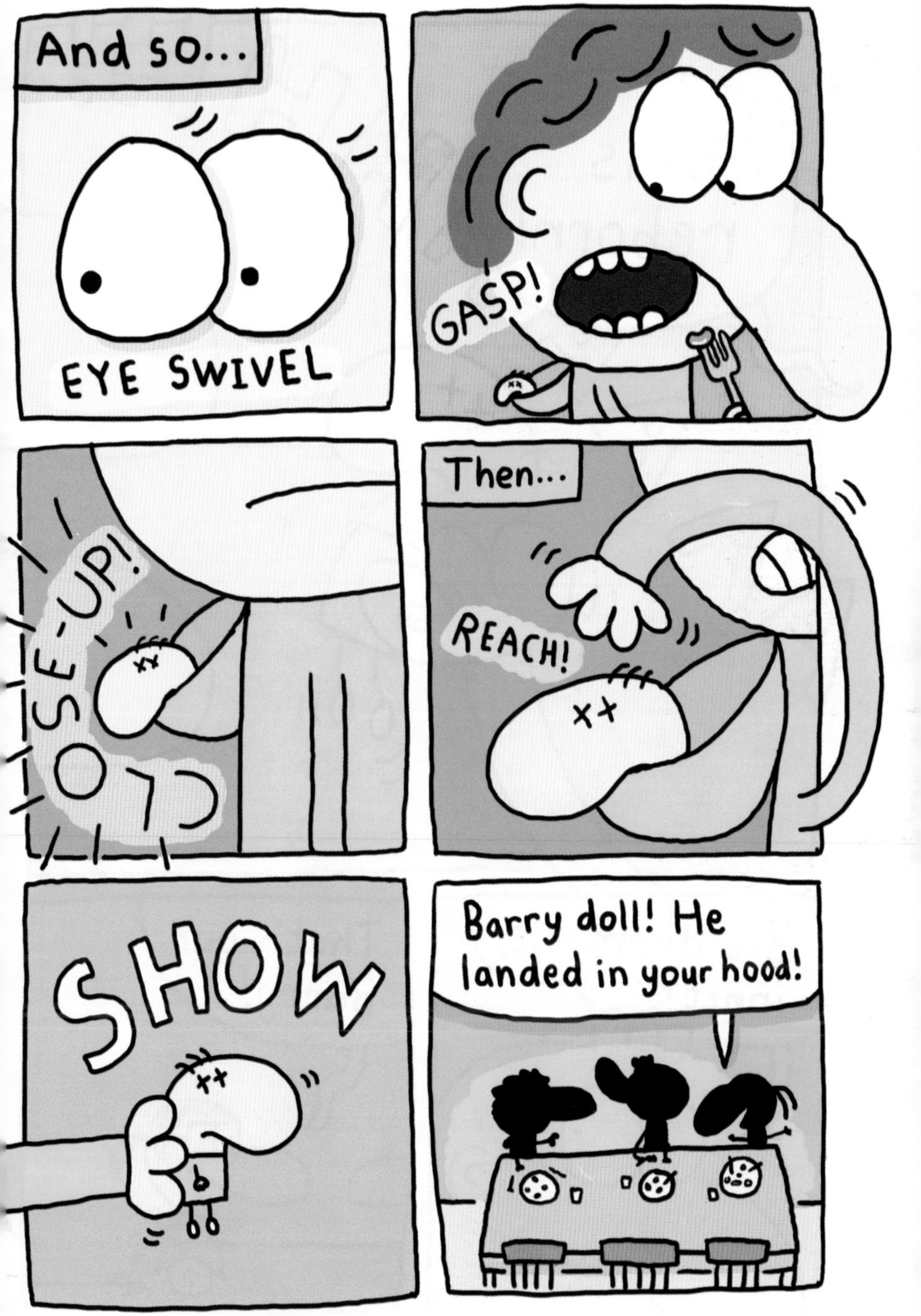
And so...
EYE SWIVEL
GASP!
CLOSE-UP!
Then...
REACH!
SHOW
Barry doll! He landed in your hood!

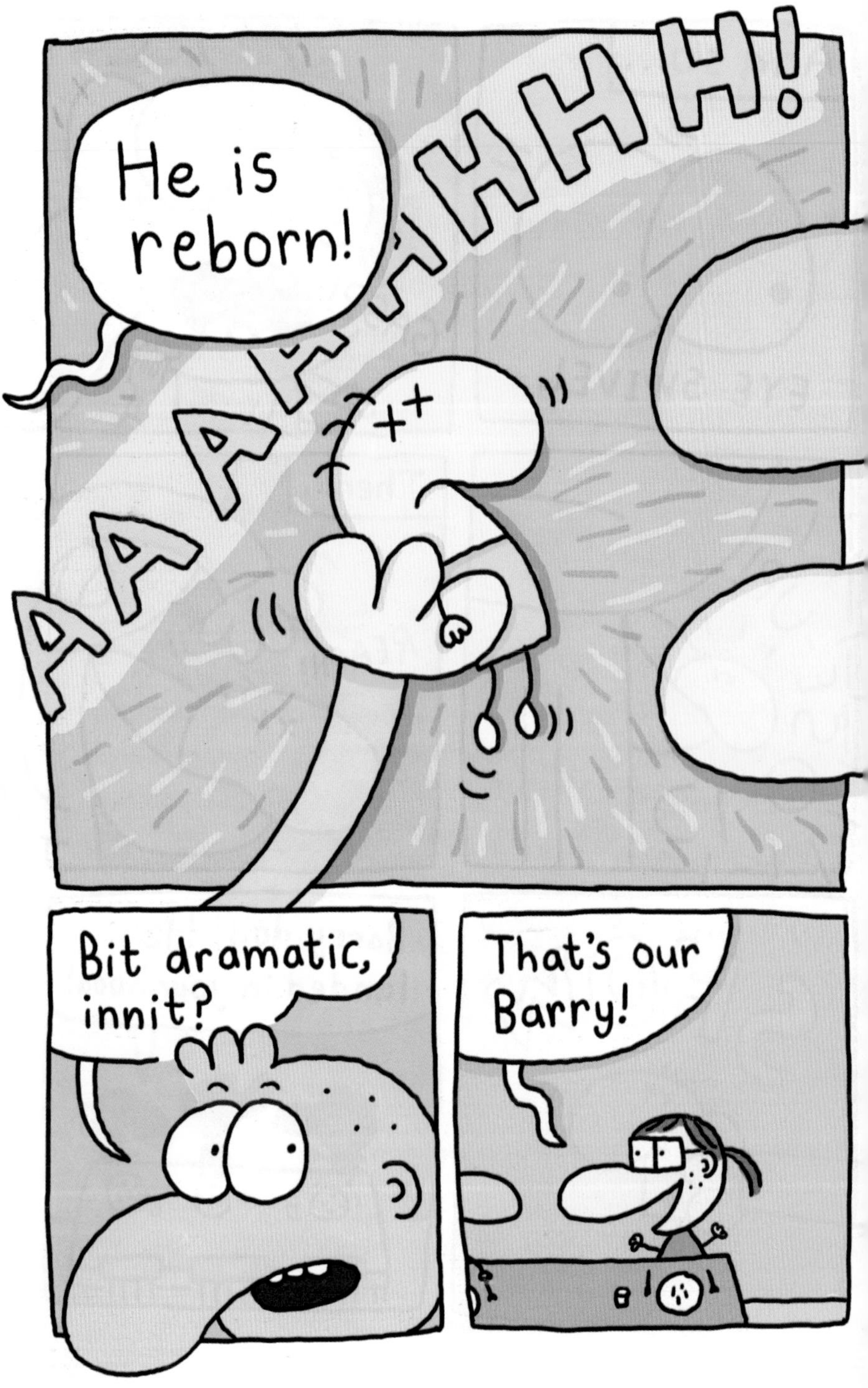
He is reborn!
AAAAAHHHHH!
Bit dramatic, innit?
That's our Barry!

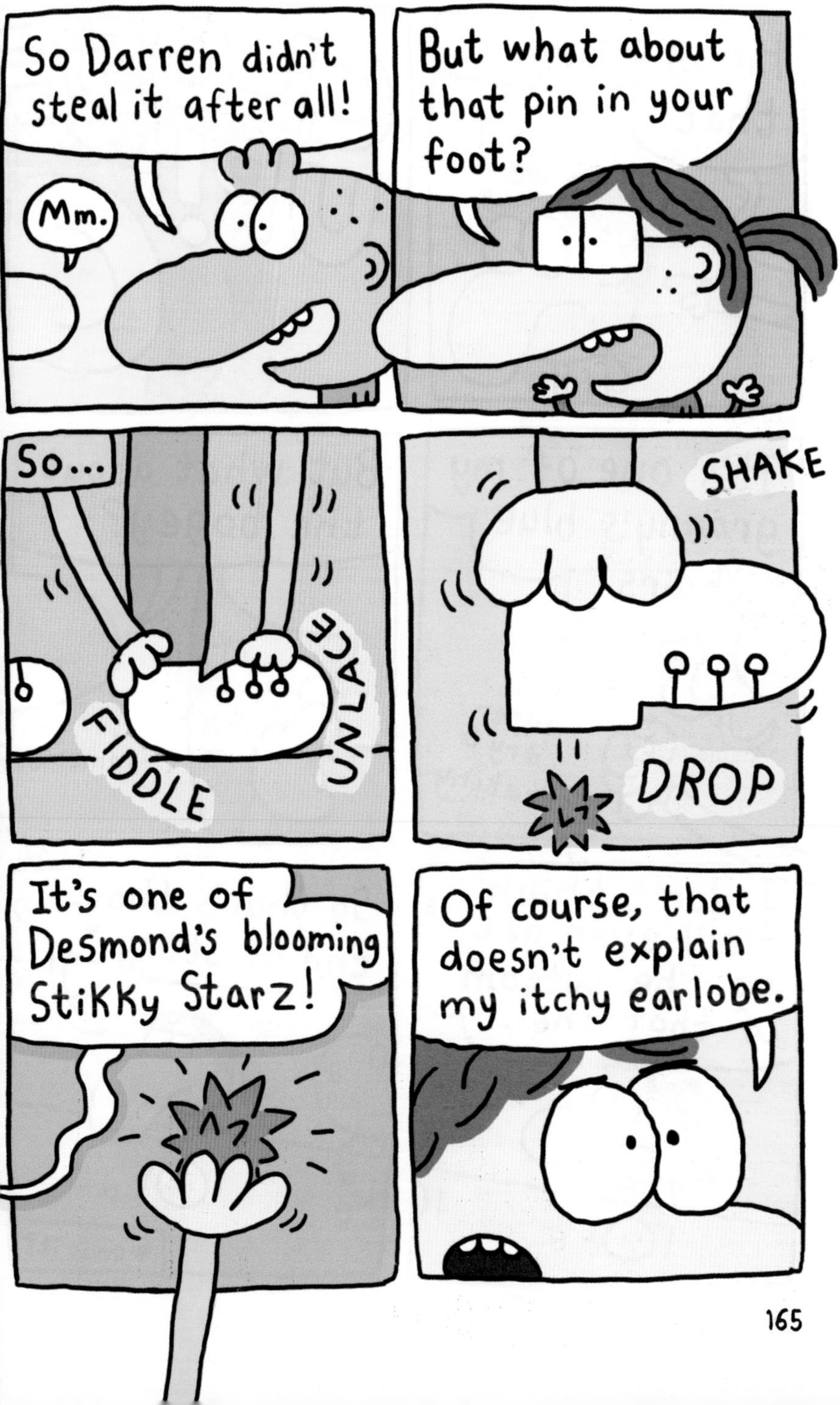
So Darren didn't steal it after all!
Mm.
But what about that pin in your foot?
So...
FIDDLE
UNLACE
SHAKE
DROP
It's one of Desmond's blooming StiKKy Starz!
Of course, that doesn't explain my itchy earlobe.

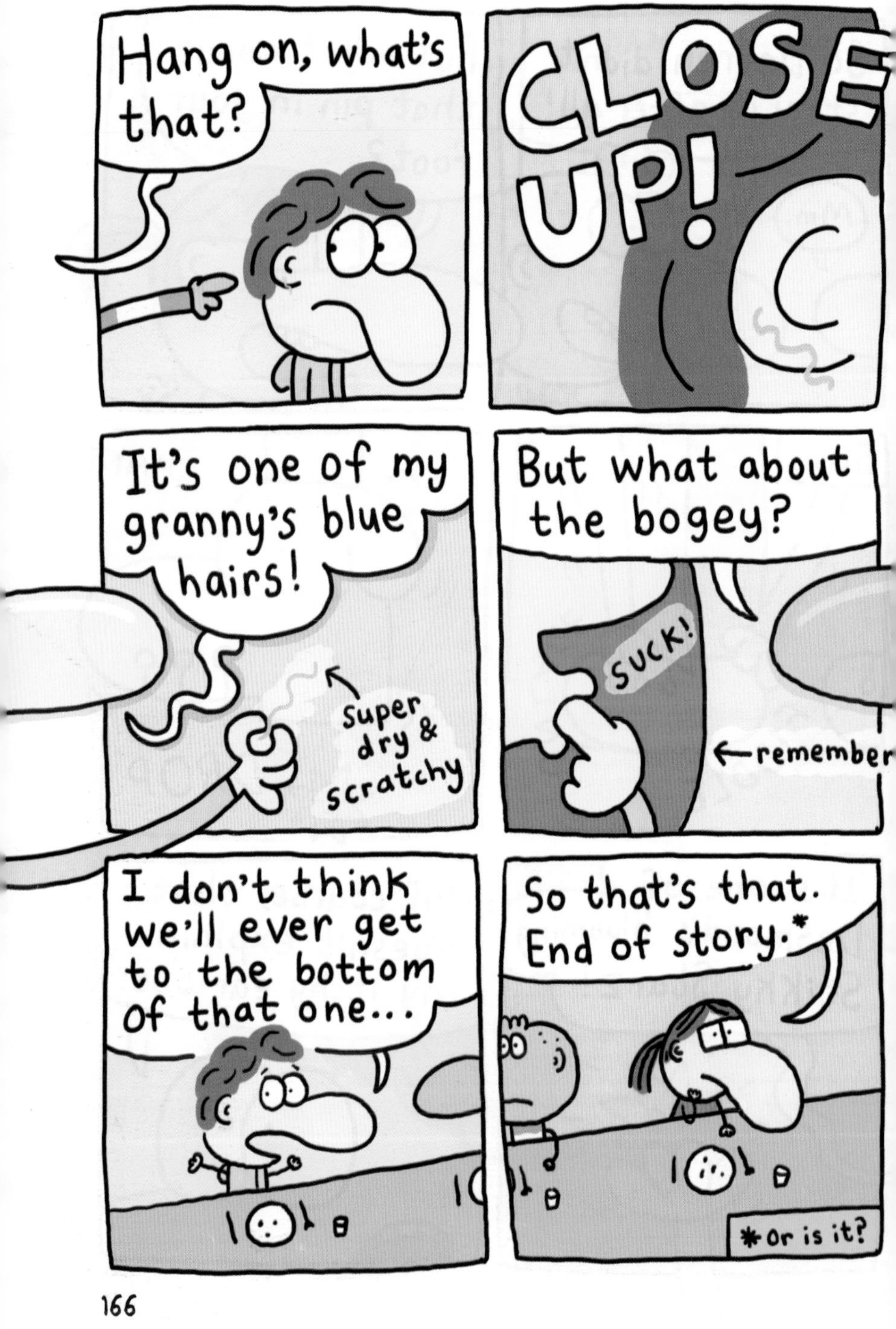

Hang on, what's that?
CLOSE UP!
It's one of my granny's blue hairs!
super dry & scratchy
But what about the bogey?
SUCK!
←remember
I don't think we'll ever get to the bottom of that one...
So that's that. End of story.*
*or is it?

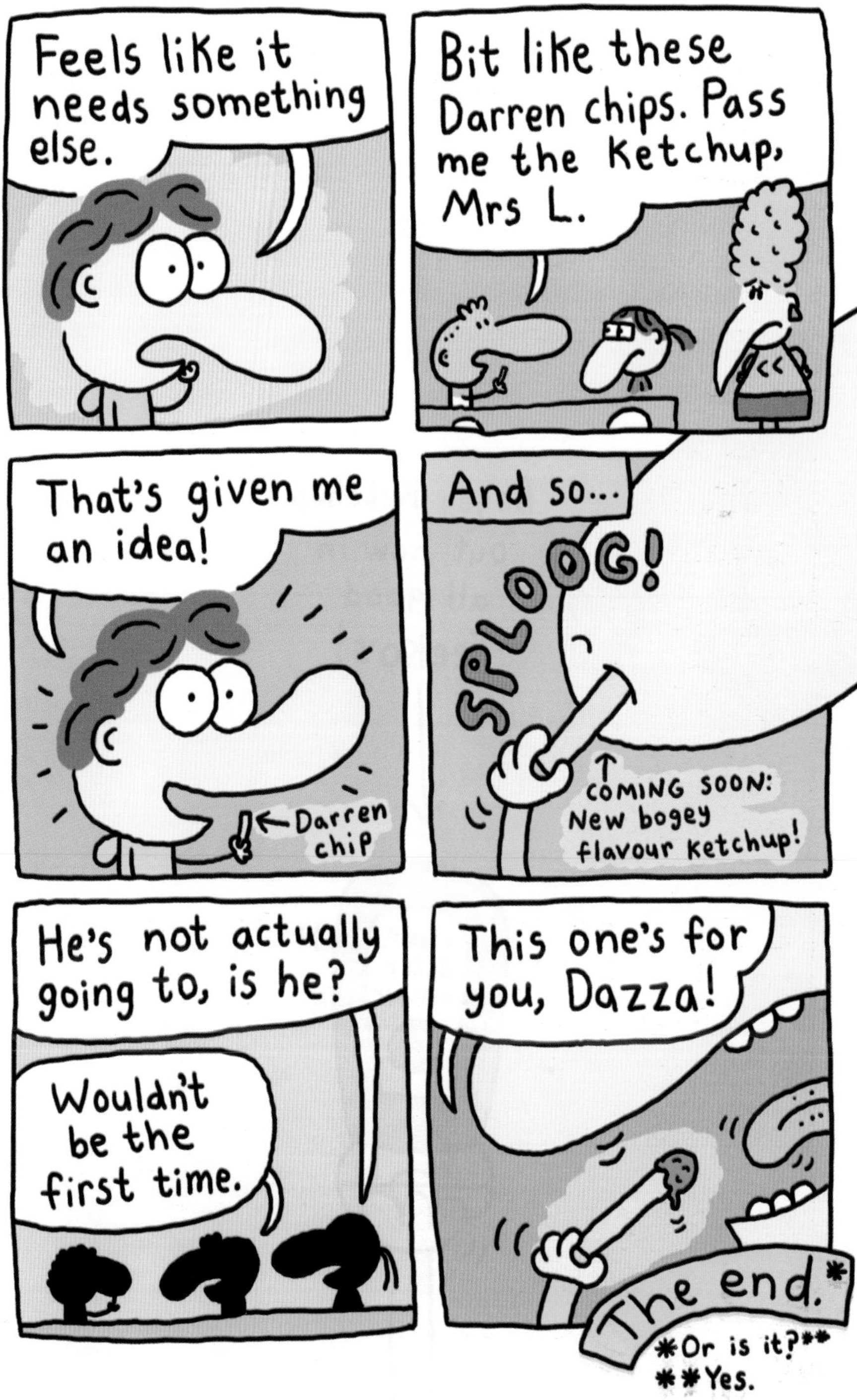

Feels like it needs something else.
Bit like these Darren chips. Pass me the ketchup, Mrs L.
That's given me an idea!
Darren chip
And so...
SPLOOG!
COMING SOON: New bogey flavour ketchup!
He's not actually going to, is he?
Wouldn't be the first time.
This one's for you, Dazza!
The end.*
*Or is it?**
**Yes.

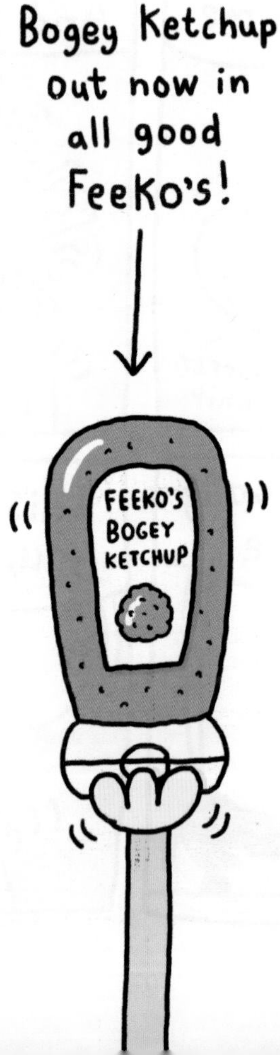
Bogey Ketchup out now in all good FeeKo's!
FEEKO'S BOGEY KETCHUP

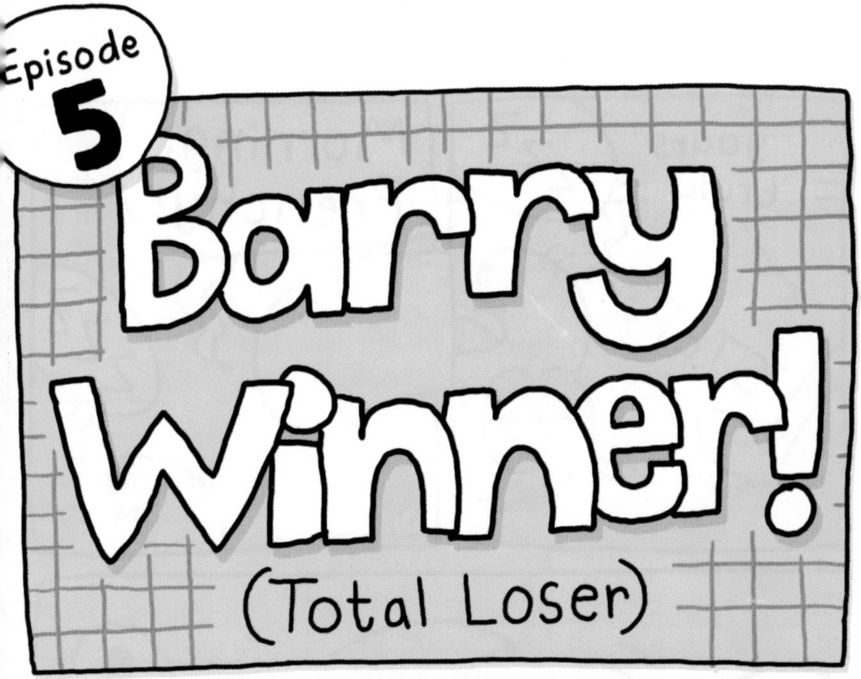
Episode
5
Barry Winner!
(Total Loser)

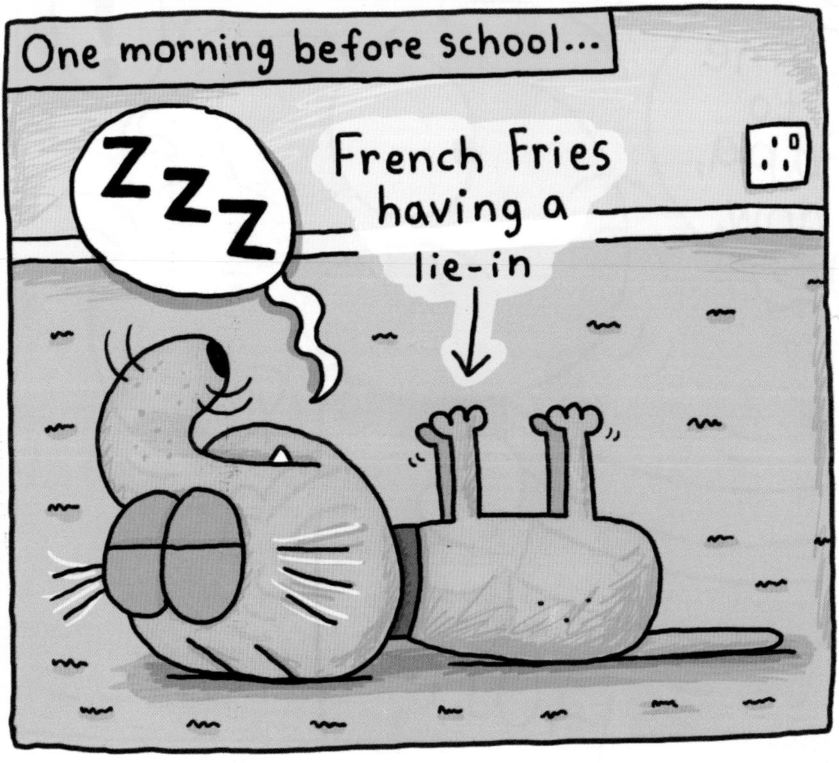
One morning before school...
ZZZ
French Fries having a lie-in

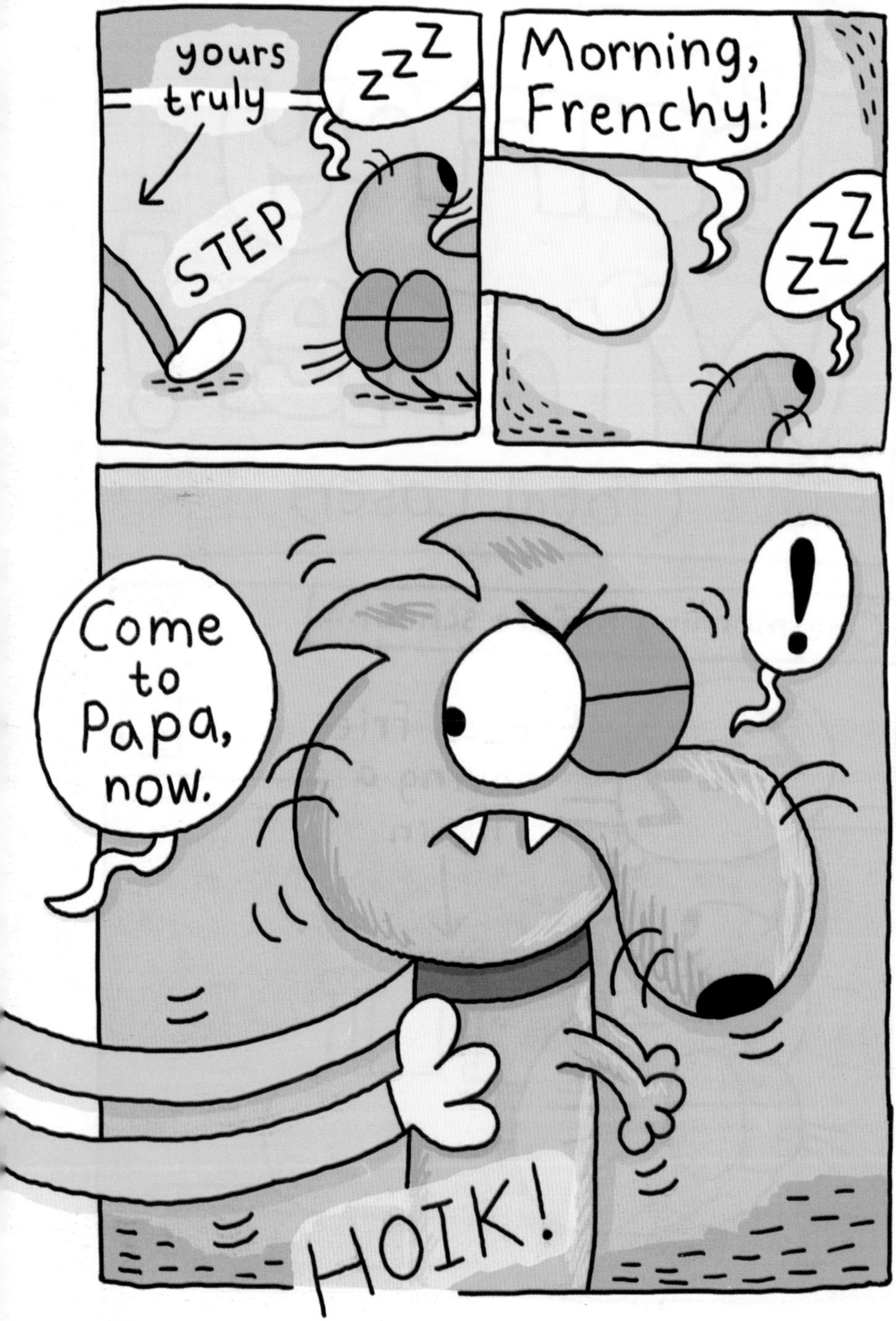
yours truly
zzZ
STEP
Morning, Frenchy!
zzZ
Come to Papa, now.
!
HOIK!

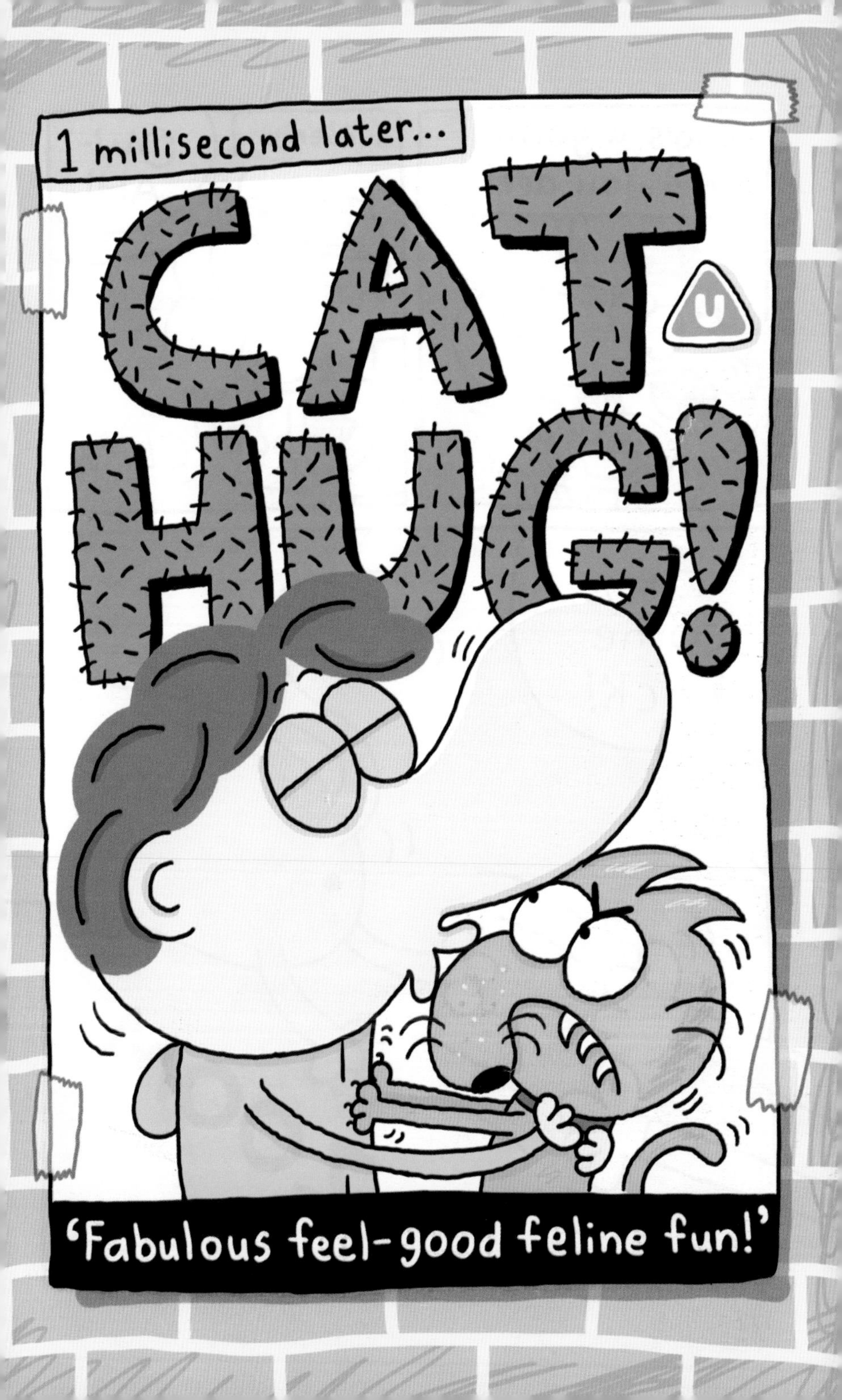
1 millisecond later...
CAT HUG!
U
'Fabulous feel-good feline fun!'

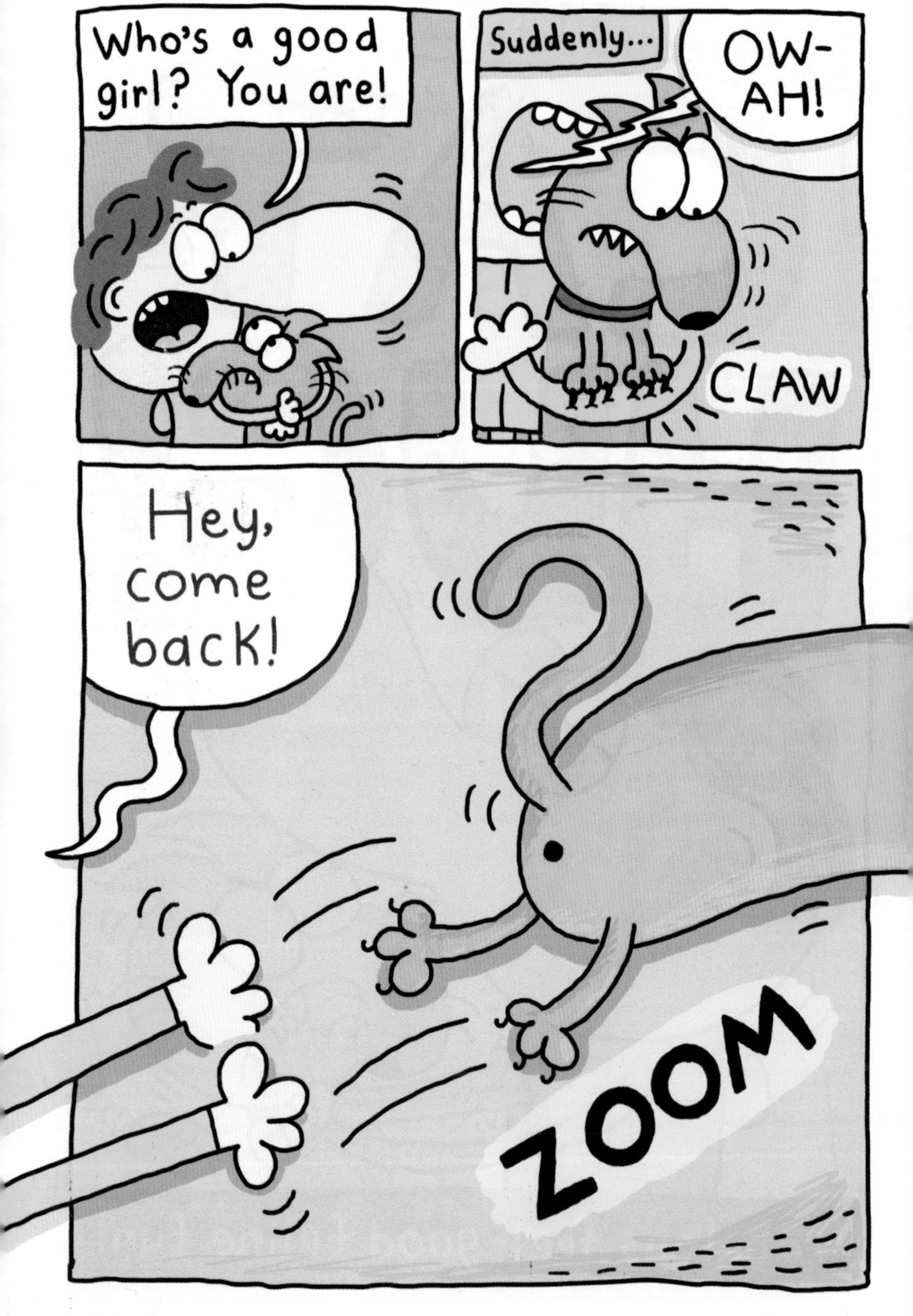
Who's a good girl? You are!
Suddenly...
OW-AH!
CLAW
Hey, come back!
ZOOM

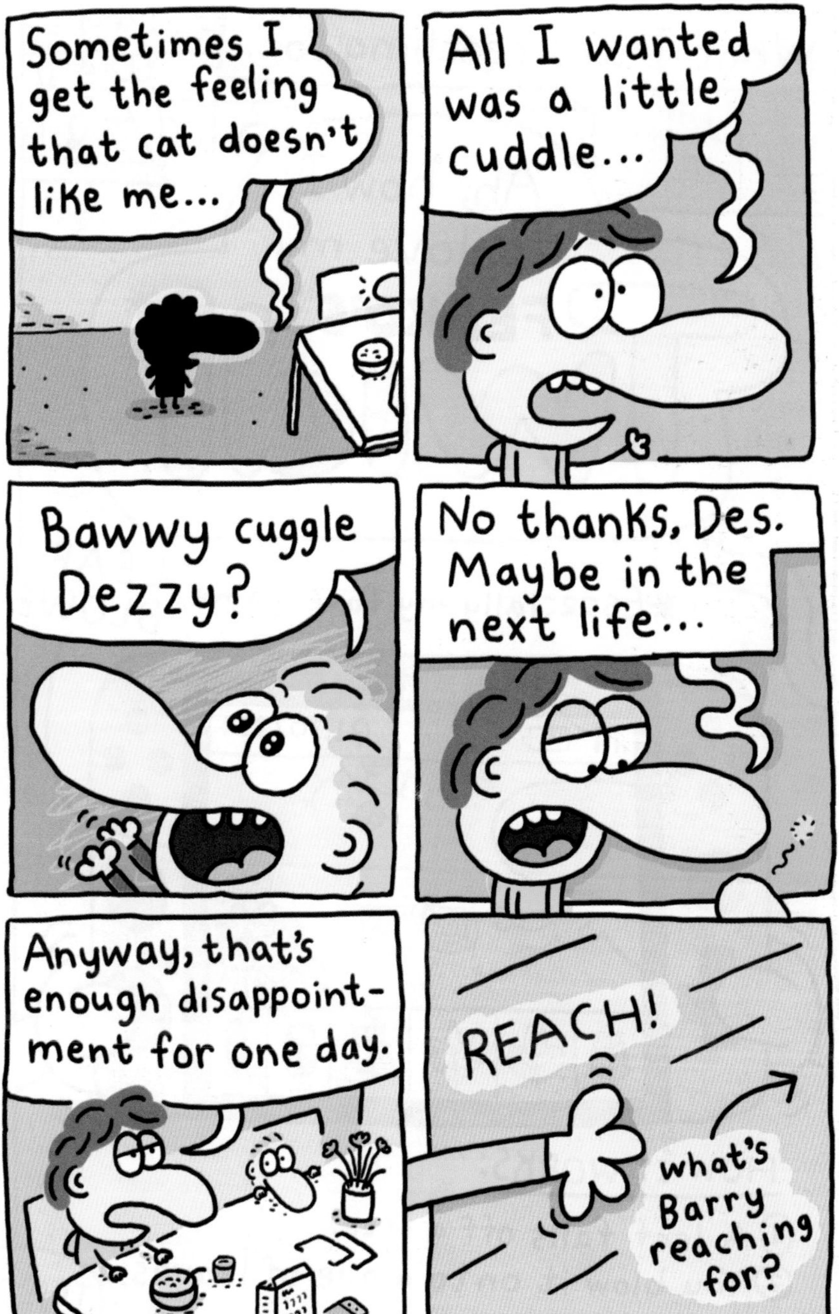
Sometimes I get the feeling that cat doesn't like me...
All I wanted was a little cuddle...
Bawwy cuggle Dezzy?
No thanks, Des. Maybe in the next life...
Anyway, that's enough disappointment for one day.
REACH!
what's Barry reaching for?

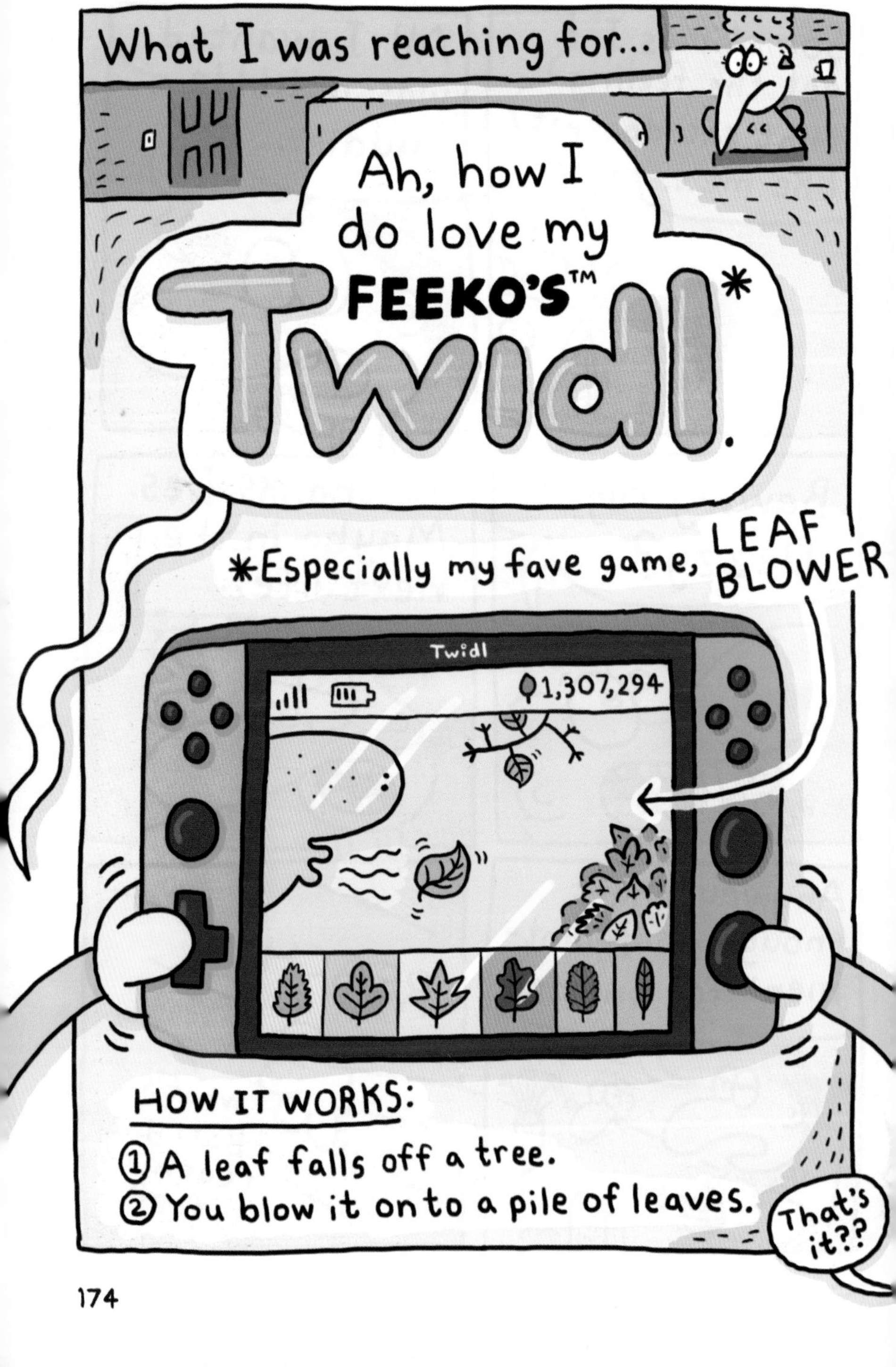
What I was reaching for...
Ah, how I do love my FEEKO'S™ Twidl.*
*Especially my fave game, LEAF BLOWER
Twidl
1,307,294
HOW IT WORKS:
① A leaf falls off a tree.
② You blow it on to a pile of leaves.
That's it??

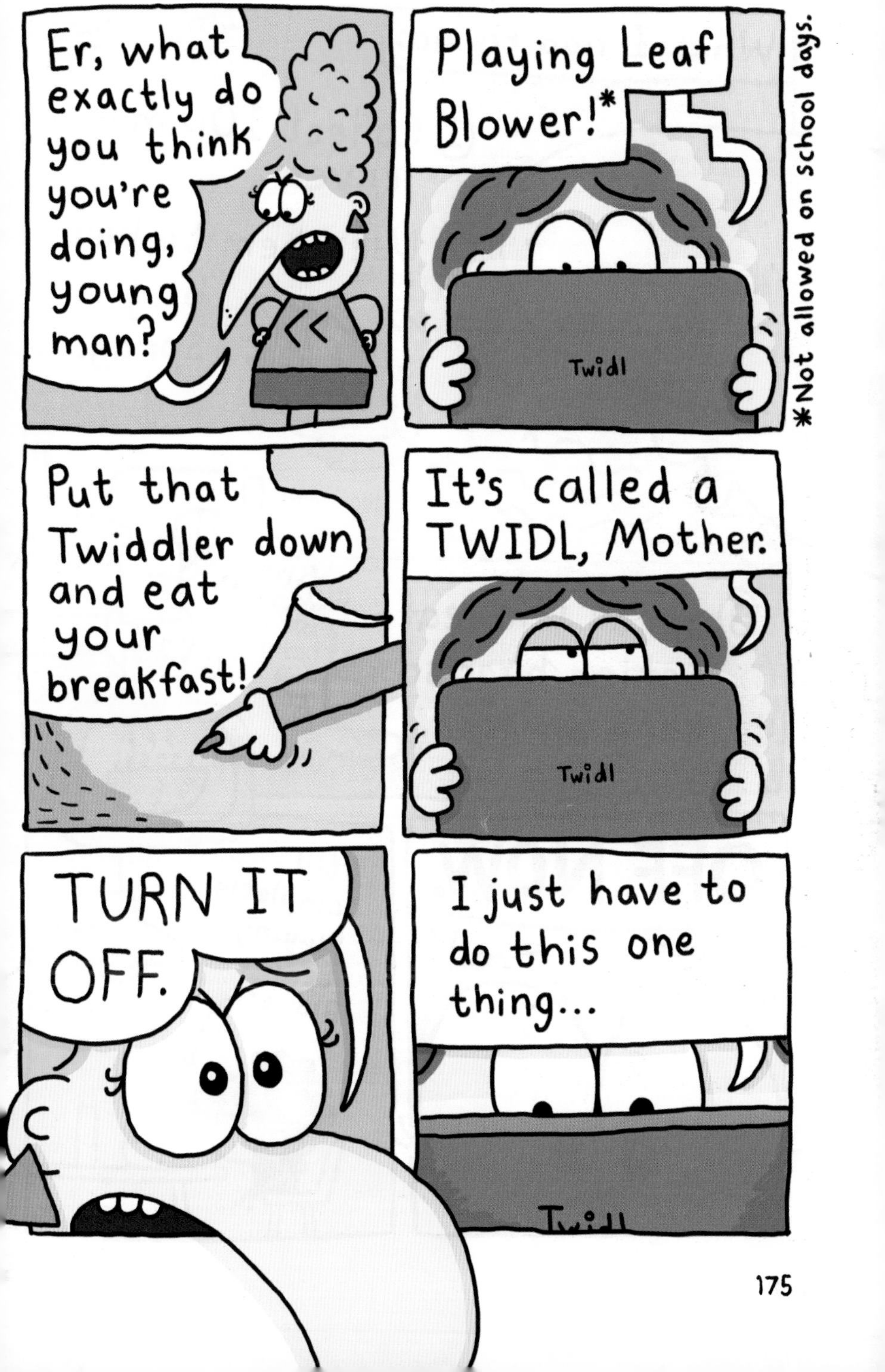
Er, what exactly do you think you're doing, young man?
Playing Leaf Blower!*
Twidl
*Not allowed on school days.
Put that Twiddler down and eat your breakfast!
It's called a TWIDL, Mother.
Twidl
TURN IT OFF.
I just have to do this one thing...

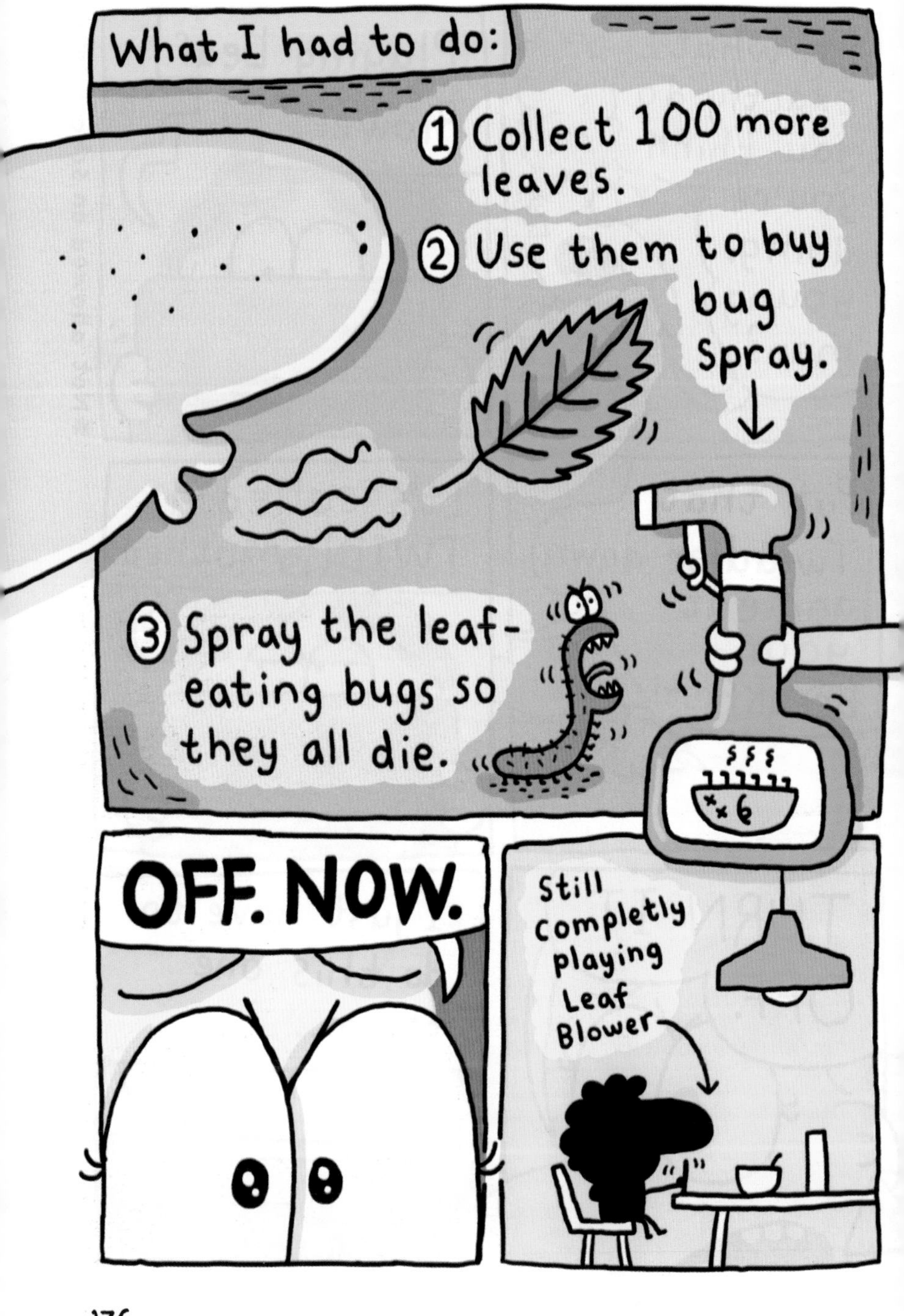
What I had to do:
1 Collect 100 more leaves.
2 Use them to buy bug spray.
3 Spray the leaf-eating bugs so they all die.
OFF. NOW.
Still completly playing Leaf Blower

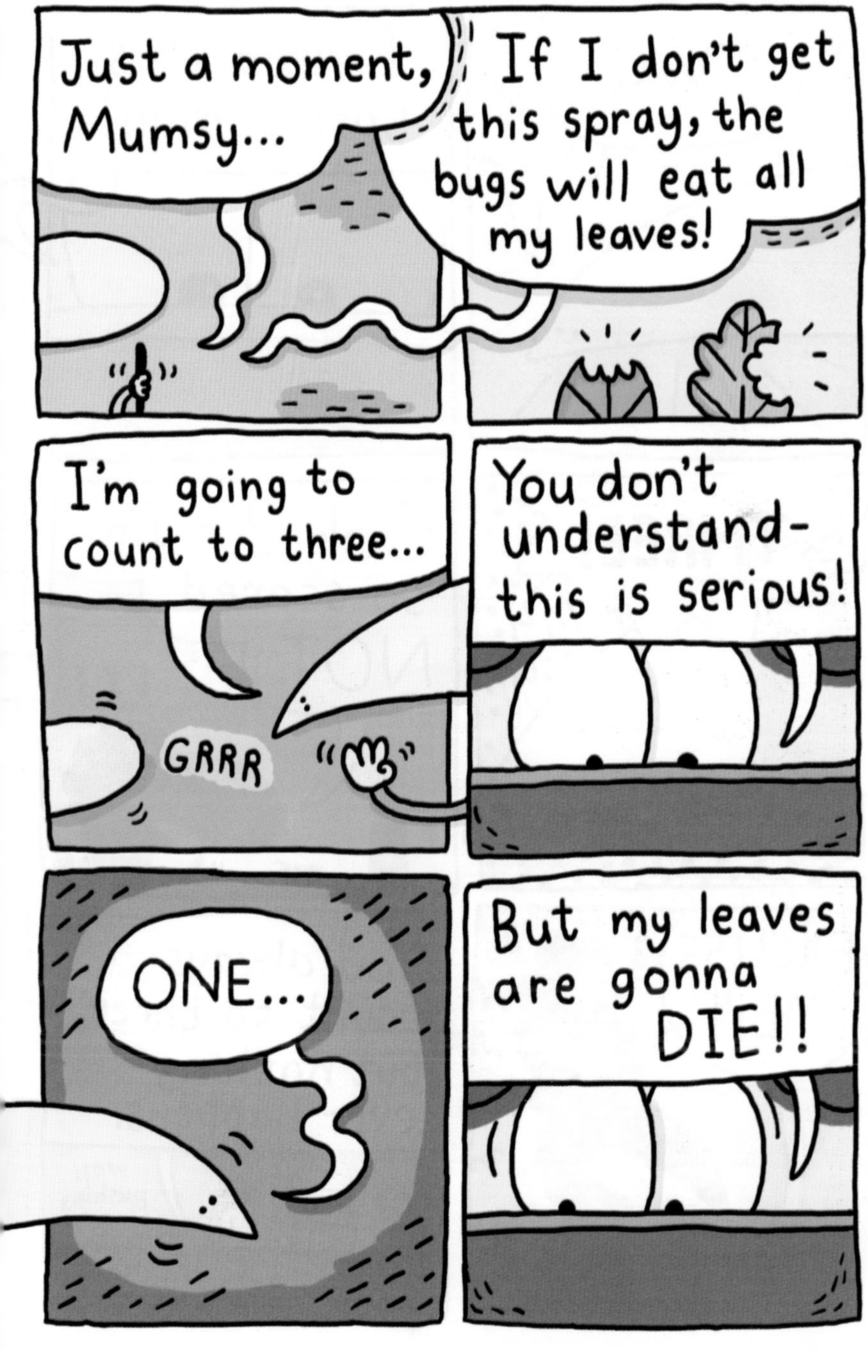
Just a moment, Mumsy...
If I don't get this spray, the bugs will eat all my leaves!
I'm going to count to three...
GRRR
You don't understand- this is serious!
ONE...
But my leaves are gonna DIE!!

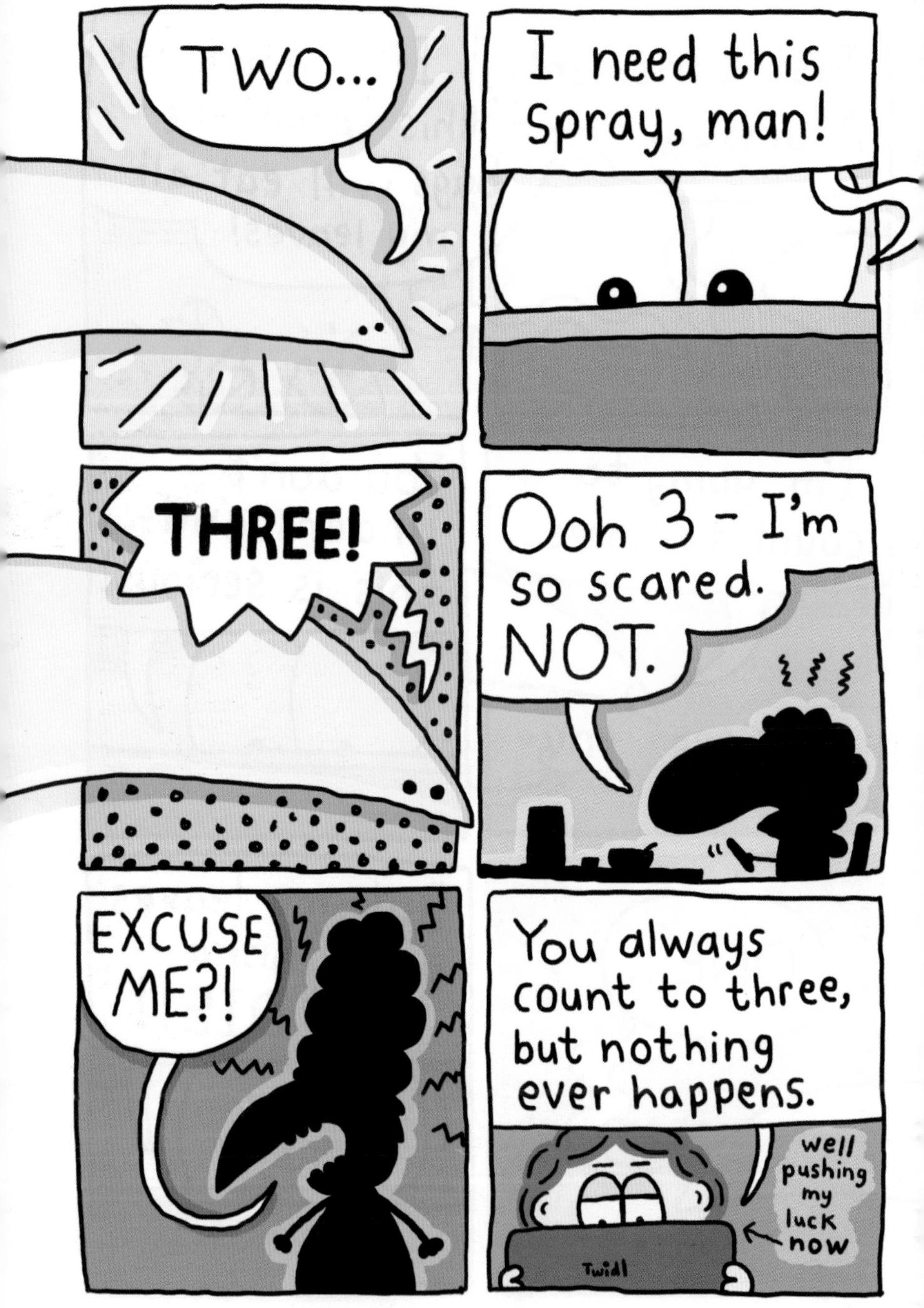
TWO...
I need this Spray, man!
THREE!
Ooh 3 - I'm so scared. NOT.
EXCUSE ME?!
You always count to three, but nothing ever happens.
well pushing my luck now
Twidl

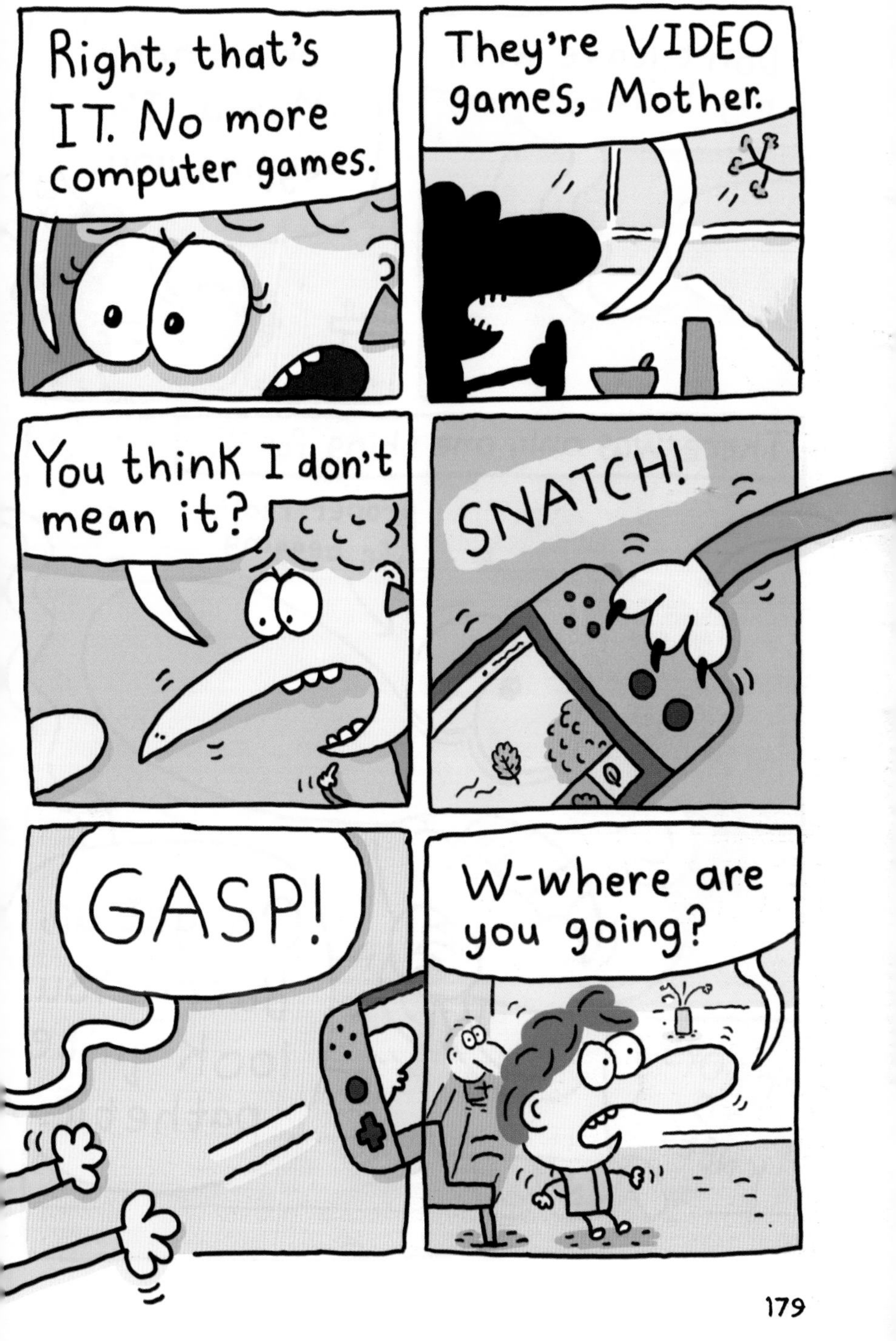
Right, that's IT. No more computer games.
They're VIDEO games, Mother.
You think I don't mean it?
SNATCH!
GASP!
W-where are you going?

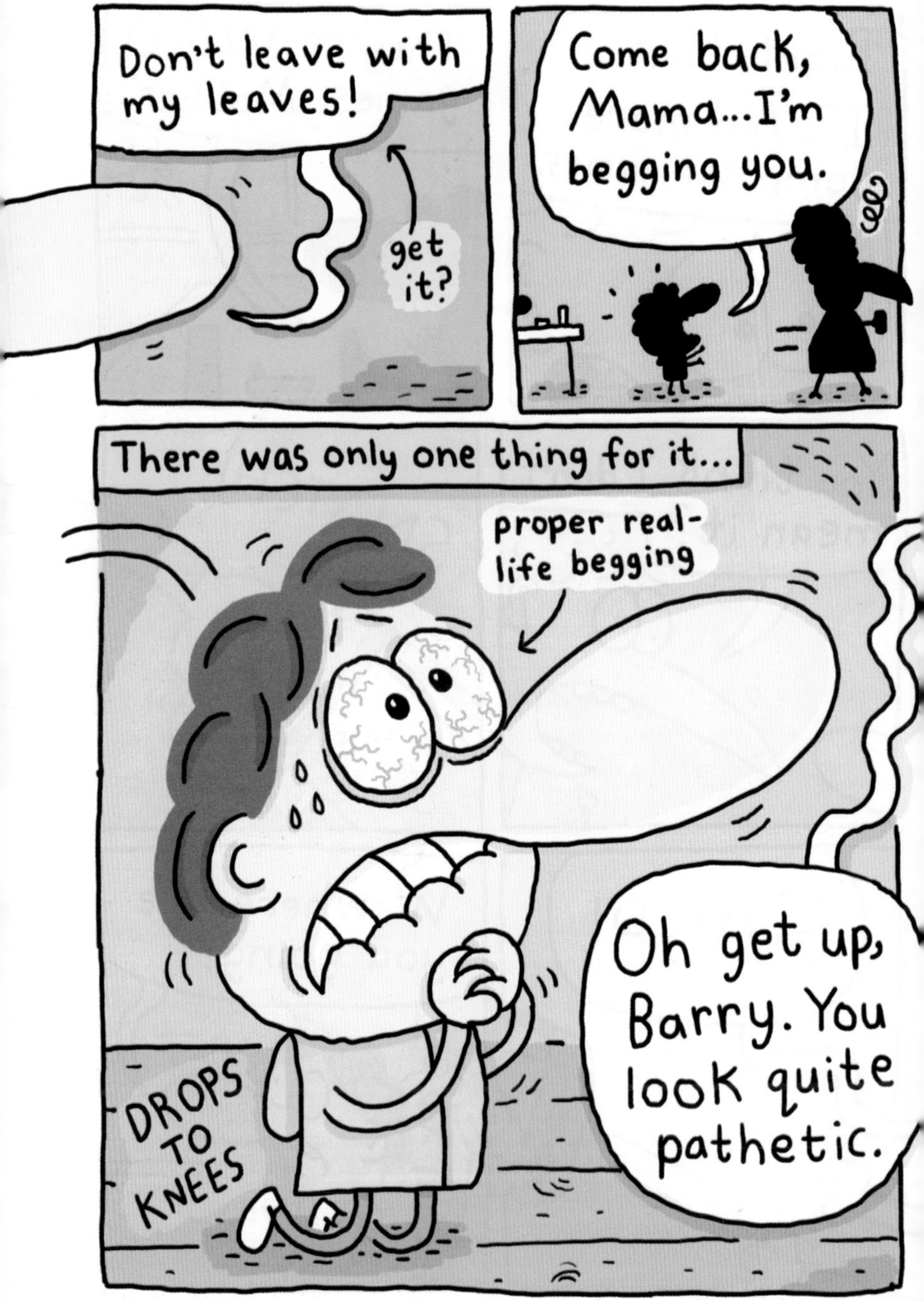

Don't leave with my leaves!
get it?
Come back, Mama...I'm begging you.
There was only one thing for it...
proper real-life begging
DROPS TO KNEES
Oh get up, Barry. You look quite pathetic.

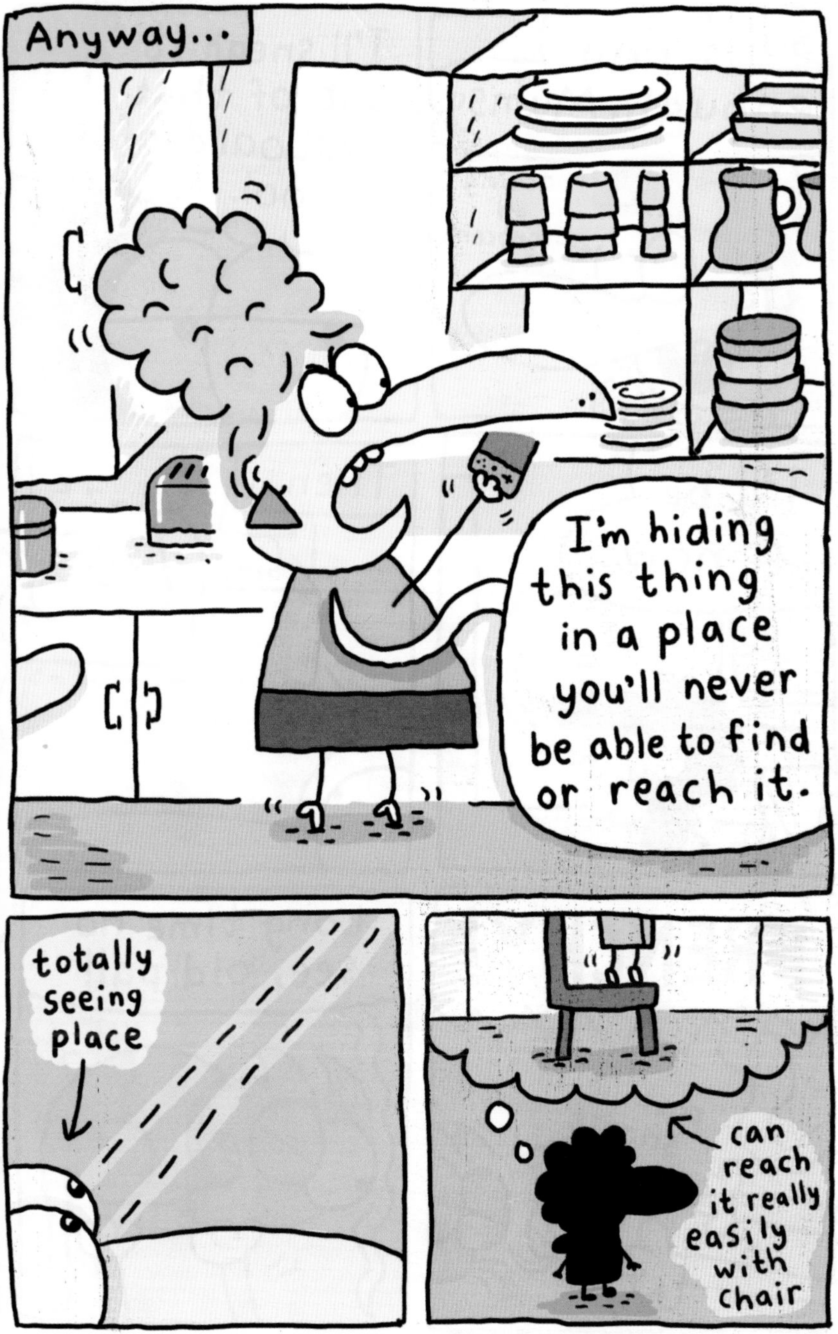
Anyway...
I'm hiding this thing in a place you'll never be able to find or reach it.
totally seeing place
can reach it really easily with chair

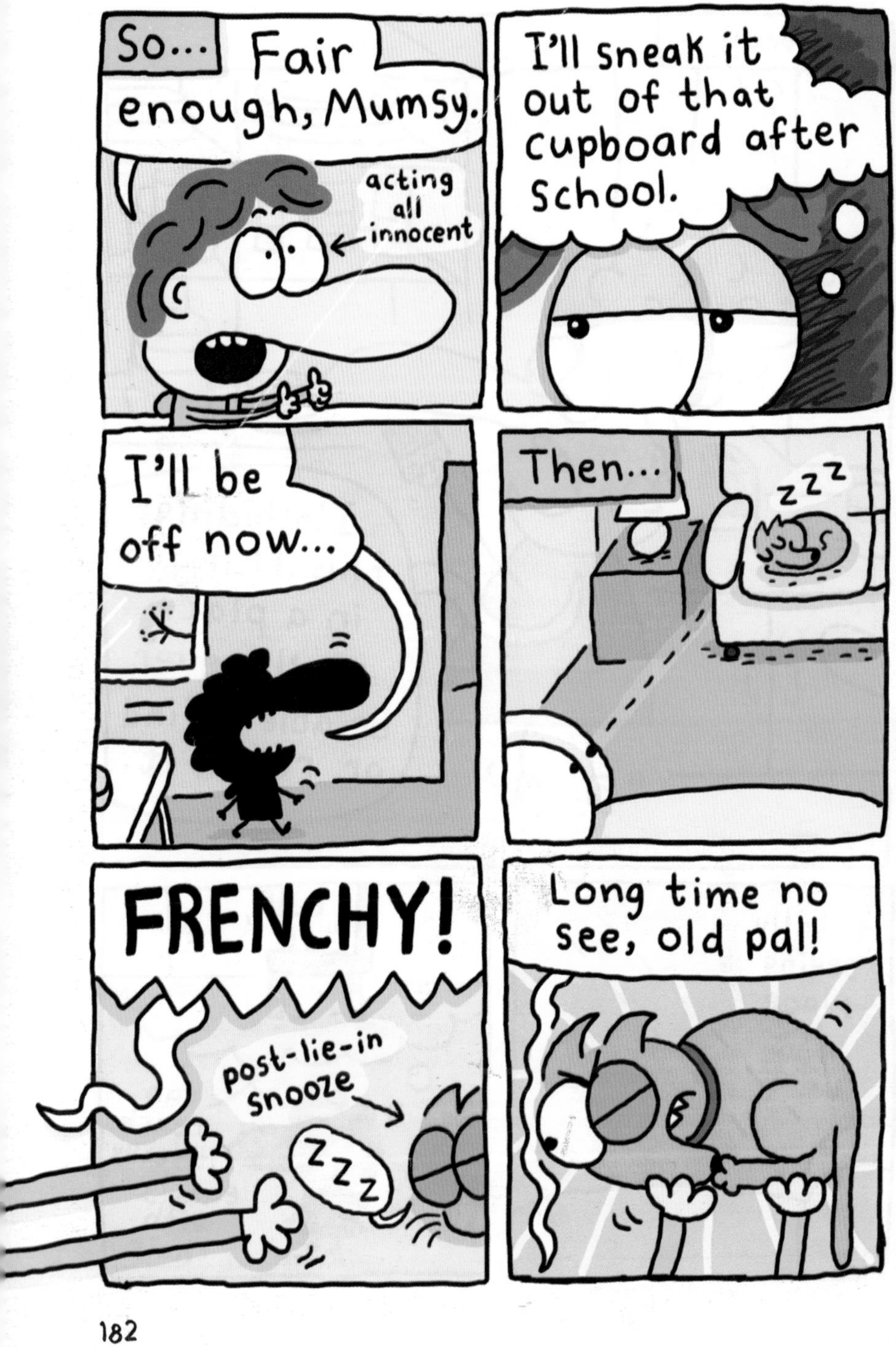
So...
Fair enough, Mumsy.
acting all innocent
I'll sneak it out of that cupboard after School.
I'll be off now...
Then...
zzz
FRENCHY!
post-lie-in snooze
ZZZ
Long time no see, old pal!

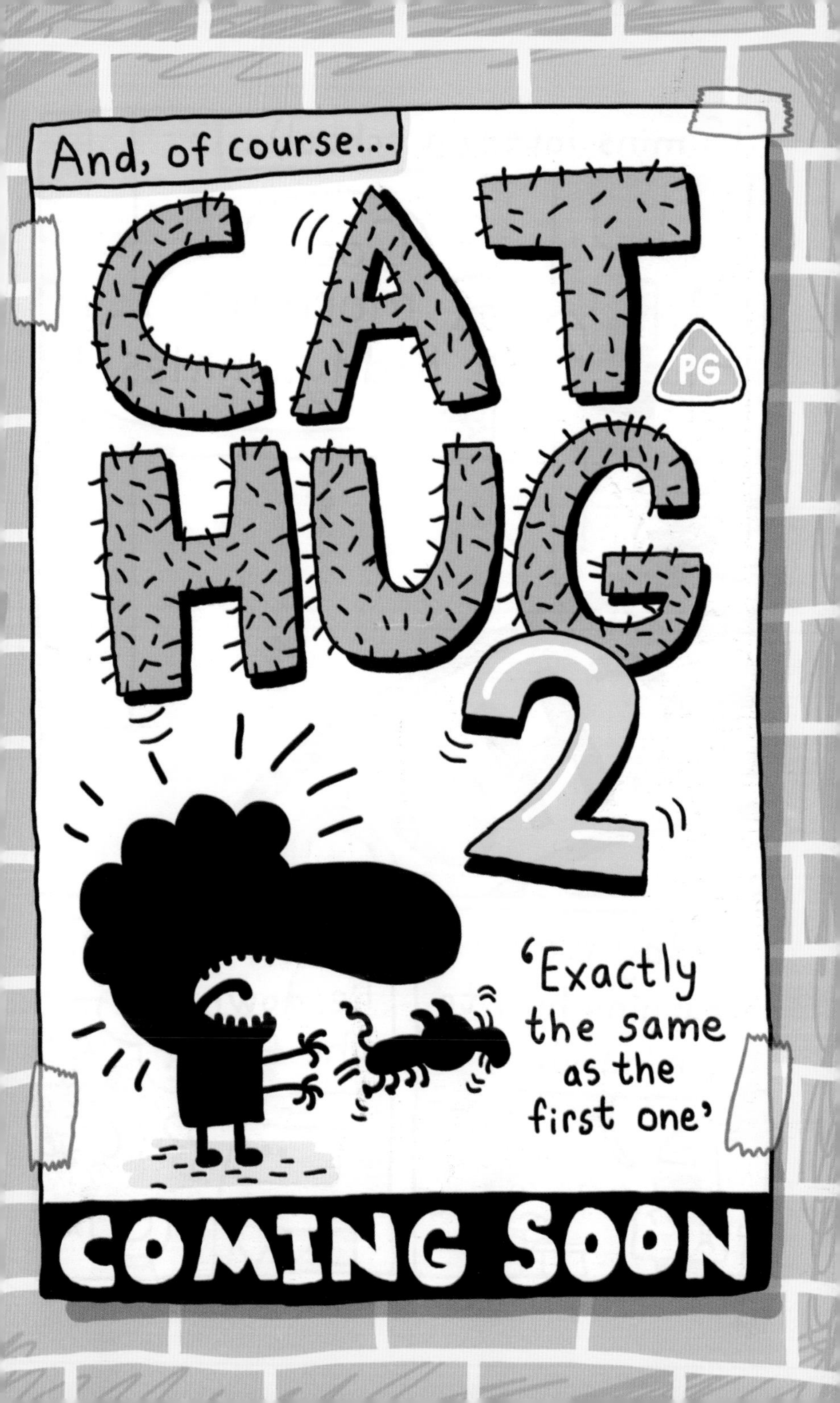
And, of course...
CAT HUG 2
PG
'Exactly the same as the first one'
COMING SOON

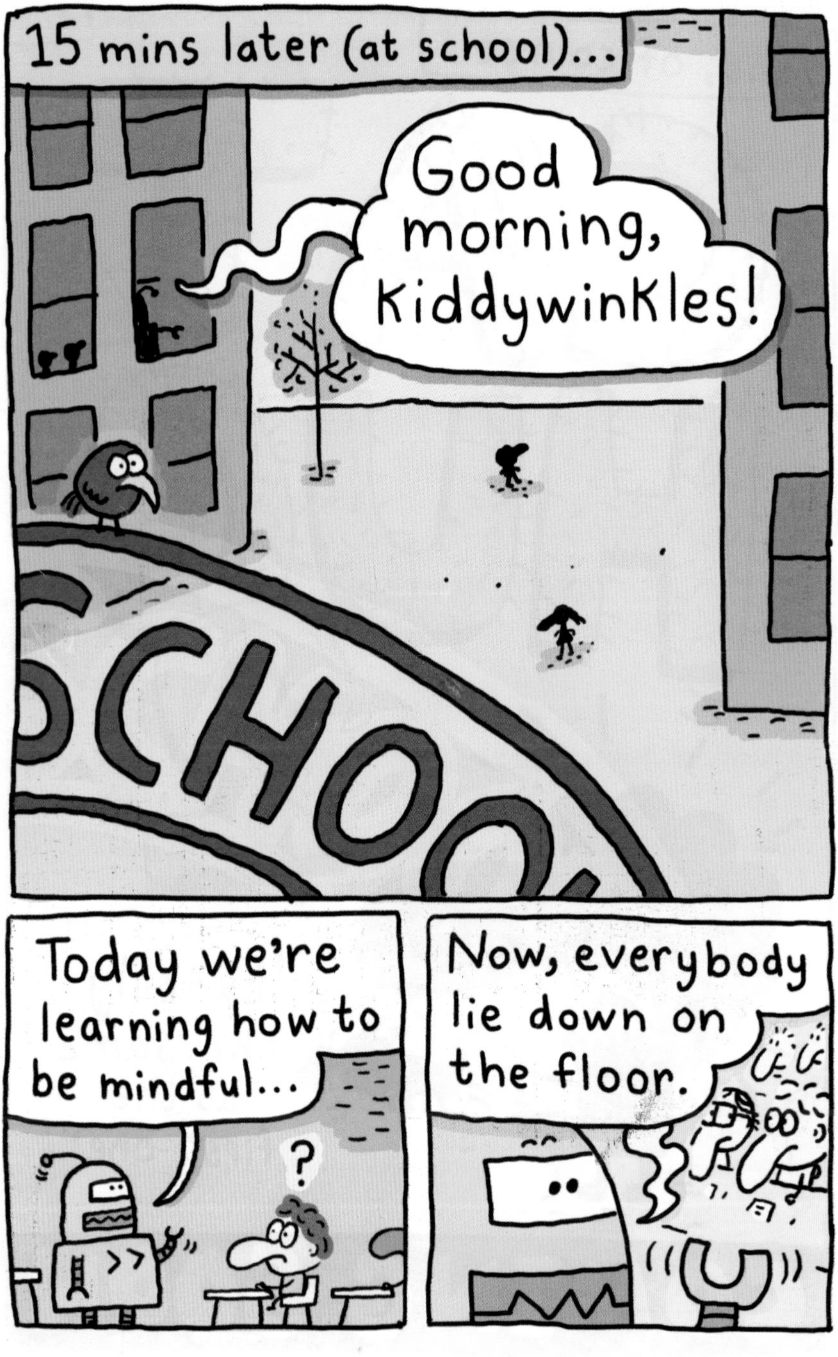
15 mins later (at school)...
Good morning, kiddywinkles!
SCHOO
Today we're learning how to be mindful...
?
Now, everybody lie down on the floor.

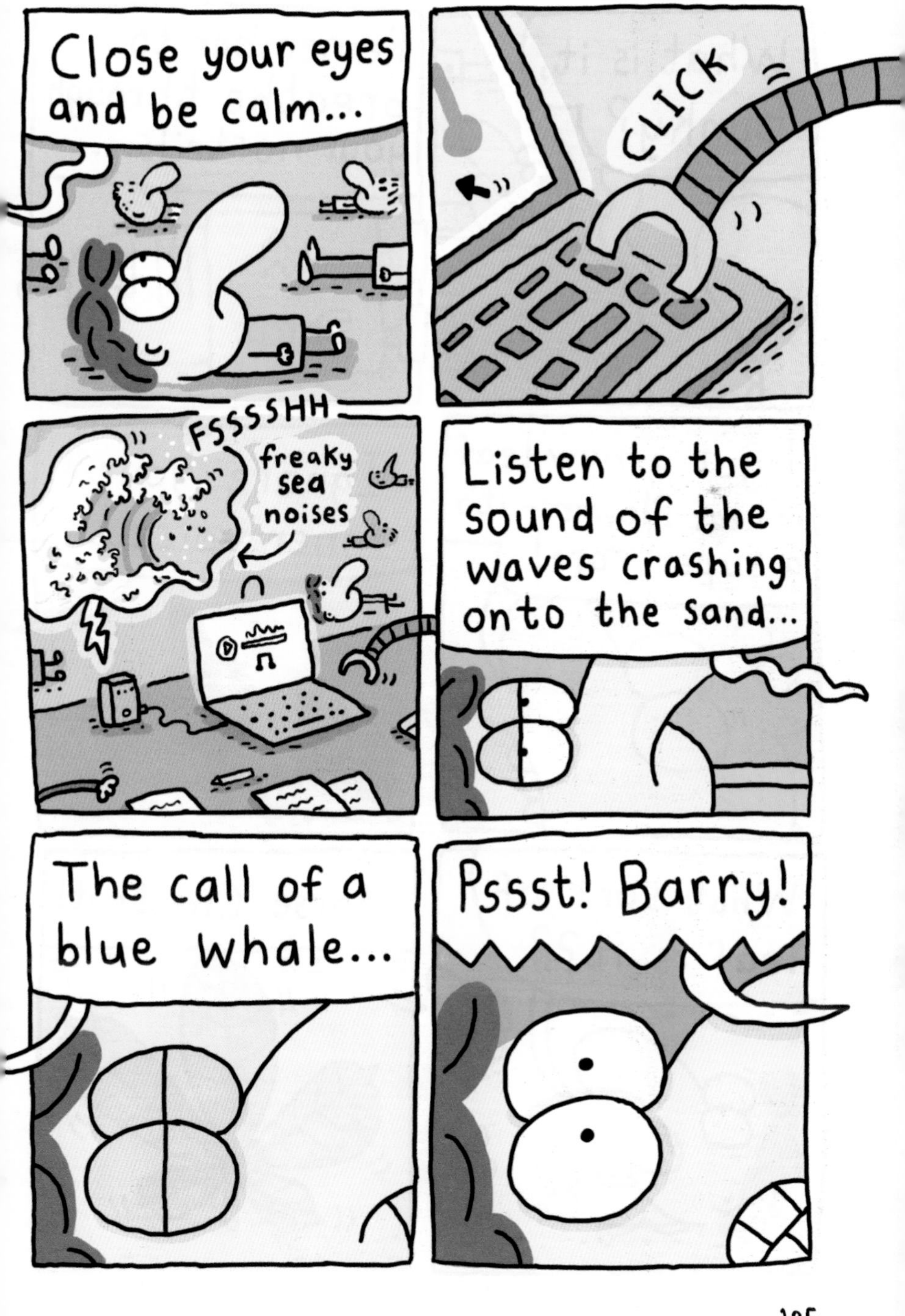

Close your eyes and be calm...
CLICK
FSSSSHH
freaky sea noises
Listen to the sound of the waves crashing onto the sand...
The call of a blue whale...
Pssst! Barry!

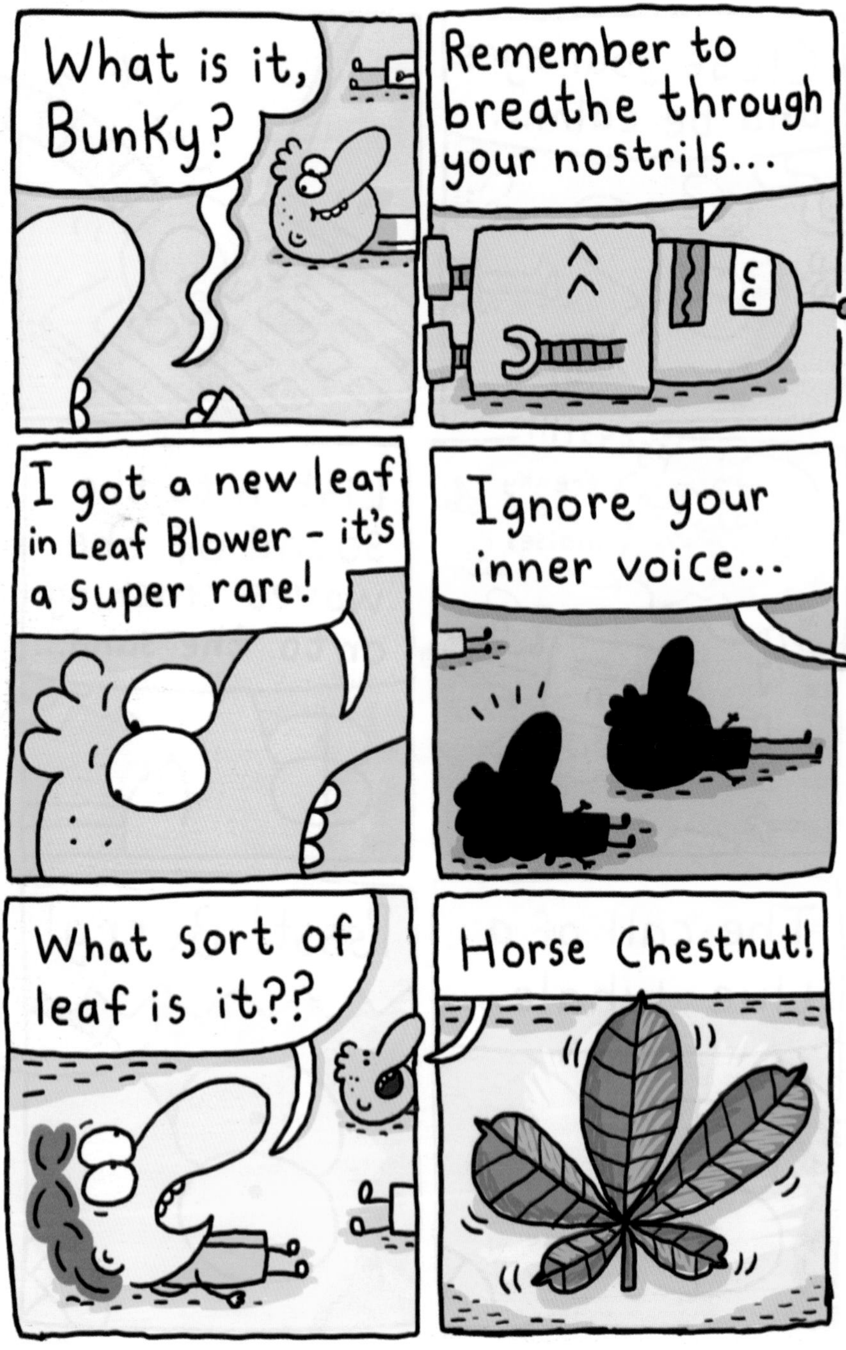
What is it, Bunky?
Remember to breathe through your nostrils...
I got a new leaf in Leaf Blower - it's a super rare!
Ignore your inner voice...
What sort of leaf is it??
Horse Chestnut!

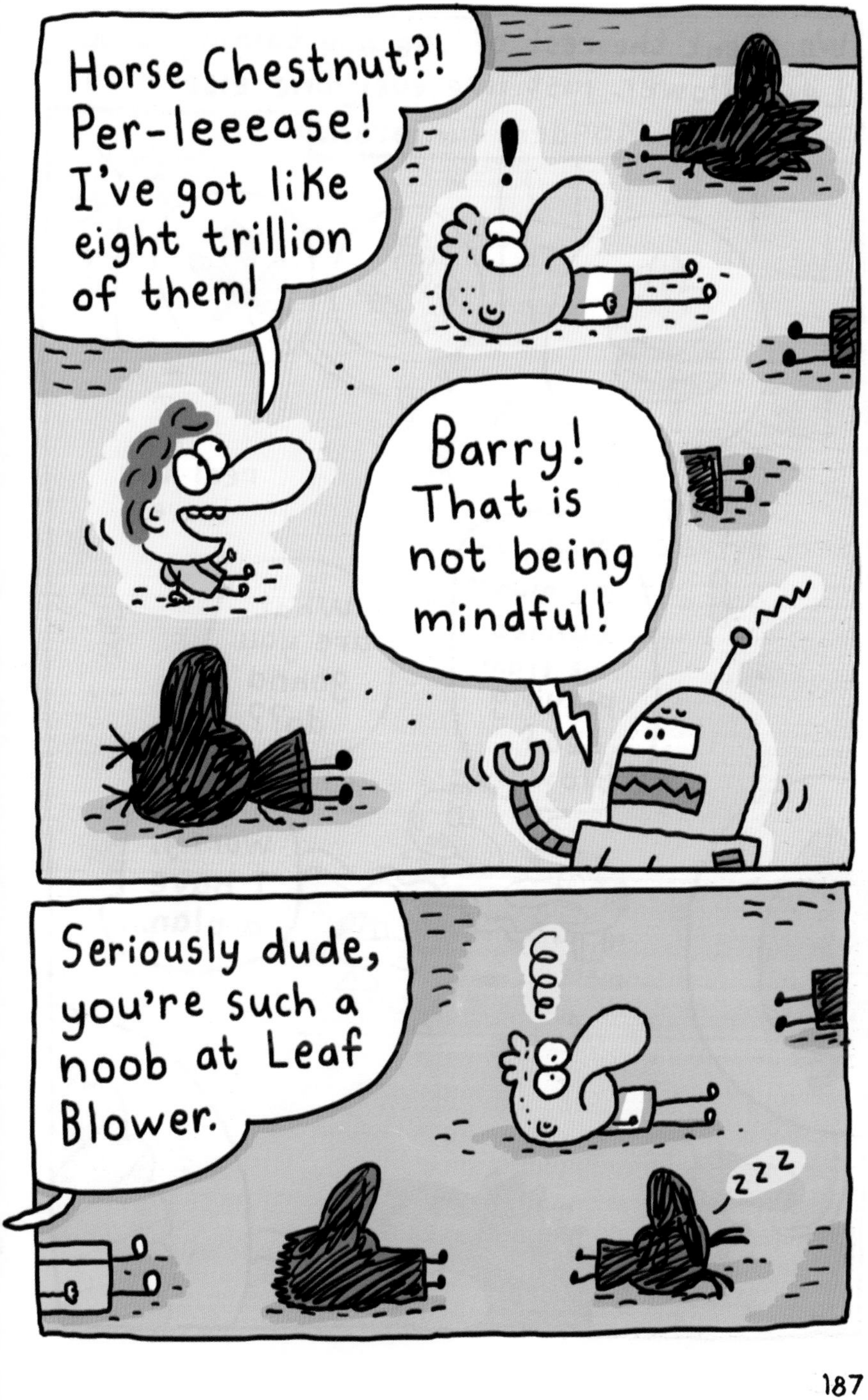
Horse Chestnut?! Per-leeease! I've got like eight trillion of them!
!
Barry! That is not being mindful!
Seriously dude, you're such a noob at Leaf Blower.
zzz

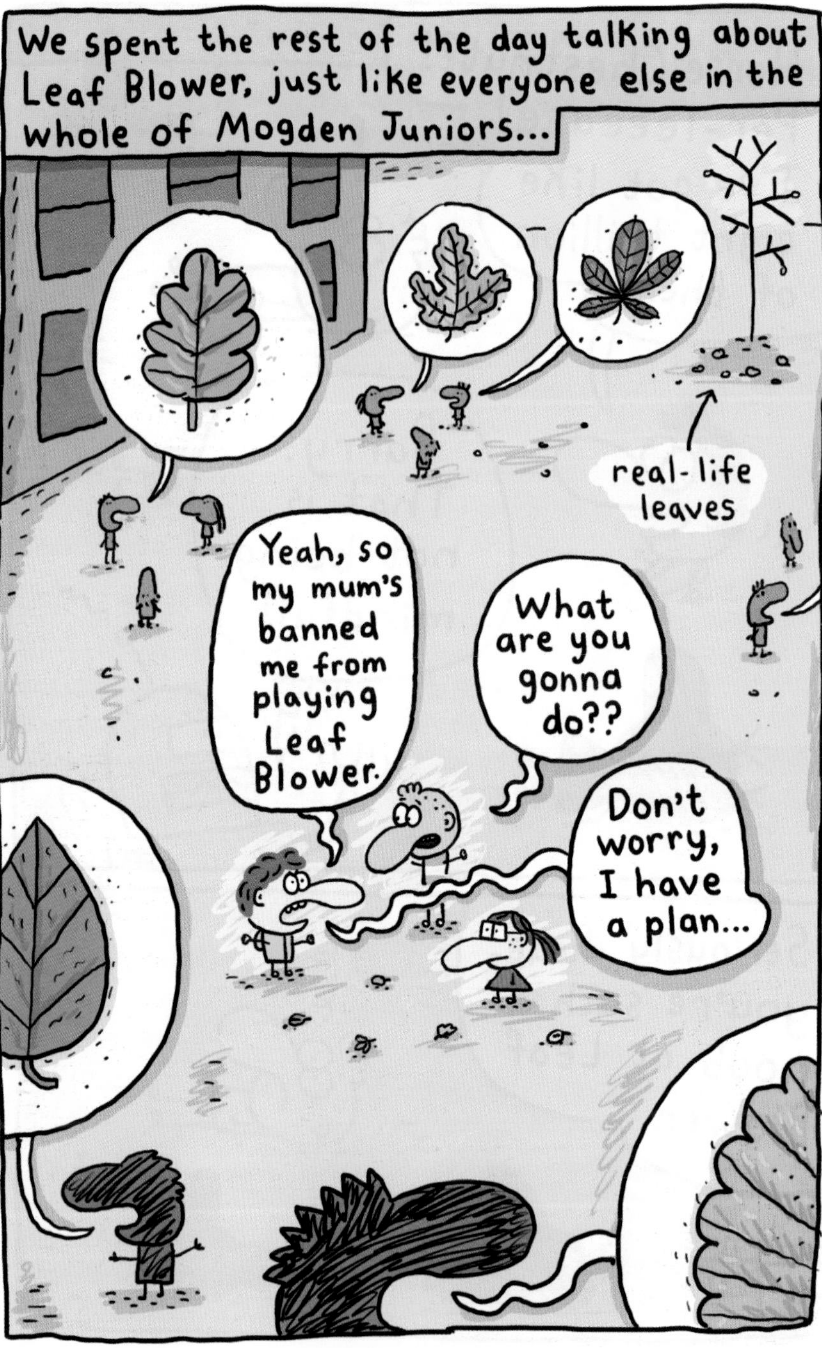
We spent the rest of the day talking about Leaf Blower, just like everyone else in the whole of Mogden Juniors...
real-life leaves
Yeah, so my mum's banned me from playing Leaf Blower.
What are you gonna do??
Don't worry, I have a plan...

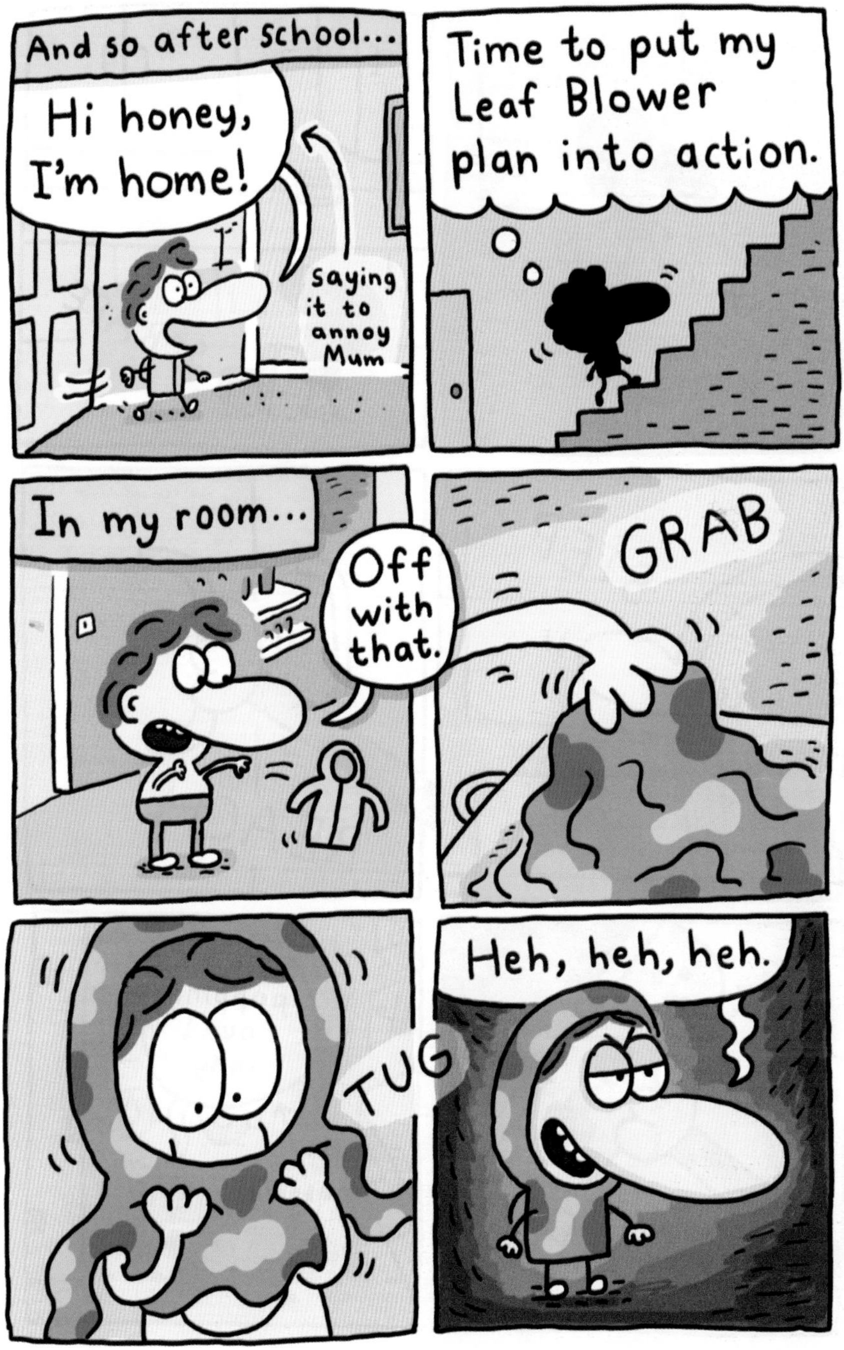
And so after school...
Hi honey, I'm home!
saying it to annoy Mum
Time to put my Leaf Blower plan into action.
In my room...
Off with that.
GRAB
TUG
Heh, heh, heh.

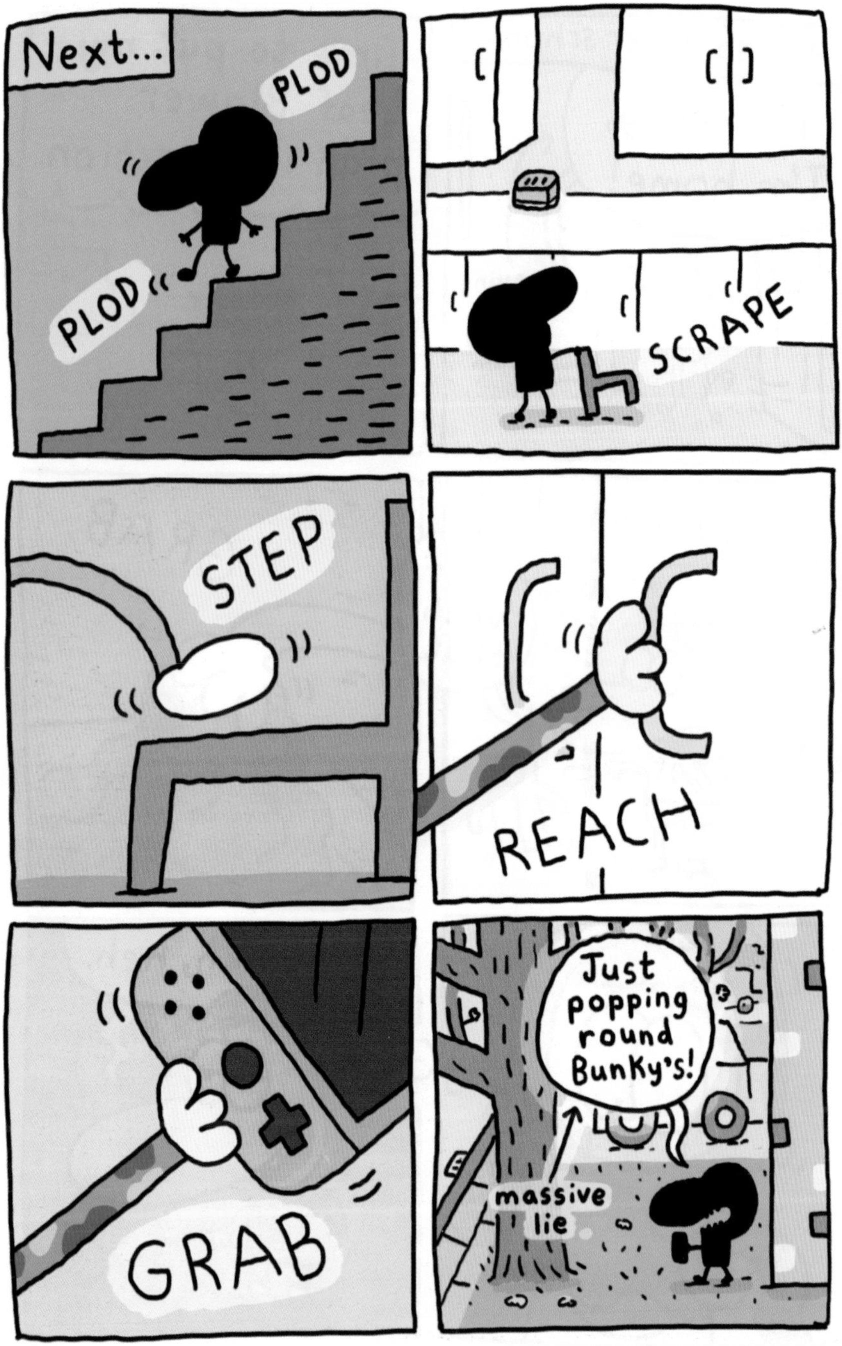
Next...
PLOD
PLOD
SCRAPE
STEP
REACH
GRAB
Just popping round Bunky's!
massive lie

Then...

CLAMBER

NNNNGH!

And...

Old Mumsy'll never spot me up here!

looks like ← giant leaf

Twidl

Just then...
Huh?
WHAT HAD I SEEN?*
FRENCHY!!
ZZZ

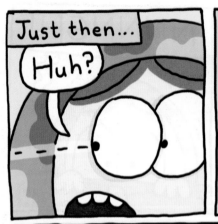

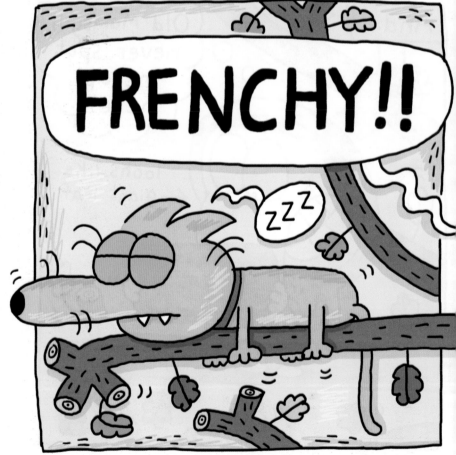

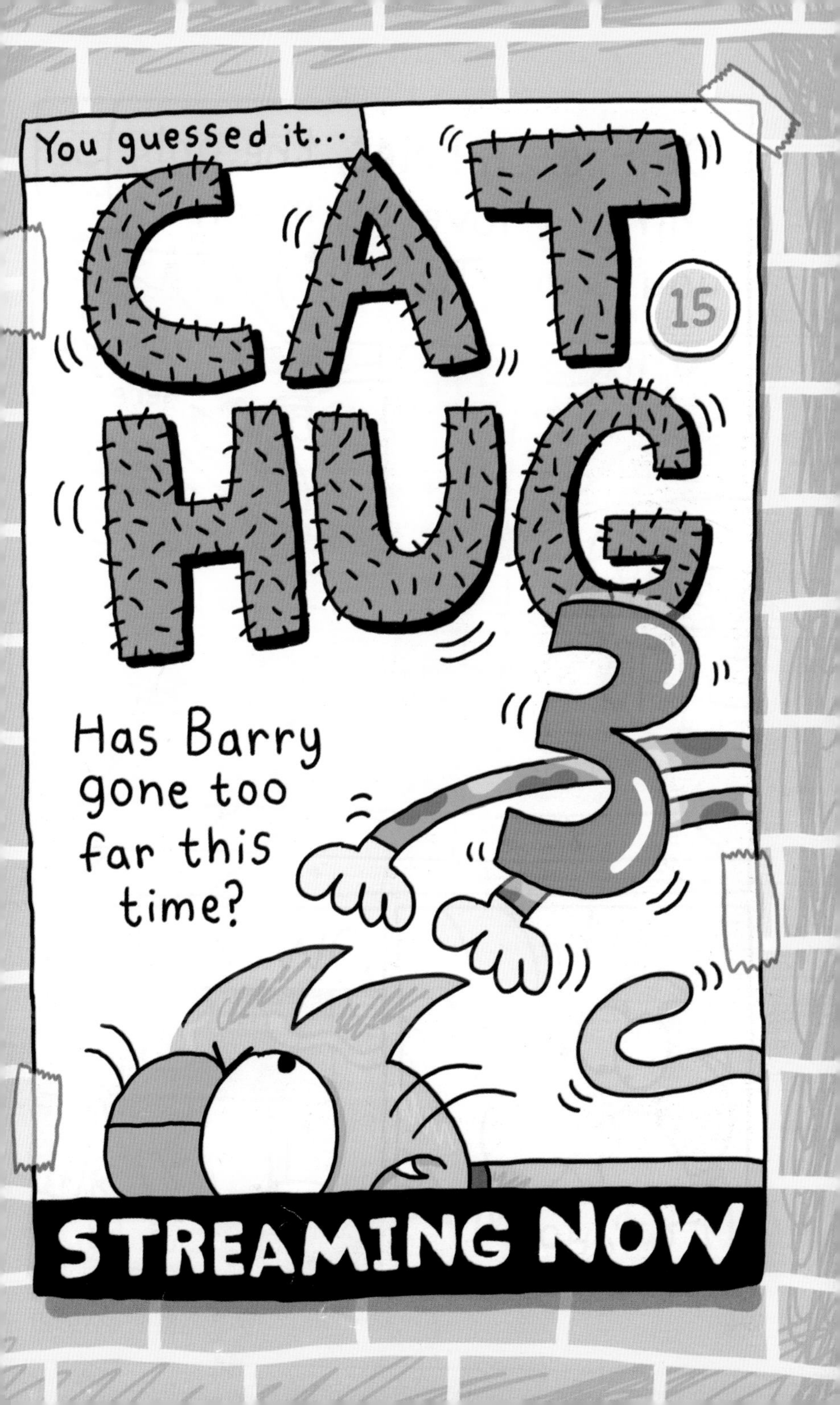
You guessed it...
CAT HUG 3
15
Has Barry gone too far this time?
STREAMING NOW

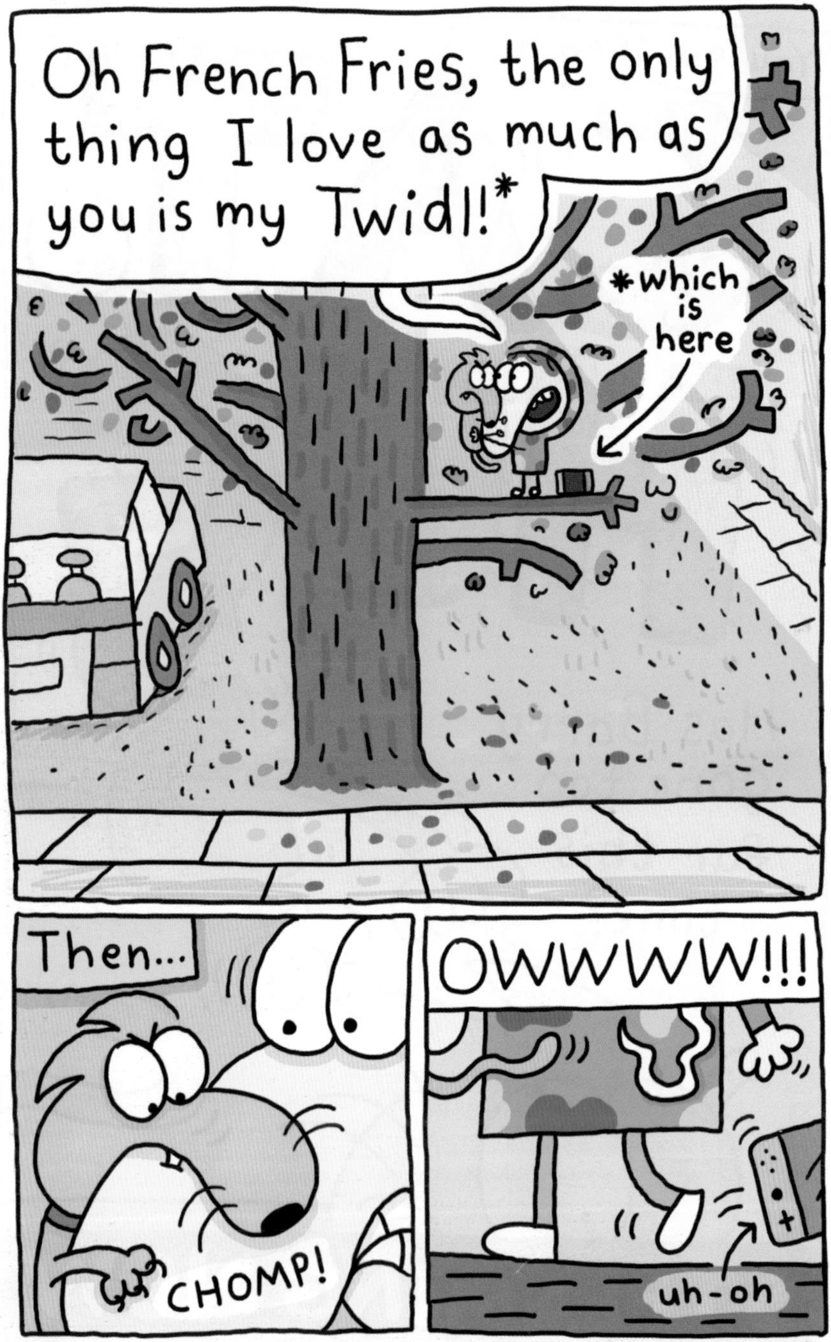
Oh French Fries, the only thing I love as much as you is my Twidl!*
*which is here
Then...
CHOMP!
OWWWW!!!
uh-oh

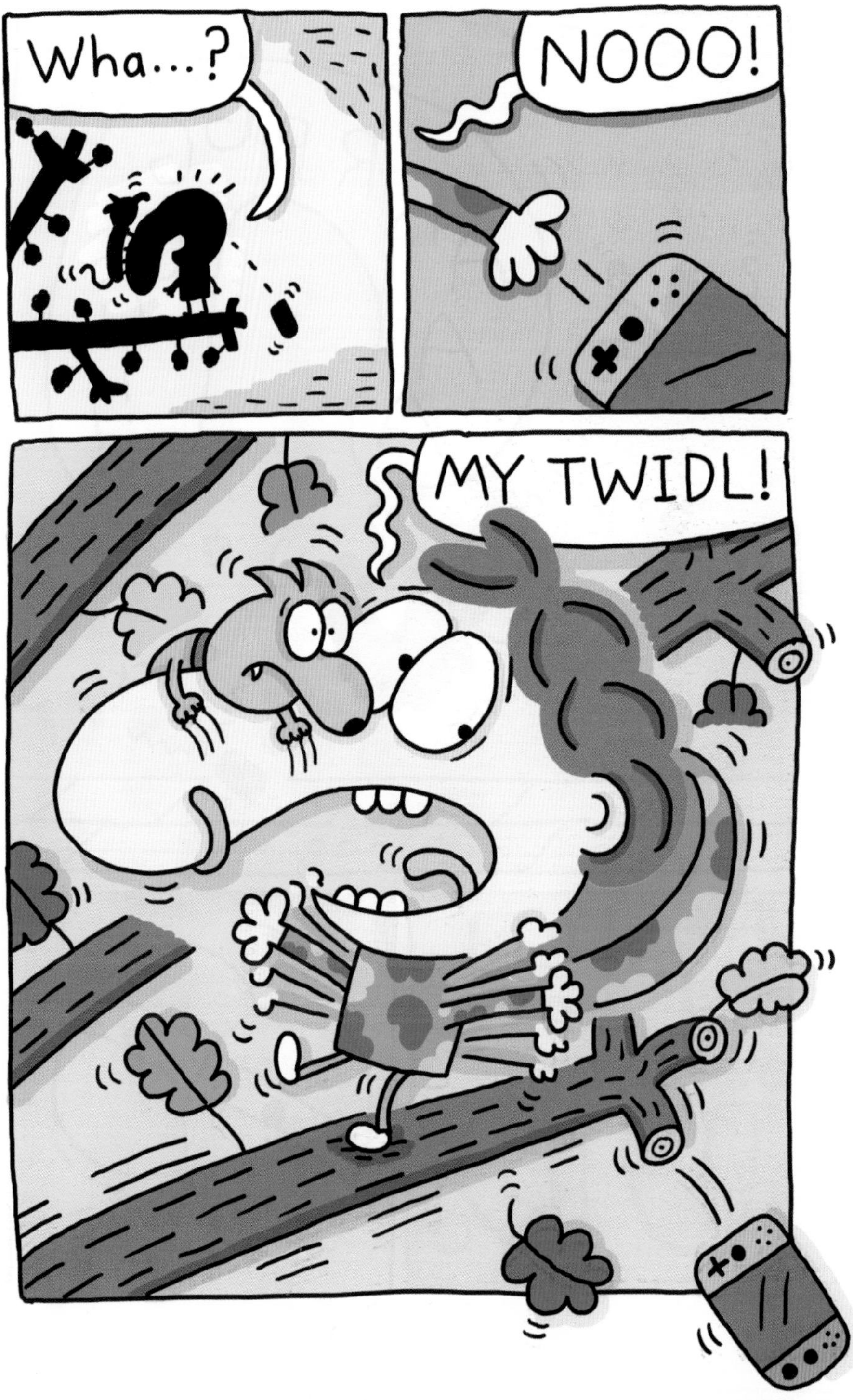
Wha...?
NOOO!
MY TWIDL!

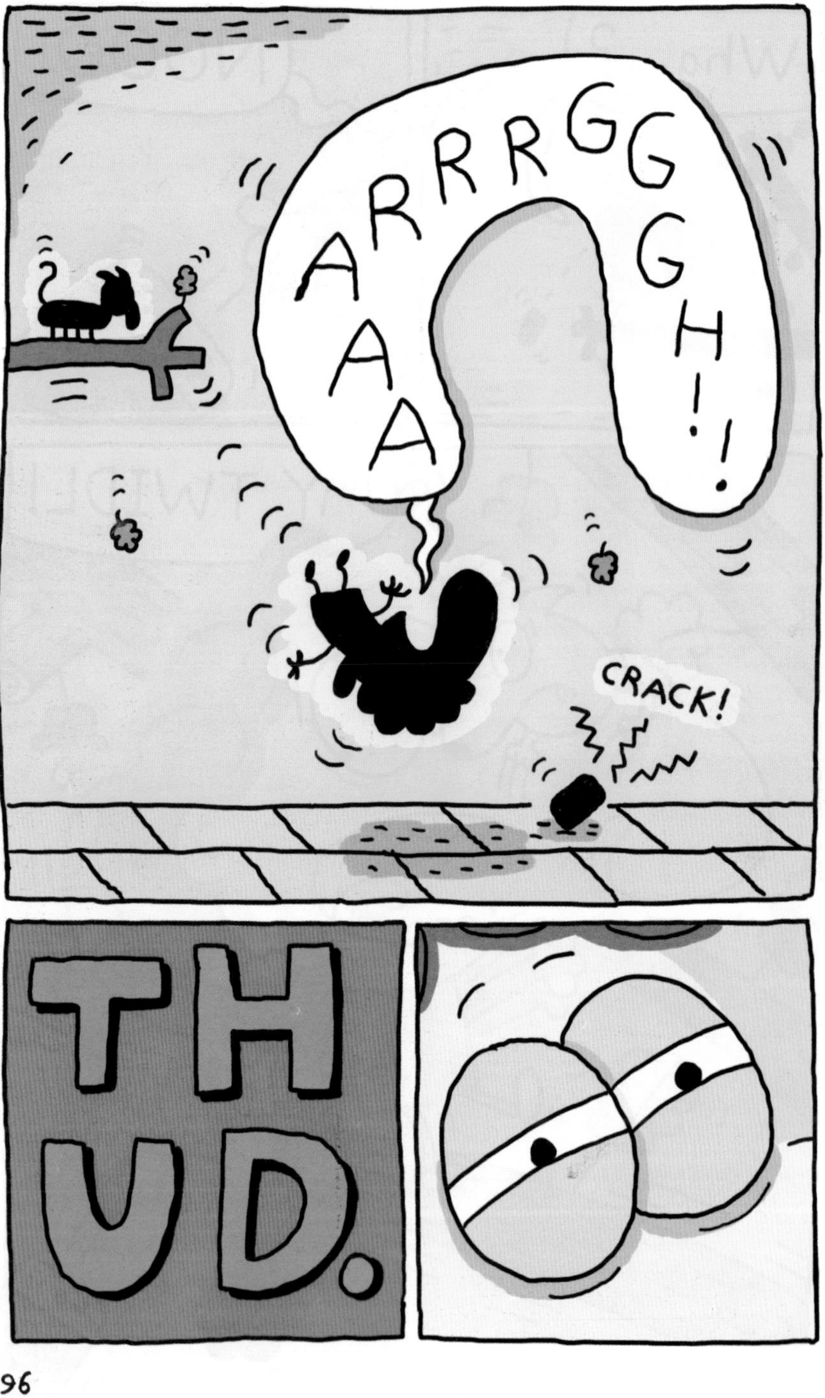
AAARRRGGGH!!!
CRACK!
THUD.

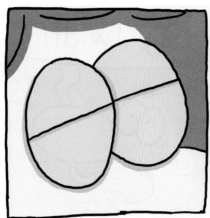

EVERY-THING WENT DARK.

BARRY?!

My Snookyflumps!

Oh thank goodness, you're alive!

Hang on, is that your Twiddler?

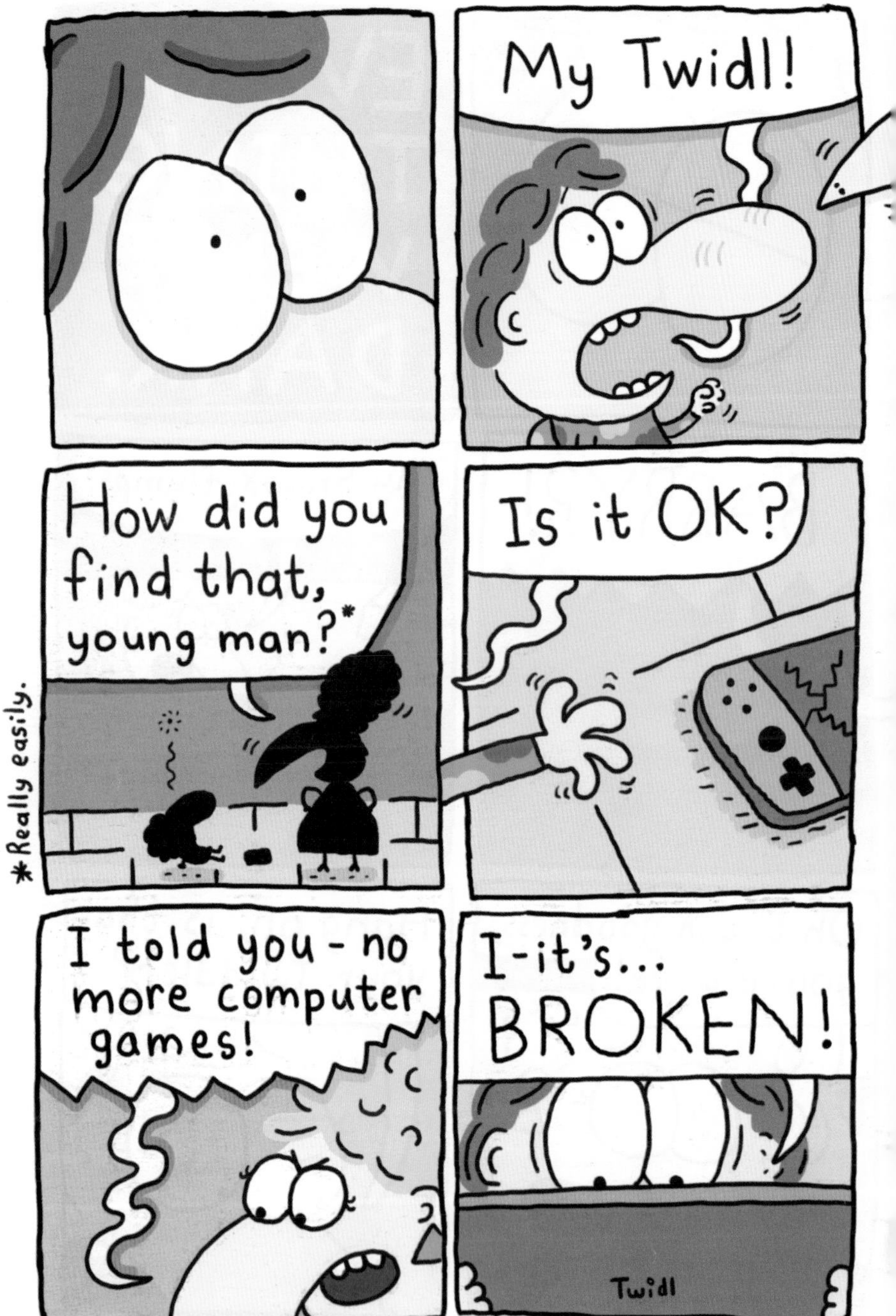
My Twidl!
How did you find that, young man?*
Is it OK?
*Really easily.
I told you - no more computer games!
I-it's... BROKEN!
Twidl

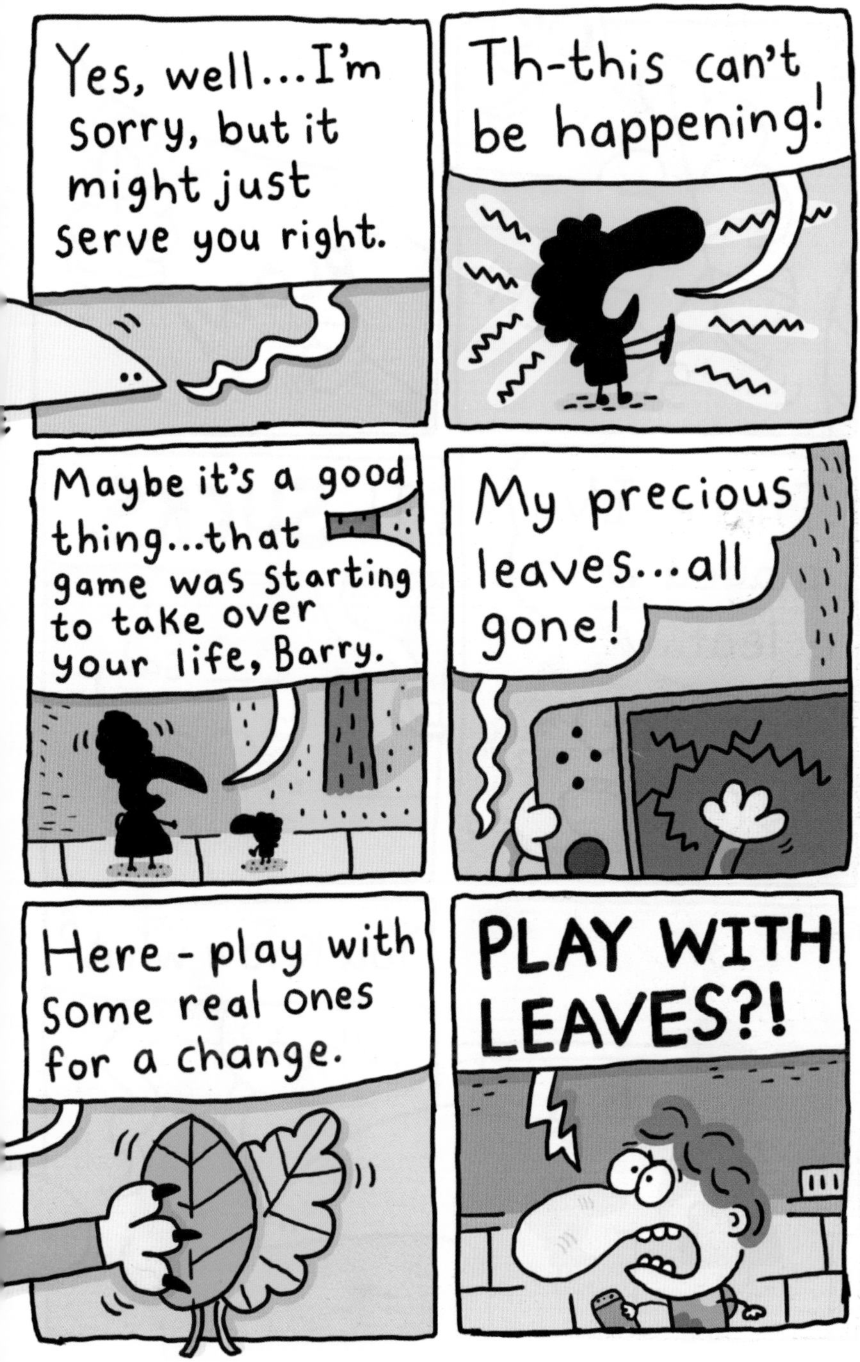
Yes, well...I'm sorry, but it might just serve you right.
Th-this can't be happening!
Maybe it's a good thing...that game was starting to take over your life, Barry.
My precious leaves...all gone!
Here - play with some real ones for a change.
PLAY WITH LEAVES?!

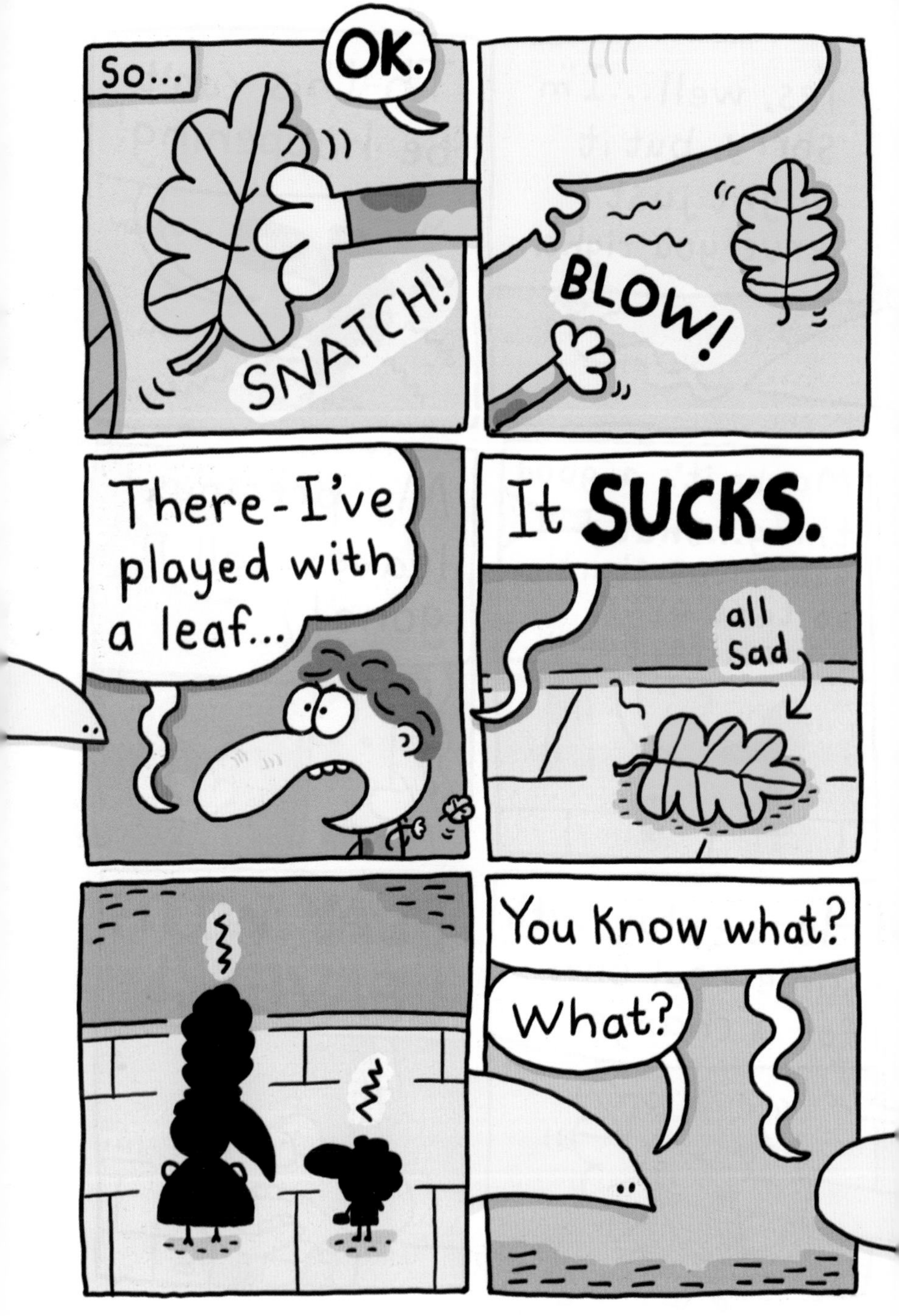
So...
OK.
SNATCH!
BLOW!
There-I've played with a leaf...
It SUCKS.
all sad
You know what?
What?

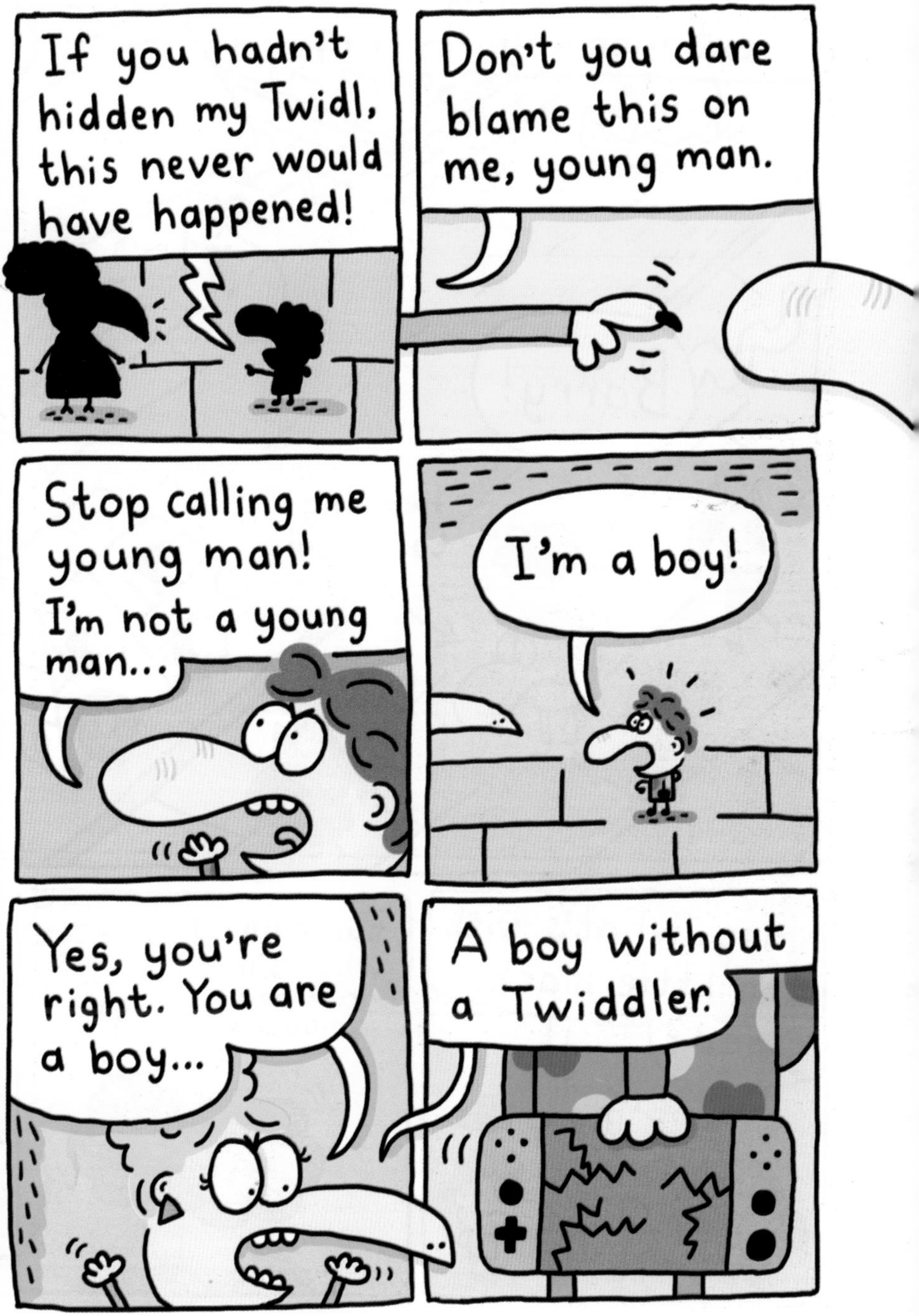
If you hadn't hidden my Twidl, this never would have happened!
Don't you dare blame this on me, young man.
Stop calling me young man! I'm not a young man...
I'm a boy!
Yes, you're right. You are a boy...
A boy without a Twiddler.

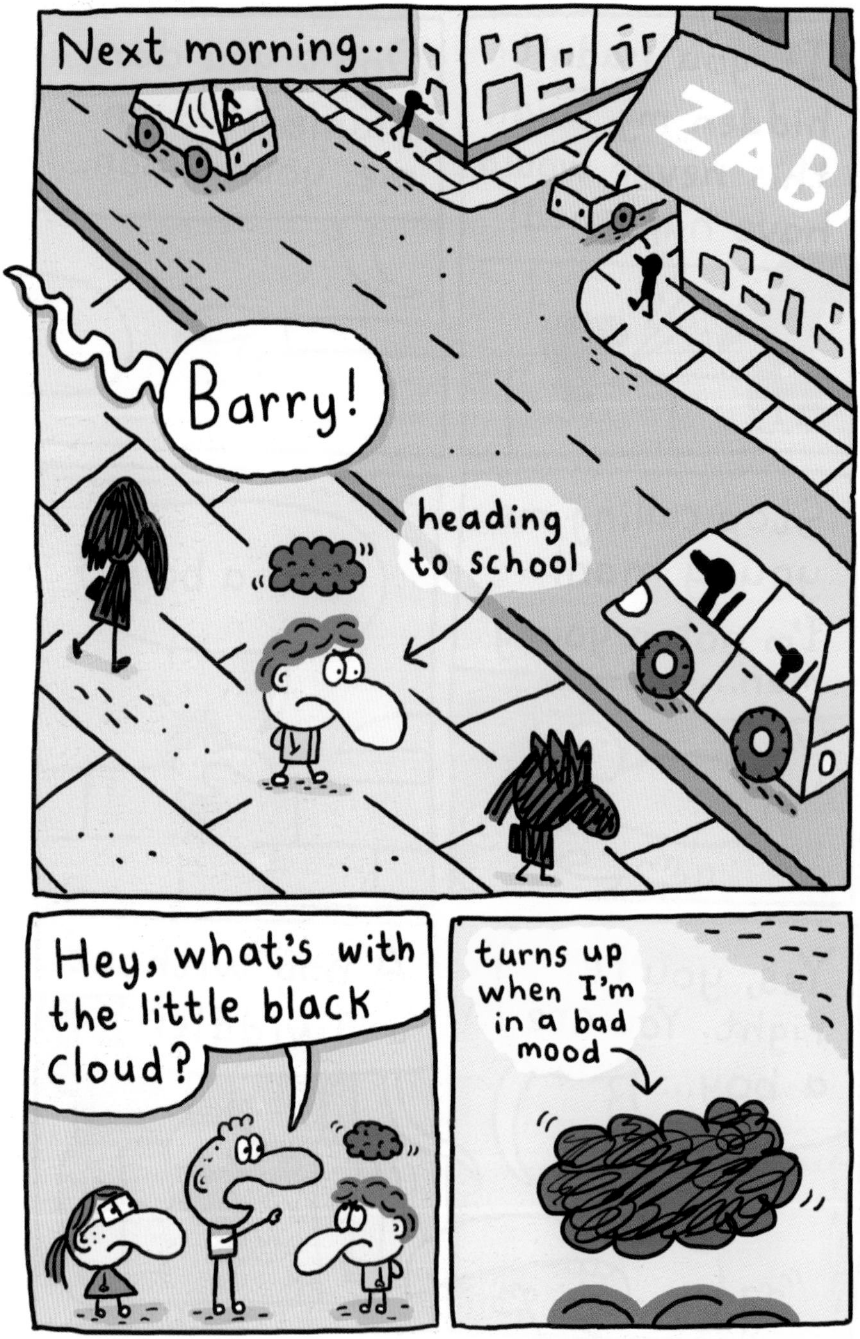
Next morning...
Barry!
heading to school
Hey, what's with the little black cloud?
turns up when I'm in a bad mood

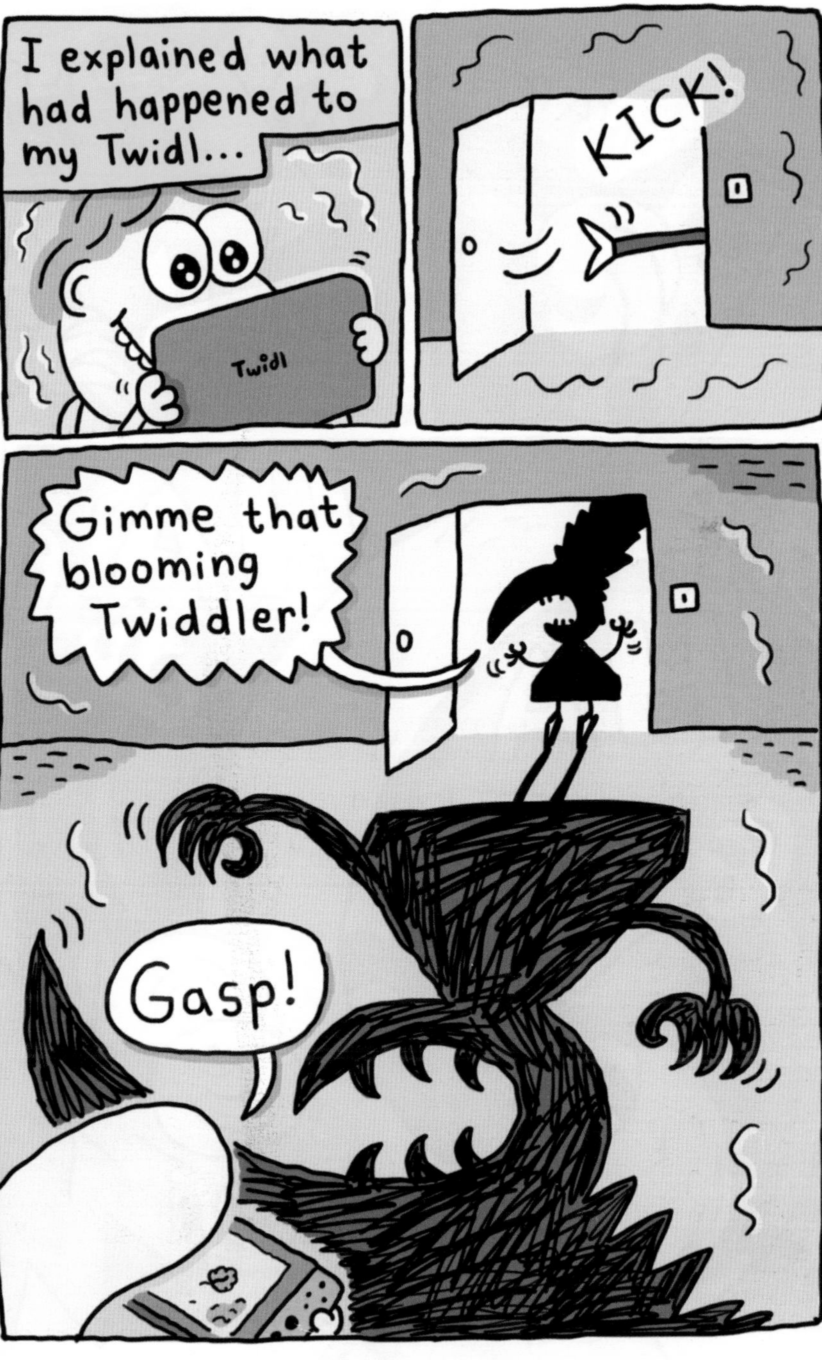
I explained what had happened to my Twidl...
Twidl
KICK!
Gimme that blooming Twiddler!
Gasp!

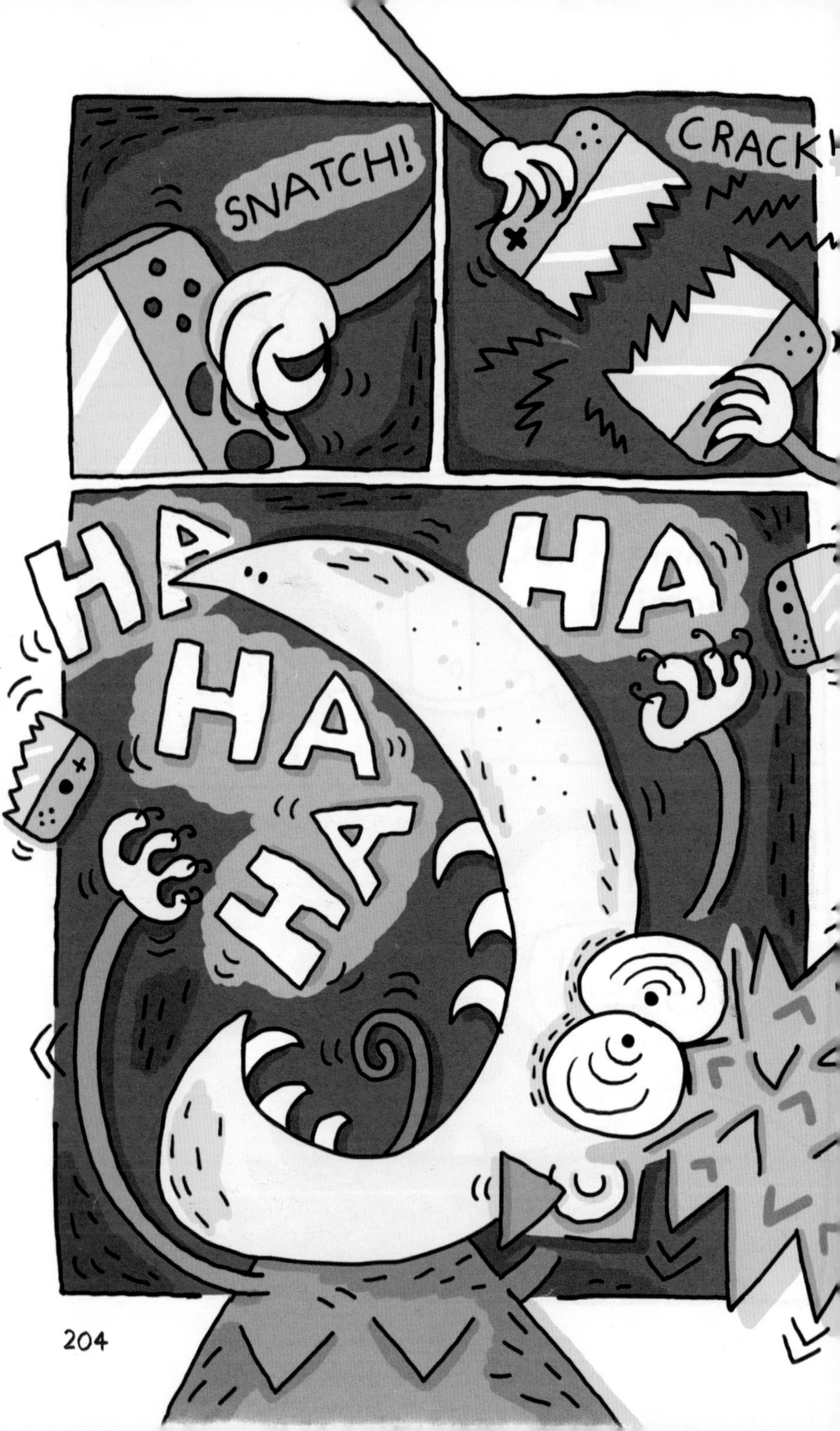
SNATCH!
CRACK!
HA
HA
HA
HA

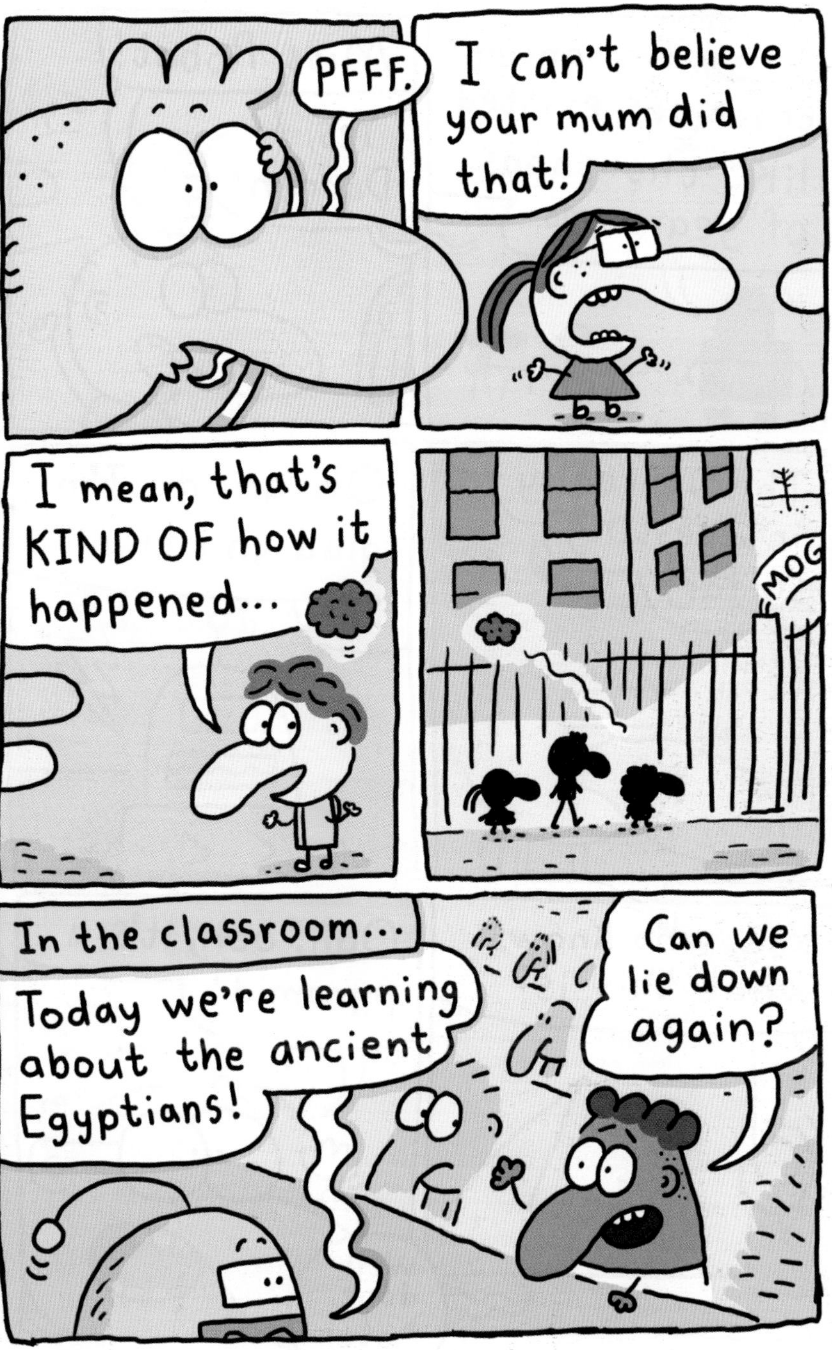
PFFF.
I can't believe your mum did that!
I mean, that's KIND OF how it happened...
MOG
In the classroom...
Today we're learning about the ancient Egyptians!
Can we lie down again?

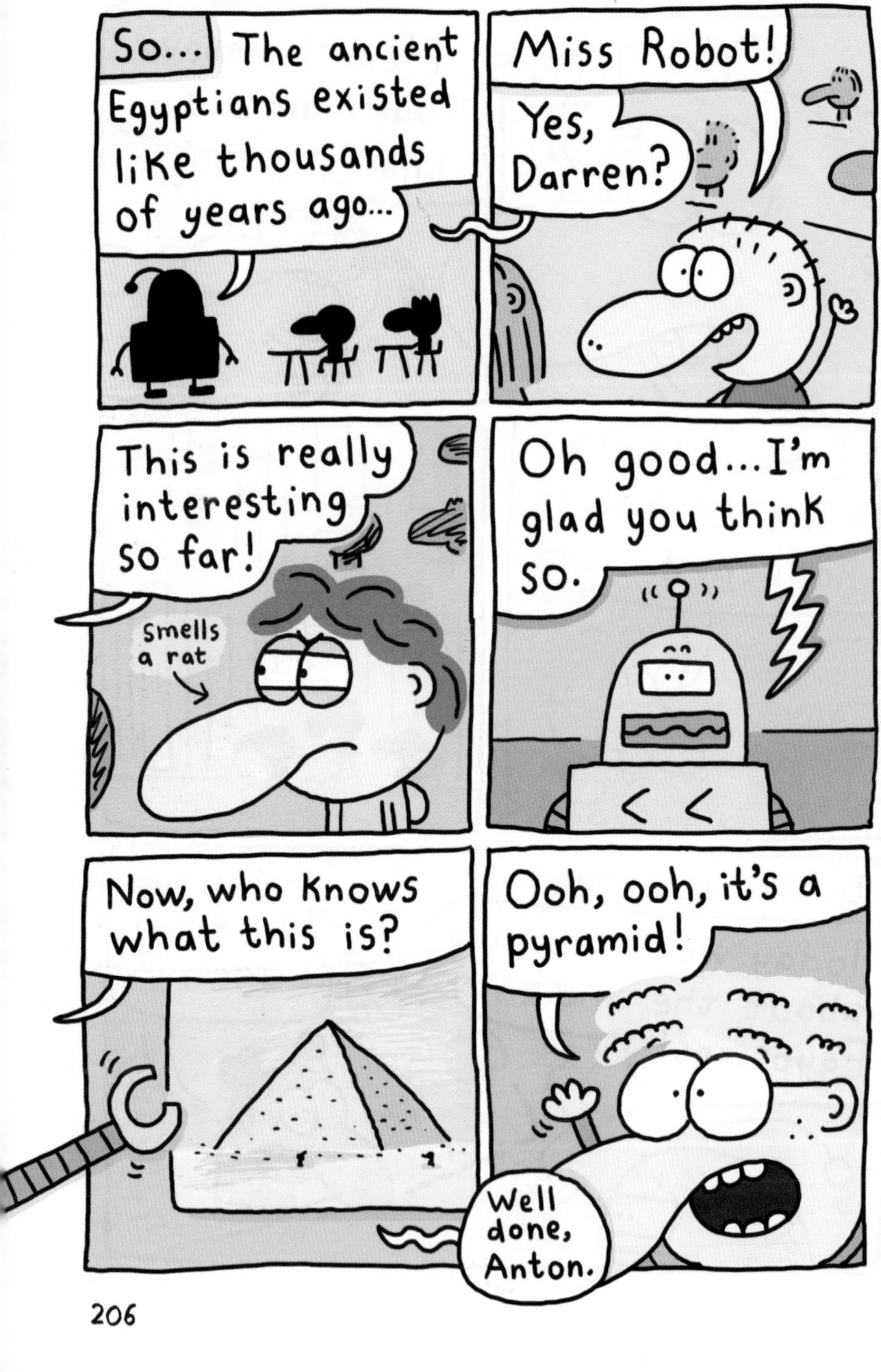

So...
The ancient Egyptians existed like thousands of years ago...
Miss Robot!
Yes, Darren?
This is really interesting so far!
smells a rat
Oh good...I'm glad you think so.
Now, who knows what this is?
Ooh, ooh, it's a pyramid!
Well done, Anton.

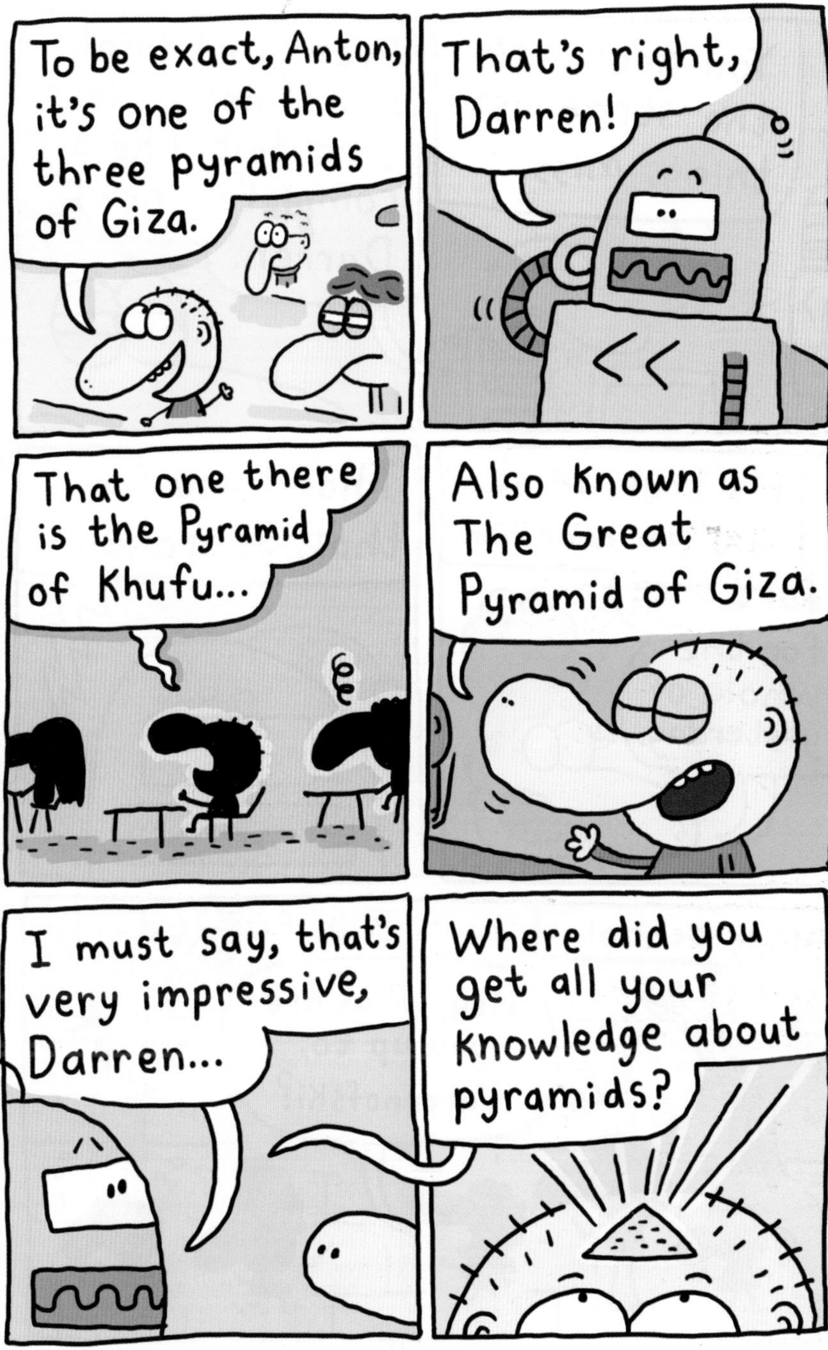
To be exact, Anton, it's one of the three pyramids of Giza.
That's right, Darren!
That one there is the Pyramid of Khufu...
Also known as The Great Pyramid of Giza.
I must say, that's very impressive, Darren...
Where did you get all your knowledge about pyramids?

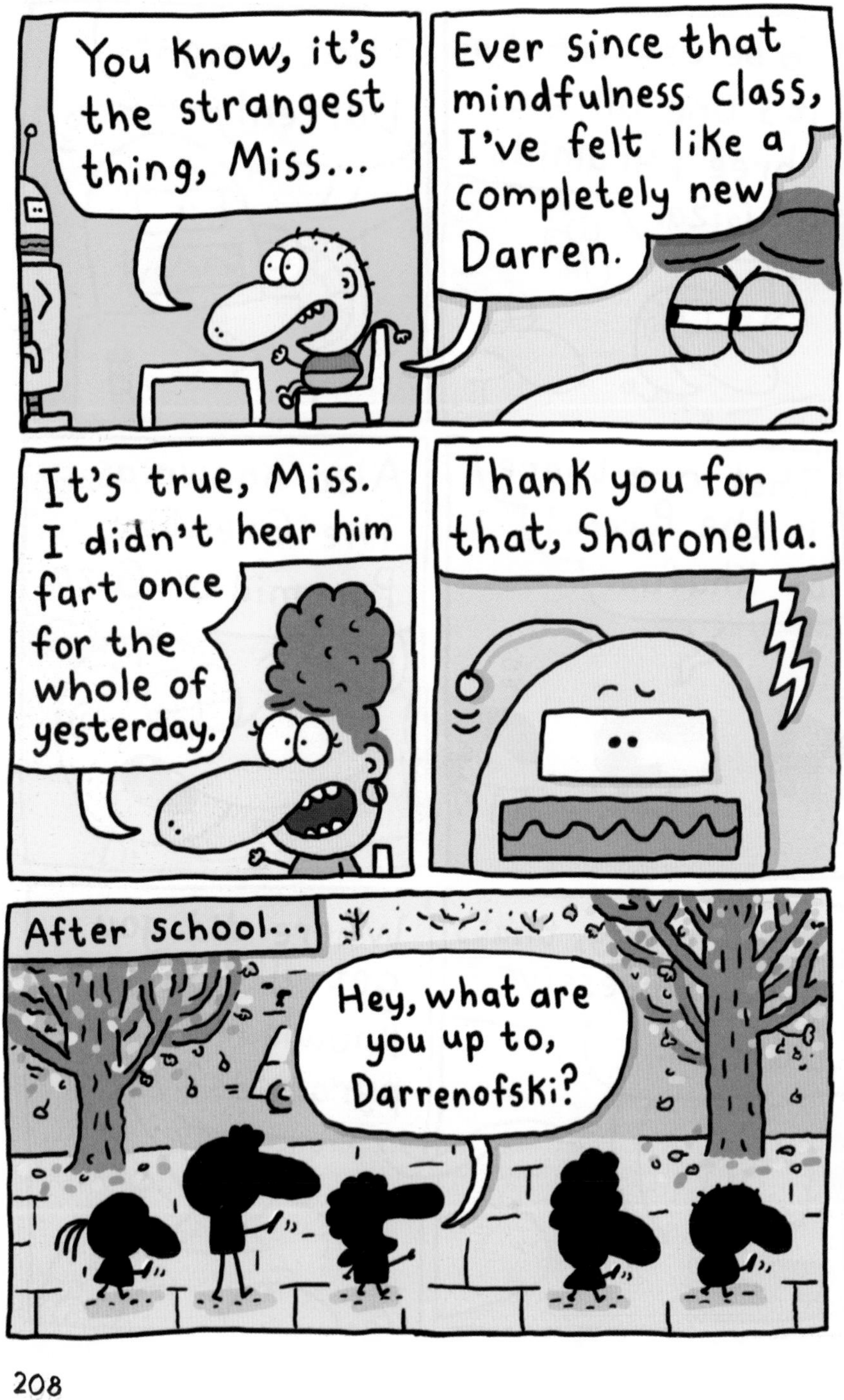

You know, it's the strangest thing, Miss...
Ever since that mindfulness class, I've felt like a completely new Darren.
It's true, Miss. I didn't hear him fart once for the whole of yesterday.
Thank you for that, Sharonella.
After school...
Hey, what are you up to, Darrenofski?

I'm playing Leaf Blower on my Twidl.

I meant all that ancient Egypt stuff...

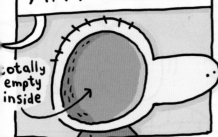
There's no way you know... well, ANYTHING!

totally empty inside

Don't be so negative, Baz...

Why not take a leaf out of Dazza's book...

He's really grown as a person these last couple of days.

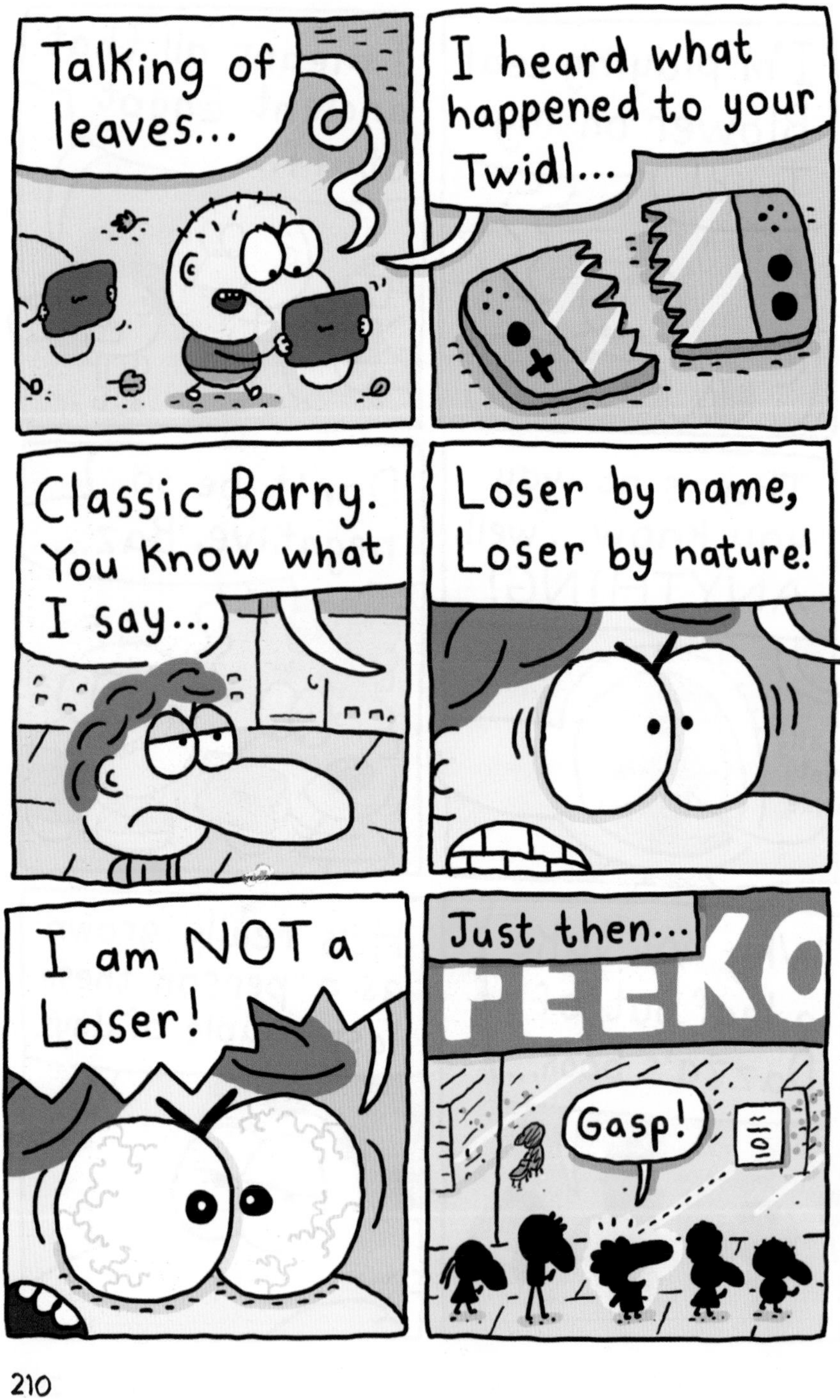
Talking of leaves...
I heard what happened to your Twidl...
Classic Barry. You know what I say...
Loser by name, Loser by nature!
I am NOT a Loser!
Just then...
FEEKO
Gasp!

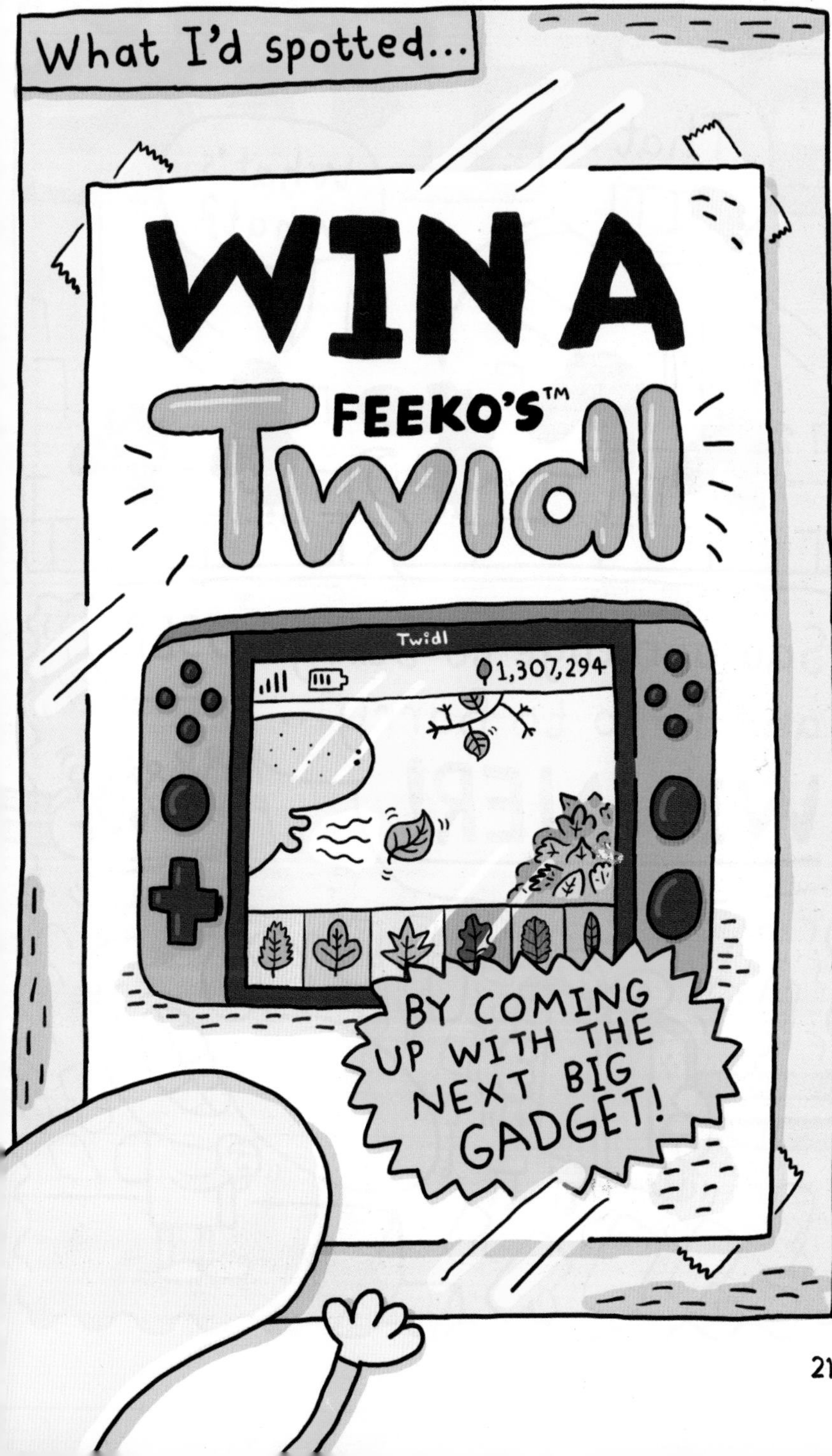

What I'd spotted...
WIN A
FEEKO'S™
Twidl
Twidl
1,307,294
BY COMING UP WITH THE NEXT BIG GADGET!

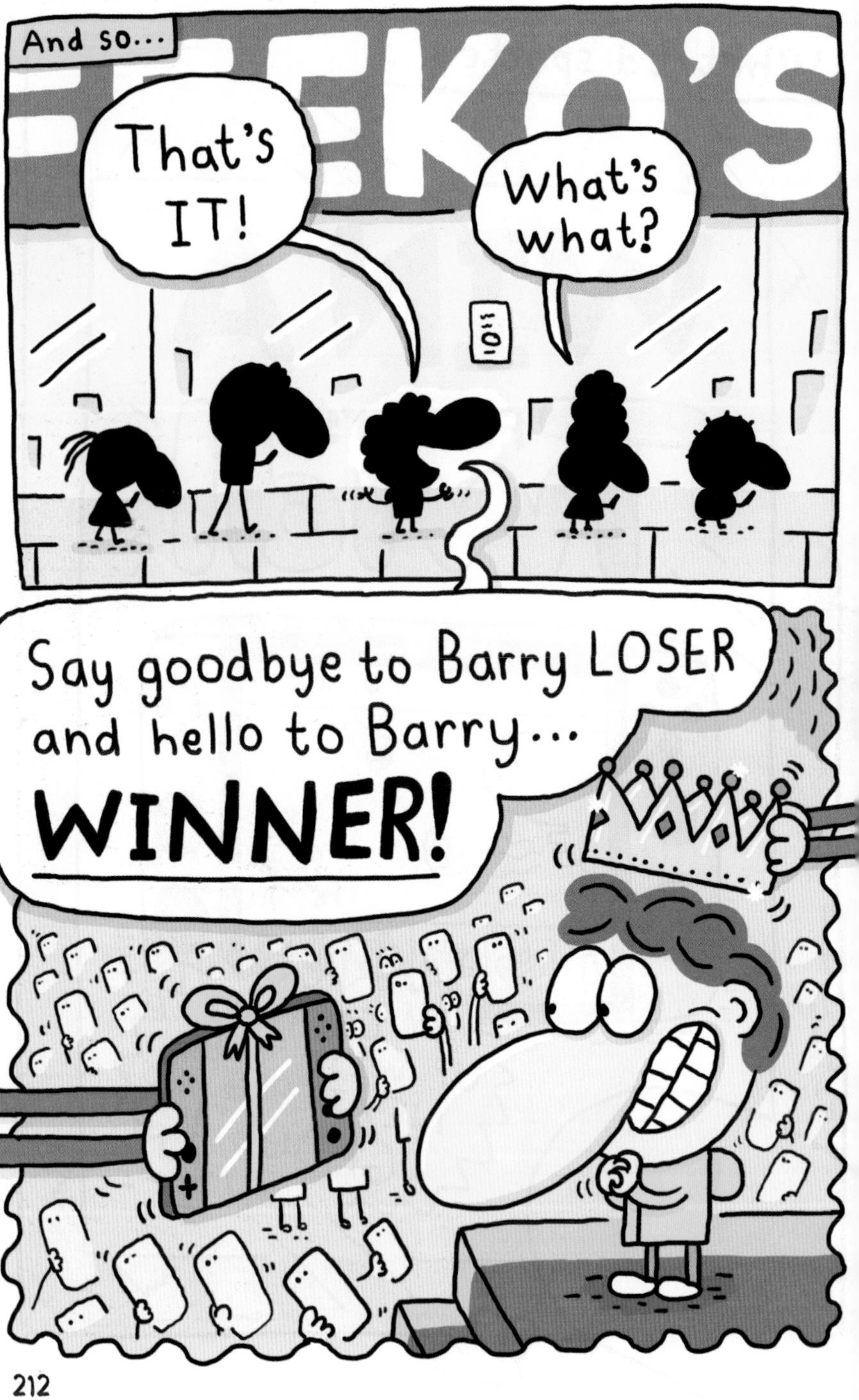
And so...
EKO'S
That's IT!
What's what?
Say goodbye to Barry LOSER and hello to Barry...
WINNER!

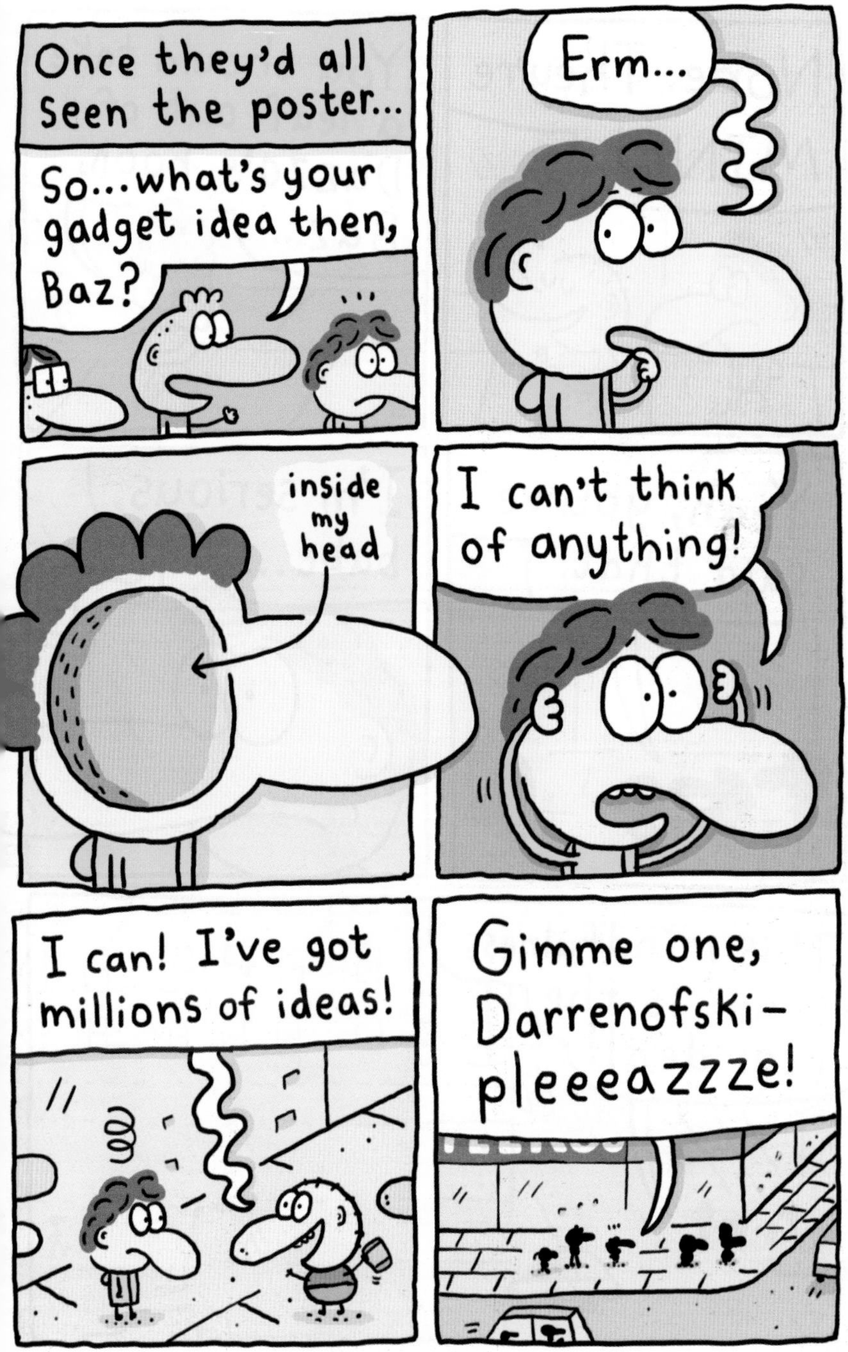
Once they'd all seen the poster...
So...what's your gadget idea then, Baz?
...
Erm...
inside my head
I can't think of anything!
I can! I've got millions of ideas!
Gimme one, Darrenofski-pleeeazzze!

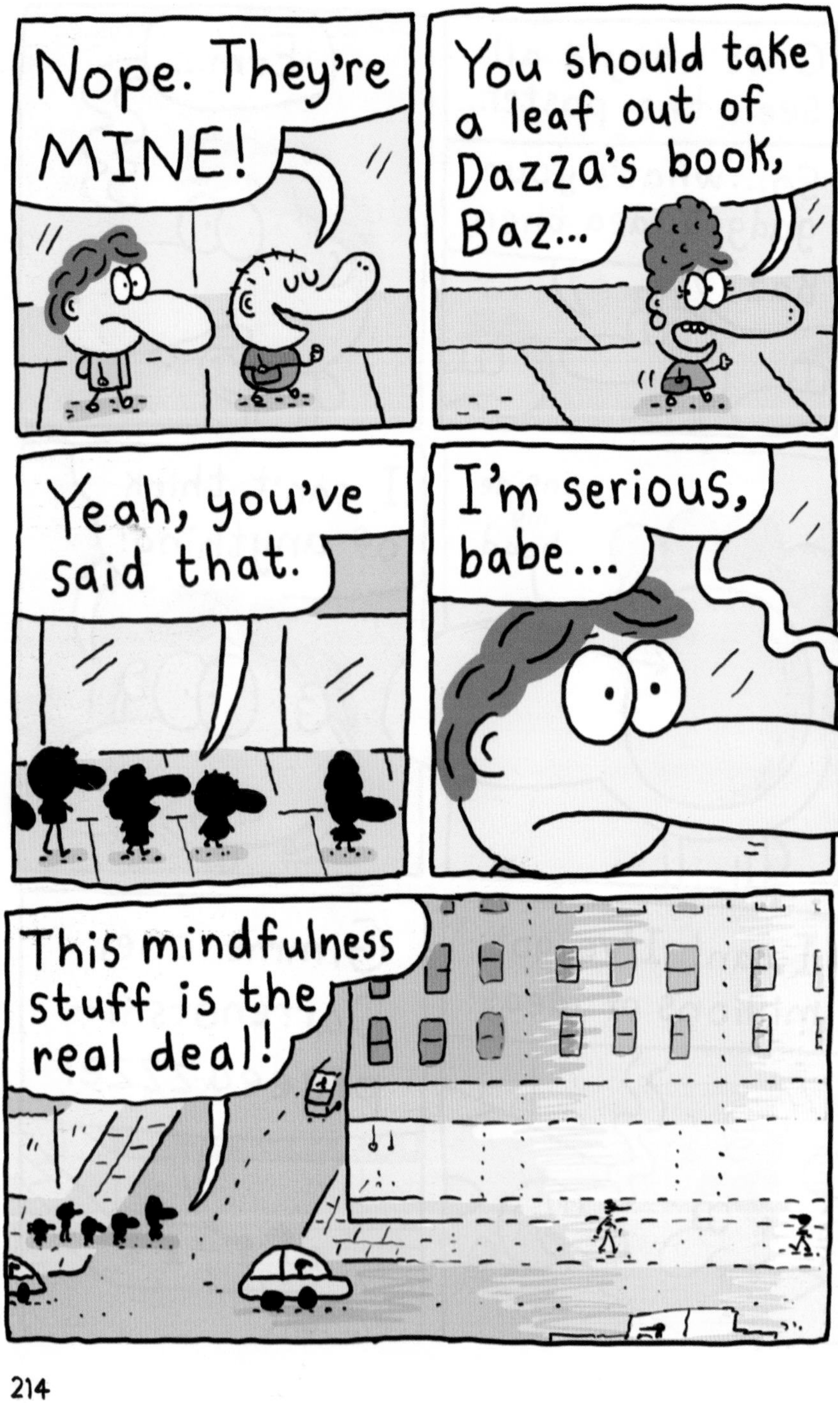
Nope. They're MINE!
You should take a leaf out of Dazza's book, Baz...
Yeah, you've said that.
I'm serious, babe...
This mindfulness stuff is the real deal!

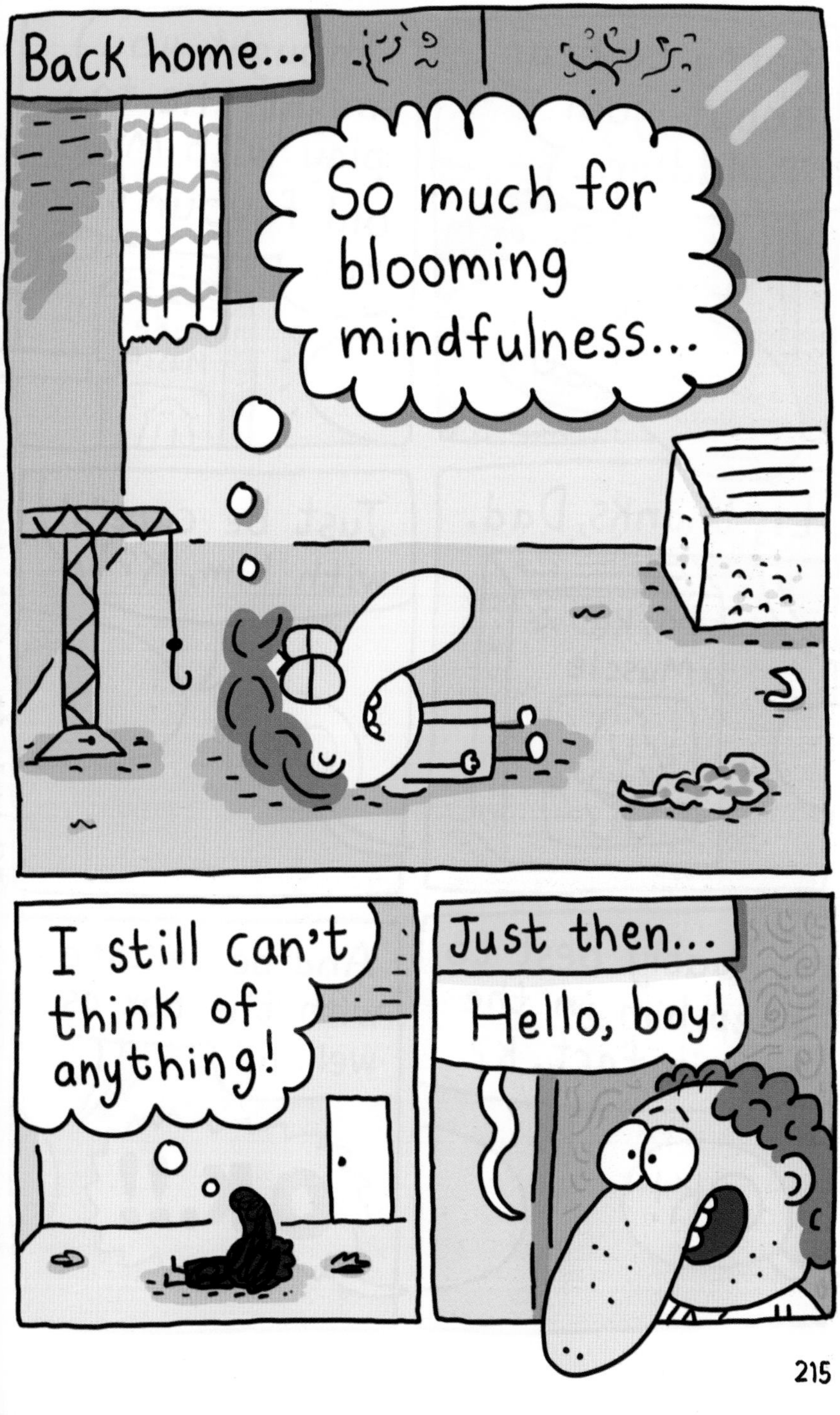

Back home...
So much for blooming mindfulness...
I still can't think of anything!
Just then...
Hello, boy!

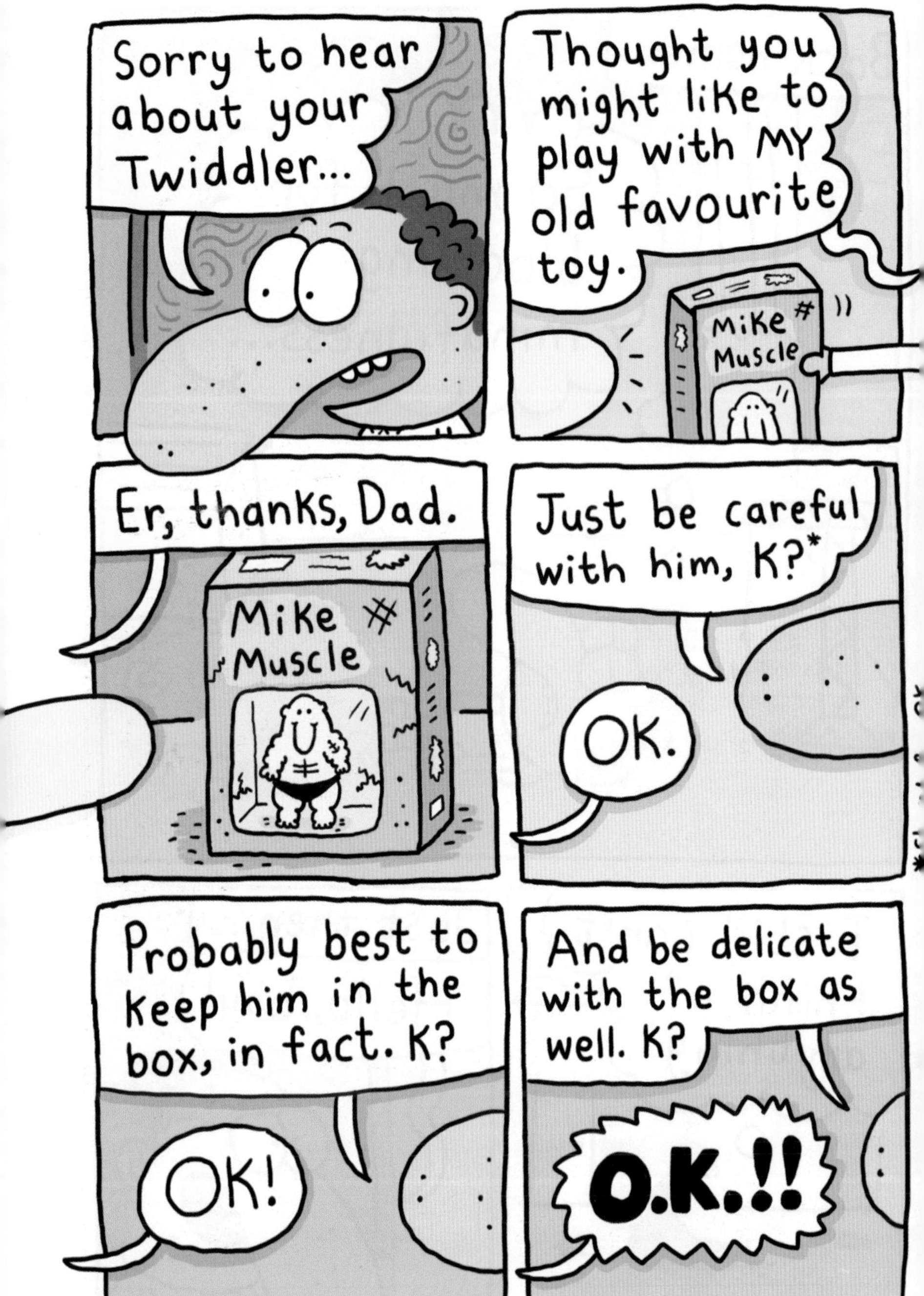
Sorry to hear about your Twiddler...
Thought you might like to play with MY old favourite toy.
Mike Muscle
Er, thanks, Dad.
Mike Muscle
Just be careful with him, K?*
OK.
Probably best to keep him in the box, in fact. K?
OK!
And be delicate with the box as well. K?
O.K.!!

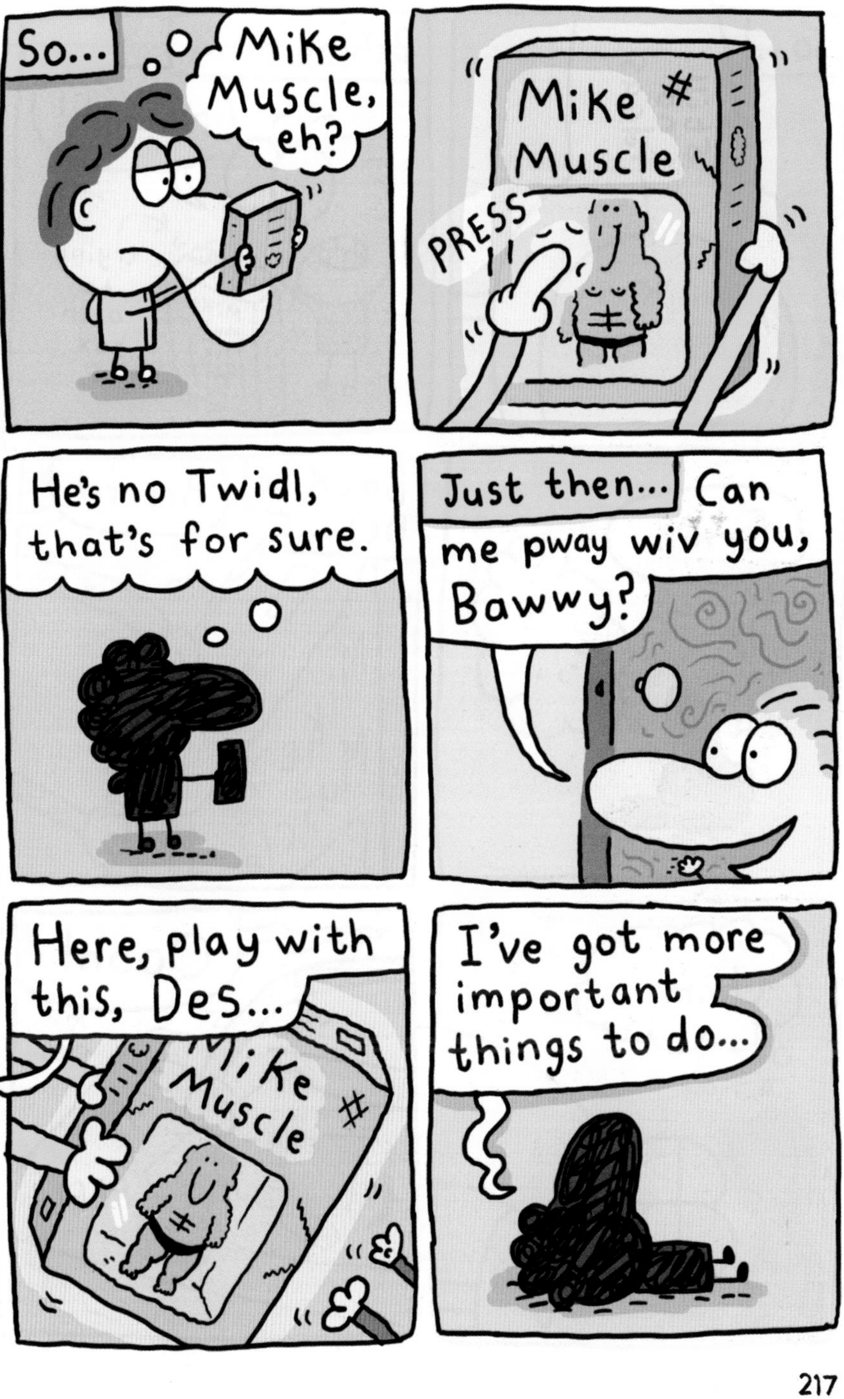
So...
Mike Muscle, eh?
Mike Muscle
PRESS
He's no Twidl, that's for sure.
Just then...
Can me pway wiv you, Bawwy?
Here, play with this, Des...
Mike Muscle
I've got more important things to do...

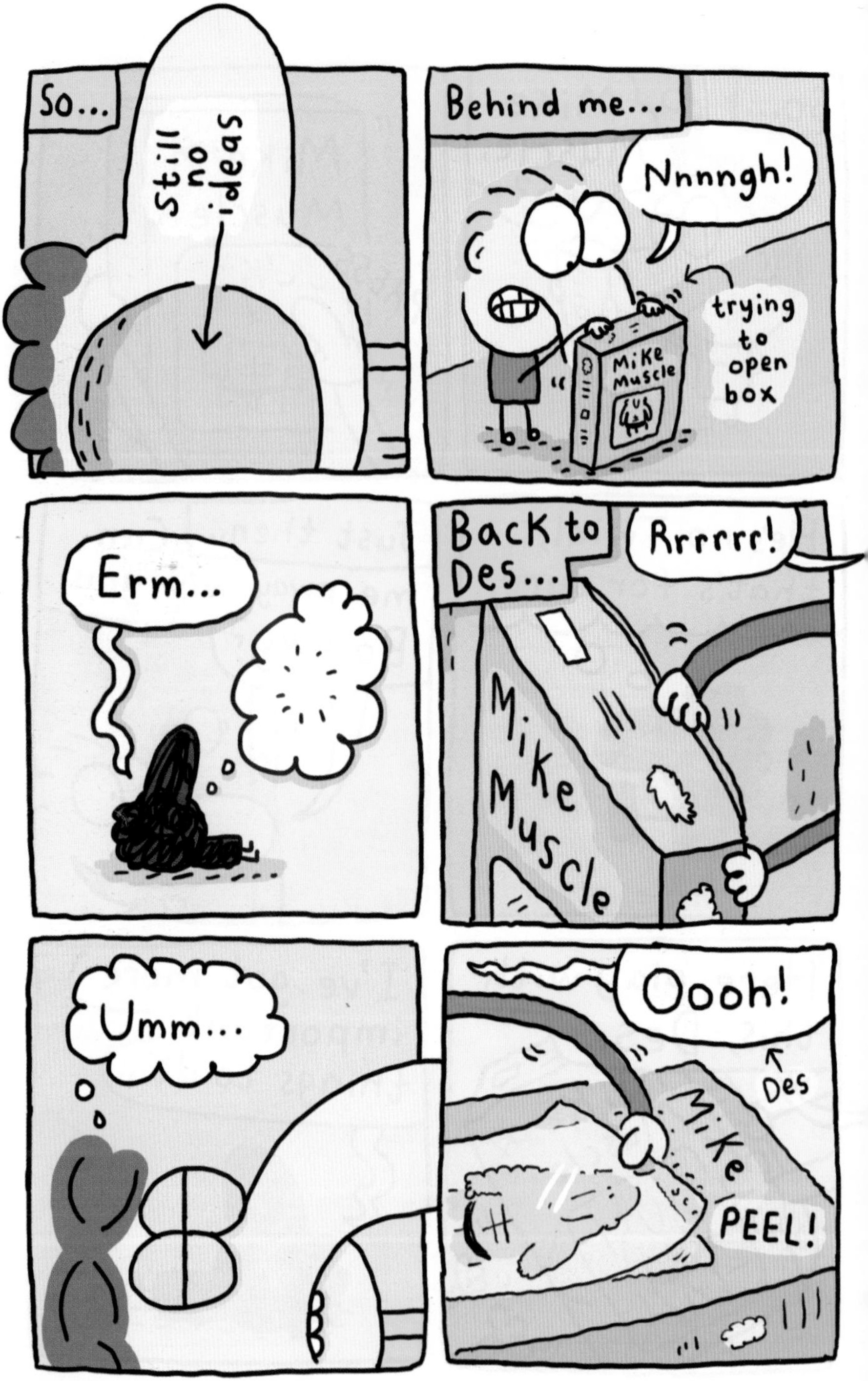

So...
still no ideas
Behind me...
Nnnngh!
trying to open box
Mike Muscle
Erm...
Back to Des...
Rrrrrr!
Mike Muscle
Umm...
Oooh!
Des
Mike
PEEL!

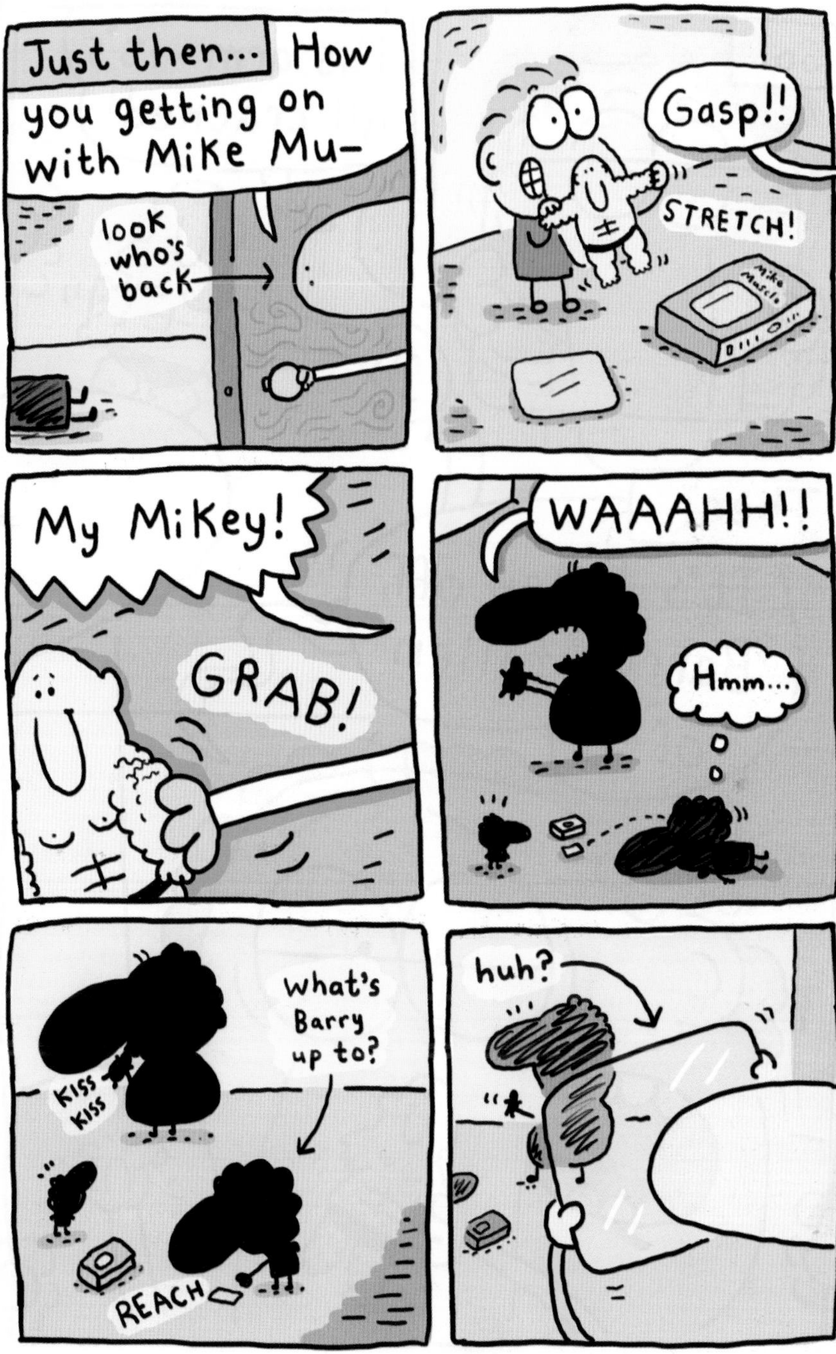
Just then...
How you getting on with Mike Mu-
look who's back
Gasp!!
STRETCH!
Mike Muscle
My Mikey!
GRAB!
WAAAHH!!
Hmm...
KISS KISS
What's Barry up to?
REACH
huh?

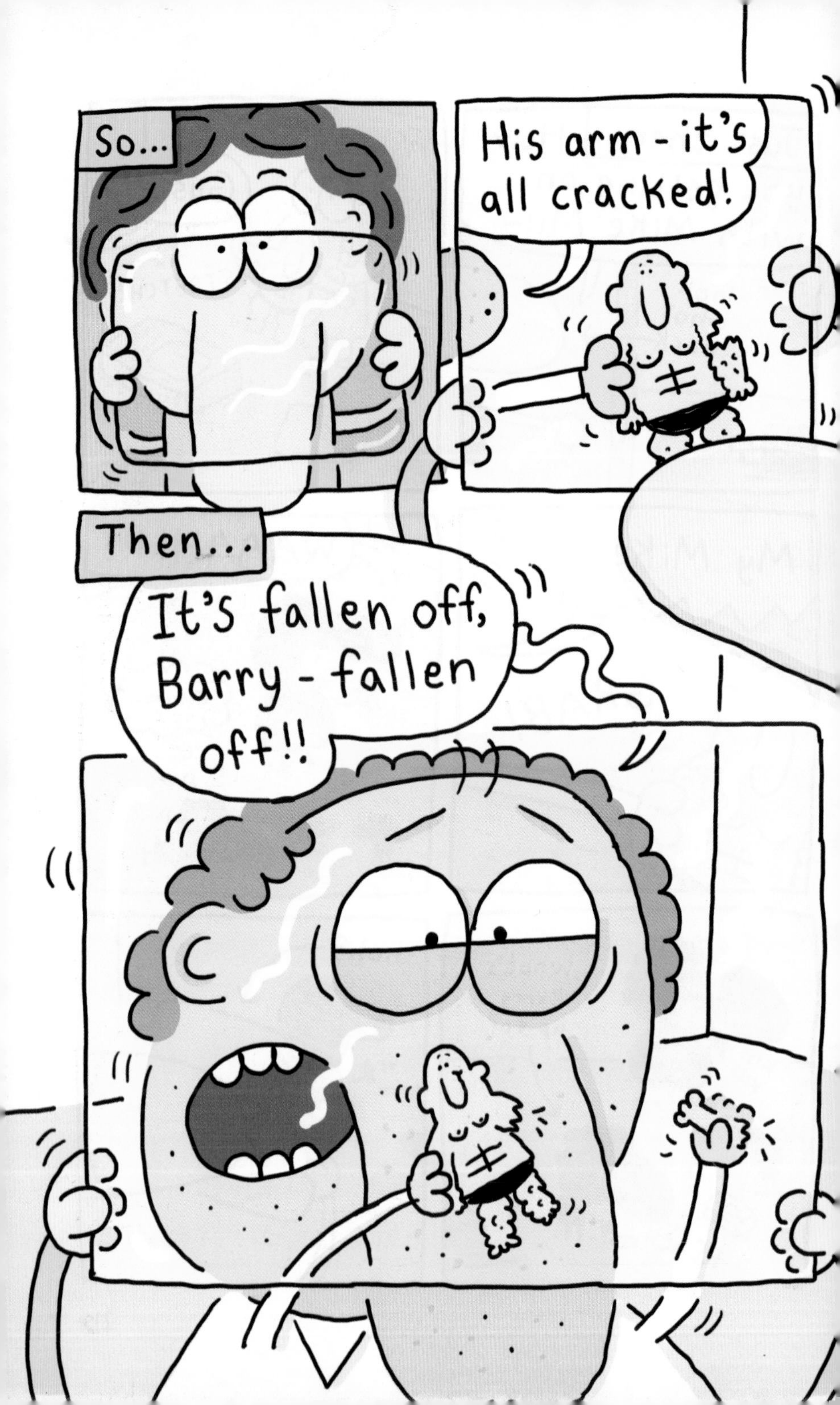
So...
His arm - it's all cracked!
Then...
It's fallen off, Barry - fallen off!!

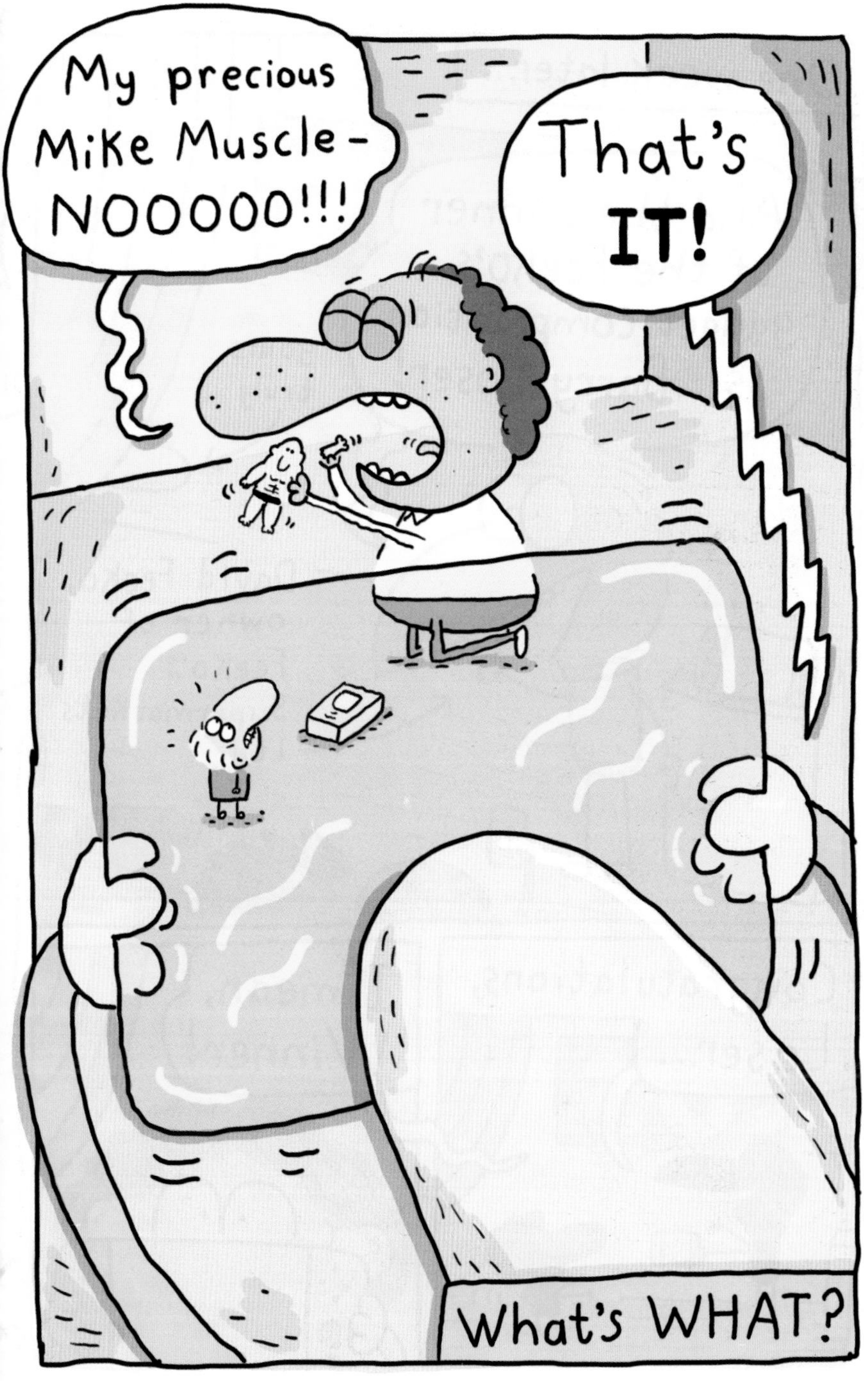
My precious Mike Muscle - NOOOOO!!!
That's **IT!**
What's WHAT?

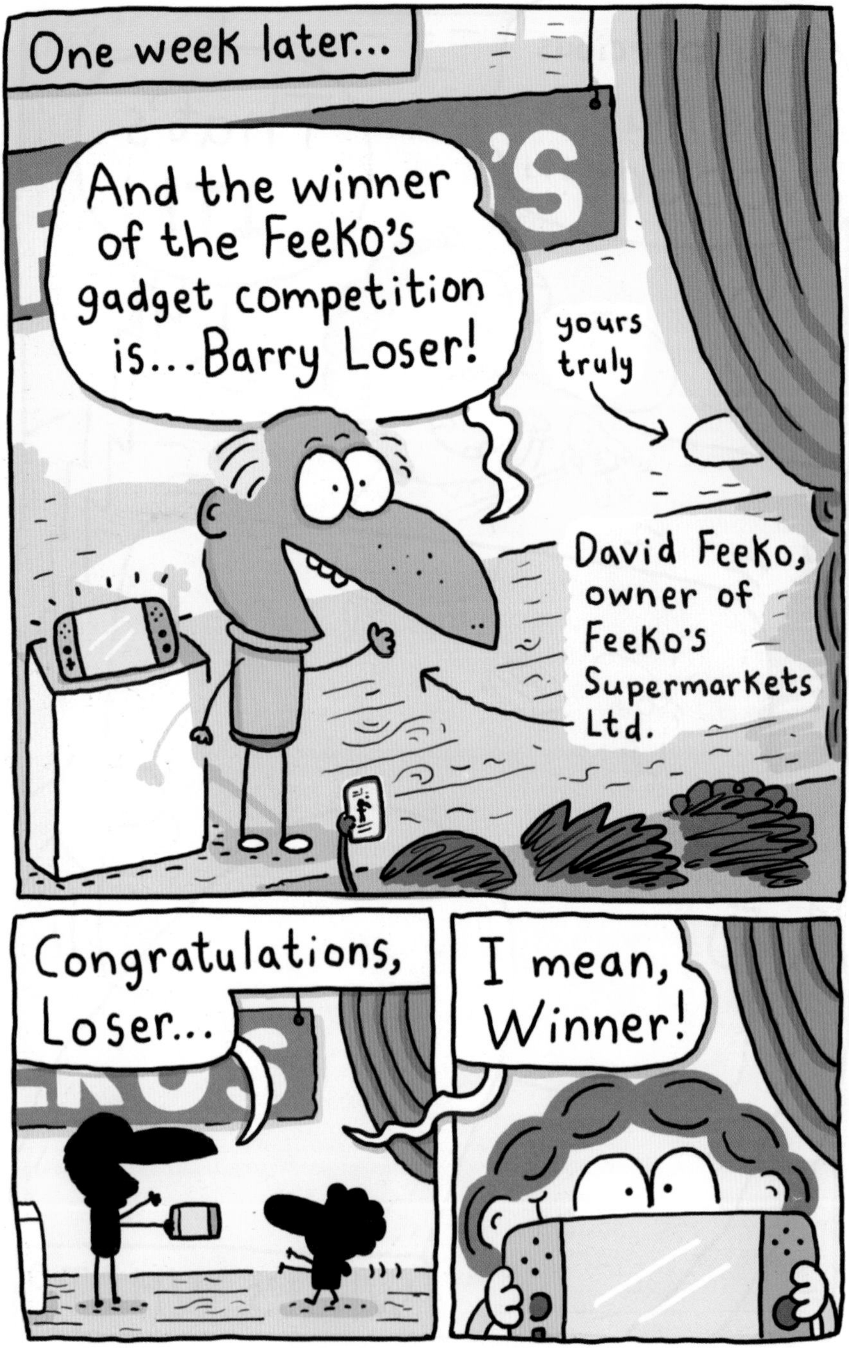
One week later...
And the winner of the FeeKO's gadget competition is...Barry Loser!
yours truly
David Feeko, owner of FeeKO's Supermarkets Ltd.
Congratulations, Loser...
I mean, Winner!

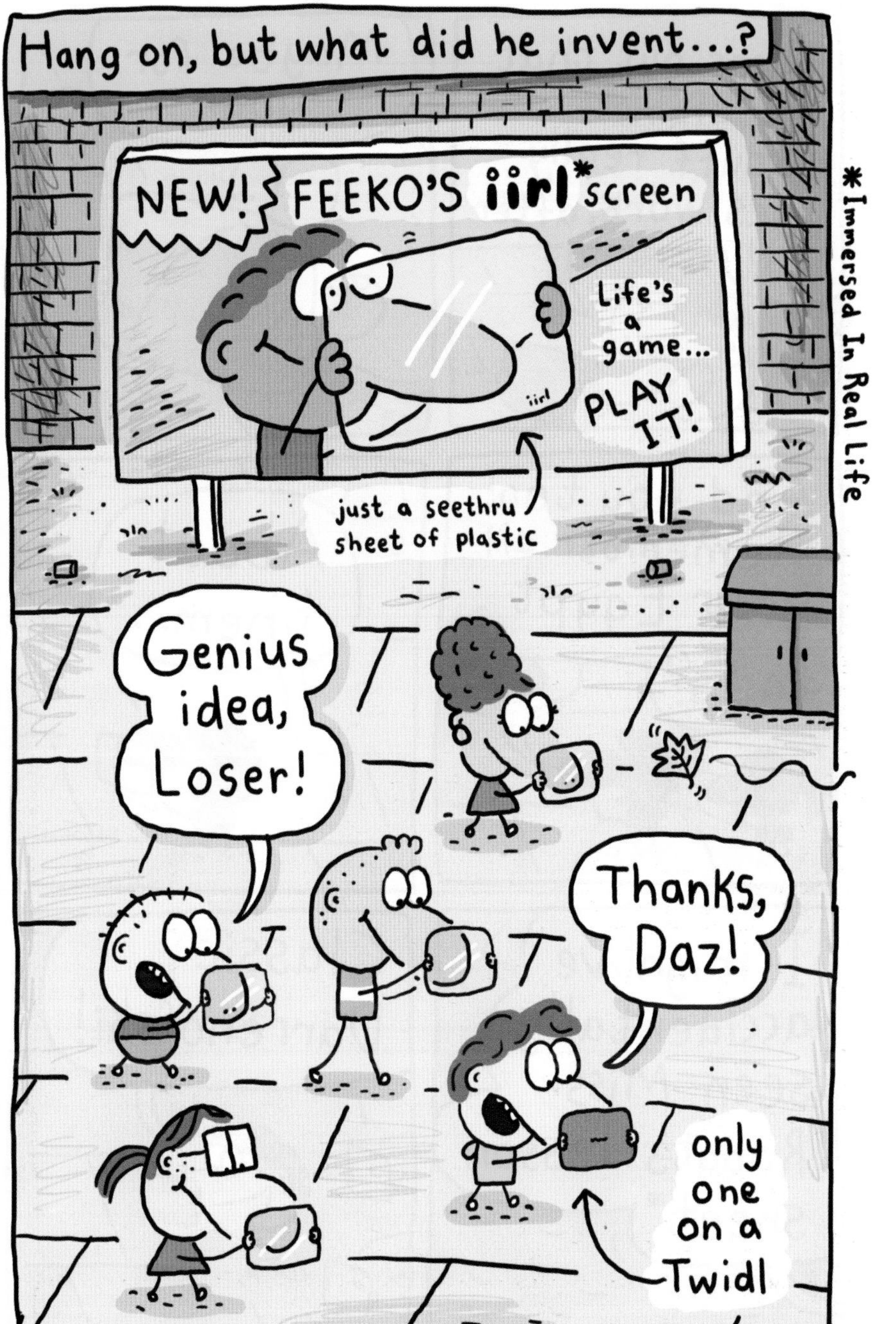
Hang on, but what did he invent...?
NEW! FEEKO'S iirl* screen
Life's a game... PLAY IT!
iirl
just a seethru sheet of plastic
*Immersed In Real Life
Genius idea, Loser!
Thanks, Daz!
only one on a Twidl

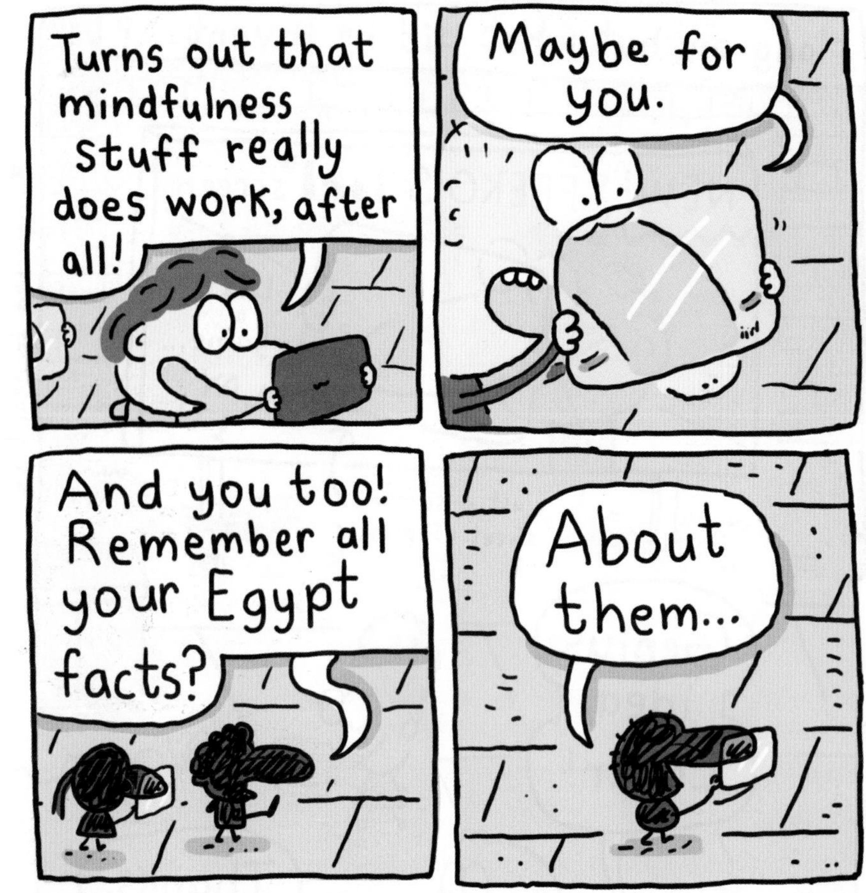
Turns out that mindfulness stuff really does work, after all!
Maybe for you.
And you too! Remember all your Egypt facts?
About them...
I might've accidentally seen Miss Robot's lesson sheet*
Classic Darrenofski!

*See p.185

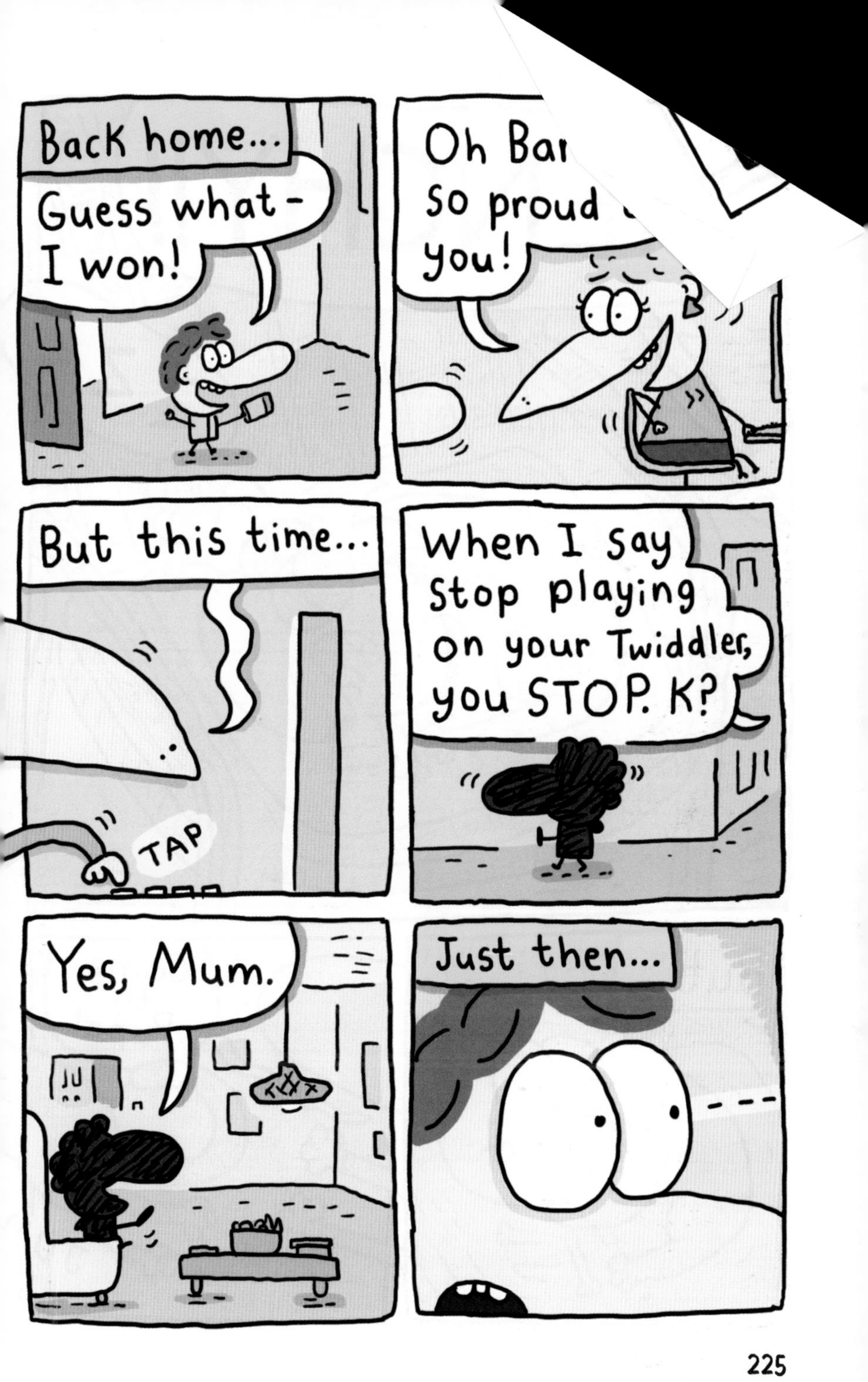
Back home...
Guess what - I won!
Oh Bar
so proud
you!
But this time...
TAP
When I say Stop playing on your Twiddler, you STOP. K?
Yes, Mum.
Just then...

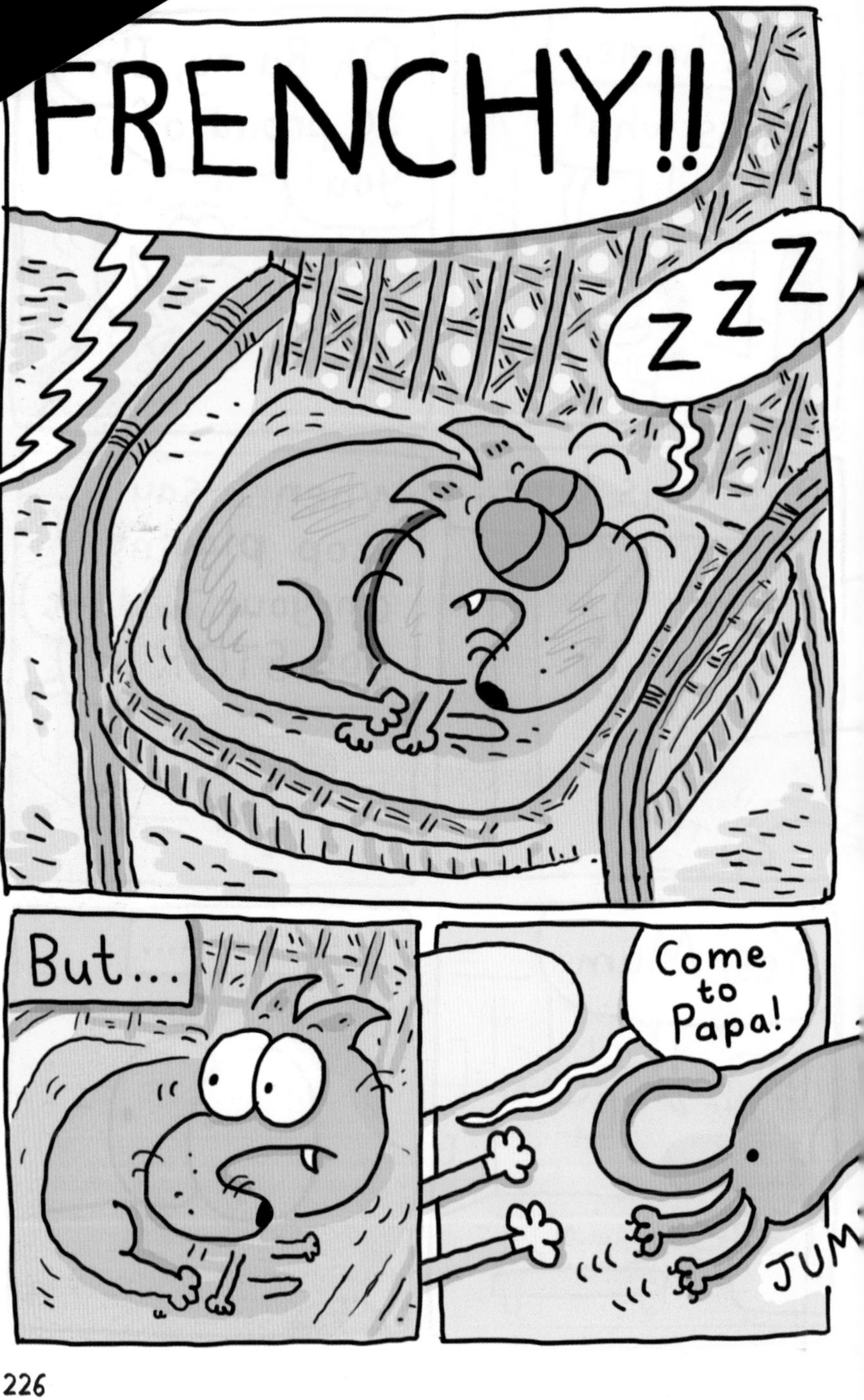
FRENCHY!!
ZZZ
But...
Come to Papa!
JUM

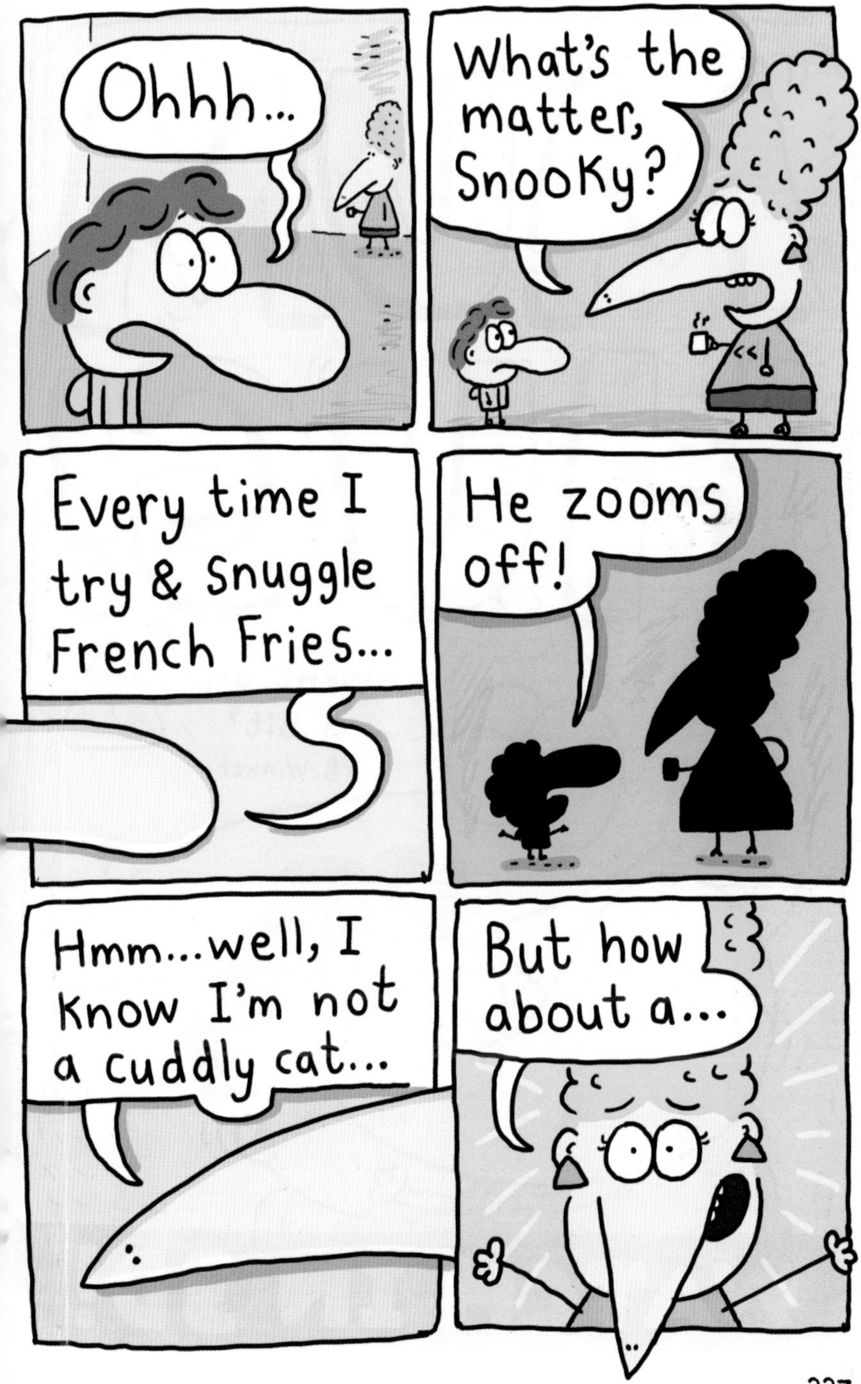
Ohhh...
What's the matter, Snooky?
Every time I try & Snuggle French Fries...
He zooms off!
Hmm...well, I know I'm not a cuddly cat...
But how about a...

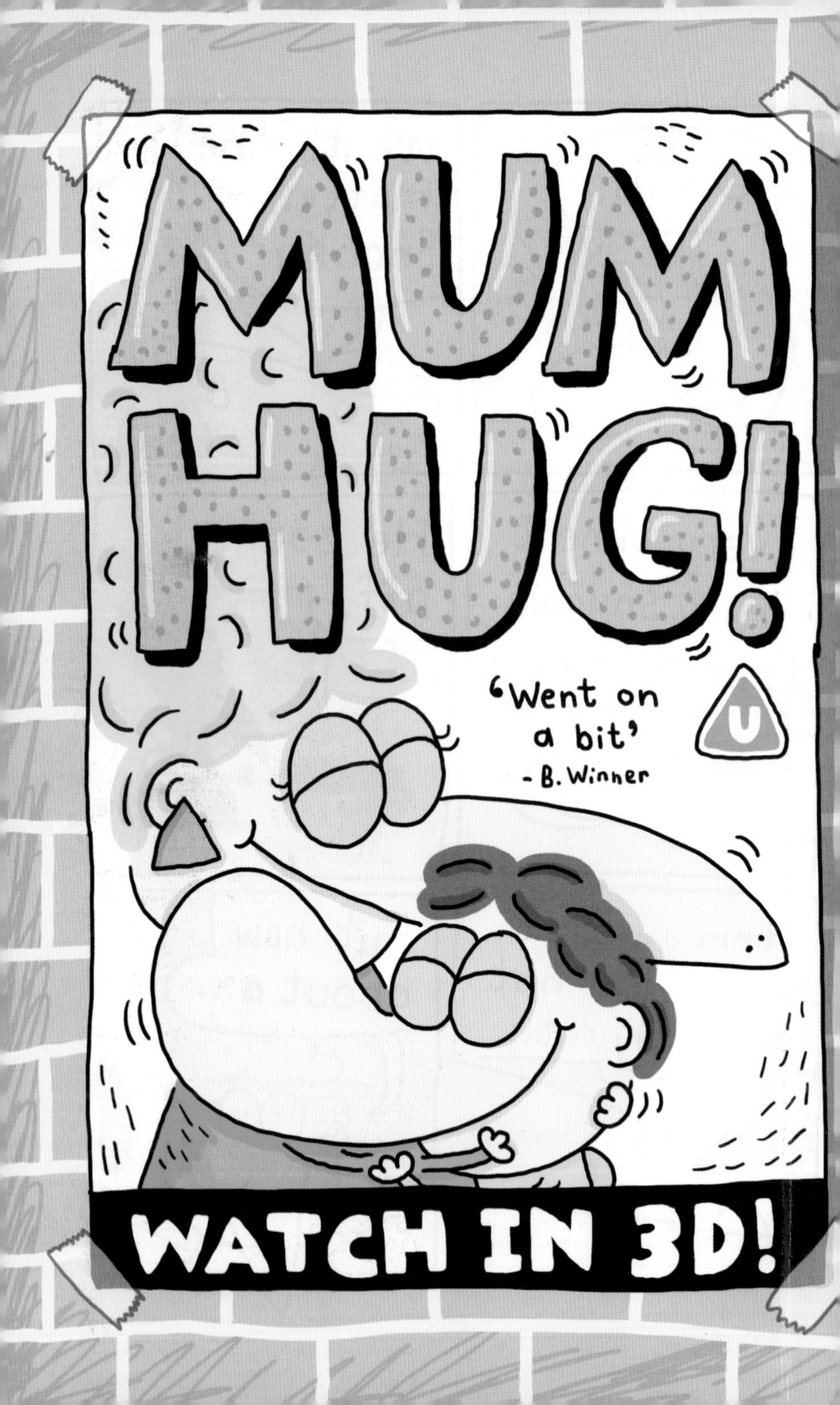
MUM HUG!
'Went on a bit'
- B. Winner
U
WATCH IN 3D!

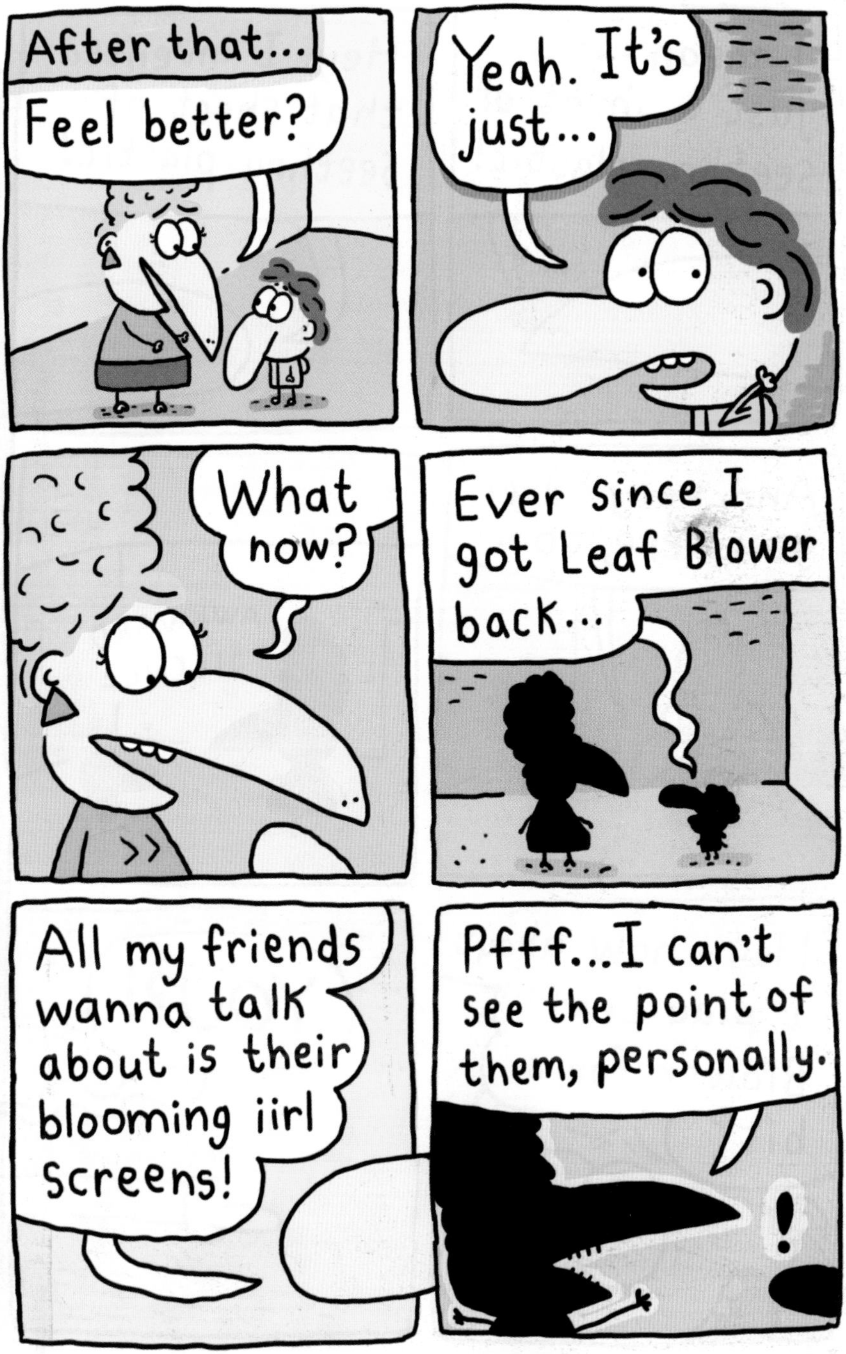
After that...
Feel better?
Yeah. It's just...
What now?
Ever since I got Leaf Blower back...
All my friends wanna talk about is their blooming iirl screens!
Pfff...I can't see the point of them, personally.
!

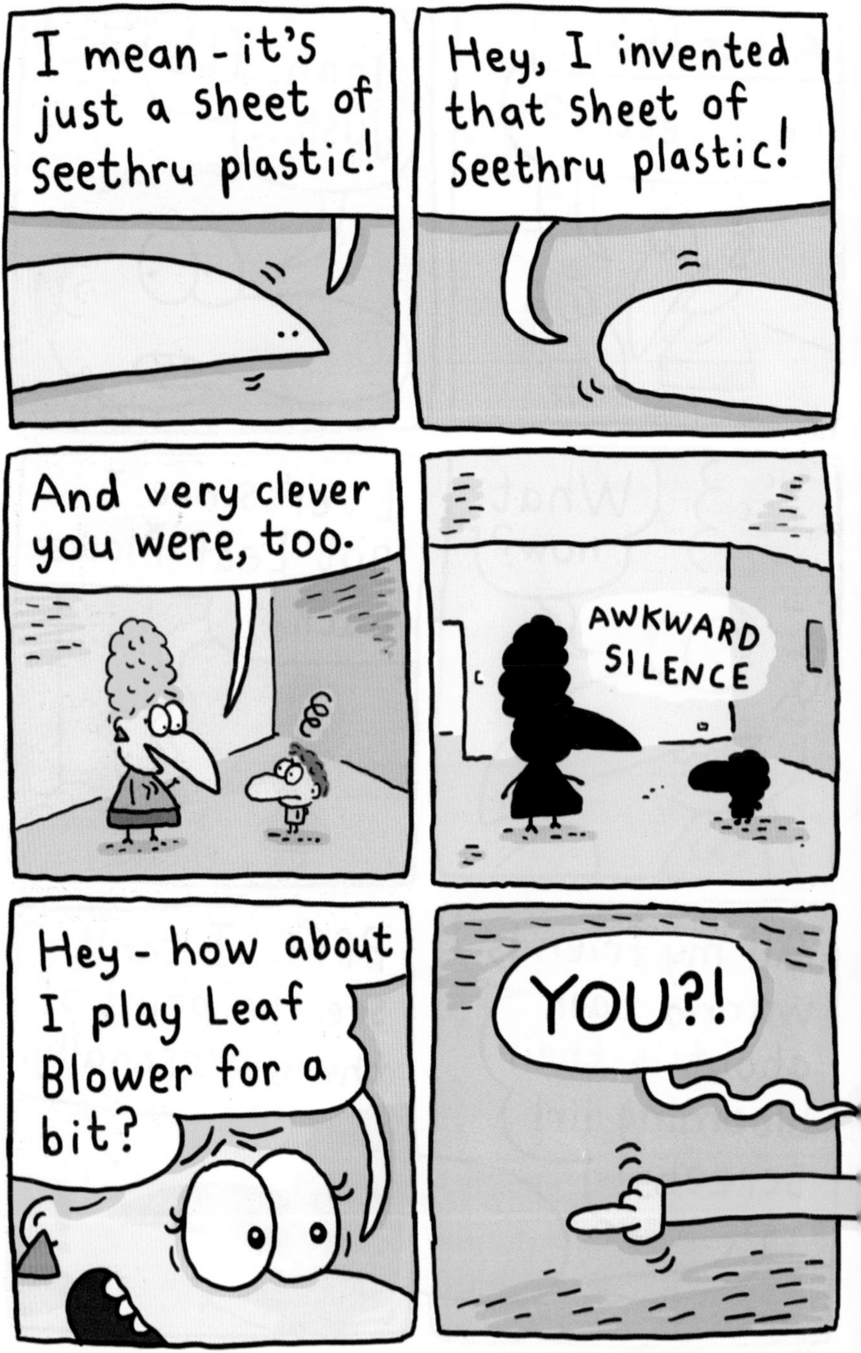
I mean - it's just a sheet of seethru plastic!
Hey, I invented that sheet of seethru plastic!
And very clever you were, too.
AWKWARD SILENCE
Hey - how about I play Leaf Blower for a bit?
YOU?!

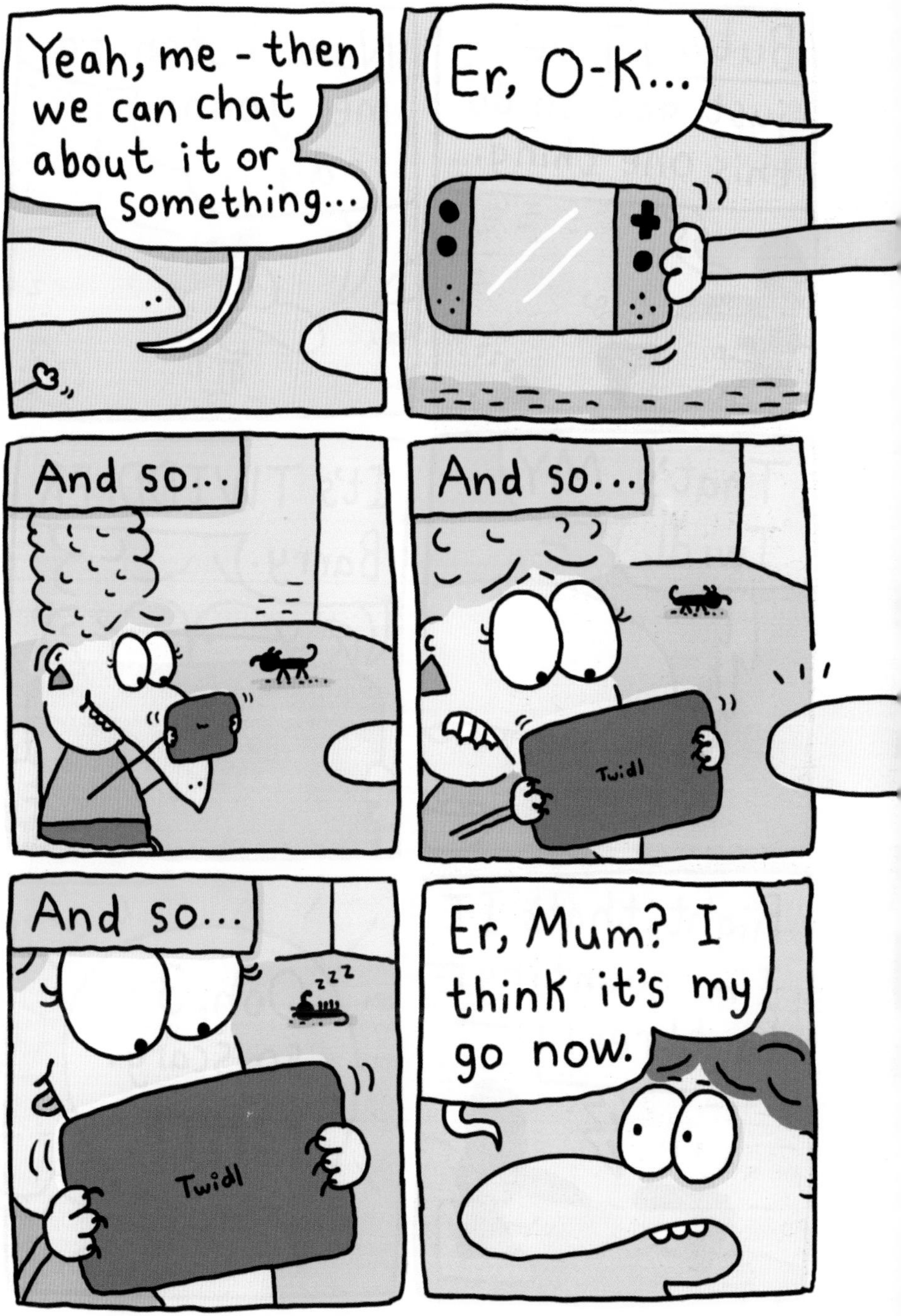
Yeah, me - then we can chat about it or something...
Er, O-K...
And so...
And so...
Twidl
And so...
Twidl
Er, Mum? I think it's my go now.

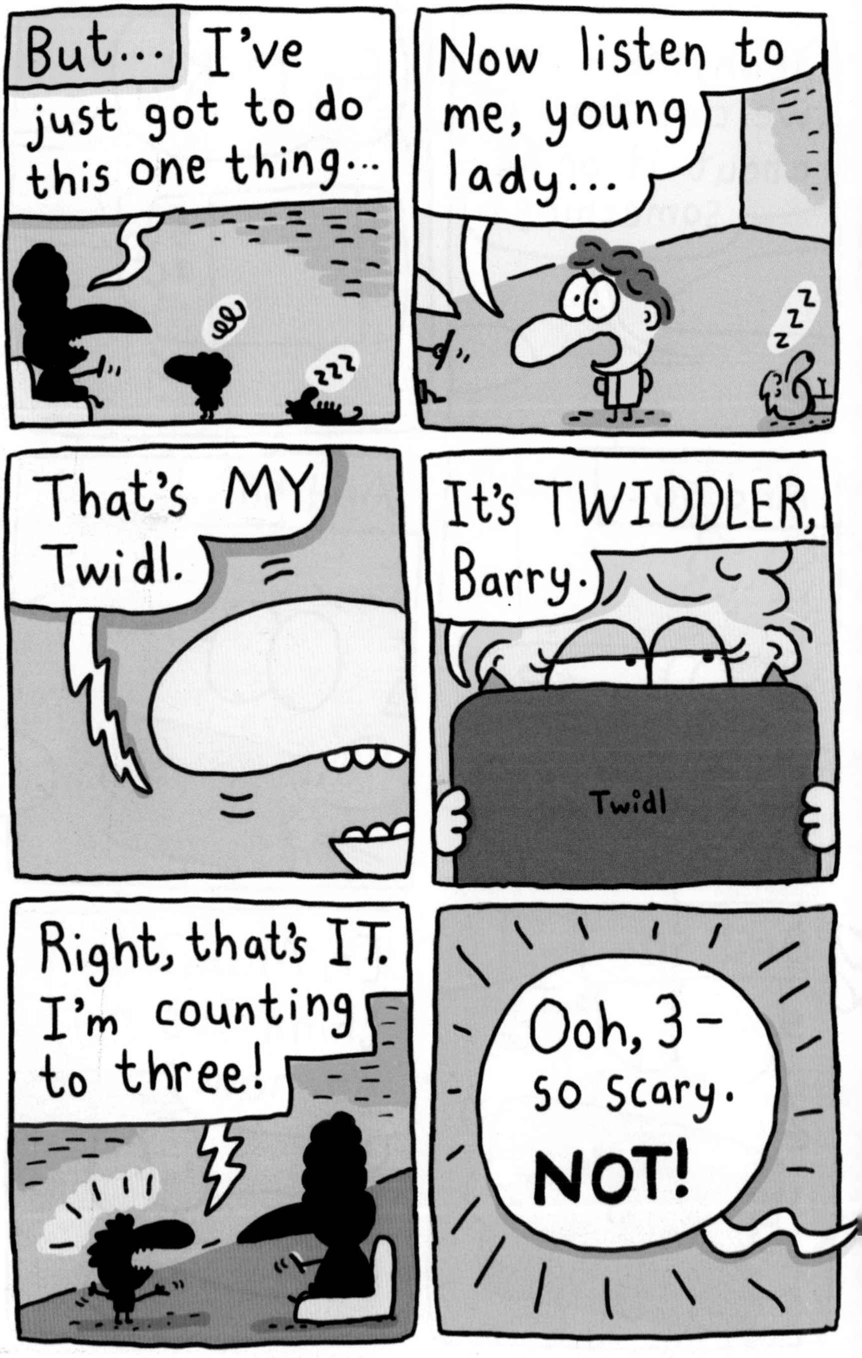
But... I've just got to do this one thing...
Now listen to me, young lady...
That's MY Twidl.
It's TWIDDLER, Barry.
Twidl
Right, that's IT. I'm counting to three!
Ooh, 3 – so scary. NOT!

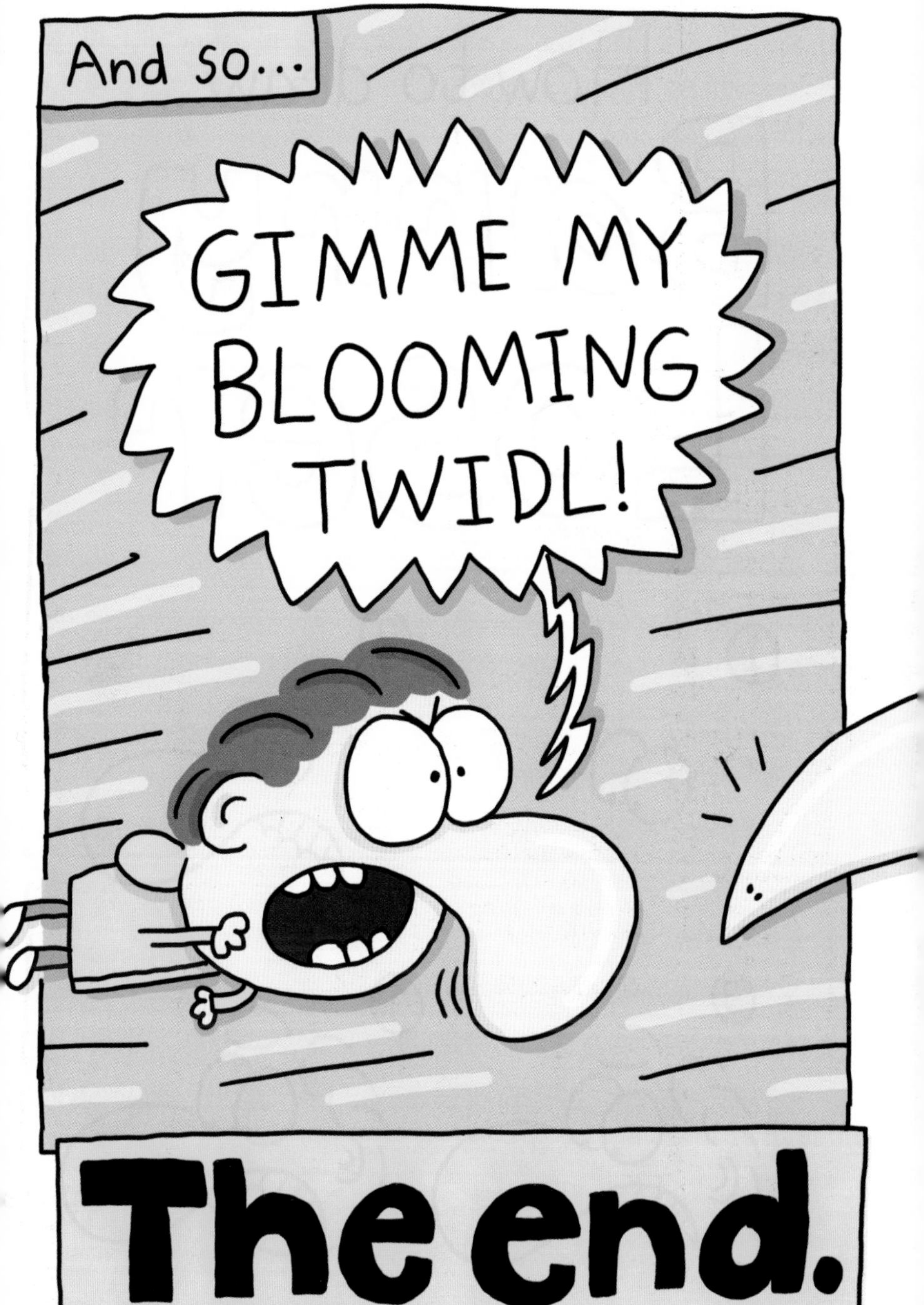
And so...
GIMME MY BLOOMING TWIDL!
The end.

How to draw...

Barry Loser

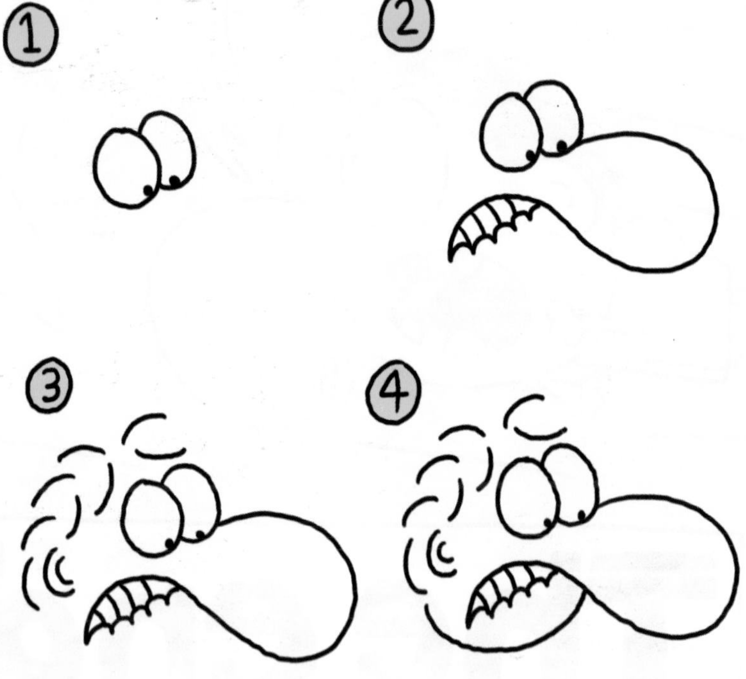

1
2
3
4

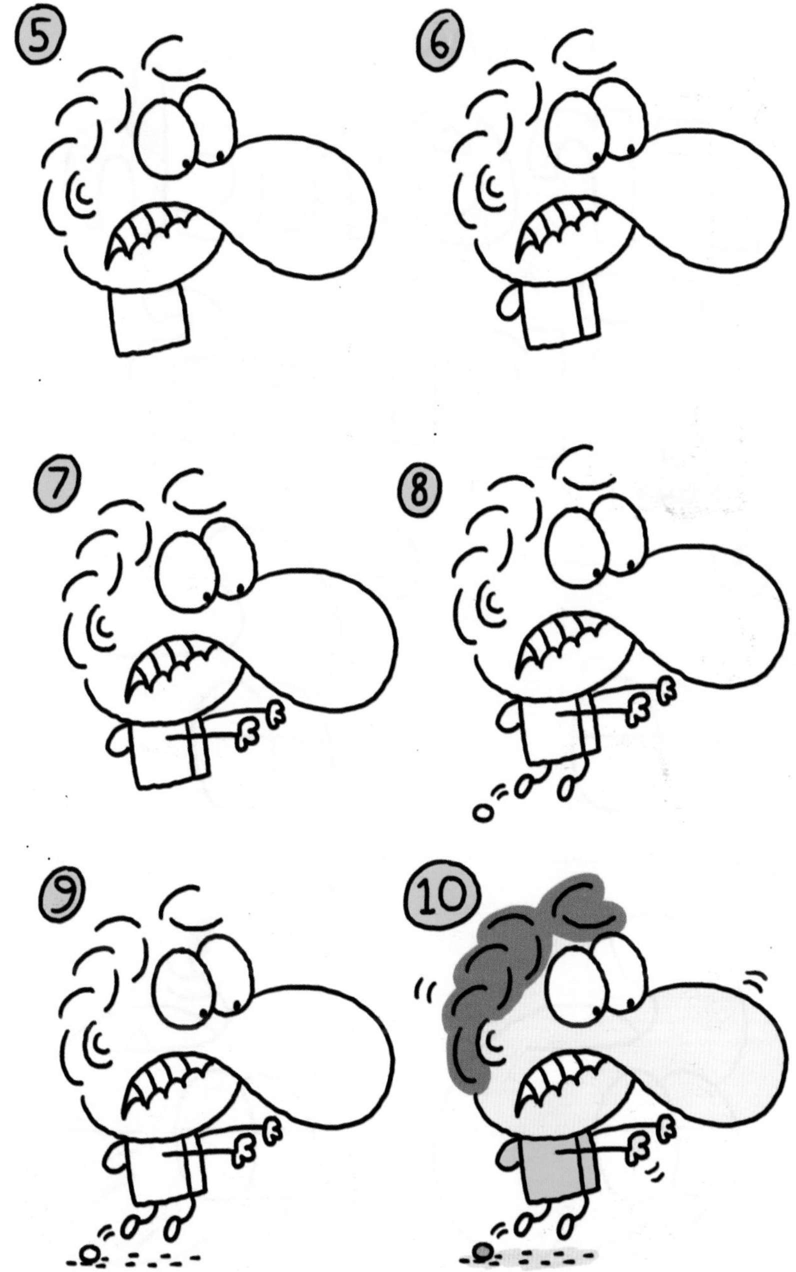
5
6
7
8
9
10

Now for...

French Fries

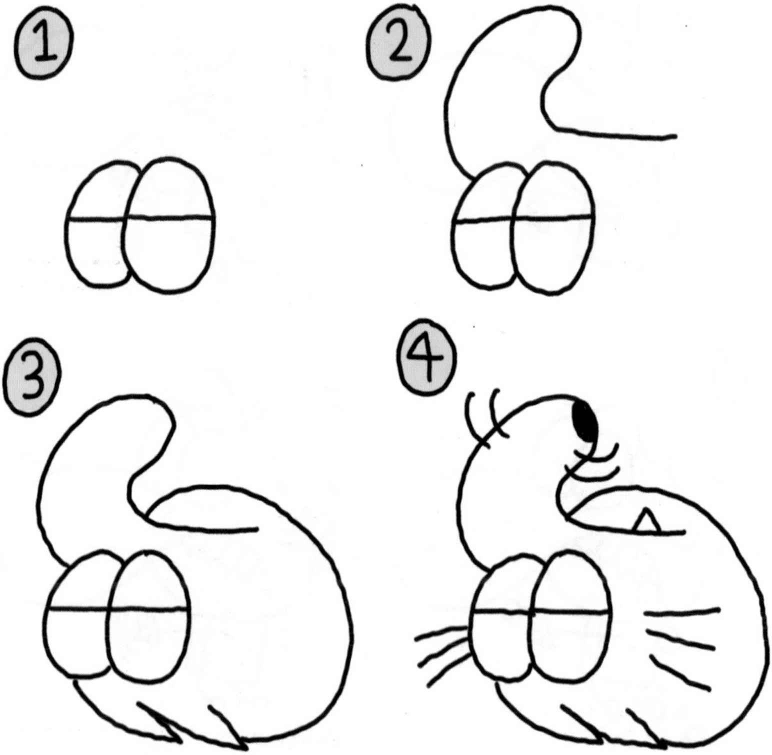

1
2
3
4

5

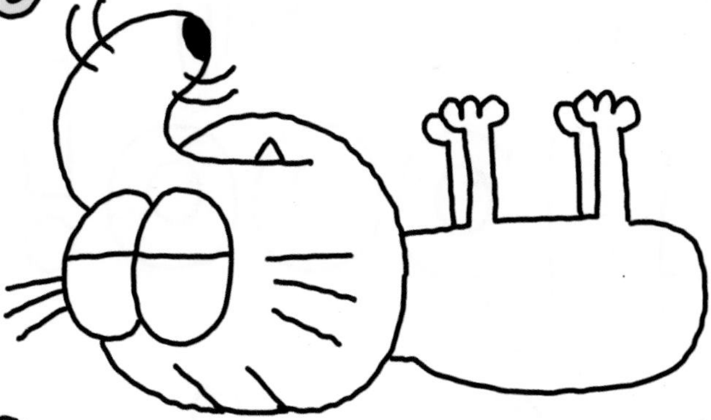

6

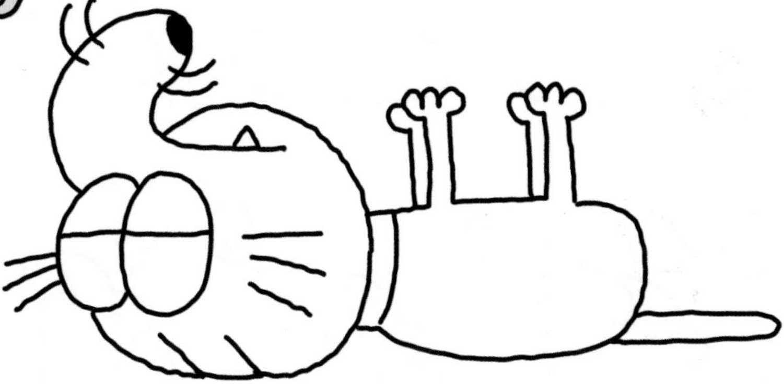

7

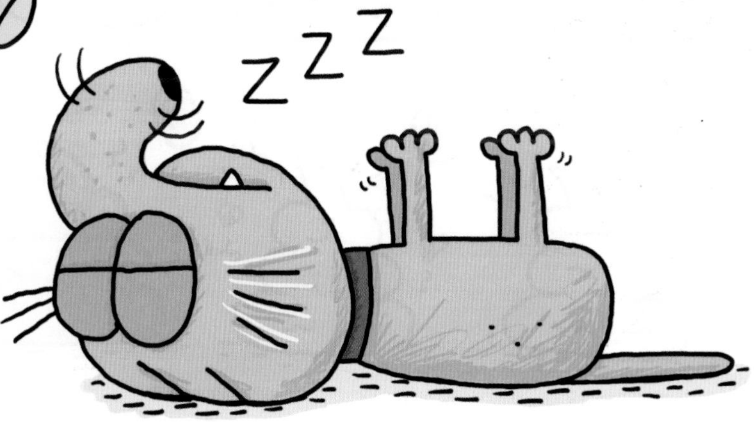
Z Z Z

And finally...
a poo!

All about Jim Smith

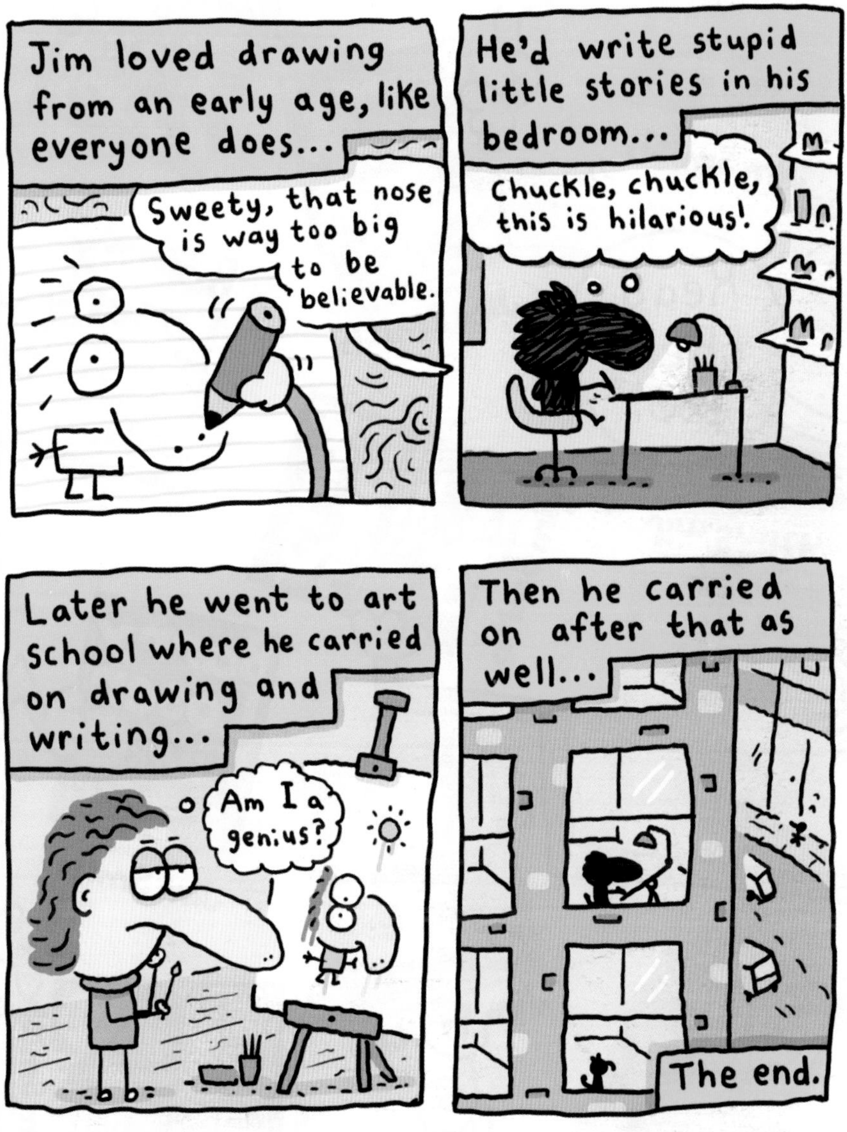

Jim loved drawing from an early age, like everyone does...
Sweety, that nose is way too big to be believable.
He'd write stupid little stories in his bedroom...
Chuckle, chuckle, this is hilarious!
Later he went to art school where he carried on drawing and writing...
Am I a genius?
Then he carried on after that as well...
The end.

Visit waldopancake.com for more Jim info (Jimfo).

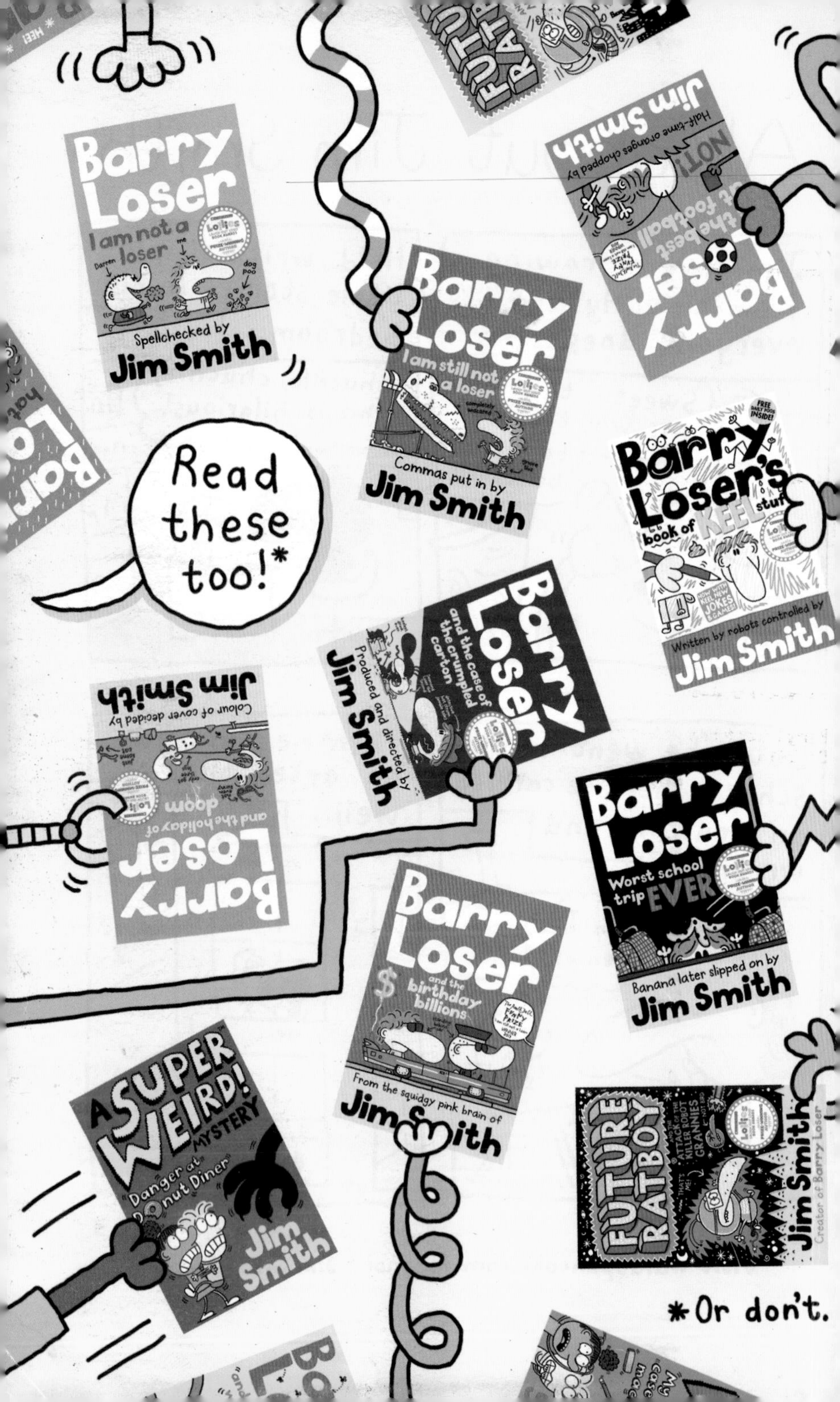
Read these too!*
Barry Loser
I am not a loser
Spellchecked by
Jim Smith
Barry Loser
I am still not a loser
Commas put in by
Jim Smith
Barry Loser
the best at football NOT!
Half-time oranges chopped by
Jim Smith
Barry Loser's book of keel stuff
Written by robots controlled by
Jim Smith
Barry Loser
and the case of the crumpled carton
Produced and directed by
Jim Smith
Barry Loser
and the holiday of doom
Colour of cover decided by
Jim Smith
Barry Loser
Worst school trip EVER
Banana later slipped on by
Jim Smith
Barry Loser
and the birthday billions
From the squidgy pink brain of
Jim Smith
A Super Weird! Mystery
Danger at Donut Diner
Jim Smith
Future Ratboy
and the attack of the killer robot grannies
Jim Smith
Creator of Barry Loser
*Or don't.